Praise for
The Bridegrooms

"Sisters. Secrets. Squabbles. Symphony and suitors. Allison Pittman's newest historical romance, The Bridegrooms, has it all. What happens when you match up an every-man hero with a conflicted heroine? You find yourself enthralled by a story full of improbable pairings that showcase love's surprising ways. Again, Pittman has me waiting impatiently for her next compelling tale."

—MONA HODGSON, author of *Two Brides Too Many* and
Too Rich for a Bride

"Get ready to put the rest of your life on hold. The Bridegrooms will sweep you off your feet and carry you over the threshold into the hearts of Vada Allenhouse and her unpredictable sisters. Mysterious romance is not the same thing as true devotion—or is it? And can one sister tell another how to choose between them? Allison Pittman's literary sparkle shines better than ever in this story of hilarious, heartfelt love."

—KAREN ROTH, author of *Found on 16th Avenue* and
My Portion Forever

"The Allenhouse sisters bear a striking resemblance to Allison Pittman's writing—feisty, witty, and intriguing, with a hint of underlying passion. This unique story of romance, secrets, and sisterly love will have you eagerly turning pages for more."

—BETSY ST. AMANT, author of *A Valentine's Wish* and
Rodeo Sweetheart

D0034988

"Allison Pittman has elegantly and beautifully drawn a cast of characters that captivate from page one. Vada and her three distinctively different sisters seek love and happiness, each in their own way. You can't help but identify with one in particular—the one most like you. Is Vada like her mother, who chooses passion over family? Will she succumb to temptation or learn that steady, honorable love brings a heady passion all its own? The answer isn't revealed until the very end of The Bridegrooms, and it'll make you ask yourself what choice would you have made."

—KELLY IRVIN, author of *A Deadly Wilderness*

THE BRIDEGROOMS

OTHER BOOKS BY ALLISON PITTMAN

Nonfiction
Saturdays With Stella

Fiction
Stealing Home

CROSSROADS OF GRACE SERIES
Ten Thousand Charms
Speak Through the Wind
With Endless Sight

ALLISON PITTMAN

THE BRIDEGROOMS

A NOVEL

MULTNOMAH
BOOKS

THE BRIDEGROOMS
PUBLISHED BY MULTNOMAH BOOKS
12265 Oracle Boulevard, Suite 200
Colorado Springs, Colorado 80921

This is a work of fiction. Apart from well-known actual people, events, and locales that figure into the narrative, all names, characters, places, and incidents are the products of the author's imagination or are used fictitiously. Any resemblance to current events or locales, or to living persons, is entirely coincidental.

Special thanks to the Colonial Dames of America for letting Multnomah Books use the McAllister House as the cover photo location.

ISBN 978-1-60142-137-1

ISBN 978-1-60142-261-3 (electronic)

Copyright © 2010 by Allison K. Pittman

Published in association with the literary agency of William K. Jensen.

All rights reserved. No part of this book may be reproduced or transmitted in any form or by any means, electronic or mechanical, including photocopying and recording, or by any information storage and retrieval system, without permission in writing from the publisher.

Published in the United States by WaterBrook Multnomah, an imprint of the Crown Publishing Group, a division of Random House Inc., New York.

MULTNOMAH BOOKS and its mountain colophon are registered trademarks of Random House Inc.

Library of Congress Cataloging-in-Publication Data
Pittman, Allison.
    The bridegrooms : novel / Allison Pittman. — 1st ed.
      p. cm.
    ISBN 978-1-60142-137-1 — ISBN 978-1-60142-261-3 (electronic)
    I. Title.
    PS3616.I885B75 2010
    813'.6—dc22

                                                    2009042392

Printed in the United States of America
2010—First Edition

10 9 8 7 6 5 4 3 2 1

For my sisters,
Barbara, Roi Lynn, and Martha.
And—of course—my parents.
Thank you, Mom and Daddy, for the life you've lived for us.

PROLOGUE

What Vada remembered most about that night was the snow, how it clung to the window one wet flake at a time.

"Look at that, Hazel. It's like God's sending down the stars."

But her younger sister was already asleep, or close to it. She muttered something and turned to the wall, pushing Vada to the edge of the bed with her contortion. *Lucky Althea,* she thought, envying her three-year-old sister. *She gets to share her room with the baby. And the baby gets a crib.*

But it didn't matter. Vada was too excited to sleep. Tonight had been her first official performance. She'd stood, alone on the stage, wearing the pale blue dress with ivory lace trim. Her hair in long, dark ringlets, her shoes shining and new, and her violin balanced perfectly on her shoulder, chin in place. The hush of the crowd, the piercing notes of "Au Clair de la Lune" wrought from her own small, nimble fingers. Not to mention her name printed in the program. Her very name!

Vada Diane Allenhouse, age eight.

Who could sleep after a night such as this?

She climbed out of bed, went to the window, and opened it an inch. Just enough so she could stoop down and breathe in deep the always-magical scent of snow.

"Close that window and get back in bed, Vada."

The command might have startled her, coming as it did from the other side of the dark doorway, but Mama hadn't spoken much above a whisper since before Vada's littlest sister, Lisette, was born.

The stillness of her mother's voice had become just another underlying sound in the house—along with the patter of three little girls in soft leather shoes and the rustle of so many petticoats.

Sometimes Mama's whispers were hidden behind the back of her hand. They snaked around in the shadows of the evening or stayed trapped behind her pretty lips. Tonight, they seemed to drift in like the flakes, and it wasn't until Vada turned to see her mother, lit on one side from the lamplight spilling from the room across the hall, that she could be sure she'd heard them at all.

"It's open just a little bit, Mama. And the snow smells so—"

"I said close it. I don't want you catching a chill."

Pouting once her back was turned, Vada obeyed, bringing the frame to nestle in the painted sill. Just as she stood to return to bed, a movement in the street caught her eye. A carriage, its black cover dark against the intermittent whiteness of the sky, pulled to a stop in front of their house. Two dark, prancing horses snorted mist into the night.

"Papa's back!"

"That can't be." The door swung open, filling the dark room with shadows. Mama rushed in, a bundle of squirming baby sister over her shoulder, and pulled the curtain aside. "He said not to expect him until the morning."

"Then whose buggy is that?"

"It's not even ten o'clock."

This didn't answer Vada's question, but Mama was speaking into her sleeve, not to her daughter. Baby Lisette's enormous eyes peered over Mama's shoulder, as she silently gummed the puff of fabric.

"Come, Vada." Mama gripped the top of her arm, tugging her to her feet. "Come away from the window and help me with the baby."

Vada followed obediently, her bare feet padding across the hall to her parents' bedroom. Mama followed behind, closing bureau drawers and scooting an open satchel to the other side of the bed.

"Are you getting a bag ready for Papa?"

"Here," Mama said. "Sit in the rocking chair with her while I go get her bottle."

"Do you want me to fix her bottle? I know how."

As an answer, Mama tumbled little Lisette into Vada's narrow lap, muttering about her return.

The windows in this room were hidden behind heavy velvet drapes, so no magic could be seen on the other side of the glass. No sound save Lisette's bubbly coo. Vada gathered the soft body closer and buried her nose in the sweet dark golden curls.

Little Lissy was restless and squirming, and Vada gave what comfort she could, but her feet were too short to reach the floor so she could not propel the chair into rhythmic rocking. Instead the eldest Allenhouse girl and the newest sat, abandoned, waiting for Mama to come back.

By the time she did, Lissy was beyond inconsolable, bucking and wailing, her little feet tangled in her long lace gown.

"Can I try feeding her?" Vada tried once again to wrestle her littlest sister still.

"Yes," Mama said, without a moment's hesitation. She knelt beside the chair, aiding Vada in settling the baby in the crook of her thin arm.

This close, Vada could see snowflakes like tiny flecks of lace, melting into watery beads on top of Mama's thick, dark hair. Damp spots speckled her shoulders. The scent of wet and cold clung to her, and a thin rivulet ran down her neck, disappearing within her collar.

"You went outside?"

"Make sure she sits up a little. Like this." As Mama readjusted the baby, Vada felt the slight burdensome weight pulling on her shoulder. "And here's the bottle." Mama settled the comfortingly warm glass between Lissy's chubby feet, and her soft bowlike mouth eagerly sought the nipple at the end of the long rubber tube.

"Papa doesn't like using bottles." Vada spoke above her sister's rhythmic, contented grunts. "He says they make babies sick."

"Your papa doesn't know everything."

"But he's a doctor."

Mama didn't answer. She sat on the floor, her feet tucked up under her heavy, dark skirt and set the rocking chair in motion with her hand.

"You're a big girl, Vada, taking care of your sister like that."

"I love her. It's easy to take care of someone when you love her."

"I suppose it is." Mama traced a finger along Lisette's chubby arm.

"I love Hazel and Althea too, but they're not babies."

"No, they're not."

"Do you think Mrs. Schaeffer has had her baby yet? If she hurries, Papa can be home in time to kiss me good night."

"I suspect he'll kiss you no matter what hour he gets home." Mama's voice was flat, like that one note in "Au Clair de la Lune" Vada could never get just right.

"Does it hurt a lot to have a baby?"

"Yes, Vada. It hurts very much."

"I don't think I ever want to have one." She waited for her mother to respond, but Mama didn't even look up from the carpet. "I might not ever even get married. I think I want to be a premier violinist and travel all over the country. And France. And Germany."

With each recited country, baby Lisette waved a chubby fist, lending emphasis to Vada's spoken dreams.

Mama reached up and caught Lisette's flailing hand and brought it to her lips for a soft kiss. "Be careful, Vada. Your heart can change."

"Not mine. I'll always love music."

"There's never any telling what you'll love from one day to the next."

Something in Mama's voice struck a fearful chord, and Vada swallowed hard, fighting back tears before she could speak again.

"You—you think I'm good enough, don't you, Mama? Good enough to be a premier violinist?"

Her mother looked up then, her large eyes rimmed with their own tears. But hers seemed harder and dried unshed before she spoke. "I'm not going to tell you what you can and cannot be, Vada."

"But did you think I was good tonight?"

"I thought you were fine."

"Just fine? What about—"

"Hush, now. If you keep talking, the baby will never go to sleep."

From then on the only sound in the room was Lisette's hungry swallows, but soon those slowed with the rocking. Heavy lids made fringed brown-sugar skirts along the top of her cheeks, and the nipple fell out of her slack mouth.

By then the arm holding her sister was numb, and Vada's head filled with unanswered questions. Those, however, would have no relief as Mama silently stood and scooped the infant up and away, leaving an empty chill where the soft, warm body had been nestled.

Lisette emitted an enormous belch as Mama placed her over her shoulder, and Vada giggled at the sound.

"Sssshhhh." Mama took gingerly steps out of the room to deposit the baby in her crib in the next room. In the meantime, Vada scooted to the edge of the rocker's seat and used her weight to dip the chair down until her bare toes hit the floor. She hopped off, leaving the chair in a rocking frenzy behind her, and ran across the hall to look out the window.

The carriage still waited.

She met up with her mother in the hall. Collided, actually, and grabbed Mama's hand. "Who do you think that is waiting outside?"

"Stay away from the window. It's late."

"But I'm not sleepy at all. Do you think I can stay up until Papa gets home? Then maybe I can play my song for him since he couldn't come to the recital."

Mama knelt then, right in front of her, and took Vada in her arms, holding her tighter than she had since long before little Lisette had been born.

"You must go to sleep, Vada darling. Remember, you can't come into your dreams unless you sleep."

"But I'm too excited! I want Papa to hear—"

Mama held her an arm's length away and looked at her with a very stern face. "Your papa will be home when he's home. Staying awake won't make that happen any sooner. And I daresay your song won't sound any different if you play it for him tomorrow. In fact, it might be better since you won't be so tired and upset."

"But I'm not upset. Are you upset, Mama?"

She glanced over Vada's shoulder toward the window, then stood. "Why don't you come and sleep in Papa's bed for tonight?"

"Really?" Such a treat it was to climb up into that big, soft mattress— something she and her sisters quarreled over on nights when Papa was out doctoring.

"Yes. Run along and lie down. I'll be in after I kiss your sisters and check the locks."

This, Vada obeyed. Funny how the minute her face touched the feather pillow, all the excitement of the evening broke up within her, dissolving and fizzing like the headache powders her mother stirred into glasses of water throughout the day.

Vada closed her eyes against the lamplight and listened to whispers coming from across the hall and Mama saying what sounded like a prayer over Hazel. Then again in the next room where Althea slept. Vada waited for Mama to come in and speak over her, but her footsteps carried her down the stairs. The front door opened and closed, and opened and closed again. Minutes later, Mama was at her side, bringing with her the essence of snow. Vada felt a cool hand on her brow, followed by a soft kiss.

"Sleep now, Vada," Mama whispered. "I'm right here."

Vada heard the creaking wood of the rocking chair as her mother settled into it, followed by a slow, lulling rhythm. She opened her eyes one final time and watched her mother's profile moving in and out of the lamplight. Just as she reached the edges of sleep, she heard faint strands of "Au Clair de la Lune," but there was no telling if they came from the memory of the stage or the woman in the chair. Either way, the notes carried her to dreaming and held her until the morning when she opened her eyes to Papa.

SATURDAY

HOME, AND WALKING TO IT

Between its walls, this tattered house
Plays host to lives held breathless.
Our dreams held ransom'd in the clouds
That drift above us, restless.
We look through windows at a world
That swiftly moves and changes.
We wait to see God's plan unfold,
~~And marvel at His strangeness~~
~~Unmindful of the dangers~~
As our lives He arranges.

Althea K. Allenhouse, 1898

1

SPRING 1898

The violins came in late at the top of the third measure. Again.

They'd been late at yesterday's rehearsal and earlier today just before
lunch. One would think a generous hour-long break, complete with mint
iced tea and citrus cake, would bring them back alert, bows poised over
the strings, ready to touch down at the mere twitch of Bertram Johann's
wrist. But once again there had been just that breath of hesitation—the
tiniest fraction of a beat—followed soon after by the cacophonous halt
of every instrument, one cellist the last to realize as a singular low note
echoed into the empty hall.

"Do you not have schools in Cleveland?" Johann's voice bore the
trace of his Austrian childhood—the one rumored to have been spent in
the greatest concert halls in Europe. "Have you not learned to count?
One. Two. Three. Four." His speech was accompanied by the small sound
of a baton striking his open palm. "Or perhaps here in America you think
you are entitled to an extra half beat in each measure? You think you are
Rockefellers of the music?"

Up in the balcony, Vada Allenhouse held the Bissell carpet sweeper
still and listened to the tirade, smiling. She would have been on beat.
Safely tucked away in the shadows, she peered out over the edge and

looked down the line of mortified musicians. Their instruments hung listlessly at their sides, resting bows and stilled mallets. One face after another—some pale, some bearded, some young, some old—all men, all lined up with nowhere to look. Their eyes darted from the conductor to the floor to some invisible comfort out in the third row.

She scanned and scanned until she found the face she sought. Even in the dim light of the stage, Vada could see the flush that crept up from the stiff white collar of his shirt. She stared until the slightest turn of his head brought their gazes together. One pale eyebrow popped above the rim of his spectacles.

"You! Third Chair!" Johann's voice brought the eyebrow back behind the spectacles and the face to full attention. "What is your name?"

"Walker?" The sound was weak and small before he cleared his throat and spoke again. "Garrison Walker."

"Do you think you could tear yourself away from whatever is so fascinating in the balcony? Or would you rather I ask Miss Allenhouse to come down and conduct you with her feather duster?"

"Yes sir. I mean, no sir. That is—"

"Enough, Third Chair." Johann struck his music stand with his baton. "We start again from the top of measure one, and—"

Vada focused her attention on the carpets and thrust the Bissell forward on the first downbeat. She moved the sweeper, keeping time with a swishing percussion as the flowers beneath her appeared and disappeared as the music swelled from below. She hummed the tune just beneath her breath and held her free hand aloft, imagining the strings of her violin beneath her fingers.

After an uninterrupted expanse of orchestration, the top row was swept clean, and she heard Johann's muted, "Much better that time."

He must have given some permission to dismiss, because soon thereafter came the sound of dozens of soft conversations, the unmistakable *click* of instrument cases, and the scooting of chairs as the musicians became a wiggling mass of dark suits.

Vada tried again to catch Garrison's eye, but he was engaged in conversation with the man beside him—a portly, older gentleman, Mr. Pennington, whose jowls quivered with each word. He was probably going on about his glory days playing with the quartet at the Hollenden Hotel. Played for presidents, he did, and Garrison would be kind enough to listen to each word, as if he were hearing it for the first time.

Just as well. The prolonged conversation would give her time to freshen up. It was hot up in the balcony, and she sensed a fine sheen of perspiration on her brow, not to mention the trickle down her back.

Once the Bissell was safely stored in the upstairs maintenance closet, Vada made her way down the steps, eager to have the vast powder room to herself for a quick splash of water on her face, and perhaps a repinning of her hair.

"Miss Allenhouse?"

"Oh, Mr. Johann. You startled me."

He was not a tall man, and he seemed always to be assuming some pose to increase his stature. He stood now at the foot of the stairs, his hands locked behind his back as he rocked on his heels. His hair had both the color and appearance of iron as it sprang, thick and straight, from all parts of his head.

"Did you take the program to the printer?"

"Not yet, Mr. Johann. I haven't had a chance to proofread—"

"Are we to assume that it will walk itself around the corner?"

"I wanted to be sure there were no errors. I didn't know if you'd want to make any changes."

"Changes in what way, Miss Allenhouse?" He looked down at her, though he had to nearly raise himself to his toes to do so. "Is there something in our current repertoire that you find lacking?"

"No…no, of course not." She wanted desperately to bring her kerchief up to wipe the sweat from her brow, lest Herr Johann believe it was his pathetic attempt at authority that had her in such a heated state. But no such indignity could ever take place in the presence of one so highly self-esteemed, so she forced a sweet smile. "If you've looked it over—"

"It is my job, now, to verify the program? I am to be both the musical director, the conductor, and the theater secretary?"

The insufferable man made himself taller and taller with each word until Vada was tempted to look down to see if his expensive shoes were still attached to the floral carpet.

She puffed herself up a bit. "I'll get them to the printer first thing Monday morning."

"Which means you can assure me they will be ready by Friday night?"

She bit the inside of her cheek. "Perhaps the printer is still open. I can take them by this evening on my way home."

Herr Johann lowered his heels to the floor and gave a curt nod before walking away, his hands still clasped at his back.

A peek through the thick double doors showed Garrison had made no progress extracting himself from the conversation with Mr. Pennington, so Vada allowed herself a quick foray into the powder room before making her way to the little office at the back of the theater. Here the faint rays of late afternoon sun stretched through the skylight, allowing her to find the large cream-colored envelope in the middle of her desk.

Four sheets of paper in all—the first proudly announcing the debut of the East Cleveland Terrington Community Orchestra, under the leadership of Bertram Johann. The second listed the five pieces to be performed, beginning with Bach's *Brandenburg Concerto no. 5* and culminating in his "Jesu, Joy of Man's Desiring."

It was a far cry from the glorious philharmonic that had filled the city with ambitious, masterful performances for as long as Vada could remember. No, the gathering of musicians on this stage was very much a remnant—some carried over from the philharmonic, but most, like her Garrison, just ordinary men who'd once abandoned their instruments to work in small, cramped offices all over the city. Their names were listed on the final pages, followed by small blocks of advertising.

After the concert, "Waltz" on into Sherm's Soda Shoppe, present this program, and receive two chocolate sodas for the price of one!

Visit the birthplace of the Viennese Waltz! Let D. S. Walters book your voyage today!

Vada sighed. What she wouldn't give to take such a journey. To visit all those places she'd dreamed about as a child.

Someday.

Now, though, she squinted to make out the time on the wall clock. Four forty-five. If she hurried, leaving right now, she should have time to make it to the printer's before they closed. She rushed out of the office, nearly colliding with Garrison in the hall.

"How did we sound?" Behind his spectacles, bright blue eyes searched for her approval.

"Better," Vada said after just a breath's hesitation. "Much better as the rehearsal wore on."

He seemed awash in relief and held his violin case up in a gesture of victory. "I thought so too. But it's hard to tell on stage. What did you think—"

"Listen." She held up the envelope. "I need to get this around the corner before five o'clock. Can you walk with me?"

His face puckered the way it always did before giving her disappointing news. "Sorry, darling. I have to get some briefs prepared to file in court on Monday. And I don't want to work on the Lord's day."

"Nor should you," she said, unfazed by his response. "I suppose that is just the price you pay to become a successful lawyer."

Garrison smiled, making him look like a little boy about to go visit his father at work. "Lawyer by day and third-chair violinist by night." He cast his gaze above. "And junior partner by the fall, if, of course, that's what the Lord has planned for me. His direction has to come first in any plans I make."

Vada stood in front of him, leaning forward ever so slightly, as if to remind him of her presence as he made his future plans. "Don't you ever want more? Does it ever cross your mind to just toss that partnership to the wind—strike out with nothing but the clothes on your back and your violin and listen to the music on every world stage?"

"You're right, Vada." He lowered his gaze. "Sometimes I think I'd go mad if I didn't have this." He held up his violin case.

"Oh." She made a vague attempt to hide her disappointment. "Well, yes, music is a great release—"

"And I know I couldn't make it through a day if not for you." He turned his head to glance up and down the empty hallway before bending to give her his familiar kiss. Top of the right cheek, his lips soft and dry against her flushed skin.

Just like that, she was third chair.

"I have to get to the printer's," she said as he drew away.

"And I have to get to the office."

They walked together down the hall and out the theater's back door, wished each other a good evening, and turned in opposite directions.

She'd lost at least five minutes.

With renewed fervor, Vada rushed down the street, clutching the envelope to her like a schoolgirl with her precious homework. The sidewalks were crowded this Saturday afternoon, and she wove in and out of those people whose agendas were certainly less urgent than hers. The printer's shop was still half a block away, and if she was to make it on time, she'd need to break into a most unladylike run.

The piercing eyes of Herr Bertram Johann still burned at the back of her head, spurring her on and, finding an opening in the mass of people, she took her first lunging step.

"Excuse me! Pardon me!" she called out over her shoulder, not once considering slowing her pace to avoid the occasional brush with a stranger. While she was thus turned around, she noticed she wasn't the only person running up the street.

"Oh, bother." Should she slow her steps or attempt a final burst of speed? But in just that brief pause, he'd caught up to her.

"Miss Allenhouse?" There wasn't a hint of labor to his breath while she clutched the envelope to disguise her heaving.

"Mr. Voyant. How…unusual to see you again."

They stood in the middle of the sidewalk, impeding the pedestrian traffic, so when he touched the fabric of her sleeve in a most gallant manner, she allowed herself to be led beneath the protective striped awning of Moravek's bakery.

"You're not an easy woman to keep up with."

"And you, apparently, are not an easy man to escape."

He touched the brim of his cap, drawing her eyes to the fringe of jet black hair beneath it.

"What can I do for you today, Mr. Voyant?"

"Well, for starters, you can call me Dave. And then, since we'll be on friendlier terms…" He reached inside his jacket pocket and produced a small notebook and a stub of pencil. "You can fill me in on the big debut."

Vada clutched the program even tighter.

His gaze lingered on the envelope. "And what would that be?"

For just a moment Vada wondered if he was more interested in what was within it or behind it. "I've told you before, *Mister* Voyant, Herr Johann won't allow any press to attend the rehearsals. And as I am merely a secretary, I can hardly be a good source of information."

"Oh, I have the feeling you're more than a secretary—"

"Nevertheless, if you want a preview of the 'Harmonic,' you'll need to conduct an interview with Herr Johann himself."

"Come on, Miss Allenhouse." He leaned closer, the deep bass of his voice underscoring the sounds of the street. "It is *Miss* Allenhouse, isn't it?"

Vada flashed her best smile, the one she knew would bring out the dimple just above her chin.

"Don't try your flattery on me, Mr. Voyant. I really can be of no help. Now, if you would like to speak to Herr Johann—"

"I've tried." He effectively blocked her exit with one side step. "Maybe it's my imagination, but I think that guy thinks I'm an idiot."

She wanted to say it wasn't his imagination at all, that Bertram Johann considered just about everybody to be an idiot, but she didn't want to hurl an insult into his sincere green eyes. Instead she said, "I'm sorry. Mr. Johann is intent on revealing as little information as possible."

"I'm begging you, Miss Allenhouse. Anything you tell me would be helpful." He held up his little notebook again, clearly revealing the time on his wristwatch.

"Oh no!" Vada stamped her foot, and the envelope dropped to her side. "Now you've made me late for the printer's, and we'll never get the program on time."

"So that *is* your precious cargo." Dave's eyes traveled the length of her, stopping short of being downright insulting. "What's on the list for the evening's entertainment? A little Bach? A little Beethoven?"

As he spoke, he moved aside to hold the bakery door open, allowing a woman and her two children to pass through. He tipped his cap and wished her a good afternoon, at which time the woman turned and sent an approving smile over her shoulder.

Vada squared herself in response, preparing to get out of this conversation. Now. After all, Mrs. Moravek, the baker's wife, had been serving Garrison and her their Sunday morning pastries for nearly a year. What would she think seeing Vada locked in conversation with another man? It was only a matter of time before she would come to the window and see—

"Maybe a touch of Mozart?"

"Honestly, Mr. Voyant. Why do I get the impression that your ability to rattle off a list of composers exhausts your vat of musical knowledge?"

He chuckled and threw his hands up in surrender. "You've caught me. I just got into town a couple of months ago, and the first assignment I get is the arts beat. So can you help a fellow out?"

"I don't think—"

Before she could finish her sentence, Dave snatched the envelope from her hand.

"Give that back to me!"

"Were you headed for Franklin's Dream Printing just around the corner?"

"Yes, until you—"

"I'll take it in for you."

"They're closed."

"They'll open for me, Miss Allenhouse. Answer one question, and I promise you'll have them in a week."

"We need them by Thursday."

"Answer two, and you'll have them Wednesday."

She studied his face. The smile was still there, but it was void of any flirtation and artifice. How much harm could one question be? Or two? Keeping her nose in the air as high as safety would allow, she walked away from the bakery window, knowing he was following close behind.

Once she was safely in front of an anonymous tailor's, she turned, planted her feet, and folded her arms in front of her. "Two questions, then."

"Great." He tucked the envelope under one arm and licked the tip of his pencil. "First, how does this orchestra compare with the philharmonic that disbanded in '95?"

Vada's mind flashed back to the missed beat at the top of the third measure. "It doesn't."

"How so?"

"Is that your second question?"

"My darling Miss Allenhouse. Perhaps you should consider a career in politics."

"Hardly likely, seeing as I don't even have the right to vote."

Dave tilted his head back, squinted one eye, and gave a studied perusal. "Funny, I didn't take you for a suffragette."

"Oh, I'm not, really. I leave that to my sister Hazel."

"Sister? So there are more of you at home?" The leer was back. "Tell me, are any of your sisters as beautiful as you are?"

"Is *that* your second question?"

He had the good grace to look defeated. "Yes. I'm dying to know."

"Well, I'm afraid there's no way for me to answer without seeming immodest, so what a shame that you wasted it. And that, Mr. Voyant, is your cautionary tale for the day." Invigorated by the exchange, she punctuated her statement with a victorious chuckle.

Without another word he flipped the cover, closed his little notebook, and returned it to his pocket as he looked at her with new, unabashed admiration. "Will you at least allow me to see you home?"

Vada wagged a chastising finger in his face. "That would be a third question. Not part of our agreement. But I'll look forward to seeing you Wednesday with the programs."

She walked away, replaying the entire conversation in her mind. Each time, her retorts were saucier, his banter more intense. Left to herself, she giggled in a way she hadn't dared before. What would Garrison think if he had heard this verbal battle with Dave Voyant? For that matter, what was *she* thinking?

Little by little, her nose descended from its perch high in the air, and her head bowed to where she could only see the tips of her shoes peeking out from beneath her skirt with each step.

Forgive me, Lord, for my inconstancy.

Feeling chastised, Vada tried to make amends by replaying her last conversation with Garrison. But it was another full block before she could recall a single word.

2

"Rotten old cow." Hazel stood on the porch, hands planted on her hips, directing her comment at the last bit of a stiff brown silk skirt disappearing behind their front door. "Some nerve showing up this late in the afternoon. She'd keep Doc down there until seven o'clock. Her and her fainting."

"Oh, Hazel, stop it." Vada paused at the foot of the concrete steps that spilled down the front of the house. As always, the conflicting tug of relief and resignation accompanied her arrival home, and she wished she'd hidden in the alcove under the stairs long enough to avoid this confrontation. "You know Mrs. Thomas doesn't like to walk down the basement stairs."

Hazel made a face. "The *widow* Thomas, if you please. Seems she makes a point of mentioning that little fact every time she shows up, lest we forget how very marriageable she is."

"Well, the widow Thomas is one of the few people who pays Doc with actual money, so we'd better be a little grateful every time she graces the door."

"Honestly, Vada. You can steal the fun out of just about anything." Hazel's glare lasted just a few seconds before turning into a mischievous grin that produced a dimple identical to Vada's own.

As young girls, they'd often been mistaken for twins, but Hazel remained two inches shorter, and at least that much rounder, until only their dark chocolate hair and that dimple remained as a shared feature.

"So, do you want to see what came in the mail today?" Hazel asked.

"Not another one?"

Hazel held up two fingers—the nails bitten to the quick.

"Unbelievable."

"Quick. Come inside." Hazel opened the front door and, after a quick scan of the entryway to be sure the distasteful Mrs. Thomas was out of sight, grabbed Vada's hand. The two ran giggling up the stairs to the second-floor landing.

"Hurry." Hazel propelled them toward her bedroom door. "I want to show you before the others get home."

"That's right." Vada crossed the threshold on her sister's heels. "Where are they? It's late."

Hazel closed the door behind them. "Althea's still at work, of course. I guess more people send telegrams on Saturdays."

"And Lisette?"

"Who knows with that one." Distracted, Hazel sorted through piles of paper on the writing desk beneath the white lace curtain-covered window. "Now how could I have lost… They just came today…ah, here!" She picked up two envelopes and studied them closely before handing one over to Vada. "Look at this one first."

Vada peered inside. "A picture and a letter."

Hazel nodded. "This is the fourth letter I've received from him. But the first picture. What do you think?"

Vada took a deep breath, bracing herself. She pulled out the postcard-sized photograph and studied the image of a man seated on a straight-backed chair. His dark hair, shining with some sort of oil, was combed, as if against its will, straight back from his forehead. Thick, dark brows formed little nests above pale eyes. There was also a nose and, she assumed, lips, although the detail of either feature was left a mystery behind the massive, thick beard. He wore an ill-fitting, rumpled suit and thick-soled boots. Something that had once been a critter or varmint had been converted to a hat that perched on one knee, as if ready to hop up and skitter away.

"Isn't he magnificent?" Hazel's voice was little more than a sigh.

"Is this the one who can only write three-letter words?"

"No, meanie. This is Barth, the one who writes the beautiful passages about the mountain pools like smooth silver coins and the thundering of the elk across the plains."

"Ah, the poet." Vada looked deeper into the pale, vacant eyes.

"But not like Althea. He doesn't write in verse or anything. He just makes the land come alive."

Vada looked up at her sister. She'd never seen her looking as beautiful as she did that moment. Hazel had always carried a certain hardness to her. Coarse hair, chapped skin. Her lips formed the same natural bow shape as Vada's own, but it seemed they'd been made with thinner ribbon. Now Hazel's face was relaxed, with just enough of a smile to bring out the Allenhouse dimple.

"You look like you're ready to hop on a train right now," Vada said, feeling like an intruder.

"Not quite. But he's a definite contender."

Hazel crossed the room to the large oak armoire and opened the door wide. The backside of it was covered in cork, and a dozen slips of paper fluttered in response to the movement. They were handwritten notes— some little more than painful scrawls—and photos. All men, all with the hard-bitten features of frontier life. Some stiff in photographer's studio chairs, a couple standing grimly next to newly killed game.

Hazel stepped back to observe the display. "Hmm. I think it's definitely time to send regrets to this one, and this one." She plucked the two pictures of the victorious hunters. "And probably this one. He looks short."

The image of the poetic, stoic Barth was pinned prominently, as scrap after scrap of hopeful correspondence was snatched off the cork.

"You know," Vada said, preparing herself for the argument to come, "you don't have to do any of this. If you want to move to Wyoming, just go. You're twenty-one. You don't need a husband to be able to vote."

"Easy for you to say." Hazel gave a pitying look to the bearded man with a bowler hat and one suspender. "You have a man. I don't want to give up my chance at marriage and security just because I want the rights this country owes me. I shouldn't have to go out there and be somebody's laundress just so I can vote."

"Who says you—"

"If I move out there alone, I'll be desperate. I'll latch on to the first man I find. I want to be wooed. I want to be courted. I want romance, like you have with Garrison."

"Yes, well." Vada remembered his familiar, dry kiss. "If that's your aim, there's no reason you can't have that here. The city's full of men—"

"Who aren't exactly piling up on our front porch. And once they've seen Lisette, what chance does an old maid like me have?"

"Watch it, sister. You're younger than me, you know."

"And you're engaged. Practically, anyway. I want a man who wants me."

"So it's not just your constitutional aspirations?"

The glint was back in Hazel's eyes. "That is the icing on the wedding cake."

The sisters stood side by side, staring at the narrow field of matrimonial possibility pinned to the armoire door. The pensive Barth stood out, untouched on all sides by an inch of reverent cork.

"Look at him," Hazel whispered. "Looks like he could walk right out of that picture."

"And you sound like you're ready to walk right down the aisle. But I thought you said you got two letters today."

"Oh! How could I forget?" Hazel ran back to her desk and rifled through the pile of envelopes again. The one she selected was cream colored and obviously a heavier weight than the others. There had been a thin wax seal at its closure, and the paper itself made a rich brushing sound against the roughness of Hazel's hands.

"Listen to this: 'My Dear Miss Allenhouse: Having seen your letter, I feel it is the sign I have been looking for, and I am compelled to meet you. I will be in Cleveland on business the week of the sixth. I will be staying at the Hollenden Hotel and would be most honored if you would join me for luncheon there on Monday afternoon. Given the circumstances, I will quite understand if you choose not to accompany me. However, it is my earnest prayer that you will grant me this chance to make your acquaintance, knowing full well I cannot expect any more than that. Warmest Regards, Alex Triplehorn.'"

Hazel topped off the reading with an uncharacteristic squeal. "Doesn't he sound mysterious?"

"He sounds…"—Vada searched for the word—"…forward."

"And dinner at the Hollenden?" She flung open the other side of the armoire. "What can I wear?"

"You aren't seriously considering going?"

"Of course I am."

"You cannot simply meet a man at a hotel for lunch. Not unchaperoned."

"So I'll get a chaperone."

Vada laughed. "Doc doesn't even know about *this*." She ran her hand along the collection of clippings. "You can't break it to him with an invitation to lunch."

"I wasn't thinking about our father." Hazel's intense stare belied her true intention.

"Oh no." Vada held up her hands. "Two ladies at luncheon aren't any more proper than one."

"Ah, but if one is accompanied by her fiancé…"

"Stop calling him that." Vada's words came out harsher than she intended. "We are not engaged. We have an understanding."

"But—"

"And that's not the point. Garrison would never leave his office long enough to have lunch downtown."

"Not even for you?"

"No."

Hazel laid her head on Vada's shoulder. "Sure there's nothing you can do to convince him?"

"Oh, Hazel, feminine wiles would never work on Garrison." Or at least she didn't think so. She'd never actually tried.

"Please, Vada." Her sister took her in a full embrace. "No one's ever wanted to take me to lunch before. Please?"

Vada's mind filled with images of ballrooms and parlors. Parties full of young people gathered around punch bowls and dance floors flashing beneath swirling skirts. All of it she remembered as a blur, as she had been the one spinning and laughing and dancing. And at the corner of her vision, Hazel sat with a cup of punch and a cookie balanced on her lap or standing in full view, trying not to look for a partner. Her dress permanently rumpled, her hair disheveled on one side, her face clinging to dignity.

She sighed. "All right, Hazel. I'll ask him."

"Oh! Thank you!" She gave Vada a final squeeze before she took a pushpin and impaled the cream-colored envelope right next to Barth's portrait.

3

During the week, Molly Keegan controlled the Allenhouse kitchen with a fearsome Irish fist. She arrived before dawn each morning with a basketful of fresh eggs, butter, and cheese from her family's small farm just outside of town and spent the day clattering pots and pans, slamming cupboards and drawers—all the while singing tales of heartbreak in her thick Irish brogue.

But every Thursday night, promptly after serving the family supper, her meaty hand swiped the pay envelope from the kitchen counter and stomped out the back door, yelling over her shoulder that she'd be back Monday mornin' if the good Lord willed it and the drink didn't kill her.

More than once the Allenhouse daughters implored her to leave a little something bubbling on the stove to get them through the week's end, but she always refused, saying it was a sorry lot of girls they were that couldn't stir a stew.

So it was Vada who found herself rattling around, finding a few of Thursday's sausage-stuffed corn muffins in a bowl covered with a blue-checked towel and the remnants of yesterday's fish wrapped in waxed paper in the icebox. Four potatoes were left in the basket hanging above the icebox, a tin of peaches in the cupboard, and half of a blueberry cobbler in the pie safe.

"It'll have to do," Vada muttered to herself. She lit the stove's burner and put a pot of water on to boil. Just as she touched the knife to the first potato, the back door opened, ushering in the third of the Allenhouse sisters, her arms full of brown-wrapped packages.

"Althea, let me help you with those!" Vada took the largest of the packages, feeling its familiar bulk within the coarse twine. "Pork roast?"

Althea's weary nod mirrored Vada's lack of enthusiasm.

"And let me guess. Yams, turnips, and carrots?"

Althea silently confirmed each item on the list, and the two busied themselves stowing the vegetables in the hanging basket and the roast in the icebox until the next morning, when all would be assembled in the oven to simmer while the family was at church.

The Allenhouse girls knew how to prepare exactly four meals: the pork roast being one, followed by pot roast (with similar vegetable trimmings), fried bacon and eggs, and corned beef hash, provided they had leftover corned beef. It made for monotonous Sunday rotations, but to linger in the kitchen for the culinary tutelage of Molly Keegan meant being at the mercy of her unpredictable temper.

Vada poured her sister a glass of water from the cool pewter jug and placed it on the table before resuming her chopping. "Anything interesting come over the wires today?"

She spoke with her back to Althea, knowing full well she wouldn't get an answer. Not that there was anything wrong with Althea's ears. She could hear a whisper in a windstorm; she simply didn't speak. She wasn't a mute—not in any medical way. In fact, she had been a normal little girl, born when Vada was nearly five years old, and the older girl clung to memories of Althea's little voice singing songs, counting pebbles, and wailing at childhood injustices. Most of all, Vada remembered the sound of Althea's voice the morning the sisters woke up to find their mother gone.

"Where'd Mama go?" Althea had asked. "Is she coming back?"

Though Vada never asked about their mother, she had followed Doc day and night around the house, trailing his gloomy footsteps from one room to another, down to his basement exam room, and up again to the kitchen where he gave them bread and sliced cheese for supper three nights in a row.

Then on the fourth night, sitting around a table full of empty, crumb-scattered dishes, he dragged his reddened face out of his hands and looked across the table at three little pleading faces. "She's not coming back. Ever."

Young Vada and Hazel clasped each other's hands, their feet swaying in tandem beneath the kitchen chairs, but Althea would not be silenced.

"But why? But where? Papa? Papa!"

Until the man rose to his terrible height. "Never!" he roared. "Never! Never! Never!" His fists slammed into the table with each repetition, making the dishes rattle and the crumbs jump off the plates. "And if you mention her again, I'll throw the whole lot of you out to the wolves!"

That was back when the family lived in a tiny town in southern Ohio—before the ugly rumors prompted the move to the city—and their father seemed just crazed enough to toss them into the whirling snow. So the little girls fell silent and remained hungry until the next morning when Dr. Allenhouse greeted each one with a hug and a kiss and a bowl of fluffy scrambled eggs.

They'd breakfasted in silence, and for Althea, the silence continued. No amount of threat or cajoling or outright trickery could bring her to speak again. So she was the ideal employee at the telegraph office, never betraying the triumphs and tragedies that came across the wire to be typed onto precise yellow papers.

Still, Vada always asked about Althea's day, more to fill the silence than to seek information, and she smiled when she looked over her shoulder to see Althea running her finger along her tightly closed lips, the final say against any further prying.

"Just as well." Vada turned her attention to the chore at hand. "There's enough excitement around here to keep a mind busy."

She prattled on, filling Althea in on Hazel's newest correspondence and Monday's lunch date, pausing only when Althea's soft intake of breath warranted a face-to-face commiseration.

"And the widow Thomas is here again." Vada pointed down toward their father's office with the knife. "I don't know why Doc can't see through that woman. She's no sicker than I am, but maybe he likes the attention."

She turned to see Althea tapping the end of her nose.

"I just hope the woman doesn't plan to be asked to stay for dinner. It's a pretty pathetic spread we have tonight." Vada dropped the potatoes into the simmering water, added a generous shake of salt, and put a lid on the pot. "It'll be hard enough to stretch it for the five of us. Speaking of which…" She wiped her hands on a tea towel and squinted at the clock on the wall. "It's late. Did you see Lisette outside?"

Althea offered an indulgent smile and shrugged one shoulder.

"Honestly, that girl." Vada strode through the swinging kitchen door, nearly colliding with the widow Thomas in the hall.

"My goodness, dear." The older woman reset her hat. "A lady really mustn't charge through a room like a rampaging bull. Why, if Dr. Allenhouse were to see such behavior—"

"I doubt my father would have much to say on how I conduct myself in my own home, Mrs. Thomas." She ignored Mrs. Thomas's breathy retort and opened the door, swinging it wide enough to usher the widow out.

The woman's nattering decreased with each stomp down the concrete steps. Vada stood in the open doorway, arms folded against the cool spring evening. She intended to stay long enough to see Mrs. Thomas round the corner but regretted her decision when she saw the look on the woman's face as Lisette turned onto their street.

The girl, as usual, sailed along in a sea of young suitors—half-a-dozen young men all jockeying for position to see who could walk closest to her, shielding her from the dangers lurking at the edge of the sidewalk.

Lisette was seventeen years old, her hair a mass of caramel curls, long and loose down her back, held from her face by a burgundy velvet ribbon at her crown. Her wide pink lips were turned down in a pout, even as her eyes, dark and sparkling, danced with mischief.

She stopped in her tracks, causing the boys who followed to nearly collide with each other in her wake, and whispered something that made the tallest of the six clutch his heart in mock agony while the others exploded in laughter.

It was at just this moment that the little group crossed paths with Mrs. Thomas, and even from this distance, Vada could sense the woman's disapproval.

Lisette managed to hold a contrite expression until Mrs. Thomas turned the corner, but the minute the train of the unpleasant woman's skirt disappeared, the youthful party exploded in new mirth.

"Lisette Allenhouse!" Vada shouted from the top step. "Supper's on the table."

The flotilla continued in strolling lockstep until Lisette had one foot on the bottom step and pivoted to dismiss her faithful tugs. "Good night, boys." She turned her back, gathered her skirt in one hand, and skipped up the stairs. She barely acknowledged the sister who followed in her wake as she washed through the front door.

"Where have you been all day?" Vada took the girl's straw boater with its long blue ribbon and hung it on the hat tree in the hall. "And don't tell me you've been to the library because I know that wasn't a study group I just witnessed."

"Honestly, Vada. You're too young to be such a nag." Lisette tossed the words over her shoulder on her way to the stairs.

"What about supper?"

"Ugh." Lisette clutched her stomach and leaned against the banister. "I couldn't eat a thing. The Britton twins were arguing over who would buy me an ice cream soda, so I had two. One vanilla and one strawberry. If I keep this up, I'll be as fat as Hazel."

Vada chose to ignore the comment. She'd had enough conflict for one day.

"Well then, at least come in and have a cup of tea with us." It was a halfhearted invitation, considering how the girl was sure to ridicule the spread in the kitchen.

"Mary Winston is having a birthday party tonight." Lisette backed up a step or two. "Did Molly press my dress?"

"Only if you brought it down to the kitchen."

"Drat!" Lisette spun on her toe and rushed up the stairs, her hair a bouncing cascade down her back.

"Watch your language!"

But by that time Lisette was at the top of the landing, and the next sound was the slamming of her bedroom door.

Moments later, Vada was back in the kitchen, draining the cooked potatoes and tossing them with the last of the cream. Althea came up behind her and silently added salt, pepper, and a handful of dried chives. Hazel made her familiar boisterous entrance, and Vada set her to work flaking the meat off the leftover fish, which she tossed in with the potatoes. The happy find of a small tin of peas completed the dish that, in the capable hands of Molly Keegan, might have been an enticing chowder. Instead, it was an irregular mass of gradient bits that didn't even have the courtesy to steam as it was ladled onto the cheap daily ware plates.

"Good evening, girls." Their father's entrance was, as usual, without fanfare. He wore a brown rumpled suit that complemented his pale rumpled face.

The photograph of him taken upon the day of his university graduation showed him to have been handsome, if boyishly soft. Now the softness had gathered into little pockets beneath his eyes, and anything left of it was obscured behind a face full of whiskers. "We're eating in the kitchen tonight?"

"It's Saturday, Doc." Vada handed a fork to each one as she took her place.

Hazel plunked the peaches—still in the can—in the middle of the plain, sturdy table. "No need to make fuss with fancy dishes in the dining room for a meal like this."

Vada winced at the comment. "Without Molly here to help with the cleanup—"

Doc closed his hand around hers as he took his fork. "It was a simple question. No more." He gave something just short of a squeeze before making his way to the head of the table, stopping to plant a brief kiss on the top of Althea's head.

When all were seated, he held out his hands and, one by one, each sister grasped the other's, with Vada stretching her arm to reach Hazel's across Lisette's empty place. Doc raised one thick eyebrow in acknowledgment of the absence.

"She'll be eating later," Vada said. "At a birthday party."

Doc's eyebrow nestled back into place without question, and each of the sisters bowed her head.

"Dear Lord," he said in his usual, whispery voice, "we thank Thee for the food we are about to eat. May it nourish us to better serve Thee…"

Vada's mind drifted from the words of the familiar blessing. She heard Lisette's waltzing footsteps above her head as the girl readied herself for an evening of gaiety and dancing. During her father's deep, thoughtful pauses, Vada caught bits and pieces of her sister's breathy voice singing a popular tune. She closed her eyes tighter and tried to hear the words. Something about gliding across the floor with a beautiful girl while the band played on.

Much as he loved music, Garrison had never been much of a dancer, and for the briefest moment, Vada's mind pictured a swirling room while she looked up into the eyes of a flirtatious journalist.

She shook her head, hoping to dispel the image, but there it stayed until a quick pinch of her fingers brought her back to her senses.

Hazel took her hand away, and the only sound to follow Doc's "Amen" was the intermittent clicking of forks against plates. Still, it was enough to overpower the music upstairs.

Vada dug into the haphazard conglomeration and put a forkful in her mouth. For just a moment, she tasted the phantom flavor of ice cream sodas and birthday cake. But the more she chewed, the more she tasted the undercooked potato, the leftover fish, and the flavorless peas.

No use longing for what she couldn't have. She'd had her days of dancing in parlors, and now she had Garrison. Once again, though the prayer was long over, Vada closed her eyes and swallowed.

SUNDAY

A PRELUDE TO A DAY OF REST

I often wonder what God sees
When He's looking down at me.
And if He hears the words I say
Before, after, and when I pray.
I wonder what my God would say
If He sat down with me here today.
And if His thoughts are always kind
Or are they sometimes more like mine.

Althea K. Allenhouse, Winter 1895

4

Up on the third floor, a flurry of ribbons and stockings were traded from room to room. Stairs bore the constant clattering of footsteps as the sisters tore up and down to the kitchen where the iron was heating on the stove. Arguments erupted as to what hat belonged to whom. Indeed, the dignity of the Lord's day seemed tremulous in the hands of four young women wielding curling tongs. They yanked each other's corset strings, stole each other's shoe hooks, yet somehow managed to stumble out the door and down the front steps looking lovely while clutching dainty Bibles in lace-gloved hands.

This Sunday, like most Sundays, Dr. Allenhouse remained behind a closed bedroom door throughout the ordeal. Vada knocked twice and said, "See you at church, Doc?" before rushing to join her sisters on the sidewalk. Vada and Hazel took the lead, with Althea and Lisette quietly following.

"You got in awfully late last night." Vada declined to turn her head to address her youngest sister.

"Just…past…twelve." Lisette barely got the words out around the yawn.

"Did you have a good time?" Hazel asked.

"Oh, the best!" Lisette regaled them with tales from the party—a small band playing on the lawn, punch chilled with frozen fruit in

cut-glass bowls, and a veritable fashion show as some of the more afflu-
ent girls modeled the latest styles.

"Honestly, Vada," Lisette poked her head between the two older
sisters, "you've got to be the last woman in America wearing mutton
sleeves."

"I can't afford to buy new clothes just because some magazine tells me
mine are out of style."

"You could ask Doc for money—"

"She's not a child." Hazel offered Vada a warm nudge with her own
voluminous sleeve. "There comes a time when a woman needs to assume
responsibility for herself."

"At least until she can land a man to take care of her," Lisette said with
a giggle.

"If she's waiting on ol' Garrison, she'll be wearing mutton sleeves into
the next century."

Vada stopped, bringing the entire party to a halt, and glared in response to her sister's mischievous grin. But Lisette's giggle was infectious,
and even Althea was grinning broadly.

"Well, it could be worse," Vada said, allowing her own little smile.
"We could be wearing hoop skirts."

They talked of fashion—rather, Lisette offered a high-spirited
tutorial—for the rest of the block. When they turned the final corner on
Cleric Street, Garrison was waiting, dressed in a pale green summer suit
that drew a snicker from Lisette to punctuate her lesson for the day.

"Good morning, ladies." He offered his arm to Vada and led the
group across the street to Moravek's bakery.

The door to the small shop was open wide, better to accommodate
the steady stream of Sunday-morning customers. A dozen small tables
were placed up and down the sidewalk in front of the neighboring busi-

nesses, all of which were closed for the Lord's day. Moravek's would close too, right after the first ringing of the bells at the Methodist church. Until then, the good Christians of Cleveland could stop by for hot coffee and fresh pastries.

One table was empty, with only two chairs, and Lisette grabbed Althea's hand and rushed ahead to claim it. While Garrison set about procuring unused seats from other parties, Vada offered to go inside and order their breakfast.

"Cinnamon buns and coffee?" Moravek's cinnamon buns came hot from the oven, the sugar melting and drizzling into the folds of the waxed paper folded over the edge.

"And a pistachio éclair," Lisette said. "I'm starving."

"Make that two." Hazel opened up her square little pocketbook and produced a dime. At the mournful stare of her youngest sister, she searched around for another one.

"Althea?" Vada held a waiting hand under her sister's nose until she'd been given a nickel to pay for her own bun and coffee.

Inside, the bakery bustled with neighborhood churchgoers in their Sunday best. Vada took a numbered card from the hook by the door. Twenty-seven.

Mrs. Moravek stood behind the counter, wiped her hands on her flour-dusted apron, and called, "Twenty-three?" just as Garrison walked in.

"Are we close?"

Vada showed him the card.

"Not bad." He moved a step closer.

When Mrs. Moravek called, "Twenty-four?" the gentleman holding that number bustled past them, knocking Vada straight into Garrison's buttoned-up vest. She caught a whiff of his shaving soap—a hint of mint permeating through the dense odor of fresh sweet bread.

"You smell good," she said, emboldened by the noise and the press of the crowd.

"It's new." A flush of pink crept up from his collar. "Twenty-five cents a bar."

"Oh, my." She leaned closer and batted her eyes. "A man with intelligence and a sense of luxury. What an irresistible combination."

He laughed—a quiet sound she might have missed entirely if not for the bobbing of his Adam's apple.

"Do you remember when we first met?"

His eyes circled around the room and came back to her. "Of course I do, darling. It was right in here. A year ago. Well"—he looked up, calculating—"sixteen months."

"You were the saddest thing with a plain cake donut and tea."

"I was just out of school. That donut was a luxury."

"And what did you think?" Vada said.

"Aside from wondering how such a tiny woman could eat so many pastries?" He took both her hands in his. "I thought you were the most beautiful girl I'd ever seen."

Suddenly, despite the enticing aroma all around them, there didn't seem to be any room inside her for a cinnamon roll. Her stomach squeezed tight and her heart turned the same fluttering spin it had the first time she saw him.

She gave a flirtatious glance from side to side and ran a finger along the pale green lapel of his suit. "What would people say if you were to kiss me right here in the middle of Moravek's bakery?"

"Twenty-seven?"

"That's you." He squeezed her hands and brought them to his lips to give her fingers a quick kiss.

"Twenty-seven!"

"That's me." Vada pulled herself away and went to the counter and rattled off her order to Mrs. Moravek. "Are you sure you don't want anything?" she asked Garrison over her shoulder.

"I had a poached egg and toast with Mrs. Paulie," he said, all earlier traces of romantic abandon gone. "You know breakfast comes with the rent."

"I just thought you might like something…sweet."

"But I'm not hungry."

Vada gave up, turned around, and gave the handful of coins to Mrs. Moravek.

The next minute Garrison was carrying a tray laden with sturdy white mugs of steaming coffee while Vada followed with a white sack of warm pastries. The crowd parted for them, and they made their way through the open door to the crowded table outside where Lisette was in the middle of an animated story about the previous night's party.

"So this woman was dressed like a gypsy with a patchwork skirt and an enormous black lace shawl. She had a scarf on her head and gold hoop earrings, rings on every finger—"

"We know what a gypsy looks like," Hazel said, rifling through the bag for her éclair. "Get on with it."

"Well." Lisette took one of the mugs off the tray and took a tentative sip before continuing. "It was late in the evening and we all gathered in the parlor. Mary turned down all the lights save for a single candle and then, when we were all completely silent, this woman speaks."

Lisette set the mug on the crowded table and assumed the posture of a gypsy fortune-teller with a low-timbered voice to match. "'Leesten to mee…'" She waved her invisibly-jeweled hands. "'I see great joy coming very soooon for all of the young gentlemen in the roooom, and the ladieeees as well. I seeee a train coming into the station, and on it are men. Many men. Soooon the town will be overrun with Bridegroooooms.'"

"Lisette, please." Vada ripped a warm chunk off her cinnamon roll. "You're making a spectacle of yourself."

Lisette wrinkled her nose and dropped the act. "Then she reached into this old velvet bag and said she had a gift for all of us."

"Like a party favor?" Hazel spoke through a mouthful of éclair.

"Exactly. We each got a ticket to tomorrow's baseball game." Lisette paused, obviously waiting for a response, but when the table remained silent, she huffed and continued. "Tomorrow. Cleveland's playing Brooklyn. You know, the Bridegrooms."

Vada swallowed. "But you hate baseball. You've never gone to a game in your life."

"I know," Lisette said. "But we're all going. The whole party. And we'll sit together and drink ginger ale, and I figure I'll have to be next to some boy so he can explain the whole thing to me—"

"But you have school."

"The game's not until one. We'll all skip out a little early—"

"I can't even imagine doing such a thing."

"Well, of course you can't, Vada." Lisette wiped a stray bit of cream away from her mouth with the back of her hand. "It would be ridiculous for a woman your age to go to a baseball game."

"My age?"

Garrison, at least, had the decency to look embarrassed, but Althea and Hazel listened in with thinly veiled amusement.

"I meant alone." Lisette took the napkin Althea offered and placed it in her lap. "Now, if Garrison were to take you…"

"Now *there's* a thought," Hazel piped in. She slapped her hand on the table, causing the cups to clatter and garnering the attention of the people around them—primarily those waiting for an open table. "How 'bout it, Garrison? Are you going to take Vada to the baseball game tomorrow?"

"Um…no." He looked just uncomfortable enough to garner a rush of protective sympathy. "I, uh, only have one ticket."

This prompted a hoot from Hazel that in turn startled a gentleman behind her so he sloshed coffee onto his exposed shirt-sleeve.

"So, you go to baseball games?" Vada tried to include Garrison in the images she had of the ruffians in the stands, sloshing beer and getting into fights.

He sat straighter in his chair. "I do."

"But what about work?"

"I'll take the afternoon off."

"Ah, he has the afternoon off," Hazel said. "Tomorrow afternoon? *Monday* afternoon?" Her face contorted to produce such an obvious wink, everybody at the table turned to stare at Vada.

"Oh, yes." Vada remembered the luncheon invitation. "About that—"

Just then the first peal of the church bells made its way through the streets, and the crowd gathered outside the bakery let out a collective disappointed moan. On cue, the Allenhouse girls gulped what they could of the hot coffee, knowing Mr. Moravek would soon be out with his giant tub, grabbing the cups out of customers' hands.

"So, what about me?" Lisette said in the midst of the flurry of finishing breakfast and brushing the crumbs off their skirts. "Can I go to the game tomorrow, Vada?"

Vada and Lisette looked at each other for a moment, both knowing that neither permission nor blessing was necessary. A small sound of a clearing throat made its way through the cacophony, and Vada looked at Althea who, in turn, gave a brief, consenting nod in Lisette's direction.

"Oh, I suppose." Vada sounded more exasperated than she really felt. "Now, you all head on to church. I need to talk with Garrison."

She offered her cup—half-full—to Garrison and took Althea's to finish. The two remained rooted to their seats while all those around them emptied. They sipped quietly, uncomfortably, until Mr. Moravek, with his stained shirt and enormous mustache, came around saying, "Get up now. Go!"

Still, they lingered behind the last of the stragglers, and even then they walked much slower than their usual, purposeful pace.

Garrison was the first to break the silence. "I'm sorry I said I wouldn't take you to the game."

"I don't care about that." Vada looped her hand through his arm.

"If I thought you really wanted to go—"

"I don't." Vada tucked herself closer. "But I do need to ask a favor of you."

The church was just a block away, every step of the journey a familiar one. As they passed the neighborhood sights, Vada told him the whole story of Hazel's letter-exchanging exploits, and if he was shocked at her behavior, he had the good grace to hide it.

"So I need you to accompany us to lunch tomorrow," Vada said, summarizing the tale.

"At the Hollenden Hotel?"

"I know it's expensive. And I've told Hazel she would need to contribute to the bill because it certainly wouldn't be proper to let a total stranger—"

They'd arrived at the church steps, and she stopped to return one morning greeting after another as friends and fellow church members passed them on their way to the ornate double doors at the top. Vada kept her face a smiling mask, hiding just how much she hated having this conversation. Hated needing him so much for such a small thing.

"I just need you to be there," she said, fighting for control. "For my sister. And for me."

"Darling, of course if it means that much to you. I'll gladly miss an afternoon at the ballpark to be your luncheon escort." Without a hint of hesitation, he took her in his arms—right there on the church steps.

She waited for the warmth that had nearly taken over her body at the bakery to fill her, but she remained stiff in his embrace, the brim of her hat keeping her distanced from his shoulder.

After a moment he placed his hands on her shoulders and stooped to maneuver under that brim to place a warm, lingering kiss on her cheek. When he stood back, she lifted her face.

"Thank you, Garrison."

"I'll call for you at noon tomorrow. Now, shall we go inside?"

And like that, it was settled. The unknown made staunchly familiar, as common as the feel of Garrison's guiding hand at the center of her back.

MONDAY

OH, WHAT A DIFFERENCE A LUNCH MAKES

Secrets spinning in the air,
Secrets, secrets everywhere.
Secrets robbing you of peace,
Secrets—wolves beneath the fleece.

Althea K. Allenhouse, June 1895

5

The maître d' barricaded the doors of the Hollenden Hotel dining room with the help of an impressive wood podium that stood a good two feet shorter than he but not quite as wide. His dark hair was plastered into two wings on either side of his round face, and his cheeks fluttered with every garbled breath.

He paid no attention to Vada, Hazel, and Garrison as they approached through the lobby. Indeed, the gaze he fixed just above their heads seemed to move higher and higher with each step, until the first feature Vada saw close up was the depth of his cavernous nostrils.

"Do you have a luncheon reservation?" he asked when it was clear they weren't going away.

Hazel looked as if she were about to be sick at any moment, so Vada took her hand, ready to turn and flee if her sister desired.

"Actually," Garrison said, posturing himself to command the snobbish man's gaze, "we are due to have lunch with one of your guests."

"And which guest would that be?" He opened the enormous leather-bound book on the impressive podium.

"Alex Triplehorn." Hazel's voice was little more than a breath.

"Mr. Alex Triplehorn," Garrison said authoritatively, as if he hadn't heard Hazel at all.

"Ah yes." The man produced a smile that involved only one lip. "Allow me to show you to his table. I see, sir, that you have already checked your hat."

Garrison's hand went up to smooth the soft blond tufts. "I, uh, don't have a hat."

"Well, that's one mystery solved, then, isn't it?" He slammed the book shut. "I'll take you myself."

Vada pinched her sister's arm in retaliation for the barely contained snicker before sending Garrison an apologetic smile. The little party followed the broad dark suit through a second set of double doors into the main dining room.

She'd seen pictures of the Hollenden Hotel before, of course. Every Monday morning the society page ran photographs of Cleveland's elite gathered to do political and charitable things. But to actually walk in and see the intricate chandeliers glistening in crystal and pearls, the ornate gold-leaf wallpaper playing host to masterful works of art, the sea of tables draped in pure white linen—she had to stop, just for a moment, poised on the threshold to take it all in.

The conversation was little more than a ripple as heads throughout the room bent low over their tables. The occasional trill of laughter escaped but soon seemed to be swallowed up in the muffled bubble created by so many ladies' feathered hats.

More distinct was the sound of silver against china—tiny *clinks* of forks and knives. Through all of this, waiters dressed in crisp white coats wove their way around, arms draped with clean white towels, carrying glass pitchers of clear water or expertly balancing trays on up-turned hands.

Beside her, Hazel took a deep breath. "Smells delicious, doesn't it?"

Vada hadn't even thought about the food.

Garrison gave her sleeve a tiny, almost imperceptible tug, prompting her to follow, and soon they too were making their way through the sea of tables. For a man of such girth, the maître d' navigated the dining room with surprising agility while Vada, slim as she was, walked with her arms tight to her sides lest she send somebody's wine glass crashing to the glossy wood floor.

They came to a stop near the back of the room, three tables away from the swinging kitchen door. "Mr. Triplehorn?" The maître d' spoke with an accent he hadn't bothered affecting earlier. "Your luncheon party has arrived."

He stood at such an angle that the man seated at the table was blocked from view, and it wasn't until a set of broad shoulders rose above their host that Vada got a good look at the man they'd come to meet.

He was tall, yes, but his height alone couldn't begin to comprise his stature. His broad chest and long arms perfectly filled the expensive-looking suit jacket that might have been tailored for a giant.

He brought up massive hands to straighten his blue silk tie, drawing Vada's gaze to his face. Deeply tanned skin contrasted the stark white collar of his shirt, and his hair was the blackest she'd ever seen. It was short and brushed forward in tiny dry fans across the breadth of his smooth forehead.

Beneath it, dark brown eyes studied her face, then Hazel's, then back to her. One black brow lifted in curiosity.

"Mr. Triplehorn?" Garrison thrust out his hand in introduction. Mr. Triplehorn's grip swallowed it down to one pale, struggling thumb. His bemused expression remained.

"I am Garrison Walker. This is Miss Vada Allenhouse and, of course, Miss Hazel Allenhouse." Garrison said Hazel's name with a meaningful nod that seemed only to increase Mr. Triplehorn's confusion.

"I believe there's been some kind of mistake." His voice was low, his words clipped.

"I do realize that Miss Vada's and my presence might come as a surprise"—Garrison successfully regained his hand after a brief tug—"but under the circumstances, it hardly seemed proper to send Miss Hazel here without a proper chaperone."

"Miss...Hazel?" He spoke, as if mastering the English language.

With each passing second, another diner dropped his fork and turned to stare at the scene unfolding at Alex Triplehorn's table. If, indeed, this was the right table. Vada felt a flush rise to her cheeks. They were at the wrong table, talking to the wrong man. It had all been a hoax, a mistake. She was just about to grab her sister's hand and run back through the heavy double doors when Hazel spoke.

"Your confusion is understandable, sir." Her voice rose an unnatural octave, making her sound like one of the actresses in the touring companies that played at the Dresden Street Theater. "You see," she looked directly at Vada, "I thought it wiser not to use my Christian name in my correspondence."

This seemed to put all but the still-bemused Mr. Triplehorn at ease. Nonetheless, moving with considerable grace for a man his size, he stepped away from his place and pulled out a chair for Hazel. Garrison promptly followed suit for Vada, and soon the four were seated, each staring at the little bowl of pansies in the middle of the table.

"You must understand," Mr. Triplehorn said after what seemed an eternity of silence, "how difficult this is for me. I know I have no right—"

"Nonsense." The trill in Hazel's voice made Vada wince. "After all, it was I who placed the advertisement."

"Perhaps it was unscrupulous to take advantage. But I saw it as a sign." Mr. Triplehorn spoke slowly, almost a full pause after every two or three words, and listening to him gave Vada the chance to study him more closely.

His eyes almost had an almond shape, and though his hair was raven black, the series of tiny lines at the corners of those eyes meant he had to be forty—at least. Possibly older. What in the world could Hazel be thinking?

"A sign?" Vada said. Certainly such a statement deserved to be scrutinized.

Before Mr. Triplehorn could answer, a waiter in a crisp white jacket appeared with a cut-glass pitcher of water and proceeded to fill each glass. He'd no sooner left the table when a second waiter in a white shirt and black vest came bearing crisp, gilt-edged menus. He delivered a well-rehearsed speech about the chef's lamb stew and ambrosia salad, to which Vada only half listened.

Instead, she looked about the table—openly—as nobody was bothering to look at her. Hazel kept her head down, staring at her hands. It was an unfortunate posture, as it brought forth a rather jowly appearance and caused a furrow between her brows.

Mr. Triplehorn seemed equally uncomfortable as he spent the entire time trying to find a place to land his gaze, ultimately turning his head to the side, watching the party at the next table.

All in all it was hardly what Vada expected, given the passionate tone of Mr. Triplehorn's letter and Hazel's eagerness to meet the man behind it. But from the moment they approached the table, there had been such an obvious air of disappointment emanating from the man, Vada couldn't help but join her sister in what she was sure was a desire for the floor to open up and swallow them whole.

She turned to Garrison, hoping his sweet, gentle nature would be able to find some way to bring ease to this moment, but he was lost in the menu, his eyes growing wider and wider as he took in the prices. Vada bored her gaze into him, willing him to look up at her, and when he did, he merely held up his menu to block his face from the view of Mr. Triplehorn and mouthed, "Just get the soup."

As the waiter came to the end of his speech, he brought forth a little notepad on which he poised a short, elegant pencil. "Are we ready to make our luncheon order?"

"We are not," Mr. Triplehorn said with such an air of finality, Vada began to think Garrison could put his mind at ease about the soup.

Their waiter gave an offended sniff at his dismissal, and his mustache barely moved when he announced his imminent return.

Left alone, an uncomfortable silence returned to the table. Vada cleared her throat. "You were saying," she reached for her water glass, "that you took Hazel's post as some sort of a sign?"

"I must have been mistaken." His voice was low, his words measured.

"Mistaken?" She allowed her fingers to rest on the elegant stem of the glass, too afraid to lift it lest her intense grip cause it to snap in her hand.

"Vada, darling, please." Garrison's gentle touch on her arm invited her to relinquish her grip, and she wanted so badly to entwine her fingers in his, grab her wounded sister, and leave.

"I was working in Cheyenne when I saw the advertisement and read the name Allenhouse. It is such an unusual name, I thought certainly…" He seemed to finally have the good grace to feel uncomfortable. "You are not—" He spoke toward Hazel, who still refused to look up, before switching his gaze directly to Vada. "She is not the young woman I expected to meet."

Vada bristled at the implication. "The *young* woman?"

"The woman in the advertisement clearly said that she was eighteen."

Beside her, Hazel winced at his words.

"Now see here," Garrison said, after a false start in which his voice got tangled at the top of his throat. "I find it insufferably rude of you to comment on the young lady's age in her presence."

"I only meant—"

"And furthermore," he straightened in his chair, "I think it's a fair enough assessment to say that, even with her misrepresentation—"

"Garrison!" Vada clutched at his sleeve.

He covered her hand and gave it a gentle squeeze. "Darling, we must concede that Hazel's true age has been, let's say, altered."

"Oh, dear Lord." Hazel planted her elbows on the table with such force that the pansies quivered in their vase, and she buried her head in her hands.

"As I was saying," Garrison continued, "even given that distortion, the lady is clearly not much more than half your own age—"

"Garrison!" Both sisters pleaded in concert.

"—so if it was the bloom of youth that so enticed you to pursue this introduction, I submit that you have not yet been presented with any reason to disavow the acquaintance of Miss Hazel Allenhouse." By the end of his speech, Garrison had taken off his glasses and used them to emphatically point to the mortified woman across the table. In the awkward aftermath, he used the edge of the tablecloth to clean the lenses.

Vada studied him—so rare was it to see him without his spectacles, rarer still to see him in the throes of such passion. Suddenly the familiar placid blue of his eyes took on the glint of pure steel, and the impressive Mr. Triplehorn seemed to have been wounded indeed.

"I have no objections to her age," he said once Garrison's glasses were safely perched on his nose. "She is simply not the woman I came here to meet."

"Oh, enough," Hazel groaned, scooting her chair away from the table. "I cannot take more of this."

"No, wait." Vada put a restraining hand on her sister's. "My sister is a lovely young person. And she may seem like some bold, modern woman ready to strike out and begin a new life in the middle of nowhere, but inside—" Tears welled in Vada's eyes, and the quivering in her chin wouldn't allow her to continue.

"After all," Garrison picked up the argument, "there is a reason they are referred to as the weaker sex. A certain gentleness is required."

"Please." Mr. Triplehorn waved away the approaching waiter, whose face was now twisted into sour disdain. "I will say only that I have made a mistake and I apologize. Now, if the three of you would like to stay, I'll leave instructions that the bill be charged to me."

"You owe us an explanation," Vada seethed.

"I owe you nothing besides the lunch to which I invited you."

"Under false pretenses and with malicious, dare I say, salacious intent," Garrison added.

"I assure you I meant no harm."

"Then what did you mean?" Hazel's voice was reed thin—so far from its usual breezy boldness that Vada felt the last of her reserve begin to crack. "Why bring me here? Why not just write to me? Perhaps if we'd become more familiar, I wouldn't seem so, so…wrong."

"All right. If you must know, I came here today hoping to meet a young woman who might be your younger sister."

"Althea?" Hazel said, her mouth hanging open on the final syllable.

Again, Mr. Triplehorn looked confused. "Marguerite told me she named the child Lisette."

Marguerite. Mama. She named the child…

Suddenly the innocuous noise of the diners around them—the clinks of the forks, the mild laughter, the rattle of the carted dishes—all melted to one oppressive roar inside Vada's head. The burning sensation at the back of her throat spread throughout her body, and it seemed the next breath would incinerate her, so she didn't take it. She held it in, fearful of bursting, as snippets of long-ago conversations bored their way through the mass of noise. And when the realization hit, horrible in its entirety, all that heat and fire turned to ice.

"Vada, dear, are you all right? You've gone white as a ghost." Garrison's voice sounded far away, as if coming through a storm. "Now see here, Triplehorn. Just who do you think you are?"

"He knows…" Vada fought the sudden dryness of her mouth. "He knew our mother."

"It was foolish of me." Whatever arrogance Mr. Triplehorn had possessed was gone, but Vada wasn't moved anywhere near to pity. "I loved her very much, and even though she told me the child wasn't mine—"

"The child? Our Lisette? You think she's—she's *yours*?"

"I've always wondered—"

"Well, stop." Vada clutched her napkin in both hands, twisting it like rope. "Stop wondering and go home."

"I have to see her."

"You've no right to see her." Garrison's calm voice offered Vada some measure of warmth.

"I need to know."

"*I* know," Hazel said, a shadow of her old self. "You couldn't possibly be her father. She's beautiful and funny and—"

"Nearly eighteen." Although he didn't state it outright, he was obviously implying a calculation.

"Now see here." Vada stood, clutching the table lest her legs give way. "You have already caused enough heartache for our family. You took away our mother. If not for you, she would be here—would have been here for all of us, all our lives. She might even still be alive."

"Ah, Vada." The sound of her name on Triplehorn's lips steeled her. "You are as strong as she said you were. She knew you would be fine—"

"Don't you dare!" Suddenly all the school-yard fights, all the scuffles endured defending her mother's soiled reputation rose up within her, and it was all Vada could do not to leap across the table and knock him to the ground, no matter what his size. "Don't you dare talk about our mother; you're horrible, awful—"

From somewhere behind she felt a restraining hand, but she shook it off, ready to relaunch into her tirade until she heard someone say, "Miss. *Miss.* I must insist—"

It was the troll-like maître d', looking positively justified at having been called in to moderate this fray.

"You'll insist nothing," Hazel said. "Take your hands off of her this minute." She always had been the one to come to Vada's aid in a fight, and soon Vada's arm was free, and the maître d' took two steps back.

"Come on, girls." Garrison stood and walked to stand between the two sisters. "We've nothing more to say here."

"Yes, we do." Vada separated herself and walked around the table, leaning closer and closer to Mr. Triplehorn. "You stay away from our home. You stay away from our sister. Do you understand?"

The man refused to so much as flinch, and when Vada stood straight again, he said, "I will be here for the remainder of the week." He looked around Vada to the maître d'. "I believe I'll be luncheoning alone after all."

Vada landed on the sidewalk outside the hotel with all the force of having been thrown there. Nothing about the ground seemed capable of supporting her weight, and it wasn't until Garrison's arm steadied her that she felt confident to stand.

"I'll get us a cab." He spoke low into her ear.

She tore herself from his embrace and spun around to find Hazel and grasped her hand. "We'll walk." She bent low, ready to shoulder her way through the crowd. Hazel was dead weight behind her—a sullen piece of furniture to be carted across the pavement.

"Hazel, come on!"

"It's twenty blocks. I'll never make it in these shoes."

Vada looked at the narrow kidskin slippers peeking out beneath Hazel's skirt. A far cry from her usual, practical flat-heeled boot, these had a dainty one-inch heel that quivered in protest beneath the foot spilling over it.

"Those are Lisette's shoes."

"I know, but they're so much prettier than any I have, and I just wanted—"

For the first time since that horrible afternoon began, Hazel's eyes filled with tears, and she crumpled, sobbing into Vada's shoulder. "How could I be so stupid?" She punctuated each word with a deep, wet gasp. "I've never been so...so...embarrassed. He looked at me like I was a monster."

The passersby on the street slowed to gawk at the emotional scene unfolding on the sidewalk, and whatever tendrils of pity Vada felt for Hazel withered with each footstep, to be replaced with a branching stem of anger.

"Now you just get yourself together, Hazel Allenhouse." She shook loose and left her sister to stand alone, fumbling for her handkerchief. "You don't have any right to cry about this now. It has nothing to do with you. Try to think about Doc for a minute, what this'll do to him if he finds out. And Lisette..."

"You don't—certainly he couldn't be—"

"I don't know." Vada burned with shame at the thought of it. "I just hope he stays away."

"We have to tell Doc."

"No, we don't. We don't have to tell him anything. It's best we keep it to ourselves."

"But what if Mr. Triplehorn—"

"We've enough demons of our own to worry about, Hazel, without bothering our heads about what Mr. Triplehorn might do."

"Here we are, ladies." Garrison stood holding the door open to a black horse-drawn cab. He bowed like a footman in a fairy tale.

It was a scene that spelled escape, and suddenly Vada was more than ready to take it. She allowed Garrison to take her hand, but still she lingered on the little extended step. "Are you sure? I hate to cost you the cab fare."

"Trust me, darling." He brought her fingers to his lips for a quick kiss. "It's nothing compared to the price of our abandoned lunch."

Vada offered a weak smile and settled inside, scooting across the seat to make room for Hazel. Garrison folded up the steps, climbed in, and shut the door, signaling the driver to commence.

For a while the only sound inside the cab came from the sounds outside the cab—the rhythmic clomp of the horse's hooves, multiplied a hundred times over, accompanied by the shouts of all those drivers trying to maneuver through the streets. Sometimes the song of a street vendor rang out, and Vada's stomach reminded her that she hadn't eaten yet that day.

She looked out the window and saw the man with a dozen hot pretzels stacked on a stick and a green grocer's display of fresh fruit. No doubt Molly had prepared a lovely dinner, but they had already told her not to expect them, and to show up unexpectedly was sure to set Molly in a fiery temper.

But in just that minute, the pang of hunger twisted, and she couldn't imagine taking even a bite to fill it.

"I'm starving," Hazel said, pouting.

"Just shut up." They weren't children after all.

"Now, Vada…" It was the voice Garrison used every time it seemed her mouth was about to run her into trouble. Sometimes she resented the stifling, but now—poised at the edge of falling to a real fight—she surrendered to the gentle rein and came to a shuddering verbal halt.

For the first time since they got in the cab, she looked at him. He offered her a warm smile through the dim light until the cab hit a jarring bump sending him sideways in his seat. When he righted himself again, his long legs stretched farther across the width between them, and she could feel the boniness of his knees through her skirt. As usual, when some unforeseen event brought them into such close physical contact, he begged her pardon and resumed his unnaturally erect posture in his seat.

That was Garrison, gallant and proper to the extreme. Usually she basked in his chivalry. But right now she inwardly cringed at his decorum. Given the circumstances of the afternoon, had she somehow been tainted by Mr. Triplehorn's revelation?

"Oh, Garrison." She covered her face with her hands. "What you must think of us."

"It certainly was…enlightening."

"I guess I never told you about our mother."

"You told me she died."

"She did," Hazel said.

"But she actually left us before that."

"So, she left with this Triplehorn fellow?"

"I don't know," Vada said, more to herself than to him. "We woke up one morning when Lissy was just a baby, and she was gone. Maybe she left both of them."

Garrison brought his hand to his chin and gazed at a point just above the sisters' heads. "Now why would they run off and leave their baby?"

"Lissy isn't *their* baby," Vada said.

"She doesn't exactly look like the rest of us," Hazel muttered.

"That's because we look like our mother." Vada didn't often allow herself to dredge up painful memories, but from the moment Mr. Triplehorn said her mother's name, she'd been haunted by that final image of the woman, sitting in the rocking chair next to her marriage bed, knowing her lover waited in the carriage on the street.

"We might look like her," Hazel shifted in her seat, "but Lisette certainly *behaves* like her. All those boys. Hanging off the arm of one with another following behind like a puppy. Next day, same scene, different boys. Both of them, no more morals than a couple of cats."

"Don't talk about our sister that way," Vada said. "Besides, how much better are you, running down strangers who answer a newspaper advertisement?"

"There's no comparison—"

"You have five pictures pinned to that armoire door—"

"Ladies, please!" Garrison actually waved his hand between them to get their attention. "We aren't going to solve anything by arguing this point."

"Well, we aren't going to waste any time speculating about such nonsense," Vada said. "I don't want to speak another word about it. Not a word." She pointed a finger in Hazel's face.

And while Vada couldn't bring herself to repeat the gesture for Garrison, he seemed to understand. The rest of the ride passed in silence, until she looked out the window and saw they were little more than a block away from home.

"Stop here," she said, relegating the actual task of communicating with the cabbie to Garrison. "If we pull up to the house in a hired cab, everybody will want to know how we've spent the afternoon." She looked pointedly at Hazel's shoes. "We'll walk the rest of the way."

Garrison poked his head out the window, and soon the cab slowed to a stop. He got out, folded down the little stepstool, then reached his hand inside to help Hazel descend. For just those few seconds, when the little door was filled with Hazel and her skirt, Vada allowed herself to take one deep, shuddering breath.

"Oh, dear Lord," she said, speaking out the window. "What are we going to do?"

The next minute her hand was gripped in a pale, smooth, capable one, and he held it long after both of her feet were firmly on the ground. Then, after she gave Garrison a little squeeze and a little smile, he paid the driver, offering up an uncharacteristically generous tip. "It's still cheaper than lunch."

Hazel was already several steps ahead, moving at a flustered pace that might have been close to running had she not been so hobbled by her borrowed shoes. Vada and Garrison strolled, arm in arm behind her. With the noon hour long waning, the neighborhood was nearly empty. They said "Hello" to a little boy playing with a set of tin soldiers on his front stoop and greeted another woman pushing her baby in a tram.

"We moved here when I was ten, you know." Vada watched door after door pass by. "We had to move after Mother left. We had to; people aren't always…kind. At the time I didn't really understand what they were saying about her, but later on…"

"It must have been hard on your father."

"On all of us. You know, Lissy's the only one who calls him *Papa*. He hired a nurse for her and didn't really speak to the rest of us for years."

"Can I ask you a question, darling?"

"Of course." She loved it when he called her *darling*.

"Did you ever hear from your mother after she left?"

"Not a word."

"Then how do you know she died?"

"Just what I've told you. One evening Doc brought us all into the parlor, sat us down, and said our mother had taken ill and died."

"How soon was that after she left?"

"Not long." They passed a lilac bush in bloom, and Vada stopped to lift a bunch to her nose and inhale its sweet scent. "About a year."

"So that's why you never told me that she'd left you."

"It's not something I—we—talk about."

Garrison looked surreptitiously up and down the street before reaching into his pocket and pulling out a folded knife. After one last peek over his shoulder, he sliced the bunch of lilacs from the bush and handed them to Vada with a bow.

"You deserve flowers today."

"But—"

"Ah." He held up his hand to stop her protest. "If the owner comes out of her front door in the next twenty seconds, I'll gladly give her a nickel for her blooms. Ready?"

They stood on the sidewalk, Garrison quietly whistling a little tune as he rocked back and forth on his heels.

"See anybody?"

Vada giggled. "No."

"Then they are yours, m'lady."

She smiled and held them close, breathing in their sweetness. No doubt Garrison believed this simple gesture could erase the shame of

Triplehorn's intrusion. Right now she never wanted to lift her nose from the blossoms, never wanted to leave the sweet simplicity of this man, this moment.

Soon, however, she felt the slightest tug on her elbow and looked up into his eyes—their pale blue somehow diminished in comparison to the vibrant blooms in her hand.

"Better, darling?"

All she could offer was a brave face.

They walked a little farther, and as they got closer to home, Vada pulled her feet slower and slower.

"How do you think your father learned of her passing?"

"I don't know." They came to the corner and turned it.

"And is she truly dead? Or did one of the parties in question simply concoct this story to dispel any hope of her returning home?"

Vada stopped short, crushing the lilacs in her hand. "This isn't a case for you to sift through the evidence. We've never heard a word—not a single word from her. What kind of woman could walk away from her children for a lifetime?"

"I only thought, if she were capable of such, mightn't your father want to spare you knowing?"

"He would never give up hope." Again, the burning sensation in her throat at the memory of her father, all those nights sitting at the window, the way he refused to let any of them touch the mail when it dropped through the slot in the door, even if it had to sit there for hours.

"He loved her, Garrison. There's never been another woman in his life. Ever. But not because he's waiting for her to come back. That night, when he told us she was dead, he died a little too. "

There was no holding back the tears now. Vada buried her nose in the flowers and sobbed.

"There, darling." Garrison's arms wrapped around her, and she allowed herself to collapse into them. "Of course you're right, and it was awful of me to have said anything at all."

His shoulder was warm from the afternoon sun, and she felt so safe there. His hand pressed tight against her back, his thumb moving in small, regular strokes. After a time, she matched her breathing to the movement of that thumb and felt the only thing holding her up was the frame of this man. If he released her, she might surrender to the sidewalk. Or float away.

Why, when a woman had a man who offered this kind of strength, would she ever leave?

"Come along." His lips moved against her hair. "Let me get you home."

"I don't want to." Her voice was muffled by his jacket. "I can't face them."

He stepped back but kept his grip on her shoulders. "Now, you'll be fine. You're a big girl."

"I hate being a big girl." She gave a playful pout.

"Nonsense. You love bossing people around."

"I'm tired of it, Garrison. I've been bossing people around all my life. I get tired of being in charge all the time."

"You know, dear, it might be that you need not be so hasty in jumping in. Perhaps you need to step back and trust the Lord to take care of you."

"Of course." She brushed the comment away with a wave of the lilacs. "I just mean that—just once, I'd like to run away. Throw caution to the wind and embark on some wild, crazy journey."

He grinned. "We did that this afternoon, didn't we? And that didn't turn out too well. But maybe next time."

"And you'll go with me?"

"Of course I will, darling. But, alas, not now. I have things to finish up at the office."

"But you took the afternoon off."

"That doesn't make the work go away, unfortunately. And if I want to come to rehearsal tonight with a clear head, I need to finish some things."

"And you're sure you're not upset about missing the game to go with me?"

As an answer, he leaned forward and kissed her. No sooner had her lips reacted to the fact that they were being kissed than he'd drawn away, pink cheeked. "Couldn't very well do that on your front stoop in broad daylight, now could I?"

Her heart gave the tiniest flutter, and she was glad he still held her up. "Yes, you could."

"Hmm…well, we'll see when we get there." He turned toward her house and held out his arm.

"No," she said, unable to bear the thought that he might *not* kiss her again. "I'd like a few minutes to collect my thoughts."

"Very well." He leaned forward again to give his customary kiss good-bye to her cheek, and she hoped she imagined the hint of relief behind the gesture.

She continued alone the few steps until her house came into view, checking over her shoulder, just once, to see if Garrison was there for a final wave, but he'd already disappeared around the corner. She should have asked him if he loved her. He did, of course. He'd told her so dozens of times, but to hear it once more might have set her shoulders straighter.

Oh, how she dreaded that first step through the front door. Her father's face—questioning where she'd spent the afternoon. Wondering why Hazel was in such a state.

Hazel!

What if she'd already blurted out the whole story? Certainly Hazel could be sly and secretive when it suited her purpose, but as upset as she was when they left the restaurant—

Oh, Hazel, please, please let me tell Doc. Let me take care of everything.

Just as Vada began to formulate exactly what to say when she walked through the front door, the door itself flew open, and there was Lisette flying out of it, her caramel-colored curls bouncing behind her.

"Vada!" She tore down the sidewalk without the least glance to the left or right. "Vada! Thank goodness you're home! Oh, it's the most terrible thing ever! Or most wonderful—I can't tell..."

Once she closed the gap between them, Lisette grabbed Vada's sleeve and tried to tug her along behind.

"Lissy!" Vada wrenched her arm away. "What in the world—"

"Shhh!" She held a finger to her lips. "It's supposed to be a secret."

"*What's* supposed to be a secret?" Vada planted her feet. "I'm not moving one more step until you tell me."

Lisette glanced over her shoulder with a mischievous grin. "Then you'll never know. But trust me; you'll want to see this."

6

Vada could hear the commotion before her foot even touched the bottom step. Lisette had left the front door wide open, and from it emitted a low, rumbling sound punctuated by the fearful voice of an irritated Molly Keegan.

"Get out! Out o' my way 'fore I toss the lot of you to the street!"

Vada followed her bounding sister up the front steps but stopped short at the Allenhouse threshold. In truth, she had no choice but to stop, as the narrow entryway was packed full of men—all different shapes and sizes—dressed in varying shades of white and gray. They wore short pants with dark socks, and it would be several seconds before the shock of the scene wore off and left Vada with a clear, if unexplained, definition of the scenario in her home.

"Why is there a baseball team in our house?"

"Isn't it wonderful?" Lisette was still clutching Vada's sleeve, and now she pulled her close. "It's not a whole team, of course. But honestly, sis, there's more than enough to go around."

"Don't tell me they followed you here?"

"You are so silly." Immediately Lisette's attention was drawn to a tall, thin man stationed at the doorway leading into the front parlor. She smiled her widest smile, the one that brought her shoulders up to her ears. He, in response, twirled the corner of his overgrown mustache.

"Well," Lisette lifted her hand in a delicate, finger-wagging wave, "maybe one or two…"

"Then what—"

"Ah, now here you are, missy hoit-n-toit finally decidin' to come home." Molly Keegan thumped down the final step and made her way through the crowd, dispersing the men like so many nine pins. "And haven't I told you more'n a dozen times that the noon dinner finds its way to the table at precisely noon? But I suppose after a fancy outin' downtown, you're just like your sister, expectin' me to keep it waitin' for ya on the off chance you'll make an appearance."

"Molly, what is going on?"

"Well, ya might know if ya'd been here at noon like you're supposed to, now wouldn't ya? But go on back to the kitchen where your Hazel is. I made some stuffed cabbage rolls, and if you're wantin' to eat today I'd make it quick. Never seen the girl tuck into nothin' like I seen—"

The woman's oblivion to the fantastic scene around them proved too much for Vada's patience. "Molly! Answer me!"

Nobody—not even their father—ever spoke to Molly Keegan with anything other than subservient gratitude, and Vada immediately regretted her outburst.

The Irish woman swelled up before them, like some mythic Celtic giant in a lace cap and starched apron. Her hands became meaty red fists at her side, and her eyes sparked, as if ignited by the tiny licks of flame at the tips of her ears.

Vada felt Lisette cower behind her back.

"And now *you* think ya can take that tone with me, missy? Well, I've got *this* to say to the lot o' ya!" Her voice boomed above the din, and there was an immediate drop to silence, as if someone had lifted the needle off a phonograph cylinder. "It is my job to see to the needs of these four girls and their father. Do ya understand me? I'm not taken in this house to care for a bunch of ill-bred hooligans the likes of you. So don't any of ya dare to ask me to fetch you *this* or tote your *that*. If you're hungry, make your way back to the trough that slops ya, 'cause not one of ya's under my lovin' care."

By the time she had finished, her face was nearly the color of her famous strawberry compote, and her fisted hand was held high, as if inviting Irish maids everywhere to follow her cause.

The skinny man at the parlor door dropped all pretense of making eyes at Lisette. In fact, he was staring at the brass spittoon in the corner when Vada noticed the telltale bulge in his cheek.

"And as for this," Molly said, making a straight line for him, his eyes growing wider with each approaching step until she was right in front of him. "I didn't sign on here to spend my days washin' your filthy tobacco stains. So you'll not be spittin' any of it near this house, and that includes the porch. Do ya understand?"

She took her thick finger and pointed, then poked the man's distended cheek, causing him to swallow, choke, and turn ghastly pale. There was a low ripple of laughter at this, and Molly's face was a mask of triumph as she made her way back to the kitchen. Before leaving the hall, though, she turned to make one last stand.

"One final thing." She was no longer yelling, as by now even her softest whisper would probably strike fear into the hearts of anyone in the room. "If I catch any one of ya layin' so much as a finger on any one of my girls, I'll strip ya down and grind ya up for sausage. Startin' with your feet so ya can watch the whole thing. And if you doubt me, poke yourselves into my kitchen and see how handy I am with a cleaver."

The next sound was that of a swinging kitchen door, and Vada, who had witnessed Molly's finesse with a knife, shuddered on behalf of those on the tail end of the threat.

"What in the blazes is all this noise?" Her father's voice drifted from the top of the stairs.

Finally, someone who could answer her questions. Vada tugged herself away from Lisette and hurried up the stairs, thankful for the relative privacy of the stairwell. "Doc, can you please tell me what's going on?"

As an answer, he beckoned her to follow him up the final steps and into the hallway to the first room on the left. Her room. The door was closed, but he opened it and stepped aside, allowing her to enter ahead of him.

At first it seemed little more than a scaled-down version of the scene downstairs. Just three men were in the room, each wearing the signature knicker uniform. They stood with their backs to the door, one shoulder to another, their feet at a wide stance, their heads bowed, caps in hand.

Doc cleared his throat. "Step aside, gentlemen. If you would." Silently, the three stepped back and parted, making way for Doc to get closer to Vada's bed. "Come see." He beckoned and Vada stepped forward.

On any given day, her narrow bed would be covered with a lavender quilt patterned with scattered peonies. Now, lying atop her pristine bedding was a man dressed in a tattered brown suit. Someone, at least, had thought to remove his shoes, which fell short of a blessing as it forced them all to see a pale, white toe jutting through a hole in the well-worn sock. The pants were frayed at the hem, and the shirt was coarse cotton, but clean. His hands lay perfectly still at his sides, knobby wrists poking out of cuffs fastened with twine.

Her gaze followed, up to his pale neck, riddled with an angry-looking red rash, to the face framed by the pure white linen of her goose-down pillow. He had broad, soft lips topped with a thin fuzz of mustache and a narrow nose with the tiniest hook at the top. But above that nose— that was the image that caused Vada to gasp.

"Oh, dear Lord!"

The man's eyes wore a mask of bruising. Deep purple orbs extended to the top of his cheeks, filtering nearly to the temple. And his forehead, where thick, blond hair had been slicked away with water, was equally discolored—a marbled pattern of red and purple and green, with a distinctive mark just above his left eye. Vada leaned closer.

Lace marks. Like someone had molded a baseball right into the flesh.

"What on earth?" She reached forward but kept her fingers aloft.

"Got hit with a clean line drive." The voice behind her was rough but warm, and it held the last three words just long enough to indicate the speaker was from somewhere south of Cleveland. Maybe Texas? And he spoke with an air of admiration, although she couldn't decipher just what was being admired.

"First home run of the season," said the second man at which the third snorted.

"Quite a price to pay for a silly game." Her father spoke from just behind her, and she felt his hand on her shoulder.

"Oh, Doc. Is he…?"

"He's unconscious," Doc said.

"Knocked clean out."

"Dropped like a sack of hammers."

"Poor sucker never saw it coming."

"Unfortunately neither did my outfield."

The ensuing laughter enraged Vada, and she spun around only to find herself inches away from a Bridegroom, according to the letters stitched across the expanse of dark gray fabric. BRIDEGROOMS. Faint lines crisscrossed each other creating a field of perfect squares, and the center was laced up in a pattern identical to the wound on the unconscious man's head.

The shirt was open at the top, revealing a triangle of sun-bronzed skin. She had to take a step back to take in the breadth of him, and she lifted her gaze to look up and up and up, past a strong, clean-shaven jaw, not stopping until she found a pair of warm hazel eyes—a mischievous marble of brown and green—poised on the cusp of a wink. Never, in all the time she'd known him, had Garrison ever looked at her in quite that way.

She squelched the unwelcome flutter his gaze invited and tried to remember why she was angry. Oh yes. The man on the bed.

"How can all of you laugh? A man is dying here." She managed to tear her eyes away from those tipped with ginger-colored lashes and looked to her father. "Isn't he, Doc? Is he dying?"

"I don't know."

Her father's words brought a quiet to the room that her outburst never could, and Vada took the opportunity to study the other men in the room. Neither stood as tall as the one directly behind her, though the three of them served to dwarf her father in their midst.

"Gentlemen, allow me to introduce my daughter. Vada, this is Mr. Oliver Tebeau."

"Most call me Patsy." He had a face as round as a chipmunk and wore a rough woolen shirt that long ago lost its battle to be white. The word SPIDERS crossed his chest in a rainbow arc of square block letters interrupted by a vertical row of black buttons.

She hesitated to take his outstretched, chapped red hand, but her self-taught good manners trumped the aversion and she took it, forcing a smile as his skin chaffed against hers.

"Third base and manager for Cleveland."

"And this is Mr. William Barnie."

"Call me Billy." He reached out a hand as soft and moist as Mr. Tebeau's was rough and dry. Mr. Barnie was bald as an egg on top of his head, with a fringe of salty blond encircling the rest of it. His eyes were pale blue, his mustache tipped with gray, and his uniform so precise—down to the crisp bow tied at the base of his throat. Probably hadn't seen a speck of dirt in years.

"And this young man," Mr. Barnie said, taking the burden of introductions away from her father, "is about the most powerful hitter you're gonna see in this league. Lucky LaFortune."

She snatched her hand away from Mr. Barnie, but not in time to conceal the most impolite snicker at the ridiculous name.

The bearer of the amusing moniker offered an odd, adorable smile that started at the center of his mouth and extended up toward his left ear, creating a half-moon of white, straight teeth.

"That ain't but my name on the field," he said, the accent more pronounced. "My given name's a whole story, but you can call me Louis." By the time he'd finished speaking, his smile was a blinding crescent in the midst of a clean-shaven, sun-kissed face. A smattering of pale freckles graced his cheeks and nose—to be expected given the red-ginger color of his close-cropped hair.

She wasn't exactly sure when her palm landed squarely in his, but there it was, nestled in a warm, strong grip. Suddenly it seemed as if all eyes—save for the ones closed behind bruises—were staring at her.

"Very nice to meet you, Mr. Tebeau. Mr. Barnie." She turned her head to acknowledge each one. "Mr. LaFortune."

Clearly, if she waited for him to release her, they might all have to bed down for the night on her floor. Resisting the urge to outright yank herself away, she slid her fingers from within his clasp and asked why the man hadn't been taken to a hospital rather than her bedroom.

"Bit more privacy here," Mr. Tebeau said. "We don't need the press snooping around, trying to make their slugger look like some sort of killer."

"Now, that is uncalled for." The corners of Mr. Barnie's mustache blustered in his outburst. "I think you are simply more concerned with maintaining this ill-gotten reputation of being a field of goody-goodies—"

"Our team has a spotless record—"

"Until a certain player of yours goes on his drunken rampages—"

"Sockalexis is ten times the player of any man in your uniform!"

"Gentlemen, please!" Her father nearly jumped out of his shoes to break up their conversation. "There is a critically injured young man here. I expect a little decorum. If you must continue this conversation, I insist you take it outside. And I don't mean *downstairs*. I mean out of my house and down the street. And take your men with you."

Mr. Barnie and Mr. Tebeau eyed each other uneasily, spun in slow unison, and wedged themselves through the door.

"If'n you don't mind, *mon vieux,* I'd like to pass some time here to see if the boy wakes up." LaFortune's smile was gone. His eyes were cast down, and he shuffled uneasily from one foot to the other.

"Of course, son."

Vada's heart ached at the tenderness in her father's voice. Maybe it was the utterance of the word *son* and the way it seemed to clutch at the top of his throat.

"I do have things to tend to downstairs. Vada?" Her father paused at the doorway, waiting for her to follow, but she still had so many questions. Now that the dueling managers had been dismissed, maybe she could get some answers.

"I'll be right down, Doc."

Thankfully he didn't press the matter, only issuing her an unmistakable warning glance before pushing the door open wider before leaving.

"He a good man, your pa-pa."

"He's an excellent physician." She focused on the wounded stranger.

It seemed the best way to keep her thoughts straight. "So he was hit with a ball."

"Yes, that."

"But he's not a player?"

"No, ma'am. Was sittin' in the stands. Must-a had him a good seat too. Right up front. Beg pardon…" His voice caught, and whatever words that were to follow were swallowed up in his welling emotion.

The sight of this tall, strapping, handsome man seemingly moved to tears and the plight of this helpless wounded soul made Vada swell with an overwhelming need to offer solace.

"Oh, you poor, poor man." Vada resisted the urge to offer a comforting touch. "Are you the one who—"

"Yes, ma'am. It was my hit. A good 'un too. Not too high. Sailin', sailin' until…boom!" He slammed his fist between his eyes. "*Frappe-à-tête* and I reckon he just gone down."

His words meandered from one language to another. French, from what she remembered from school. The poor, wounded one temporarily forgotten, she tilted her head and batted her eyes. "*Vous êtes français?*"

"*Pas du tout.*" He puffed with pride. "Slithered out of Louisiana swampland, bayou born."

Vada's mind leaped to stories of ports and pirates, powerful, dangerous men. She tried to picture Lucky Lou LaFortune sporting a red head kerchief and gold earring and found it a surprisingly easy picture. After all, here he was, tall, broad shouldered, able to knock a man unconscious with the swing of a bat. Once again, she dragged her thoughts back to the matter at hand.

"Did you…*see* him fall?"

"Too busy runnin'. But I hear tell after that he just dropped."

He was once again overcome, bringing the back of his hand to his mouth to stifle what might have become a heartfelt sob. This time, Vada did not resist.

"There, there…" She put a gentle hand on his forearm, right where he'd pushed his sleeve up to his elbow. The feeling of his skin seemed too intimate for this setting, however, with only a comatose chaperone, so she moved her hand up, resting lightly on the firm bicep.

Perhaps he too was uncomfortable with her touch, because he flexed his muscle not once but twice. The feel of it was thrilling. Too thrilling, and she took her hand away after the fourth. "I'm sure there was nothing you could have done."

"Maybe he couldn't. But *I* could."

Startled, she spun around, but nobody was behind her. Nobody in the open doorway either.

"I shoulda caught that ball. Didn't even call it."

The muffled voice came from behind the open door. Vada moved it aside to see yet another young man in a Spiders uniform—himself a rumpled mass against the wall. Long, dark hair fell into a red-blotched face. He'd been crying for some time apparently, and he was crying now, though he attempted to stem his tears with balled fists thrust into his eyes.

"Ah, see here *bougre*." Lou walked over and crouched down to come nearer to speaking with him face to face. "You don' know you coulda caught that ball."

"I didn't even try," the Spider said. "Didn't even put my glove up. Didn't even *see* it. I was too busy looking at her."

"Who?" Lou asked.

"Vad-aaa!" Lisette's singsong voice announced herself. "Papa says for you to come downstairs!" She skipped into the room wearing a naughty grin that grew more mischievous as she looked between Vada and LaFortune.

At Lisette's entrance, the young Spider scrambled up the wall, bringing himself to his full height, which put him just to Vada's shoulder. The poor boy looked terrified as he worked to smooth the hair from his face and plunk the cap back on his head. His eyes, dark brown pools of leftover tears, drank in the vision of Vada's youngest sister.

"Actually, Papa says *both* of you should come downstairs and let the guy have some quiet."

"What—" The Spider cleared his throat and tried again at a lower octave. "What about me?"

Lisette looked at him, her eyes trailing from cap to toe, as if deciding whether or not to squash him. "What about you?"

"Should I stay here? Or go downstairs with you?"

Lisette shrugged. "I hardly think it matters."

She flounced out of the room. The Spider, none the worse for the slight, trailed behind her.

Vada followed suit, assuming Mr. LaFortune was in tow, but a gentle sound brought her up short. She didn't recognize the tune, or the words, but the essence was unmistakable.

She turned to see Mr. LaFortune sitting square on his haunches, his hands gripping his cap loosely between his knees. He leaned close to the wounded man's ear—as close as his posture would allow—and half whispered, half sang:

> *Fais do do, petit frère,*
> *Fais do do ce soir.*
> *La lune t'aime, et moi la même*
> *Fais do do, petit frère.*

"That's beautiful," Vada said when the last note—such as it was—faded away. Her mind scrambled for a translation. "What does *fais do do* mean?"

He smiled that crescent smile and stood, crushing his cap in his hands. "It mean, 'go to sleep.' I singin' 'go to sleep, little brother.' But I guess that don' make much sense, singin' such to a man already sleepin'. But it what my *maman* sang to me many a night, and it just seem—"

"It's beautiful," Vada repeated. "And that line about the moon."

"Ah, that." He took a step closer, ostensibly toward the door, though she stood in his path. "The moon love you."

"Yes." If she'd taken one more step back, she wouldn't be this close to him now, wouldn't be smelling the scent of sweet grass on his shirt or noticing the single dark freckle on his earlobe.

"*Et moi la même.*"

"And so do I," Vada said, translating.

"You *parlez bon français?*"

"Oh, I don't speak it as well as I understand. Besides, it's a simple song."

"Did your *maman* sing such simple songs to you?" Mr. LaFortune asked.

All that had been flowing warm and loose within her froze and grew tight in her throat. "No. Not since I was very, very little. I suppose I outgrew such things."

"*Pah!* How do a child outgrow a lullaby?"

"That's easy, Mr. LaFortune." She placed one foot behind her, and the rest of her body followed suit until she could freely breathe the air of the open hallway. "When she's forced to start singing them."

7

It was Molly Keegan who decided that the first course of action to be taken with the comatose spectator was to strip him of his tattered clothing and bathe him the best they could.

"No matter what happens," she said, filling a clean bucket with boiling water from the kettle. "If he wakes up, he's not bearin' the shame of such filth. And, Lord forbid, if 'twere to go the other way, it's a clean soul we're sendin' to meet Saint Peter at the gate."

Hazel, Lisette, and Vada all sat at the kitchen table, where the two older sisters peeled and sliced potatoes for that night's beef stew, and Lisette, at Vada's insistence, read the second act of William Shakespeare's *The Tempest* to make up for having missed that day's lesson at school.

"You'd better check with Doc," Vada cautioned, wishing somebody would have thought to do so before soiling her pretty bedclothes with this stranger. "We might need to be careful in how we treat him."

"*Ach.*" Molly made a guttural noise at the back of her throat and slammed the empty teakettle back on the stove. "Not enough now I have the four princesses to see to, I'm takin' on the care of foreign invalids."

The kitchen had a door leading down to the doctor's office, and Doc had warned Molly several times not to disturb him during his working hours with household questions. Still, without hesitation, Molly flung it open and stared down the dark staircase before turning to Hazel. "You. Run downstairs and see what your father has to say."

Hazel, who hadn't said more than two words since leaving Vada and Garrison at the corner, set down her knife and wiped her hands. Once the sound of her footsteps faded, Molly took her place and began digging out potato eyes.

"Now tell me, Miss Vada. What's gotten into that one? She hasn't been the same since you got home from your mysterious outin'."

Vada shifted her gaze to Lisette, whose mouth silently twisted around the words of the Bard. "Lissy, why don't you take your homework upstairs to your room? It's much quieter up there."

Lisette wrinkled her nose. "It's *too* quiet, if you ask me. And what if that guy," she looked from side to side before leaning over the table to whisper, "*dies*? And it's just the two of us up there?" She shuddered. "No, thank you."

Vada sighed. "It's nothing." She returned to the task at hand, managing to peel off one long, curling piece of skin while leaving much of the potato itself intact. "Hazel and I just thought it would be fun to have lunch at some fancy place downtown, and it was…well…awkward."

"And why wouldn't it be? What business do ya have goin' to some stranger's kitchen when you can get the best of all cookin' right here in your own home?"

"Oh yes." Lisette's voice was primed for sarcasm. "Beef stew. Quite the culinary accomplishment."

"That's enough with you." Molly gestured with the knife, a small chunk of potato clinging to its tip. "I'll have you know I had something a wee bit grander planned before those ones come trampin' in with Sleepin' Beauty upstairs."

"Speaking of which," Vada said, grateful for the change in subject, "do we have any idea what his name is? Did he have any sort of identification?"

"Sure'n I'd be the last to know if he did," Molly huffed.

"Perhaps we'll have to go through his pockets later, when we," Vada shot another cautionary glance toward her youngest sister and mouthed, *undress him*.

"I'm not an idiot." Lisette had resumed reading her page. "And there's no need to worry—I can't imagine anything more disgusting than looking at that man naked. So you both feel free to keep the bathing party all to yourselves."

Molly and Vada laughed as the last of the potatoes were peeled and the skins scooped into a bowl to be taken out later to compost the garden. Molly then set aside the paring knife in favor of her large butcher knife and began turning each potato into bite-sized chunks with just one or two decisive blows.

Lisette, not taking her eyes off her book, held out an open hand, and Vada knew exactly what to do. She snatched a potato from Molly's unchopped pile and cut it in half, lengthwise, then trimmed the rounded side off, leaving her a full-length flat slice.

She took the saltshaker from the middle of the table and shook a generous amount onto the glistening white potato slice and wordlessly dropped it into Lissy's outstretched hand. Soon the only sounds in the kitchen were those of Molly's knife, Lisette's crunch, and Vada's fingers drumming on the heavy wooden table. Soon added to that were Hazel's footsteps.

"Doc says it's fine." She reached over Molly's shoulder, grabbed a chunk of potato, and salted it for herself. "And he wrote up a list of things we'll need to get for…him."

"Let me see." Vada took the scrap of paper from Hazel's hand and squinted, trying to better focus on her father's scrawl. "Two yards thick cotton batting and *three* waxed sheets? Why three?"

"If it turns out he lasts more'n a day, don't want him soakin' up the mattress."

"Oh, my." Vada shook her head, trying to dispel the image. She refrained from asking the purpose of a sea sponge and cornstarch. "Hazel, why don't you and Lissy go right now and get these things so you can be back by the time Molly and I have him ready." She reached for Hazel's hand and ignored Molly's scowl when Hazel flinched at her touch.

"Why do I have to go?" Lisette licked the salt from her fingers. "I'll never get my homework done."

"Not at the rate you're going. You've been on the same page for thirty minutes."

"Come on, Lissy." The tender tone in Hazel's voice clutched at Vada's own heart. "We can get an egg cream at the drugstore."

"Don't you be spoilin' your dinner, now." Molly got up from the table and dropped the sliced potatoes into the pot of simmering water, heedless of the splashes that sizzled on the stove. "Though you might stop by Moravek's and get a cream cake for dessert. It's a hard day we've had, and I think we're due a little sweetnin'."

"I'll go get my hat."

Vada watched Hazel walk out of the kitchen, noticing she'd changed back into her own wide, sensible shoes. Vada wanted to take time to warn her not to say anything to Lisette or Althea or anybody about their lunch with Alex Triplehorn, but the sadness that emanated even from her slumped shoulders told a story that Hazel had chosen to keep buried deep inside. At least for now. And if nothing else, the young man upstairs was proving to be a welcome distraction.

"And you, littlest miss," Molly said, busily crumbling herbs into her stew, "take them peelin's out to the compost heap."

"Can't Vada do it?"

"Vada's got her own unpleasant chore waitin'. Now go 'fore your sister gets back downstairs."

Lisette sighed and pushed herself away from the table. She somehow managed to hold the bowl of peelings with just two fingers, the others distended in a dainty display of distaste. Holding the bowl as far away from her as possible, she opened the door leading out to the backyard.

Then came the commotion—Lisette's high-pitched scream, the clattering of the bowl, the scattering of the peelings, and the boy in the Spider uniform falling into the kitchen.

Vada jumped up from her seat and was standing by her sister's side before the bowl came to a spinning stop on the floor.

The poor Spider, looking equally confused and embarrassed, immediately began to scoop up the peelings to put them back in the bowl.

"I'm dreadful sorry, Miss Allenhouse." He acknowledged Vada, then Lisette. "Miss Allenhouse." He looked over his shoulder and up at the looming Molly Keegan and began scraping up the peels a little faster.

When the last one had been dug up from between the floor boards, he brought himself unsteadily to his feet and raked the dark curly hair away from his face, leaving behind a tiny bit of peel in the process.

To Vada's horror, Lisette reached out and plucked the peel straight from the boy's hair and shook her hand, sending it fluttering back into the bowl. "Just what were you doing out there?"

"I couldn't leave. I couldn't go not knowing if he… How is he?"

"He hasn't woken yet," Vada said gently. Something about the boy touched her; everything about him seemed hungry. "Perhaps you'd like to stay for supper, Mr. …"

"Cupid." He extended a hand, looked at it, wiped it on his pants, then extended it again.

Lisette snickered. "Cupid? Honestly. Of all the—"

He stumbled over his words to answer. "No, honestly. I mean, yes, that's my honest name. Kenny Cupid. Sometimes they just call me Kid, 'cause I'm so young. Well, not that young. Almost twenty. But I'm not one of these guys that gets the slick nicknames. Which is a good thing, I guess, since *cupid* rhymes with—"

"Stupid?"

"Lisette Allenhouse! How could you be so rude?" Vada turned to Kenny. "I do apologize for my younger sister. Sometimes she is just terrible."

"Like she's taken over by the devil himself." Molly spoke over her shoulder, having turned back to her stew.

"Ah yes." The way Kenny looked at Lisette was nothing short of longing. "But wasn't Lucifer the fairest of the angels?"

Lisette rolled her eyes. "I don't have to stand here and take this, you know." She pointed through the open door out into the yard. "And you can take that right out to the compost pile. It's a big heap of stinky, festering trash. So you should have no trouble finding it." She spun on her heel and flounced out of the kitchen.

His eyes never left her, even staying transfixed on the swinging door she left behind. "She's the most beautiful creature I've ever seen."

"Don't be fooled by that pretty face," Vada warned. "This isn't even her worst behavior."

He dropped his gaze to stare longingly into the potato peelings. "I guess it wouldn't be a good idea for me to come to supper after all, then."

Molly slammed the lid on the pot. "I'll be decidin' who stays to dinner and who doesn't. Now," she approached, wiping her hands on her apron, "you take those out to the yard, then pick up this bucket an' the kettle an' meet me upstairs to help wash up the man. You'll be sparin' Miss Vada here the chore no young woman should see."

"Yes, ma'am."

"An' do ya have a decent shirt to put on?"

"Not with me, ma'am. But this one's clean."

"Then it'll have to do." Molly stepped into the mud room briefly to retrieve a large washtub, then made her way to the back steps.

"Don't be afraid of Molly," Vada said.

He looked up, and for the first time, she saw a certain light in his eyes.

"Don't worry about me, Miss Allenhouse. I haven't met a fear I couldn't conquer yet."

Relieved to be free of the responsibility of bathing the patient, Vada met up with her sisters at the front door with a hastily scribbled note. "While you're out, will you stop by the theater and give this to Herr Johann? I want him to know that I won't be coming in this afternoon or this evening for rehearsal."

Hazel put the final pin in her hat and took the note. "We'll be back in an hour."

Vada stood in the empty entryway, unsure exactly what to do, when Molly clumped her way through saying, "An' look at the mess they've made down here. I feel I've lived three lives this very day." She held a length of clumsily folded waterproof tarp under one arm and still carried the empty washtub. The young Kenny Cupid followed close behind, carrying the steaming kettle.

"Are you sure you don't need my help?" Vada called up after them.

"'Tis not a fit job for a lady." Molly's words were no fainter at the top of the stairs than they'd been at the bottom.

Vada escaped to the parlor and slumped into the nearest chair. In truth, nothing she'd done today was fit for a lady. Sneaking off to lunch with a stranger, confronting her mother's sordid past, kissing Garrison on the corner in the middle of the day. Touching Louis LaFortune.

She sank further into the chair and clutched her own arms at the thought of it. Noticing how thin they were brought forth the memory of the thick strength of the Bridegroom's biceps. The sound of his lilting, playful accent kept time with the ticking of the mantel clock, and soon her feet were tapping and she was humming the little tune he'd whispered in the ear of the wounded man before they left the room.

Who knew a man could have such a big heart *and* such broad shoulders? Why, he'd nearly been in tears at the bedside. She'd never seen Garrison—

Garrison.

She jumped up and looked around, as if anybody walking into the room might have been privy to the ideas swimming around in her head. Gracious, *she* didn't even want to acknowledge them. What kind of a woman would entertain such thoughts when she had the affections of a warm, generous man such as Garrison? Why, they had an understanding. Practically engaged. They'd declared their love for each other, and some-times—quite often, actually—Garrison's kiss was almost as thrilling as what she imagined a kiss from Louis LaFortune would be.

Stop it!

She paced around the room. Compared to most parlors she'd seen, the décor was downright sparse. There were no corner whatnot shelves packed with figurines. Rather, there was a simple, worn sofa and two up-holstered wing-back chairs. In the corner by the window, a small round table hosted a chessboard, the players abandoned in the last battle be-tween Hazel and her father.

One tall bookcase was stuffed with various tomes. All of the intricate medical books had been moved down to Doc's office, lest any of the girls run across an inappropriate anatomical illustration, but a few scientific volumes remained. Althea, once fascinated with insects, had spent hour after silent hour watching them through a magnifying glass, and the *Entomological Classification* text was just as lovingly tattered as father's prized copy of *David Copperfield*.

Visitors often commented that the room lacked "a woman's touch," and then seemed embarrassed, given that four women lived in the home. Vada looked at those women now, their photographs lining the mantel-shelf above the fireplace. Two on each side of the simple ticking clock. The three older girls had sat for a photo at the time of their graduation. In hers, Vada smiled the sweet, closed smile that brought out the dimple just below her lip. The color of her eyes was lost to the photograph, but she knew its lavender hue was identically reproduced in Hazel, who looked out at her from the next frame. Taken just a year later, this could have been a picture of Vada herself, given Hazel's slender figure at the time.

Althea remained the tiny wisp of a thing she was in her photograph, where she wore an intricate black dress with tiers and tiers of ruffles. Her hair was parted down the center and rolled on each side with a flower pinned above her left ear. More than anyone, Althea appeared the same in the picture as she did in life. Maybe because so much of her time was spent in silent stillness.

Next to the photograph of Althea was an ornate silver frame with a green velvet mat behind the glass. The mat revealed two oval-shaped cutouts, and within one of those ovals was a photograph of Doc. Taken nearly thirty years ago, he was a young man, hair slicked down and whiskers neatly trimmed. He wore a white carnation in the lapel of his jacket, as the picture was taken on his wedding day.

The image in profile, Vada remembered as a little girl loving the way her father seemed to be looking with such longing at the woman who, in her own profile, looked back at him. Her childish imagination thought of the thin strip of green velvet mat as some sort of mythical valley the two lovers must cross in order to find each other in the terrestrial world.

But the photograph of her mother had long been removed. In fact, it lay tucked away inside the top drawer of Vada's bureau, where it had been since the night she snuck down into the parlor to remove it from its frame. She used to look at it every night, turning her face to the side, trying to look into the woman's eyes and beg her to come home.

Soon enough, that image of her mother gave way to the profile Vada could never forget—that of her mother in the lamplight, rocking in the chair, humming her final lullaby. That was an image that could never be framed.

Now, instead, the image of her father looked at one of a little Lisette in a photograph taken when she was just twelve years old. Even the dullness of the picture couldn't hide the coppery shine of the curls pinned to the side of her head with large white bows.

Where Althea, Hazel, and Vada all faced the camera with winsome, thin-lipped smiles, Lisette showed no such restraint. Her eyes were wide, her bow-shaped lips parted, her hand the tiniest blur in her lap.

Molly Keegan always said that the three eldest Allenhouse girls could be a set of those Russian nesting dolls—so alike they were in feature and so graduated in size. But Lisette never fit into that image. She was at once as tall as Vada, as buxom as Hazel, and as thin waisted as Althea.

Vada took a deep breath and stared once again at the head of the mantel, craning close, looking into one face, then the next, then the next—the horrific words of Alex Triplehorn echoing in her mind.

"Oh, Mother," she whispered to Doc's boyish profile. "Certainly you couldn't."

But then she thought about herself this day. Comfortably kissing one man and thrilling at the touch of another within the hour. "Or maybe you could."

The light touch on her shoulder startled her, and she spun around, stifling a cry as she saw it was only Althea, a bewildered expression on her face.

"You've got to learn to take heavier steps."

In response, Althea ripped a slip of paper off the little notebook she wore suspended from a ribbon around her neck.

Are you aware that Molly and a man named Cupid are giving a sponge bath to a naked man in your bed?

The tears that Vada had been so close to just a moment before disappeared, set free with the release of laughter. "Oh, my goodness," she said once she caught her breath. "Nothing you read in the telegraph office could even come close to the excitement we've had here today."

Vada put her arm around her younger sister's slim shoulders and led her to the sofa where they both collapsed, legs tucked up underneath them, and began to tell her the story, beginning her narrative on what she imagined happened the moment Lucky Lou LaFortune's bat hit the ball.

By the time Hazel and Lisette came home from their errands, Althea was smiling broadly at the image of Kenny Cupid meekly following Molly up the stairs.

But Alex Triplehorn and their fateful lunchtime conversation appeared nowhere in the tale. After all, he'd been kept a secret for the past seventeen years. No need to add him to the mix today.

TUESDAY

AMEN TO YOU TOO

If I could speak, and set all women free,
My voice would ring from tree to tree.
If I could sing, and thereby cure disease,
Our home would ring with melodies.
If this poem were the best of all my pen,
I'd never write a poem again.

Althea K. Allenhouse (though she's
loathe to claim it), November 1897

8

Most of the room was still hidden in predawn shadows when Vada opened her eyes. The first thought to register was surprise that she'd slept at all, given how uncomfortably crowded sharing a bed with Hazel had been. At some time during the night, she'd rolled off the bed and onto the floor, taking her pillow and the blanket with her.

Groaning, Vada eased up onto one elbow until she was eye level with the mattress. There Hazel lay curled up within the flannel gown that was the only covering she had against the cold. Her face was smashed against the pillow, and as Vada's vision adjusted to the darkness, she realized one violet eye was open and staring straight at her.

"I tell you one thing," Hazel said, her voice thick with sleep, "that boy'd better wake up or die today, 'cause you're not sleeping in here again."

It was a wicked thing to say, let alone laugh at, but Vada couldn't help herself, feeling such relief at seeing the spark of her sister return. It had been a long time since laughter was the first utterance of the day. In the last breath of it she asked, "Is it time to get up yet?"

"Nope. The clock downstairs chimed five just a few minutes ago."

"How long have you been awake?"

"Awhile." Hazel scooted to the far side of the mattress and patted the newly vacated space.

Vada climbed up, ignoring the protest of her aching back, and settled gratefully into its softness. She brought up the blanket to cover them both, and they snuggled together. Vada tried not to squeal when Hazel lodged two icy feet against the backs of her legs. "Your feet are like icicles."

"You always were a cover hog, but I've never known you to actually take the blankets *away*."

They twisted and turned, seeking each other as much as warmth and comfort, and when they finally settled in together, their breathing became deep and even. Perfectly synchronized when the parlor clock sounded quarter past the hour.

"I'll never get back to sleep," Hazel whispered to the shadows.

"Hmmm…" Vada was already drifting.

"I'm sorry to have been so horrible yesterday. It was all just such a shock."

Vada patted her sister's leg. "It's all right."

"After dinner, Doc cornered me in the hallway and asked what was wrong."

Now fully alert, Vada propped herself up on one elbow. "What did you tell him?"

"Nothing, really. I told him I didn't like the way Lissy treated that Cupid boy at dinner."

"She was terrible, wasn't she?" And she had been, countering Kenny's every attempt at conversation with some withering, sarcastic retort.

"Yes, but still…did you see the way he looked at her?"

"Poor kid." Vada settled back down and stared straight up at the ceiling.

"I wonder what it would be like to have a man look at me that way."

"Like he doesn't have a brain in his head?"

Vada could sense Hazel's smile. "No, like he doesn't have any thoughts in his head besides loving you. Consumed."

"Kenny Cupid plays baseball. He has to catch, throw, and hit. No thinking required."

"That's just it," Hazel said. "One look at Lissy, and he couldn't even do that much." They were silent for a while before Hazel continued. "Garrison doesn't look at you like that."

"Garrison's a lawyer. He needs to keep *a lot* of thoughts in his head."

"I know but—" Hazel shifted, and this time when her feet touched Vada, they were warm. "Has he ever? Even when you first started courting?"

"Of course he has. I mean, he did." She was almost sure.

"I'm afraid our Lissy's going to break that kid's heart."

"That's what our Lissy does best."

Another bit of silence and it was Hazel's turn to prop herself up, only this time Vada followed suit and the two looked into each other's eyes, barely discernable in the darkened room.

"Tell me, Vada. What do you really think, now that you've had a night to sleep on the idea?"

"I think I need another night of real sleep," Vada said. When Hazel showed no sign of responding to her little joke, she reached out her free hand and touched her sister's face, her fingers touching the lace of the nightcap Hazel insisted on wearing every night. "What do you want me to say?"

"What are we going to do?"

"We aren't going to do anything, Hazel. Not anytime soon."

"But Doc—"

"May already know that Mr. Triplehorn is in town. Goodness knows he's never felt the need to share any of this sordid tale with us over the years. I see no reason why we should share our little chapter with him."

Vada hadn't meant for the words to come out quite so bitter, and she steeled herself for Hazel to leap to their father's defense. Instead, Hazel just lay back down and pulled the covers up to her chin.

"But you have to stop moping around the house about it, or everybody will know for sure that something is wrong."

"I'll try." The words were lost in a yawn so big, Vada feared Hazel's jaw would unhinge.

Unable to stop herself, she followed suit, burying her head deep into the pillow. Somewhere downstairs, the sound of the kitchen door signaled Molly's arrival to prepare breakfast. Vada allowed herself one quick thought about getting up and going downstairs to help, but it disappeared as quickly as it came.

The next time Vada opened her eyes, a strip of sunshine pierced through the curtains. The rattling of pans had bloomed into Molly's familiar morning warning that if the family wasn't at the table for breakfast in ten minutes, she'd be wanderin' the streets lookin' for a dog to feed it to.

Vada was alone in Hazel's bed. Alone in the room, in fact, and she stood up and stretched, grateful for the last bit of sleep. Once the lingering kinks were worked out, she went to her knees at the side of the bed and bowed her head to pray. It was a ritual she'd held to since she was a child, since the first morning after her mother left when she'd prayed to find her downstairs in the kitchen.

This morning, no matter how tightly she closed her eyes against distraction, she could not bring her heart to focus.

She thanked God for the restoration of peace between Hazel and herself and asked Him for wisdom about how to handle the problem of Alex Triplehorn.

But even as she asked for guidance, her mind swirled in anxious circles as she entertained the possibility of his outrageous claim. She prayed that Doc's heart would be protected even as she wondered how or if she would ever tell him about yesterday's lunch at the Hollenden Hotel.

Just as she asked for healing for the stranger in her bed, she realized she had no idea what the man's condition was. With a quickly uttered "Amen," Vada was up on her feet and reaching for the dressing robe she'd draped over Hazel's bedpost last night.

"Amen to you too." Hazel stood just inside the doorway, dressed, her hair haphazardly pinned at the nape of her neck. "Molly sent me to ask your highness if you would like your breakfast sent up on a tray."

Vada debated for a moment which would rouse greater anger in Molly—showing up at the breakfast table in her dressing robe or taking even more time to go downstairs. "I just need a few minutes." She tied her belt. "Have you checked on…?"

"Doc's in there now. I don't think there's any change."

"I guess we'll have to take that for good news." She gave Hazel a quick hug in the doorway. "Tell Molly I'm on my way."

The door to Vada's bedroom was partially open, and she tapped on it before poking her head around the corner. "Good morning, Doc."

Her father was standing at the foot of her bed, his hands in his pockets as he studied the still form. He looked up at Vada's greeting and beckoned her inside.

"No change?"

He shook his head. "But his pupils are responding better to light—less sluggish. Heart rhythm is good. I have to admit, I've never treated a patient in this condition before."

"What else could you be doing?"

"Could be a thousand things. Maybe nothing. I just don't know."

Vada sidled closer and linked her arm in his. "Do you think maybe you should call in another physician? As a consultant?"

He patted her hand absently. "I gave those men my word I would treat him here and that I'd do it privately. No need to make a scandal out of it until…"

"What can we do?"

"Just keep watch. And pray."

"Of course." She let go of her father's arm and leaned in to look closely at the patient. A fine layer of beard formed along his jaw, though his cheeks were still quite clean. The mask of bruising had taken on a greenish hue, and the lace marks on his forehead were starting to fade. His breath was slow but even.

Molly had left him in a state of undress with the blanket pulled up over his chest. But his thin, white shoulders were exposed, as were his long, thin arms. Nothing muscular about this man. No sign of a life of hard labor. Yet his clothes were nothing like those of a man of privilege.

"I wonder who you are."

"Pray to God that he'll tell us soon enough," Doc said behind her. "When he wakes up."

"Of course."

They were quiet for a moment together. Had her father meant for them to pray right at that moment? She bowed her head and kept her eyes closed until she heard his uncomfortable shifting behind her. "Amen," she whispered.

"Amen, indeed."

He walked out of the room then, leaving her alone to sift through her armoire to find a clean shirtwaist and skirt. Once those were decided upon, she moved to her bureau, constantly checking over her shoulder as she chose her undergarments and stockings.

She clutched these close to her, covering them with her other clothes, and backed out of the room, keeping her eye on the gentle rise and fall of the blanket folded across the man's chest, and nearly collided with Althea in the hallway outside the door.

"Still no change," she said, responding to Althea's inquisitive glance toward the door. "Come with me into Hazel's room." When she spied Lisette at the top of the stairs, she motioned for her to follow them in.

"Girls," Vada said, closing them all inside the room, "we need to have a plan."

Lisette immediately reached for the door. "I don't have time for a plan. I have school."

Vada took a deep breath before answering. "Well, when you get *home* from school, we'll need you to take a shift."

"Shift?"

Hazel jerked her thumb in the direction of Vada's room. "With him."

Lisette cringed and whispered, "Is he still here?"

"Of course he is," Vada said.

"Then I've got to go. That crazy Kenny Cupid said he wasn't going to leave this place until that guy wakes up." Lisette nudged Althea out of the way to peer at herself in the mirror hanging over Hazel's dresser and fingered the curls on her brow. "'Night and day,' he said. So I'm leaving now before he gets here, and if I see him on our front porch, I'm not coming home."

"Oh no you don't, Lissy. You come straight home from school. Now I have to be at the theater first thing this morning, and Hazel and Althea can split up the day, but Althea has to work at the telegraph office tonight, and I have to be back at the theater for rehearsal. So we need you."

"Papa's the doctor."

"He has other patients," Hazel said. "And I have work to do with him down in his office."

Sensing Lisette's growing anxiety, Vada went over and stood behind her, their eyes meeting in the mirror. Any other day, the image presented to her would mean nothing, but today, even while trying to ignore her own disheveled hair next to Lisette's youthful, fashionable coif, Vada was struck by just how little the two resembled each other. For a fleeting moment, the image of Alex Triplehorn joined their reflection.

"Listen," she shook the thought away, "there's nothing to be nervous about. You don't have to do anything but sit in the chair. Just be there."

Lisette muttered something that could be taken as an affirmative response as she spun herself around and breezed out of the room.

Vada devoted the next few minutes to getting ready. Hazel stepped in to help lace up her corset, and by the time she finished brushing and pinning her hair, Vada looked upon her own reflection with almost as much appreciation as Lisette looked upon hers.

Later she sat at the kitchen table buttoning her shoes, grimacing her way through a plate of cold scrambled eggs and biscuits already slathered with blueberry jam—her least favorite—under Molly's watchful eye.

"I'm hopin' you'll see to it you're home in time for lunch today." Molly eyed the last bit of egg until Vada stabbed it with her fork.

"Don't worry." Vada swallowed. "I've learned my lesson."

She opted not to go upstairs for one last check, knowing the sooner she got to the theater, the sooner she could get back. There were ticket receipts to reconcile with the cash box, the ushers to schedule, and Herr Johann's suit to drop off at the laundry. She prioritized her tasks as she pinned her hat and hollered to the house in general that she'd be back before noon.

The first thing she saw upon opening the front door was the figure of Kenny Cupid on the front step, sitting with his arms braced on his knees.

He jumped up immediately, clutching his cap in his hands. "G'morning, Miss Vada."

"Why, good morning, Kenny. What are you doing here so early?"

He looked up, almost pleading, seeming even shorter given that Vada was several steps above him. "How is he?"

It was a terrible thing to see such pain on his youthful face. She attempted a reassuring smile. "How long have you been here? I hope you didn't spend the night."

Kenny grinned. "Nah, just awhile this morning. I was waiting for someone to come outside so I could ask."

"Didn't Lisette tell you? She's already left for school."

Again the grin, and he smoothed back his unruly hair. "She opened the door, took one look at me, and turned around. I think she snuck out the back."

"Well," she said, pulling on her gloves, "there's no change, and we have everything well at hand. Now, I'm sure you have better things to do with your day beside sit on our front porch."

"Is that your way of telling me to leave?"

He looked down at the cap in his hand, turning it over and over as something akin to melting happened inside Vada's heart.

"Have you had breakfast yet?" Molly would certainly succumb to his artless charm.

"Not yet, ma'am. No."

"Then go around to the kitchen door. Tell Molly I sent you. And don't be surprised if she asks you to empty the ash can before she cooks breakfast for you."

"Thank you, Miss Vada." He scrambled down the steps, practically running to the side gate.

"What a sweet boy," she muttered in his wake and began to make her way down the steps.

"Tell you what. I'm a sweet boy too. Think I could get some of Miss Molly's breakfast?"

She recognized the voice but saw no one until she got to the bottom step and turned to see Dave Voyant, little notebook in hand, lurking in the alcove under the stairs.

The surprise of seeing him here, at her home, knocked her into stunned silence for a moment until, for the second time that morning, she found herself saying, "What are you doing here?"

"Just happened to be passing by." He came out into the sunlight. "Thought I'd drop by to see what the story is."

"There's no story here." She looked anxiously up and down the street before moving closer. "So you can just go home."

"I'm not sure I agree." He flipped back a few pages in his note-book. "Had a buddy at the game who said there seemed to be some sort of disturbance. Guy got hit with a ball. Carried him out of the stands, then it seems like he just disappeared. Next thing we know, both team managers and a handful of players are seen heading down this street."

"There you have it. Your story. If you'll excuse me—"

"Come now, Miss Allenhouse." He leaned in uncomfortably close. "You know no story is complete without the happy ending."

"We don't have a happy ending, Mr. Voyant."

"Meaning we don't have an ending? Or not a happy one?"

Vada steeled herself and leaned in even closer. "I guess that's something for you to ponder throughout the day."

They were so close now that had either craned their neck, their lips would touch, and something inside her dared him to try while she her-self refused to budge. There they remained, locked in near battle, until Dave finally broke their gaze and took half a step back.

"Something else I'll be pondering," he said from a much safer dis-tance, "is what Kenny Cupid was doing camped on your front step."

"He seems enamored with my youngest sister."

One dark eyebrow shot up. "Is that so? And do you know who he is?"

"Of course. He's a very nice young man."

There went the second eyebrow. "Fair enough. He just seemed a little upset, and I thought maybe it was because—"

"Maybe you should ask him."

He took the pencil stub that had been stashed above one of his ears. "That's just it. Nobody's talking. Makes me wonder if someone's not covering something up."

Vada thought about the nearly lifeless form in her bed, Kenny's guilt at not having prevented the accident, and the undeniably strong arms of Louis LaFortune. If the man never woke up, if he—God forbid—*died* in her bed, would that make Louis a killer? Or Kenny? Or her father for harboring the wounded man in his daughter's fourposter bed rather than taking him to the hospital downtown?

She closed her eyes to clear her head and refocus, not wanting a bit of her doubt to seep through.

"You're the journalist. Why weren't you here yesterday?"

Again he flipped the pages of his notebook. "If you must know, I was covering a very important story. Miss Mannaheim's dance studio was giving their spring recital, and the daughters of several of our city's finest citizens were onstage performing amazing feats of ballet."

"Then it seems your evening was equally dull." She prepared to move past him. "Now if you will excuse me, I have much to do to prepare for Friday's concert. You remember that, don't you? Three days ago you were hounding me for information, remember?"

"Of course I remember." He pushed his hat back off his brow as his face took on a look of surprise and delight. "You aren't insinuating that I'm making these inquiries in an effort to get closer to you, are you Miss Allenhouse? Especially after you made it so abundantly clear that your heart was spoken for."

She opened her mouth to protest, then shut it again, wishing she'd kept it so in the first place.

"Tell you what." Dave dropped his notebook into the breast pocket of his jacket and tucked the pencil stub back behind his ear. "A lot can change in three days. Let's just chalk it up to that."

"All right. Let's."

There seemed to be an implied, if temporary, surrender in his words, and without worry that he would pursue his disturbance, she wished him good morning and turned to walk away. Not five steps down the sidewalk, and he was at her side, cap doffed in greeting.

"May I escort you to the theater?"

"You may not." She didn't slow down.

"May I accompany you as far as Moravek's bakery? It seems my plan to have breakfast in the home of a certain Cleveland physician fell through."

She turned her head away so he wouldn't see her smile, and they remained silent with each other for the remainder of the walk. And once they came upon the familiar tables scattered on the sidewalk, she told herself she wasn't disappointed that he didn't invite her to stay.

9

Though it was just past nine in the morning, it may well have been the middle of the night when Vada arrived at the Dresden Street Theater. She let herself in with the key she'd earned from Herr Johann two months ago and found herself to be the only soul in the place.

It was a wonderful feeling to be able to walk up and down hallways without bumping up against another person. Sometimes, when she was alone like this, she would throw her arms out and run full out through the dark corridors, knowing there was no obstacle to cause her to fall.

This morning, however, she felt a need for stillness. She leisurely took the back stairs up to the third floor and popped her head in her little office. Sunshine poured through the skylight, creating a grid over the top of her tidy desk. At least it should have been tidy, but now it was littered with paper—most likely illegible notes scribbled by Herr Johann and tossed through the door in one of his characteristic rants.

She should rifle through them and prioritize, especially after failing to give any of it a second thought yesterday, but Monday's escape had been anything but restful, and today begged to be put off a little longer. Instead she kept her eyes averted so as not to accidentally read any of the scattered documents as she made her way behind her desk to open the deep bottom drawer.

There, left since Saturday when she'd rushed out of the office to deliver the programs, she found it. Her violin. Her fingers curled around the handle of the case, lifted it out, and clutched it to her, closing the drawer with her foot.

She put her lips close to the case and whispered, "You're in for a treat." Then, without bothering to close the door behind her, she stepped into the dark hallway, made her way down the back stairs and, once her eyes adjusted to the near-total darkness, maneuvered through the backstage area. Her fingers traced the length of the heavy velvet curtain until she found its end, and she walked out onto the stage.

The only light in the auditorium came through the open doors that led to the lobby, which was fine with Vada. Her footsteps echoed in the darkness, and the very sound of opening the latch on her case seemed magnified a thousand times. There was no chair, no stool, so she lifted the violin and bow out and held both in one hand as she gingerly lowered the case to the floor. Again, the echo of leather on the boards and another few steps as she moved away.

Friday's concert would include Beethoven's *Pastoral* from his Sixth Symphony, and she summoned that music now. The instrument settled on her shoulder, her chin smooth against the silken wood. She touched the bow lightly to the strings and found her first note. Wincing at the sound, she readjusted, found the correct one, and launched herself into song.

Within the first measure she closed her eyes, taking away the hundreds and hundreds of empty seats. Whether alone in her bedroom or in the parlor surrounded by her family, Vada always preferred to be locked away with all of her senses attuned to her music. When she was younger, she'd imagine herself on a grand stage wearing a beautiful white gown and playing for an audience gape mouthed in awe. Instead, that winter recital when she'd fumbled through "Au Clair de la Lune" had been her final stage performance. The end of her education.

Still, music called to her, and at this moment it filled her. No room now for the threatening visage of Alex Triplehorn or the haunting scene of the young man possibly dying in her own bed. She imagined herself third, no, maybe second chair in the midst of Herr Johann's East Cleveland Terrington Community Orchestra, settled in between Garrison and Erik Vlasek, whose square, scowling face would take on an expression of red-faced shock.

Alone onstage, she dreamed a wall of harmonious sound, and when her mind hit a blank and she couldn't remember the next note, her invisible conductor tapped his stand and directed the entire orchestra back to the beginning of the second measure, where the notes were entirely more comfortable.

At some point the imagined tapping sounded entirely too real, and Vada opened her eyes to see Herr Johann standing directly in front of her. Her eyes traveled the short distance down his stocky frame to find the source of the tapping in the heel of his gray calfskin boot.

Her right hand dropped, bringing the bow with it, and her left soon followed, holding the poor violin uselessly by its neck. "Good morning, Herr Johann."

"You did not tune your instrument?"

"I—well…"

Herr Johann held out his hand and, like a guilty child, Vada gave over her violin. He held it in front of him like a ukulele and strummed one string with his stubby thumb, twisting the tuning peg until, satisfied, he moved on to the next string.

Uncomfortable watching, and not knowing where to look, Vada scanned the theater seats, grateful in a different way for their emptiness.

When Herr Johann cleared his throat, she looked back to him and handed over the bow. He brought the violin up to his shoulder, wedging it within the thickness of his neck, and launched into the piece Vada had been playing just moments before. Each note carried with it her dreams—those she'd abandoned and those stolen from her. A musical picture, really, of the swift fleeting of time. Each touch of the bow a year then lifted, a decade gone. Though he played only a few seconds, she felt a lifetime had passed when he stopped, holding the bow poised above the strings.

"Sounds better, doesn't it?"

"Yes," she whispered. "Much better, thank you."

He played one final, triumphant run of notes before relinquishing the violin. Embarrassed for herself and the torture the poor instrument endured at her touch, Vada immediately stooped down to open the case.

"You are putting it away?"

She looked up at him, confused. "I have work to do."

"What work could possibly be more important than music?" When she started to explain, he waved her off. "How often do you get a chance to play Beethoven on a stage?"

"Never," she said, straightening. *Maybe if you allowed women to play in your orchestra—*

"Then play!" He was already walking away, repeating "Play! Play!" and directing the air in front of him more vigorously with each step and humming the tune until it disappeared with him into the darkness.

Vada remained in the center of the empty stage for a few minutes more, the echoes of *The Pastoral* still lingering, but she couldn't bring herself to lift her instrument and play. Instead, she knelt and placed the violin lovingly in its case, the clicking of the latch once again the only sound.

Then, following Herr Johann's example if not his footsteps, she left the stage in the opposite direction. She'd learned long ago to be satisfied with what she could easily have. This was no different. Humming, she made her way through the darkness and up the stairs until the case itself was once again tucked inside her desk drawer.

Now to work. First she read through the series of Johann's notes, instructing her which laundry to use for his tuxedo, where to make reservations for a late supper after Friday's performance, what color velvet to use in making the "reserved" drapes for those seats set aside for Cleveland's elite. There were a few less-important ones, like the scrawled rant about the first cello's unruly hair and the frayed carpet on the stairs leading up to the stage, but as these were issues well out of her hand, she simply tossed them into the small wastebasket in the corner.

For the next task she reached for the accounts ledger and opened it to the entry from last Friday. Mrs. Greenville, who worked tirelessly in the little box office in front of the theater, had left a small envelope bound with string on her desk. In it was a receipt for Monday's sales and seven dollars in cash that Vada promptly locked in the petty cash box in her top desk drawer.

This is when she should reconcile the numbers in order to give an accurate count to Herr Johann when he came by with his daily question, "So, are we going to play to an empty house?" But every time she attempted to work out the math in the margins of the ledger, she found her mind wandering, first to Alex Triplehorn, the man who'd been able to steal away her mother's affection, then to Louis LaFortune, who seemed capable of the same feat for her.

The fitful night's sleep began to take its toll, and she rested her tired eyes on the heels of her palms. It was a different darkness here than that of the stage; there was nothing to chase away the haunting images of yesterday.

Oh, Lord. How am I going to get through all of this? I need…

Her prayer, silent as it was, dissolved within her, and the little office filled with the notes of a simple tune. She listened, head cocked at the unfamiliarity, though she herself hummed it. Her mind searched for lyrics, and before she could stop herself, her lips formed the foreign words: *"Fais do do, petit frère…"*

Mortified, she clapped her hand over her mouth to stifle the lullaby.

"Oh, Lord," she tried again, speaking a prayer to fill the room. "I've never felt so…inadequate. You took Mama away and that was fine. I was fine. And now—I need You to take Alex Triplehorn *away*. And Mr. LaFortune too. I haven't the strength to fight these battles. I need…"

But she knew exactly what she needed. She stifled the whining words and drummed her fingers on her cluttered desktop. It was a simple matter, really, of confronting Mr. Triplehorn and avoiding Mr. LaFortune. What an utter waste of prayer, given the gravity of the young man so near death's door back at home. *That* she could leave in God's hands. The rest of this—well, He'd seen to it that she'd grown up capable of confronting life's complications, hadn't He?

By now the light streaming through the skylight made the little office quite warm, and she stood to twist the handle to open the window and let in a breeze. Too late, she realized she'd forgotten to secure the series of notes from Herr Johann, and they scattered across the desk, landing on the floor.

"Oh, bother." She went down to her hands and knees to retrieve them. Just then there was a light rap on her door and a muffled voice from the other side.

"Miss Allenhouse? You have found the notes I left on your desk?"

A quiet second later the door opened, and though she couldn't see over the top of the desk, the faint whistling sound of Herr Johann's breathing was unmistakable.

Lest her own breathing have any such telltale presence, she held it, keeping herself quite still until, after a short inquisitive snort, the door was closed again and he was gone.

There, finally, in a patch of sunlight cooled by a spring breeze, Vada found a moment of pure peace.

True to her word, Vada walked into the house at noon sharp, having left her meeting with Mr. Messini, the ushering coordinator, as soon as the last assignment had been resolved.

"Molly Keegan!" she cried the minute she walked through the front door. "What is that delicious odor?"

The two nearly collided at the door to the kitchen as Molly came bursting through, her finger held tight to her lips. "What kind of a lady is it comes hollerin' into a house such as that?"

"I'm sorry." Vada dropped to a whisper. "I just don't think I've ever—"

"It's sausage and peppers is what it is." She placed her fisted hands on her hips, looking quite pleased. "With a nice butter-and-garlic sauce. Thought maybe a strong odor waftin' up might do some good in wakin' himself upstairs."

"Still no change?"

"None 't all. And the little one sittin' at his side all mornin'."

"Althea?"

"You best fetch her downstairs. I don't think otherwise she'll leave his side."

Vada left her hat and gloves on the front hall table and raced up the stairs, stopping at the top of the landing when she heard a soft, familiar sound coming from her room.

Although Althea hadn't spoken a word since their mother left, sometimes, when she thought no one could hear her, she would hum. Mournfully, tunelessly when she was sad, high and sweet in moments of contentment. Whenever Vada happened upon such a time—when Althea was in her room or straightening the parlor—she would lurk outside the open doorway and drink in this little bit of sound.

So did she now, walking on her toes as she hugged the wall, then standing flat against it, listening to the remnant of Althea's voice until she finally recognized the melody within.

> *Sweet hour of prayer! Sweet hour of prayer!*
> *That calls me from a world of care,*
> *And bids me at my Father's throne*
> *Make all my wants and wishes known.*

Each note was clear and perfect, capturing the essence of the song the way no lyric ever could.

Calls me from a world of care. Indeed. Who could know how many hours of Althea's silence were really hours spent in prayer? Vada thought back to the minutes spent back in her office. She'd left bringing every care with her.

She peered around the open doorway, expecting to see her sister's head bowed in the posture of prayer the song summoned. Instead, Althea sat in the chair next to the bed, the young man's head cradled in one hand while the other moved a snippet of sea sponge across his parted lips.

Even though this was obviously a scene of some medical necessity, Vada couldn't help feeling like a voyeur having stumbled upon some precious, private moment. Still, there could be no doubt what *wants and wishes* Althea was making known to their Father.

Althea none the wiser, Vada withdrew from the doorway, backed down the hall, and approached again with a great clattering of heels. "Althea? Are you up here?"

This time when she walked into the room, the man's head was once again nestled in the pillow, and the sea sponge floated in the glass of clear water on the small table next to the bed. Althea's hands twitched in her lap.

"Any change?" Vada whispered in deference to the patient.

Althea gave a quick shake of her head, then stood and motioned for Vada to follow her to the dresser. There, looking very pleased, she gestured to a gathering of items in one of the shallow soup bowls from downstairs.

"What's all this?" Vada touched each item carefully. There was a single key; a handful of coins; a pencil stub; two shirt buttons; a shiny, smooth stone; and a single folded piece of paper. "Are these his? You found them going through his pockets?"

Althea nodded in response to each question. She picked up the piece of paper and handed it to Vada who unfolded it slowly, as if it were some precious antique document and not a brief note scribbled on cheap stationery.

"Eli," she read, then held the note closer trying to make out the rest. What she first attributed to a problem of penmanship soon manifested itself to be another language entirely, and not a single word was recognizable to her.

"His name is Eli?"

Althea read over her shoulder and pointed out the last word in the letter.

"Katrina. The note is from someone named Katrina. What do you suppose it says?"

Althea gestured broadly, palms up, and resumed her place in the chair next to the sleeping man. The patient. Eli.

Vada turned back to the contents of the dish. The coins were American, adding up to less than a dollar. The key looked like any other, without any sort of chain or fob to identify its origin. She wondered if the pencil had been used to write a reply to Katrina—perhaps on the back of some postcard featuring two blushing lovers. And the buttons...

"Are the buttons from the shirt he was wearing?"

Althea got up and walked out of the room, returning shortly with the grimy shirt, probably retrieved from the bin in the bathroom. She inspected the cuffs first and then, seeming satisfied, ran her fingers along the buttonholes and then the buttons before presenting the garment like a piece of evidence.

"All intact," Vada said, holding one of the buttons from the dish next to one on the shirt. They differed in size, shape, and color. Althea frowned, shrugged, and left to return the shirt to the soiled clothes bin.

Finally Vada looked at the stone. It was small—about the size of the end of her thumb—and gray. Smooth as silk. Moving over to sit in the bedside chair, she held it in her hand, running her thumb along the cool smoothness of it, wondering just how often this man—Eli—did the same thing.

"Now, Eli," she leaned close, "if you don't wake up, we'll never know why you have these buttons."

She sensed Althea behind her and turned. "You know, it might help him wake up if we talk to him. If we say his name enough, maybe he'll hear us."

Althea clutched the little notepad hanging on the ribbon around her neck.

"I know. It's hard for you. But do you think, for him, you could say his name? Just his name?"

Now it was Althea's turn to back out of the room and run down the hallway with a great clattering of heels.

Sighing, Vada turned her attention back to the man resting on her pillow.

"Eli? Eli." She repeated his name over and over, drawing it out, "Eeeeeeeeeliiiiiiii," sounding like a mother calling her son home for supper. She leaned in close and whispered, sat back in the chair and sang it out like a yodel, all the while looking for any sign of change. The twitch of an eyelid. The slightest movement of a finger.

Nothing.

"Well, that's it for now, then." She rose to go downstairs for lunch. She walked over to the dresser to put the small stone in the bowl with the rest of Eli's worldly possessions but then turned back, struck with an idea.

"I'm leaving you alone for a little while, Eli," she whispered close to his ear, "but I'll leave this with you."

Though Molly had done a good job of scrubbing him down, Eli's fingernails were rimmed with dirt. Still, his hands were pliant and warm as Vada lifted one off the sheet and curled the fingers around the stone.

"It's good to have something to hold on to."

"It's Czech," Doc said definitively after glancing at the folded note for only a few seconds. "I saw and heard enough of it tending patients in Maple Heights."

Lunch that day turned out to be a special treat, not only because of the sausage with peppers and garlic tossed with macaroni, but also because it was one of the rare noontime meals when the entire family gathered together. Minus Lisette, of course, who insisted on taking only a piece of fruit and a waxed-paper twist of crackers to nibble on under the big oak trees in the school yard. The informality of the hour brought them to eat in the kitchen rather than the dining room, and often, like today, Molly bustled around, refilling and taking away dishes the minute the action was needed.

"Can you read it?" Vada asked.

"Shouldn't be too hard to find someone who can." Molly placed a dish of olives in the middle of the table. "City's fairly crawlin' with them people, fast as they can leavin' the Church—"

"That's enough, Molly." Doc took the rare stand against Molly who was as stern about her Catholicism as she was about her kitchen.

Hazel was the last to enter the kitchen, popping an olive into her mouth as she took her seat. "We could take it to Moravek's."

Althea held up a cautionary hand reminding everybody at the table that today, being Tuesday, was the one day of the week that Moravek's was closed to the public.

"I'll take it tomorrow then," Vada said. "Early. I have errands to run for Herr Johann anyway."

"Or," Doc said, "perhaps the young man will wake up and tell us himself."

Vada prayed for that very thing as she led the family in asking the meal's blessing. In fact, the thought seemed to linger on everybody's mind as they quietly loaded their plates and tucked in.

The spicy flavors of the sausage and peppers were a departure from Molly's more reliable fare, and under other circumstances Vada would be quick to rave, but now she could only think of that thin, pale mouth open to take in the smallest sips of water. She glanced over at Althea who speared a bit of pepper and was pushing it around her plate and knew they were sharing the same thoughts.

"Now what's the matter wit' the lot of ya?" Molly stood behind Doc's chair glowering down at the table. "I try a new bit o' somethin' and I can't get a word of thanks?"

"It's delicious, Molly, really," Hazel said, happily plopping a bit of sausage into her mouth.

"We're just worried, that's all." Vada turned to her father. "It's been twenty-four hours, hasn't it? What does that mean?"

"What it means," Molly said before Doc could answer, "is that the boy's sleepin' in the Lord's hands, and none but He will wake him. Ain't that so, Dr. Allenhouse?"

He looked up and over his shoulder. "No physician could have said it better, Mrs. Keegan. All we can do is watch and wait."

"Right now all of ya need to eat and keep up your strength. I'll go sit with the prince upstairs. And not that I don't trust your doctorin', mind you, or the good Lord Himself, but I might be sendin' up a prayer at the church this afternoon."

"That would be just fine, Mrs. Keegan," Doc said, though the kitchen door was already swinging.

"I suppose this means we'll have our little visitor this afternoon again," Hazel said. "That kid hung around all morning, pacing around, close to crying. Nearly had me in tears too every time I tripped over him."

Althea gave Hazel a look of gentle chastisement, and Vada, too, jumped to his defense. "I think it's sweet he's so worried about Eli. I notice the brute who swung the bat hasn't given him a second thought."

"Now, Vada darling," Doc said, "we can't assign any blame."

"No, but we can measure compassion. I mean, yesterday he seemed so moved. So concerned. And today? He can't even be bothered to darken the doorstep." She shoved a forkful of peppers and macaroni into her mouth and chewed, patently ignoring the surprised expressions on the faces around her.

Indeed, she was a bit surprised herself at the outburst. Why should she care if Mr. LaFortune came by the house? In fact, maybe this was God's own hand, keeping them apart by bringing him here to visit when she was locked away in prayer. Or maybe during the very moments she was meeting with old Mr. Messini, deciding which octogenarian would be assigned to what row, Louis LaFortune was in this very house—up in her very room—wringing his big, strong hands in grief.

Still, somehow, the thought of missing his visit was more upsetting than the idea that the visit had never taken place, and she swallowed her bite of lunch, fighting back the tears brought on by the spices.

"Actually," her father said, "both Mr. Tebeau and Mr. Barnie telephoned my office earlier. They're quite concerned."

"Maybe about the scandal." The conversation with Dave Voyant echoed in her mind.

"What scandal?" Hazel asked.

"Never mind." Doc shot a warning look to Vada, who immediately returned to her lunch. "Both men have asked me to come and speak to their teams this afternoon before the game. To reassure them, if you will. Hazel, I don't have anybody scheduled to come in, but could you call on a few patients at home for me?"

"Of course, Doc." She didn't sound the least bit enthused, and Vada alone knew just how much she hated calling on Doc's patients in their homes.

"Very good. And Althea, you can sit with our patient until it's time for you to report to the telegraph office?"

Althea nodded, the slightest smile at the corners of her mouth.

"And Vada? You can come with me to assess their level of remorse. That is, unless you have more pressing matters at the theater."

She thought of Herr Johann's tuxedo, the "Reserved" seat coverings, the final housekeeping briefing, and the host of other duties littering her desk, not to mention the afternoon rehearsal.

"No, Doc. Nothing at all."

10

Although most of life for the Allenhouse family was confined within a comfortable walking distance of their home, Doc still owned a fine pair of horses and three carriages, which he housed at Darvin's Livery on Huntington Street. There Mr. Darvin was free to rent them out in exchange for the fee he would otherwise charge Dr. Allenhouse, and whenever Doc needed conveyance, one of Darvin's sons would drive it right up to the front door.

Today it was Darvin's youngest, Pete, a slow, lumbering boy of fourteen who stood on the front step, chewing what was left of his thumbnail.

"Brought your two-seater and the bay." He never once took his thumb away from his mouth and, oddly enough, his thick lips never budged.

"Very good, Pete," Vada said. Doc followed her out onto the front step and gave Pete such a generous tip the boy was still staring at it as Doc handed Vada up into the backseat of the carriage.

"Tell you what, boy," Doc said, his foot on the running board, "how'd you like to make twice that?"

"Yessir?"

"Hop up and drive Miss Allenhouse and myself to League Park."

"Yes sir, Dr. Allenhouse."

Doc settled in beside Vada, and they'd barely pulled away from the house before she began peppering him with questions. First about Eli: How long could he live in this condition? What damage would linger after he woke up? What would they do if, God forbid, he were to die? To each of these, Doc answered with some weary variance of "I don't know."

They spoke quietly, knowing the noise of the street would drown their conversation from the prying ears of Pete. The boy's cheerful whistling further protected their conversation, as it seemed unlikely he could drive, whistle, and listen all at once.

"I still don't understand why you need to go to the park." Vada tilted her head away to hide her face from the woman out tending the lilac bush Garrison raided the afternoon before.

"I call on all my patients, Vada. Not only to care for them, but also to give reassurance to their loved ones."

"Yes, but the patient is back at home, and we have no idea who his loved ones are."

"It's a difficult situation."

"But why? I don't understand why we have the need for such secrecy. This was a simple accident, and everybody's acting as if we're covering up a crime."

"That's precisely why I wanted you to come with me today, so I could get you alone and explain. Hazel doesn't spend much time outside the house, and we know Althea won't…tell."

"And Lisette is hardly aware of his existence," Vada added, grinning.

Doc responded with a rare chuckle. "Exactly. But I know you are often out in the community, and it could well be that someone might ask you about the incident. There were, after all, spectators who saw the, er…accident. And they may well assume—correctly—that the young man was brought to my home for care, and they may ask—"

"That's just it, Doc. What if they do ask?" Her mind flashed to the image of Dave Voyant tapping his pencil against his flirtatious smile. "What could it possibly harm to tell them what happened? We might encounter someone who can tell us who the man is."

"I gave Mr. Tebeau my word that I would protect him. At least until we have an outcome."

"Protect him from what?"

"Publicity, mostly. You know how cutthroat the newspapers can be. Can't you just picture the headline?" He positioned his hands as if holding an imaginary newspaper. "Anonymous Immigrant Killed in the Stands."

Something told Vada that Dave Voyant would come up with something infinitely more clever.

"Tebeau's worried it'll make the team look bad. Scare people out of the stands. The more attention called to it, the more people will examine what led up to the moment the boy got hit. And then they'll pin blame on the player, and that could ruin him."

She thought of those massive arms, muscles bulging as he gripped the bat, slamming the ball through the air and straight between young Eli's eyes. "Oh, that poor Mr. LaFortune."

"No," Doc said, "it'll fall on Cupid."

"Because he didn't catch the ball."

"He didn't even put up his glove."

Because he was smitten with Lisette. Did her father know that?

"The man wants to protect his ballpark and his players. So until there's anything else to report, all those spectators who saw young Eli get hit just know that some fellow got knocked out by a stray ball. It happens."

"Often?"

"Often enough that, from what they told me, people around him were laughing as much as anything else."

"And when there's something else to report?"

"Well, then, that'll be a great story, won't it. When he wakes up, he can be some sort of hero."

"And if he doesn't?"

"Let's just pray that he does."

By now young Pete had eased the carriage onto Euclid Avenue, and Vada was distracted by the obvious display of wealth that lined the street. One mansion followed the next, each with elaborate front gardens peeking through ornate wrought-iron gates. Looking down over all from its place on a hill just beyond was the snow white, garreted home of John D. Rockefeller. The Homestead. As he always did when an occasion brought them to ride past this place, Doc tipped his hat to the house and said, "Mr. Rockefeller? If you're feeling poorly, feel free to call on me."

"You can bet people would know if *he* got smacked in the head with a baseball."

Doc chuckled and Vada scooted a little closer to him, tentatively reaching out to loop her arm through his and, when he didn't pull away, tucked herself next to him as they silently took in the sights.

"Didn't you ever want to be rich, Doc?"

"No, my dear." The rare endearment came with a pat on her hand. "I have always been able to recognize when I had enough. And there's no greater lesson you can learn than to be happy when you simply have enough."

She could not remember another time when she felt this close to her father—not just physically next to him, the closest she'd been to being in his lap since before her mother left. And as they had since the moment she'd heard them, the words of Alex Triplehorn echoed in her ears.

Her mind waged war, trying to shut that horrific experience out of this moment while wondering if this might be the time to ask. And then, as if lulled by the rhythmic clomping of the horse and Pete's mesmerizing whistled tune, one side of the battle surrendered.

"Is that why our mother left?"

She felt his body go rigid against hers and hold itself still for one, two breaths before seeming to dissolve as he took his arm away and recreated space between them.

Pete ceased his whistling and looked over his shoulder. "Be at League Park in five minutes."

"Thank you," Doc said, staring straight forward.

Vada studied his profile, the slight uptilt to his nose and the heavy brows that tufted out above his eyes. Everything beyond that was obscured in whiskers. Without seeing his eyes, there was no way to know his thoughts. Not unless she asked again, and she wouldn't ask again.

She too fixed her eyes ahead, staring at the back of the seat in front of her, noticing the poorly patched elbow of Pete's sleeve. Then, almost as soft as the breeze itself, she felt the tickle of whiskers against her cheek and heard her father's voice close to her ear.

"I will never fully understand why your mother left us. It hurts me every day."

He shifted then, drawing her close so her head rested on his shoulder, and there they remained until Pete hollered, "League Park!" with a voice worthy of a conductor.

Once Vada sat up straight, she realized why her father had drafted Pete to drive them. Fifty yards away she saw the two-story red brick box-office building standing at the helm of a chicken-wire fenced-in field. Standing between them and the park entrance, however, was a sea of jam-packed carriages—even a few horseless ones—parked at chaotic angles. Men of all shapes and sizes, some in suits, some in short sleeves, milled through the mess. There were a few women too, wearing broad-brimmed hats to protect against the sun.

A narrow path intersected the jumble, and Doc ordered Pete to drive on, eventually dropping the two of them at the front gate.

"Meet us back here in thirty minutes," he said to the boy, raising his voice above the din. "Do you have a watch?"

"No sir. But I got me a kind of head-clock right here." Pete tapped the top of his cap. "So don't you worry."

"I won't give it another thought." Doc let himself down and offered his hand to Vada, who heard a few whoops and hollers as her leg extended out from the bottom of her skirt.

"Animals," Doc said, but with enough humor in his voice to show that whatever melancholy had passed between them before, it was now something to be put away.

They approached the front gate, merging with the shuffling line of spectators. When they got to the front, a wide-open hand, its palm the size of a shovel, halted any further progress.

"Tickets, please." The man behind the hand had a thin cigar pasted to his bottom lip that bobbed as he spoke.

"We are not here to see the game." Doc tipped his hat. "I am here to meet with Mr. Tebeau."

"Now there's one I ain't heard before. G'wan, pops. You look like you can cough up a buck."

"If you will just send word to Mr. Tebeau—"

"Look, mister. I ain't got an in with Patsy to go askin' him—"

"Never mind, Doc." Vada tugged his sleeve. "You can telephone him later."

"Wait a minute." The massive hand pinched the cigar and took it out of the man's mouth, leaving an oddly dainty, sausagelike pinky extended. "You say *doc*?"

"I am Dr. Marcus Allenhouse—"

"Aw, why didn't you say so? Patsy's been goin' crazy lookin' for you all morning. Hey, Grimley!"

From nowhere emerged a scruffy-looking man wearing a soiled news-boy cap and a tobacco-stained shirt stretched over a protruding belly.

"Take these two to the dugout. This is the doc Patsy's been waiting for."

Grimley gave his belly a leisurely scratch, studying them both, before he crooked his finger and stepped back into the crowd.

Doc grabbed Vada's hand and followed. Once through the front gate, they took a sharp left and entered a narrow covered concourse lined with vendors' carts set up to sell hot sausage links, popcorn, and beer. At least, those were the ones whose calls rang out above the din of the crowd. She also saw patrons walking with enormous pretzels and pickles wrapped in waxed paper, and several little boys ran pell-mell through the crowd clutching sticks of horehound candy.

At first she kept her eyes firmly fixed on the back of Mr. Grimley's neck, terrified of losing him in the crowd. After all, it seemed every man in the place looked just like him. But when the closeness of the crowd forced them to slow their progress, she noticed several men in expensive suits standing elbow to elbow with those in tattered shirt-sleeves.

The women too seemed to have strolled in from every walk of life. For every feminine voice heard uttering the rough talk more suited to a sailor, another lifted a lace-gloved hand to sweep a strand of hair back in place.

So caught up in the sights around her, she soon forgot all about fol-lowing Mr. Grimley and might have wandered off completely if not for the clutch of her father's hand. It wasn't until she collided with Doc's shoulder that she realized he had stopped moving, and the three of them stood at the entrance to what looked like a long, dark hallway.

"Youse have to wait," Mr. Grimley said pointedly to Vada. "Can't allow a female such as yerself into the clubhouse."

"Oh." She clutched Doc's hand.

"You'll be fine, Vada." He gave her a little pat as he released his grip. "I won't be but a few minutes, and I'll meet you right back here."

She watched her father and Mr. Grimley disappear through the dark opening, then smoothed her skirt and, rooted in place, allowed her eyes to roam as they would, taking in the posted bills along the walls.

Then, wafting above the noise of the surrounding conversations and the hawking calls of the vendors, she heard music. Perhaps it had been playing all along, but once her ear caught the first note, the melody unfolded, carried through the bellows of a pipe organ.

Soon her foot was tapping and her head filled with the sound of her youngest sister singing the familiar song as she readied herself for a night of dancing.

When you hear dem a bells go ding, ling ling,
All join 'round and sweetly you must sing
When the verse am through, in the chorus all join in,
There'll be a hot time in the old town tonight.

Unaware that she was moving toward the music, Vada turned her head to the left and found her view had completely changed. Somehow, carried along by the crowd, she'd stepped out of the openness of the concourse and found herself standing under a red-brick arch. Here the sound of the crowd took on a muffled echo, though the organ music was distinctly clearer. When she turned fully toward the open arch, hints of green compelled her farther and farther until she stood nose to chicken wire.

The glimpse of green became a vast expanse of emerald grass surrounding a perfect red-dirt diamond. Two men walked the baseline raking straight, narrow furrows, another pushed a rotating mower in the background. Here the sweet green smell took over the odors of the vendors' wares, and she closed her eyes and inhaled deep.

"Miss Allenhouse? Psst! Miss Allenhouse?"

His voice, already disturbingly familiar, called from somewhere behind her, just over her left shoulder. No, her right. There was a break in the crowd and he called again. She searched for his thatch of red hair but saw nothing, heard nothing until he called again.

"Down here!"

She moved farther along the fence and looked down to see him, his head, now sporting a gray cap, level with the walkway. At this point the fencing was no higher than her waist, and the chicken wire was replaced by sturdy, wide-placed planks. Steadying herself by gripping the top rung, she crouched down, bringing his nose level to her knees.

"Good afternoon, Mr. LaFortune. Just what are you doing down there?"

"Why, down here be the dugout, Miss Allenhouse." His smile was just as lopsided as she remembered, and his accent just as disarming.

"Of course," she said, even as she wondered exactly what he meant.

Suddenly there was an eruption of children's voices behind her yelling, "It's him! It *is* him!" and a clattering of footsteps came to a halt all around her.

"Well, hey there, boys!" LaFortune took a few steps back and to the side, offering a big, friendly wave. "You lookin' forward to seein' a game today?"

"That depends." One of the ragamuffins squatted down, a bony, dirty knee poking out of his pants. "You gonna kill another guy?"

The boys erupted into a disorganized chant, "Yeah! Killer!"

LaFortune grabbed the cap off his head and crushed it in his fist, his face just two shades lighter than his hair. "Hey! *Fermez vos bouches!*" He pumped his fist in the air and took a running lunge at the fence, leaping high enough to grasp the top rung and, biceps ready to burst through his sleeves, managed to haul himself waist high to the walkway.

Gritting his teeth, he brought one foot up and seemed intent on bringing up the other, with the unveiled intent of leaping over it and killing the boys themselves. But there would be no boys to kill, as they let out a collective scream and tore into the crowd, weaving in and out of the startled, disgruntled spectators, not once looking back. He stood on the walkway, on the inside of the rail, gripping its top with one hand, pumping his fist with the other.

"Possedes," he muttered. "Crazy kids."

By now Vada was standing upright, craning to see the last of the boys disappear into the crowd before turning her attention to the bully on the other side of the railing.

"Shame on you, Mr. LaFortune. They're just children."

"Pah!" He made a dismissive gesture and, in a graceful move she'd never think a man his size capable of, jumped down to the ground below, bouncing just once on his heels to retain his balance. "Been hearin' that all day."

"How? It wasn't in the papers."

"Don't make no matter if it in the papers. People know."

"Still, it's no reason to scare a bunch of little boys."

LaFortune looked to the left and to the right, as if checking to be sure they wouldn't be overheard. He stepped forward, rose to his toes, and planted his elbows on the walkway, beckoning Vada to bend low again, which with some trepidation she did.

"How he be?"

"His name is Eli."

LaFortune burst into a smile, mouth wide, eyes bright. "He tell you that?"

"No," she said gently. "Not yet."

He buried his face in his arms, his shoulders rising as he heaved a deep sigh. It was all Vada could do not to reach down and place a comforting hand on his head. Instead she remained very still, gripping the rail and balancing on her heels.

"He gonna die because of me." His voice was muffled, forcing her to lean even closer to hear, which is why when he did look up, she got startled and rocked back. Only her grip on the bottom rung of the rail kept her from toppling outright.

"He'll be fine," she said once she was sure of her balance.

"Him, maybe. Me, *non*. I need you to help me."

"Help you? How could I possibly do that?"

"I need you give me somethin'. To carry in my pocket for this game—for luck."

"Oh, Mr. LaFortune. Certainly you don't believe in such nonsense."

"I ain't talkin' no voodoo magic or nothin' like that. Just one little ol' token."

His smile was already working its charm, transporting her back to some of the novels she'd read as a child, where knights approached the fairest ladies, looking for a silk scarf or some such small banner to carry to the jousting field. Was a wooden bat so different after all?

She let go of the rail and fumbled in her little purse for her lace-edged handkerchief and dangled it in front of him. "Will this do for your silly superstition?"

He took a corner of the handkerchief between his thumb and first finger. "This his?"

"No." She snatched it back. "It's mine. I thought you…" She left the thought unfinished. The afternoon had grown uncomfortably warm, and the tiniest bit of sweat broke out on her brow. Still, she ignored it as she worked to stuff the handkerchief back into her little purse.

"Sorry there, *ma chou-chou*." LaFortune reached up and put his hand on her knee—*her knee*—something Garrison had never dared do after nearly two years of courtship.

She should have stood right away, but there was the beginning of an odd cramp at the back of her left thigh, so instead she shifted her weight just enough to knock his hand off her skirt entirely. "Why would you possibly need something of his?"

"Well," he said, dragging out the syllable, "I know you prone to shake it off like a lot of nothin', but if I had a little somethin' of his, somethin' that showed he was gonna wake up sooner rather than later, might give me a bit of hope this afternoon."

Having made his request, he looked up, his whole face transformed from the sly flirt to a piteous supplicant. He stood flat footed again, grasping his cap in both hands, as if any minute he would tip it out for her to toss a few coins.

Coins.

"He had nothing, Mr. LaFortune. Just a few coins, some buttons, a key to who knows where—"

He brightened. "Any of them such would do fine!"

"Unfortunately I don't have any of those items with me here. Now if you will excuse me, I need to find my father—"

"Wait." He covered her hand that gripped the railing with his. "Do you think you could bring me back a little somethin'? You see, I got this feelin' deep in the pit of me that I won't be able to make any kind of play today without me havin' even a nickel that come outta that man's pocket."

"Certainly not." She stood now, ripping her hand from beneath his and trying to maintain a placid expression even as her legs protested the unfamiliar—and unwelcome—contortion. "I will not hand over some poor soul's worldly goods to be your talisman."

"Ah, *cher*, then it's fo' sho' I'm to be cursed this game." But the fringes of humor still twinkled in his eyes, and he clutched his hat to his heart before bowing deep and backing away like Romeo exiting from beneath the balcony.

Vada watched until he disappeared beneath the walkway's overhang, then smoothed her skirt as she defiantly ignored the sidelong glances from those milling behind her. Honestly, the nerve of that man. Bad enough he had a devilish grin. Now he had to do the superstitious bidding of the devil himself?

I'm trying to avoid him, Lord. I really am. But You're not making it any easier, throwing him in my path every time I turn around.

Head held high, she merged with the spectators and retraced her steps to the place she'd promised to meet her father. Within a few minutes, there he was, vigorously shaking a grateful Patsy Tebeau's hand.

"Thanks for that bit of good news there, Doc."

"It's the best I can offer, under the circumstances," Doc said, clearly uncomfortable with the man's effusion. "I will telephone you with any new developments."

"You do that." He let go of Doc's hand and, spotting Vada, offered her a tip of his hat.

"Good afternoon, Mr. Tebeau." Vada nodded, but he had already turned around and continued with his jaunty step back into the clubhouse.

"Strange breed, these fellows." Doc took his watch from his pocket. "It's been twenty minutes. Our ride should be at the gate shortly. Shall we?"

"Of course."

He held out his arm, and Vada took it. She opted not to tell him about Mr. LaFortune's strange request. After all, she didn't want to worry her father about her brush with taboo. He might worry that she wandered off at all. Plus she had so few moments in her life that were truly, privately her own. This was one that she would keep, even as they made their way back to the gate.

When they got to the concourse, they strolled right by a man wearing a crisp white apron over his suspenders, shouting, "Cold beeeeer! Get your cold beer! Nickel a glass!"

He stood next to his associate who filled one mug after another from the tap, handing the frothy drink to the next eager customer.

"Now, I'm not much of a drinking man," Doc leaned toward Vada with the air of a conspirator, "but nice cold beer on a warm day like today is mighty tempting."

"Well, why don't you get one? Mr. Tebeau would certainly want you to."

"Oh no." He didn't even hesitate as they walked past. "Sometimes when you're faced with temptation, the best thing you can do is just keep walking."

Vada thought of warm hazel eyes against a soft green field, not to mention a certain spot on her leg that could still feel his touch, and quickened her step in agreement.

Vada wrote down the final tally of the day's box office take and handed the stack of bills back to Mrs. Greenville who was charged with making the bank deposit for that day.

"It seems we may have a full house after all," the older woman said, full of unrealistic optimism.

"Let's keep hoping," Vada answered, her reply much more closely attuned to what the receipts suggested.

She bid Mrs. Greenville a good evening and set about tidying her desk. The pile of notes setting her agenda for the next day would thankfully leave little time for any impromptu visits to League Park. She folded them neatly, put them inside her pocketbook, and snapped it shut.

She heard the first strains of the instruments tuning up and remained rooted to her seat, willing Garrison not to come up for a visit. He rarely did, as his own office hours kept him so late he was often tuning up before he took off his hat. Besides, he might not even know she was here; she hadn't spoken to him since yesterday.

In fact, part of her wanted to take the back stairs out to the alley and sneak home now, But she needed to see him. Not here in her office, where the proximity of the small room would surely wrangle out a confession, nor in the hallway where the narrowness might force the two to brush against each other. And she couldn't imagine talking to him. Not yet, anyway. No, she simply needed a good safe distance where she could peer at him through a sturdy wall of music.

Once the sound coming from the stage became full enough that it seemed all the musicians had arrived, Vada took her violin out of her desk drawer and brought it to her chin. She strained to hear the notes from the auditorium one floor below and pulled the bow across the strings in an effort to match it.

There was a gap of silence where she imagined Herr Johann was tapping his baton on the stand, feverishly preparing the musicians for their first number. Vada didn't know what to expect—he rarely played through the program—so she waited for that first sure note. Then the next and the next before she realized it was *The Pastoral,* and she sat, poised to touch her bow down at the top of the next measure.

Not surprisingly, the music downstairs came to an abrupt halt, but Vada, free from the whims of a perfectionist conductor, continued on, filling her little office with music fit for a stage. Maybe not Herr Johann's stage, but certainly her own. She joined in at the top of the next few in-ceptions of *The Pastoral,* but soon became frustrated as she was sure every-body downstairs was.

Assured that Garrison was safely tucked away in his third chair by now, she returned her violin to its case and tucked it under her arm. She took one final look around her office, then locked the door behind her.

As usual, the empty auditorium welcomed her. Something about the echoes and shadows made her feel safe—embraced by the solitude. She didn't give the slightest glance over her shoulder at the orchestra, focusing instead on her unofficial assigned seat: center section, row five, seat six. Once there she sat down, smoothed her skirt, and looked up to see Garrison gazing straight at her.

The violinists on either side of him had their eyes fixed directly on Herr Johann, who was conducting from the tip of his toes. But Garrison stared right at her, and even from this distance she could see his blond eye-brows raise above the rims of his round glasses, questioning.

She lifted her hand and waved, hoping the darkness of the audito-rium would hide the fact that her own smile was weak and forced. It must have been because Garrison smiled back, wide and warm, satisfied enough to look away and up at his conductor.

Later, when the last note had been wrangled from the amateurs, Herr Johann dismissed them with the dire warning that tomorrow night, Wednesday, would be their final rehearsal before Friday's performance.

"Don't you want to have a good evening's rest before your debut?"

The men agreed heartily that they did, indeed, and they made their way backstage to gather coats and cases.

Vada waited for Garrison at the foot of the stairs leading down from the stage, staring at the rose-patterned carpet until she felt the gentle touch of his hand on the small of her back.

"May I walk you home?"

He asked her that question every evening. Sometimes she'd respond with a flirtatious threat about waiting for somebody better to come along, but tonight she simply said, "Yes," and they headed together for the side door.

"I thought we sounded fine tonight," Garrison said after steering her through the throng of "good nights."

"Best you've ever had." Though she couldn't recall a note.

"Tomorrow should only need a little fine-tuning before—"

"I won't be there tomorrow."

"Oh?" He didn't sound hurt or disappointed or even mildly curious, but still she felt compelled to offer an explanation. "We have our patient to tend to, you know. His name is Eli."

"Is he awake, then?"

"No, not yet." It occurred to her that this was the exact conversation she'd had with Mr. LaFortune just a few hours ago, and she needed a quick change of topic before allowing her mind to linger on this afternoon's encounter.

"It's just that Althea has to report to the telegraph office, and Hazel would have been with him all day. If I'm not home, that leaves him in Lisette's care, and I don't know how reliable she is—"

"Hold on!" Garrison said, chuckling. "Do I need to worry that this man is stealing you away from me?"

"Of course not." She spoke a little more quickly, a little more loudly than the question warranted. "Why would you say that?"

"Because you seem to be in an awful hurry to get back to him."

It was then that she realized how quickly she was walking, with Garrison trailing half a step behind her.

"I'm sorry." She came to a full stop and held up her violin case. "I thought I'd try playing a little music for him, see if that might get through."

"Now I am jealous." He eased her back to walking. "You never play for me."

"You're not in a coma." She looped her free arm through his and they continued, the humming of the streetlights swelling and dwindling as they passed.

As they approached the light that illuminated "their" corner, their steps slowed. By the time they reached the curbside, they were already nearly stopped. They turned toward each other, and Vada looked up, seeing the familiar planes of his face made sharper in the lamplight.

Garrison cocked one ear up toward the lamp. "Sounds like G minor tonight."

"And a little out of tune." She joined in the familiar banter. "Herr Johann would have a fit."

"That streetlight would get fourth chair. At best."

Vada forced a weak chuckle, but it died just as slowly as their steps, and here she was with Garrison again. Standing still and silent.

"Well, then, darling. Until Thursday, I guess."

He was bending to kiss her, and where she usually would have presented her cheek, she lifted her hand and braced it against him.

"Garrison." Her fingers curled around his lapel. "I have to know. Have you ever been—" She stopped, not only to gather her thoughts, but to step a bit to the side so when she looked up, she didn't need to see his face framed by a halo of light. "Have you ever been…tempted?"

"Of course I have." The warmth of his smile drew her in, making her a part of him, though there was a hint of something much more serious in his eyes.

Last week such an admission might have made her furious, but tonight, it ushered in a feeling of camaraderie, and for a moment she felt poised to offer her own confession.

"Why do you think we stop walking together at this corner?" He brought his hand up and stroked her cheek. "My beautiful girl." He dropped one soft, lingering kiss on her lips. "There are nights when I never want to let you go. And I worry that if we were alone, in the shadows, even that close to your house, there might be a time when I simply wouldn't."

His voice had dropped to a huskiness that was little more than breath itself, and she still held fast to his coat, but now more as a means to bring steadiness to her legs.

"But never by anybody else? You've never felt yourself…drawn to…"

"Not since that morning I saw you in Moravek's bakery."

It wasn't what she wanted to hear, this expression of desire. If anything, it magnified her own wandering thoughts. His eyes were searching hers now, and she knew he wanted to ask her the same question, and she knew she would die on the spot if he did. Maybe not die, but surely confess. Though, really, what was there to confess? The stray touch of an arm? A knee? Or the unsettling smile? Or that churning, craving core?

Ah yes, that was the seed of it, the essence of what she would profess should Garrison return her inquiry. Make a clean breast of it, she would. Begging his forgiveness, and God's too, in one sweeping leap of repentance.

Seconds passed, though, and Garrison said nothing. Vada's heart and head were near to bursting with revelation, but she kept it close, fearing the uninvited pain. There, in Garrison's embrace, she felt ready to scream or run or die.

Instead she reached her arm around his neck and pulled him close, bringing his mouth fully against hers, leaving little room for doubts, less for questions, and none for confession. There was a clumsy moment when their violin cases collided as the two attempted to wrap around each other. The humor of the moment brought Vada to her senses, and she stepped back, still bearing his kiss on her giggle.

"So much for the passion of Vada the temptress." She looked to see that none of the neighbors were at their windows. "I think you're safe to see me home."

"Ah no." He brought her hand to his lips and kissed it. "You see, that would deprive me of one of my greatest pleasures."

"And just what would that be?"

His eyebrows did a devilish dance above the rims of his glasses. "Watching you walk away."

"Why, Garrison Walker!" She snatched her hand away and cooled her face with an imaginary fan before swatting him with it. "And here I was thinking you were such a fine, upstanding gentleman!"

She stepped off the curb, aware of every movement as she crossed the street. When she got to her house, she looked back, and there he was, as always, standing in a pool of light. It was rare for him to wait that long, to see her all the way home, and it wasn't until she was backing up the concrete steps, offering a wave and a smile—both too slight to carry the distance between them—that he planted his hands in his pockets and turned to walk home.

"Good night, Garrison."

Now it was her turn to watch him walk away, but she felt no equivalent satisfaction. His footsteps were slow and reluctant, scraping against the pavement. So much so, it seemed odd that their sound would carry this far.

Those weren't Garrison's footsteps she heard. Her breath caught as the bearer of those steps emerged from the shadows beyond the streetlight.

"Good evening, Miss Allenhouse."

She gripped the handle of her violin case, hoping her voice would come across stronger than she felt.

"What are you doing here, Mr. Triplehorn?"

"I've come to talk with your father."

"It's late."

"This isn't a social call."

"It's late for any kind of call."

By now his foot was on the bottommost stone step, his hand, massive and dark, resting on the concrete banister. Vada stretched in his presence, stretching her shoulders to fill the door frame and staring him down, daring him to take another step.

He declined, retreating back to the sidewalk.

"I tried earlier this afternoon, but he was out. Your housekeeper said he was visiting patients."

"So, you met Molly?" She smiled, remembering the fate of unwanted visitors in Molly's path. If Molly had been here seventeen years ago...

"I did." He was smiling too. "She requested that I return tomorrow."

"So, why are you here tonight?"

"I'm not sure."

Of course *she* knew why he was here tonight. He, no doubt, felt the same torment that haunted her. But just as she protected Garrison from the pain of such confession, she now extended that shield to her father, her sisters, and stood her ground in the porch light.

"Go home, Mr. Triplehorn. And I don't just mean back to the Hollenden Hotel; I mean home. To wherever you came from, and leave us alone."

He chuckled, an oddly comforting, nonthreatening sound, and she puffed up more in defense of it.

"Quite the mother hen, aren't you?"

"Only because of you."

He had the good grace to look ashamed and stepped farther away, taking his hand off the banister completely. "I can see you need more time to think."

"I've had a lifetime to think," she said. "Nothing is going to change."

"Perhaps tomorrow—"

"No."

"What I was going to say is that I'll be in town all week. If you'd like to give me a chance. To talk—"

"I won't."

"Very well." He stepped away then, positioning himself squarely in the glow of the closest streetlight, and raised his hand. Within seconds, a black cab pulled by a prancing black horse arrived, and like a man used to such a conveyance, Alex Triplehorn swung his long body inside.

He didn't wave as he drove away, but he didn't need to. Something told Vada this wasn't the last she would see of him.

WEDNESDAY

ANOTHER SECRET TO KEEP

I could not leave your side this night—
Nor could I seek sleep's sweet asylum.
Content, instead, I pray I might
Embrace my hopes. Yet all belie them.

Saying, for you, death approaches.
It tarries, soon to take you from me.
Darkness on our joy encroaches
To sever, nay, seal our destiny.

Althea K. Allenhouse, Spring 1898

11

Hazel still snored her funny, whistling snore when Vada first opened her eyes the next morning. She'd said nothing to Hazel about Mr. Triplehorn's visit the night before, nor would she today. Some problems were easier handled with fewer hands, and as far as Alex Triplehorn was concerned, her two were completely capable.

Downstairs in the kitchen, Molly sang an Irish ditty about young lovers frolicking in the foam of the emerald sea. Because Molly rarely sang, Vada knew that particular song meant one thing. Pancakes. She'd learned that one morning when, having risen early due to a bad dream, she sat in the kitchen watching Molly prepare the light, fluffy cakes. Apparently the verse was just long enough to cook one side and, after flipping, the chorus long enough for the other.

This morning would have no time for lag-a-bed conversations. She gingerly crawled over the form of her sleeping sister and padded across the hall to draw a bath. While the water filled the claw-foot tub, she peeked through her bedroom door to see if there was any change in Eli.

The room was still dark but light enough to reveal Althea's form kneeling on the floor, arms folded on the mattress, her head buried in them, sleeping soundly. She still wore the same dress she had when she came home from the telegraph office yesterday evening. In fact, she was still wearing her shoes.

Vada thought back to the night before. She never got the chance to lure the man to consciousness with music. She'd sat with him for a while after supper, trying to read her Bible. But the words kept blurring in the lamplight, and by the time she'd given up and was settling the violin on her chin, Althea was standing there, silent at her elbow, and would not be turned away. By the time Vada was ready for bed, Althea was sitting contentedly, scribbling in her journal.

Apparently that was the same image everybody had seen as they popped in to say good night before turning in to their comfortable beds while here the poor girl was merely crumpled on the floor.

Mindful of the water filling the tub, Vada walked into the room and knelt beside her sister, gently shaking her awake. "Althea? Althea, wake up."

Initially when Althea awoke, there was no change to the peaceful expression she had in sleep. After a few blinks, though, her eyes opened in wide surprise, and she pushed Vada aside, scrambling to lay her head on the sleeping Eli's chest. She must have found the heartbeat she sought because she closed her eyes tight and released a long sigh.

Vada righted herself. "You've been in here all night?"

Althea nodded, not lifting her head.

"Doc didn't come in to spell you?"

She nodded again, but this time it seemed less a response to a question than a simple sleepy reflex.

Vada stood and looked down at the two, again feeling like an intruder on some sweet, intimate moment. She tiptoed over to her bureau and repeated the previous day's routine, taking a clean chemise, stockings, and pantalets from the top drawer. Holding these close, she was about to back out of the room but made one last stop at the bed.

"I'm getting a little tired of this, Eli. It's time to wake up." She waited, wondering if maybe that was all he ever needed—a direct command. But neither he nor Althea moved, and the bath water was surely near the top by now. "And we'll deal with the propriety of this later, young lady."

Althea merely smiled.

Later, downstairs, smelling of her favorite strawberry-scented bath salts, Vada dug into a pile of hotcakes smothered with warm maple syrup. She ate with a napkin tucked into the throat of her blouse and hadn't spoken a word since coming to the table.

One by one, other members of the Allenhouse family trickled in. Hazel first, her face freshly scrubbed to a pinkish hue, then Lisette looking like she just came off a magazine page advertising a youthful beauty crème. Finally Althea, listing a bit to the left, her hair in yesterday's disarrayed coif.

"Ah, what a joy 'tis to see all my pretty maids in a row." Molly scraped and flipped pancakes, the song long abandoned. "Nothin' like havin' you all here at once when I can only cook so many at a time."

The girls mumbled apologies and settled into their chairs, Hazel with a cup of strong coffee.

"And I suppose your father'll keep me waitin' here at the griddle until he decides to make a show?"

The question didn't warrant an answer, so nobody volunteered one. As each sister saw the plate of steaming cakes placed in front of her, she bowed her head in blessing, then dove her knife into the ball of butter in the center of the table.

"What does Doc have to say about our patient today?" Vada asked, sensing he was waiting for the second floor to empty itself of vulnerable young ladies before conducting his exam.

Nobody answered, in fact Althea wouldn't even look up. Eventually Hazel broke the silence saying, "It can't be good. It's been three days—"

"Oh, what I wouldn't give to be able to sleep for three days." Lisette broke into a cavernous yawn and stretched her arms high above her head. "Wouldn't it be wonderful?"

Althea raked her fork across her pancake.

"Lissy!" Hazel hissed. "How could you be so insensitive? That man upstairs is probably not going to live through the day."

A fork clattered onto a plate, and Althea stood and ran from the table.

"What's wrong with her?" Lisette asked, reaching for the molasses.

"Both of you," Vada said. "Can't you tell? I think she quite likes our Eli."

"*Our* Eli, is it? Oh, Hazel, isn't that the sweetest thing you've ever heard?" Lisette rolled her eyes and batted her lashes. "And wouldn't they make quite the chatterbox pair? My goodness, if they got married, the minister would have to say their vows for them."

Hazel laughed outright, and Vada waited for the amusement that pinched the inside of her cheeks to fade away before pointing a chastising fork at her youngest sister.

"You, my dear, are truly awful. And you," she leveled the prongs at Hazel, "should be ashamed of yourself for encouraging her. You're older and should be wiser."

"I'm wise enough to know how Doc feels about his patients," Hazel said. "And I have to say, when it comes to this one, I don't see a lot of hope."

"Now don't you be takin' it upon yerselves to decide just where your father does and doesn't have hope." Molly kept her back to them as she spoke. "I've known the man to lose a patient or two in his time, but I've never seen him lose faith that God would bring a healin' he couldn't bring himself."

"Molly's right," Vada said. "We all have to have that same faith. Do you know where I found Althea this morning? On her knees at his bedside. She'd been there all night praying. Do any of us have that kind of dedication?"

"None of us are in love with him."

"I didn't say she was in love with him, Lisette. I said that she likes him."

"Like you *quite like* Garrison," Hazel contributed with a smirk.

"Well, in that case you're right," Lisette said. "It's not love."

Vada slammed her fist on the table, causing Molly to turn around and give a disapproving scowl.

"Of course I love Garrison! What a terrible thing to say."

"Relax." Hazel patted Vada's arm. "She didn't mean any harm."

"Well, the both of you are the last two people on the face of the earth who should be considered any authority on love. You," Vada looked at Lisette, "with your bevy of boys following you everywhere you go. A bunch of lovesick puppies they are, and if they had any idea what a shallow, meanspirited girl you are, they wouldn't look twice at you."

"Vada, please." Hazel's soft gesture now turned into a strong grip, but Vada would not be deterred.

"And you've got even less to say, Hazel. With your—"

She was about to embark on a diatribe about Hazel's pathetic letters, but the panic and hurt in her sister's eyes quelled her tongue.

"I'm sorry," she said, though the two of them were the only ones in the room who truly knew the depth of her apology. She turned to Lisette. "And I didn't mean any of those things, Lissy. You know that. I'm just…tired."

Lisette pouted. "Am I really mean?"

"Of course not, dear."

"Well, I'm sorry for what I said about you and Garrison. In fact, I think it's fine that he doesn't marry you because the two of you are like a doddering old couple already."

Somehow Vada knew Lisette meant no harm and, unable to ignore the truth of the statement, she chose to ignore the statement itself. "Still, girls, I think we need to be strong for Althea's sake. We need to take our fair share of time sitting with Eli, so she knows we believe he'll wake up."

"I'll sit with him this morning," Hazel said. "Doc'll be out visiting patients, so he won't need me in the office. Besides," her eyes twinkled, "I have some letter writing I need to catch up on."

They needn't worry this last bit of conversation would pique Lisette's curiosity as she was busy asking Molly to please pour her more tea.

"And Lisette?" Vada prompted. "Can you sit with Eli after school?"

"I was going to—" Vada and Hazel glared at her. Even Molly poured her tea with decided hostility. "Fine. I'll be home by four."

Vada held up her own cup as a request for more tea, and in response, Molly set the pot down firmly in the center of the table. It wasn't a complete slight, though, because just at that moment there was a knocking at the back door. Probably a delivery boy—with ice, milk, groceries, something—so what a shock to hear Molly's voice dripping with affection, saying, "Well, come in me boy-o, and just in time for some good hot breakfast."

Kenny Cupid stepped into the kitchen, cap in hand, his face fresh from a scrub and a shave, tinged pink with a tiny scabbed-over cut on the tip of his chin. "I hope I'm not bothering anybody, coming this early."

"Not disturbin' a soul, sonny. Come sit." Molly whisked Althea's plate away and patted the seat of her abandoned chair. "Right next to our Lissy. And I'll get a stack comin' right up for you. How about I fix y' an egg to go with it?"

"I don't want to be a bother, ma'am."

"Oh, please," Lisette said. "Don't tell me I have to sit through a meal with him at this very table."

"Not at all, missy." Molly said. "I'd be more'n happy to scrape your plate and send you off to school."

Lisette looked at her plate, pancakes stacked four high in a moat of rich molasses. She gave Kenny a seething sidelong glance, never taking her eyes off him as she dug her fork into her food.

"You'll have to forgive our youngest sister," Hazel said. "She's just a horrible person."

"I'll never believe that a day in my life." Kenny was settled at the table, cap dangling on the chair post. He looked straight at Vada. "And is he—"

"No change. But you can go up to visit after you've eaten if you like."

"I'd appreciate that."

Molly set a crowded plate of eggs and pancakes in front of him. He closed his eyes, made a rapid sign of the cross, and said, "Lord, bless this food and the hands that prepared it. Shine Your love on all who share it." Another quick cross and, "Amen."

When he opened his eyes, he offered a sheepish grin to the three Allen-house sisters, especially to Lisette who stared, fork firmly lodged in her mouth. "I'm sorry," he said. "That must sound a little silly to you."

"Nonsense," Vada said, silently imploring the other two not to laugh. Hazel's smirk was dangerous enough. "It's sweet."

"It's something my nan—er, mother taught me."

"Which makes it all the more special." Relieved to see Lisette quietly chewing, and Hazel's smirk reformed to a small, soft smile, Vada excused herself from the table, asking Molly to put Althea's breakfast on a tray that she could take upstairs.

"Already done." And it was, with a silver dome covering the plate to keep the food warm, a cup of steaming tea, and tiny dish of butter and jam.

Vada bade them good morning as she backed out the door and carefully maneuvered up the stairs where she met her father on the landing. The grave look on his face made the tray she carried almost unbearably heavy.

"Doc?"

"I'm at a loss." He scratched his chin, or would have scratched it if not for the springing tufts of whiskers. "If the injury had caused any bleeding or swelling in his brain, he would be dead by now. And if it wasn't a severe injury, he would be awake by now. Instead, he just..."

"Sleeps?"

"And there's nothing more to be done. But don't be startled when you see him. I've propped him up to keep fluid from building up in his lungs."

"Do you think it's time to take him to a hospital?"

Doc shook his head. "There's nothing to do for him there that we can't provide here." He offered Vada a weak smile and made his way past her to go downstairs.

She walked straight into her room, expecting to find Althea at her post. Instead, there was Eli, pale against the sea of pillows that surrounded him. His lips were parted, and the room was filled with a sound eliciting both comfort and concern: his breath, deep and regular, but accompanied by the softest rasping rattle.

She shifted the weight of the tray to one arm and glanced at the smattering of items on top of her bureau.

"Forgive me, Lord, if You consider this stealing." She grabbed the folded note found in his pocket and dropped it into her own. Then, after the slightest hovering, she closed her fingers around the two buttons and dropped them in too.

Althea's room was at the end of the hall — more of a large closet really, but it seemed to suit her small, silent needs. The door was shut tight, and Vada knocked softly before opening it and peeking in.

The sound in here was eerily like that of the room she just left but without the fixed rhythm. Instead Althea, facedown in her bed, took in one long, wet breath and seemed to let out only half of it before gasping two or three more short ones.

Vada set the tray down on the little writing desk wedged into the corner and went to her sister, kneeling and placing a hand on the sobbing girl's back. "Oh, sweetheart. He's going to be just fine. I know he is."

But when Althea didn't answer, it was more than just a matter of silence. Despite the tortured breathing, the girl was sound asleep, and no amount of breakfast, no matter how delicious, seemed worthy of disturbing that slumber.

Vada turned to the opposite end of the bed and, one by one, unlaced Althea's shoes, setting them gently on the floor. Then she took the blanket folded across the foot of the bed and spread it over Althea's narrow shoulders, administering slow, smooth circles around her back until the quaking slowed.

Satisfied of her sister's slumber, Vada rose to leave and, in her movement, knocked Althea's worn journal to the ground. Under any other circumstances, Vada would never have pried into those hidden writings, but the book landed to an open page, and she took in the first lines:

I could not leave your side this night.
Nor could I seek sleep's sweet asylum.
Content, instead, I pray—

She looked away, uncomfortable with this revelation. And, truthfully, a bit envious. When was the last time she'd felt she could not leave

Garrison's side? Last night, of course, but her reluctance had nothing to do with contentment. More of a desperate grasping, really.

Quickly, before she could be tempted to read further, she closed the book and set it beside Althea's pillow. Breakfast could wait, maybe until lunch, and she picked up the tray once more to take to the kitchen.

She arrived downstairs just in time to meet Lisette at the front door, her schoolbooks bundled in a leather strap. "You managed to make it through breakfast with your newest admirer?"

Lisette rolled her eyes. "Papa and Hazel are filling him in on all the grisly details about our coma boy. I couldn't take it anymore."

"Well, if you'll wait for just a minute, I have an early morning errand to run. I could walk to school with you."

Lisette pulled back the lace curtain covering the front door window and peered out. "No, thanks. The Britton twins are outside waiting to walk with me."

Vada noted the hint of wistfulness in her youngest sister's voice. "You don't seem too excited about that."

"It's fine." She dropped the curtain but did not turn around. "It's just, after so much conversation at breakfast, maybe I wanted a little peace and quiet on the way to school."

"Do you want me to shoo them away for you?"

"Are you kidding?" she said over her shoulder. "You're so beautiful, they'd probably forget all about school and follow you on your silly errand."

With that she opened the door, giving Vada a glimpse of the two earnest young men waiting at the bottom of the stairs, their identical faces lighting up at the sight of Lisette in her pale green spring coat with her long, caramel-colored curls streaming over her shoulders.

"I hardly think so, my dear." Vada turned to go into the kitchen. Suddenly, the front door was open again.

"Oh, Vada!" Lisette's sweet voice turned the summons into a song. "There's a certain man here this morning to see you too. I don't want to say who, but he's awfully handsome, has red hair, and his team just lost to our little Spiders yesterday."

Vada tightened her grip on the tray to keep from dropping it. "Tell him—" *What? To go away? To come back at a more appropriate calling hour? To leave her alone before she lost her head entirely?* "Tell him I have an errand to run."

"Tell him yourself," Lisette said, all of her sweetness gone. "I have boys waiting for me."

"Lord," Vada prayed to the empty hallway, "if You won't keep Mr. LaFortune away from me, I'll just have to work harder to keep *myself* away from *him*."

She headed for the kitchen, hoping to offer to help Molly with the breakfast dishes. Not something she would normally do, but this morning she needed an excuse to keep herself inside the house. Instead she walked in to see Molly and Kenny side by side at the sink, happily sharing the chore.

Hearing the swing of the kitchen door, Molly swung around. "Just leave those on the sideboard, darlin'. We'll get to them in just two ticks."

"All right," Vada said, a little taken aback by the scene. "Where are Hazel and Doc?"

"Down in your father's office, plannin' out the day."

Kenny said something under his breath, and Molly joined him in a private chuckle.

"Do you need anything from me?" Vada set down the tray.

"Oh, no, dearie. You just go and get on with your mornin'."

Vada eyed the back door, thinking for just a moment that she could escape and double back through the alley. But who knew how long Mr.

LaFortune would wait on the front porch. He might even be there when she got back.

No, no. On second thought, best to nip this problem in the bud and send him packing right off.

She lifted the large silver batter spoon from where Kenny set the dried dishes, making a joke about looking for spots while she gave her reflection a quick check before heading for the front door. Another glimpse in the mirror beside the coatrack in the entryway reassured her—eyes bright, face free of anything sticky, bodice clear of crumbs, and dark hair arranged with the perfect combination of smoothness and puff.

Not that any of it mattered.

Rather than pulling on her light wool jacket, she opted for a bright plum-colored shawl from the hall closet, and with this securely clutched around her shoulders, she walked out onto the front step, looking straight ahead of her in order to be surprised. In fact, she jumped a bit at the high-pitched little howl he gave the minute the door closed behind her.

"Hoo-cher."

There he was, standing on the sidewalk, one foot up on the third step, leaning forward with his forearm resting on his knee. The moment she looked at him, though, he straightened up and took off his cap, clutching it to his head. *"Gardez voir la belle!"*

A pack of boys on their way to school turned and looked. Although it was doubtful they understood the French vocabulary proclaiming Vada as the man's "sweetheart," the tone of his voice was unmistakable. The boys made exaggerated kissy noises among themselves, bursting into full-out laughter when Mr. LaFortune raised a fist and feigned a chase down the street.

"Honestly, Mr. LaFortune." Vada made her way down the stairs. "That's the second time I've seen you threaten children. Be careful, or I'm prone to think you some kind of a brute."

"Think anything you want, *cher,* as long as you thinkin' about me."

His eyes tracked her down every step until, by the time she joined him on the sidewalk, she felt positively pulled there.

"I'm afraid I don't have time for a visit," she said, ready to brush right past him, "I have a very important errand to run."

"Then I run right along with you."

He offered her his arm, which she declined, although she made no objection as he fell into step beside her.

"Don't know if you heard, but we lost yesterday."

"I heard." She stopped short of saying she was sorry, because she wasn't sure she was.

"'Course you don't care, bein' a Cleveland girl and all."

"My lack of concern has nothing to do with being a 'Cleveland girl.' I simply find the end result of a baseball game to have little impact on my life."

They were crossing the street now, and for the briefest moment, she found herself standing with Louis LaFortune on the corner where, just a few hours ago, she had been kissing Garrison Walker. Her pancakes flipped themselves in her stomach, and she should have told LaFortune to leave her there and go find someone else to sympathize with, but he was already asking if they were to turn left or right. Without answering, Vada spun to the right, up the familiar trek to Moravek's.

"It all my fault, you know. That we lost."

She kept walking, knowing exactly where this conversation was going.

"When I get up to bat, I just freeze. Don't even take one swing. Let them all fly by, *un, deux, trois.* All this muscle," he held out his arms, "and I can't move a-one."

Vada allowed herself one sidelong look at his arm, then picked up her speed. He had no trouble matching it.

"So you see, *belle*, why I need those buttons."

They were on Commercial Street now, weaving their path through men and women on their way to shops and offices. She nodded to a few familiar faces, ignoring their curious glances to her left, hoping they would think the handsome man beside her was nothing more than a coincidence of proximity.

For the first time that morning, it occurred to her that she might run into Garrison himself. She never had, given the rigidity of his routine, but how unlucky would it be for this, of all mornings, to be the one he decided to start his day with a delicious pastry instead of Mrs. Paulie's poached egg?

She clutched her shawl more closely around her and took one wide step to the right, increasing the distance between them. And while it would be easy enough to avoid his company on the streets, the bell-strung door of Moravek's bakery loomed ahead, and there would be no escaping him in that small space.

"You need to leave now." She spoke out of the side of her mouth. "You can't go in there with me."

"*La boulangerie? Pourquoi?*"

She stopped and looked at him, full in the face for the first time since seeing him in front of her house. "I have a note." She pulled the folded paper out of her skirt pocket. "It's his. And I need it translated so I can know something…"

"And this knowin'," he said, the sideways grin back, "it will make him better?"

"Of course not."

"But it will make you feel better?"

"I suppose."

"So you see, it is not so silly for me to want two little buttons. To think how I might hit the ball if I had this kind of treasure." His fingers inched toward the folded square, and she snatched it close to her before he could take hold.

"This is a private, intimate correspondence. You will not turn it into some good luck charm."

"And how you know it be so intimate?"

Heat rose to her neck. "It's-it's s-signed by a woman. Named Katrina."

"Well then, by all means *belle,* go inside and find *l'amour.* I await you here. But I make one request." He inhaled deeply, expanding his chest, and rubbed his narrow belly. "It smell *si bon* in there, you must to bring me a little something sweet."

The way he looked at her made Vada feel as if she herself were sprinkled with sugar, about to be devoured right there in the street. She tried to squash the deliciousness of the feeling and set her lips firm.

"Then you'll need to give me a nickel. Or a dime if you want two. What would you like?"

LaFortune dug deep into his pocket and produced a dime. He lifted her hand and pressed it into her open palm, and that sumptuous feeling crept over her again.

"I trust you to know."

She walked inside before she could melt.

There was a modest line at the pastry counter—not more than four or five people. Vada was acknowledged by the gentleman directly in front of her, allowing her to wander off to the side and study the contents of the glass case. She finally decided the swirled buns with raisins and cinnamon would be perfect, seeing the cinnamon color so closely matched the color of his hair, and its sprinkling across the bronzed, baked surface was not unlike the pale freckles that dusted his cheeks—

"Miss Allenhouse!"

Vada straightened and looked into the flushed, impatient face of Mrs. Moravek.

"Tell me. Tell me. We got more peoples."

Two more people had come in behind Vada, one of whom she knew from the Ladies' Auxiliary luncheon committee. "Why don't you all go ahead of me?" she said. "I'm still deciding."

Hoping no more customers would come in, she waited patiently as Mrs. Moravek filled their orders, and when the little bell rang on the closing door behind them, Vada stood alone on the customer side of the counter.

Approaching shyly, as if she'd never been in the establishment a day in her life, Vada took the folded note and handed it across the counter.

"*Vat* this?"

Last night Vada and Hazel had spent the last few minutes before sleep concocting the story. "It's a note. We found it near our home and were curious to know what it says."

Mrs. Moravek looked at the open paper, then at Vada. "You know who is?"

"No. It might belong to one of our father's patients. We thought if we knew, we could return it." She was struck by how easily the lie came to her.

"It not my business."

"But if it's important, and we know whose it is, we can return it. And it might be important, Mrs. Moravek. So I promise you, whatever the note says, it will stay between us. I won't tell a soul."

By now Mrs. Moravek's own curiosity was shining through, and she inched the note across the glass before picking it up and bringing it first close to her nose, then out a little farther, until finally settling on a proper reading distance.

"Oh," she said. Then, "Oh my. Oh, is sad. Is too, too sad."

Vada was now on her toes, ready to leap across the counter but, trying to remain true to her story, she rocked back on her heels and waited for Mrs. Moravek to lift the corner of her apron and dry the tear that left a thin track down her flour-dusted face.

"Well?"

"Oh, is tragedy."

Breathless, she asked, "Can you read it to me?"

Mrs. Moravek took in a deep breath. "It say, 'My dear Eli. I wish you had found me here in the way we dreamed together. But I was a silly girl then. And so young. Mother say never believe the promises of youth. I did love you, of course I did. But was the love of a child for another child. And when your heart has mended, I wish you to find a woman worthy of your love. Always your fond friend, Katrina.'"

By the time she finished reading, Mrs. Moravek's voice was thin, and Vada felt her own throat burning with the threat of tears.

"I do not believe that young man who dropped this note ever want to have it back. I go trow it in oven."

"No!" This time Vada did leap, snatching the paper right out of the woman's hand. "Let me ask my father if he has a patient named Eli. If he doesn't, I promise I'll throw the note away. But if he does, well, he has a right to know…"

Before Vada could finish, Mrs. Moravek stomped out to the back room and came back with a tray full of warm *kolaches*. She opened the back door to the display case and began tossing them onto the shelf.

"Dat evil, evil girl. Breaking dat poor boy's heart. And he love her so much."

"You don't know that." Vada's hand shook as she repocketed the note. "Maybe he didn't really love her either."

"Of course he did. For years he did."

"If he loved her, he would have married her."

"What, marry? They was children."

"See?" Vada fumbled with the note, clutching for truth. "They grew out of it. That happens sometimes, doesn't it?"

"She grow out. He don't. Oh, it is so, so sad."

Vada folded the tragic little story and stashed it back into her pocket.

Evil girl. Evil, indeed. Perhaps Katrina had simply found somebody else. Somebody not an ocean away. Nothing evil about that. In fact, it could be downright divine.

Vada continued her musings until, the shelf restocked, Mrs. Moravek wiped her hands on her apron and, with a voice full of business, asked Vada what she would like to order. One glance out the window revealed the ever-present Mr. LaFortune. He stood, hands clasped loosely behind his back, his expansive chest puffed out, his lips puckered as if whistling.

Evil girl.

At once, the rows of swirled cinnamon had lost all their appeal. "Nothing, thank you. I just needed you to read the note."

"Next time, then? And you bring dat nice young man with you."

"Of course." She forced a smile and turned to see an elderly woman standing impatiently behind her. Funny, she hadn't heard the bell ring.

Outside, LaFortune was at her elbow the minute she stepped onto the sidewalk. "And did you find out what you want?"

"Yes." She stared at the ground, nearly choking on the word.

"Hey," he said, making a show of searching around her. "Where my treat?"

She dropped the dime, warm from her hand, into his outstretched palm. "Go on in and buy your own. I didn't know what you wanted. And here"—she opened the clasp on her little purse and found the two buttons—"take these." She pressed them against the ten-cent piece and closed his fingers around them. "Now you have no reason to speak to me again."

If he protested, the sound was lost in the ringing bell of the bakery door. And it never occurred to Vada to look back.

12

Vada didn't go straight home, harboring some irrational fear that LaFortune might follow. Instead she made her way around the block, weaving in and out of people, stepping in and out of shops, hoping to lose herself in the crowd.

She found her feet following the familiar path to church. The distinct sound of laughter and rejoicing called her attention, causing her to slow her steps, then stop altogether at the sight that came out from behind the building.

First came a little girl, her hair a mass of thick sausagelike curls that flew behind her as she ran. She had an enormous pink bow on top of her head, and she wore a dress of pure white silk with a matching pink sash.

Behind her came a little boy, not nearly as elated as the girl. He wore a little sailor suit fashioned of pale blue silk with a wide white collar. He trailed his steps, dragging one foot behind the other, causing the little girl to turn back and run circles around him, as if herding him to the front steps of the church.

Vada laughed at the sight. *Here, then, is the picture of marriage in miniature.* She made a note to remind herself to share this with Hazel when she got home and was about to leave when the rest of the party came around the corner and took her breath away.

Half-a-dozen older girls—young women, really—walked as one ruffled, feathered mass, their dresses identical sweeping things with pale striped skirts and lavender bodices. They carried bouquets of purple lilies and wore hats made of purple straw festooned with long curling feathers. And in the midst of them, the bride, her arms encased in close-fitting white silk, flounced broad at the shoulder. Her skirt smooth, pure white silk, trimmed in white silk roses. The thin veil hid her face, but nothing could disguise the face of her father. He appeared set in stone as he looped his black jacketed arm through his daughter's.

Vada allowed herself a luxurious moment to imagine her face behind the veil, looking out at the world through yards and yards of delicate lace. She could picture her father beside her, Hazel, Althea, and Lisette trailing behind. And she longed to believe that Garrison would be behind the church door, waiting at the top of the aisle. More than that, she wanted Garrison to imagine the same thing. To want the same thing.

She looked closer, trying to make out just who was getting married. She didn't remember an announcement in the recent weeks, and she certainly hadn't received an invitation. But she supposed there were those who wouldn't come to church to worship but would use it for a wedding.

And what a morning for a wedding—bright and cool, a promise of warmth later in the afternoon. Inside the church there would be promises, later there would be dancing. This was the day that would change that woman's life, and Vada was half tempted to follow the party inside and join in the celebration. After all, her shawl practically matched the wedding party's colors.

Instead she simply stood, watching, while the girls got the children in order and the first strains of organ music could be heard through the doors. It wasn't until all had filed in and the doors were once again closed, the music muted, that Vada took the next step. She may have stumbled upon this scene through aimless wandering, but she left it with a new sense of purpose and an urgent one at that.

Continuing up Cleric Street and over to Chancellor, she found herself outside the door of Garrison's office building. He was three floors up, and if he were to look out his window at that precise moment, he would see the top of her hat. He might even recognize the plum-colored shawl, though he might be disconcerted by the sloped shoulders beneath it.

She looked straight up, willing him to come to the window. But he wasn't the type of man to take a frivolous glance on a chilly spring morning. So, against all logic, she walked not only to the door, but through it and up the stairs that creaked under every step until she reached the landing of the third floor and a door etched with Benedict, Parker, and Hughes, Attorneys-at-Law in swirling gold letters. It wouldn't be easy to add Walker to the door, should Garrison ever realize his goal of making partner.

Inside, everything was uniformly dark, heavy, and brown, save for one crooked, amateurish painting depicting a studious boy studying under an apple tree. A brass plate mounted to the frame read: The seeds of the future are planted in youth.

Beneath the painting, a thin, pale man sat at the desk in the front office, pounding the keys of a typewriter. Vada had to clear her throat several times to get his attention. When she did, he extended a single pinky to hold her at bay, never interrupting his rhythmic typing.

"There now," he said after a final, flourishing stroke. "With whom do you have an appointment?"

"Nobody, really. I'm here to see Garrison Walker."

"Ah, you have an appointment with Mr. Walker?"

"Not an appointment. I am just here to see him."

"Without an appointment?"

"That is correct." Smile frozen on her face, she matched his game of formality.

"Well, this is highly unusual." He tapped his fingers in a circular pattern across the top of his desk with the same enthusiasm he'd used earlier in his typing. "And whom shall I say you are?"

"Here." She opened her pocketbook and took out one of her calling cards with her name written in raised calligraphy surrounded by green, winding ivy. "If you will just give him this."

He studied the card, then looked up at her, his pinched face betraying the tiniest fraction of recognition and pleasure. "Ah, Miss Allenhouse. Of course. If you'll wait right here."

He fairly glided out of the office, his shoes making no noise on the hardwood floor. Now that the typewriter was silent, she could hear the low, muffled voices humming out from the doors around her. So many grave, important conversations. She imagined Garrison was quite happy here—nothing silly or superfluous. Even the apples in the painted tree were precise and symmetrical.

Four straight-backed chairs lined the wall on either side of the door, and she was about to take a seat in one of them, when she heard, "Vada?" Garrison's voice had an echoing quality in the Spartan room. "Sweetheart, is anything wrong?"

She was grateful for the watchful eye of the secretary who was back in his desk before she could reply. Otherwise, she might have collapsed right then, melting into a puddle of confession, begging for either a proposal or forgiveness. She allowed Garrison to take her hand in a most proper manner and told him she was simply in the neighborhood and decided to stop by.

"You've never stopped by before."

"Sometimes you just—I just need to see you." She took his other hand.

"Well, then. Isn't this nice?"

The two had certainly shared moments of conversationless quiet over the years, but Vada had never felt quite so awkward. Maybe it was the stale odor of wood and paper, or the creaking floorboard as they shifted their weight. Soon the intermittent *clack* of the typewriter popped into the midst, and they shifted their eyes toward the young man, who quickly looked away.

"I was wondering," Vada said at last, "would you like to slip out for a moment? Maybe get a cup of coffee?"

"It's ten-fifteen in the morning."

"I know."

"It's two hours until my lunch break."

"Do you have an appointment?"

"No, not at the moment."

"Later this morning?"

"I'm not—" He looked at the secretary who shook his head, never taking his eyes from his typing. "But it's just ten-fifteen."

"Honestly, Garrison." She squeezed his fingers, surprising herself at how close she was to pleading. "Is it unheard of to have a cup of coffee at ten-fifteen?"

"If you like, sir, I can pop across the street and fetch you a cup. Or two."

"No, thank you, Rod," Garrison said. Then to Vada, "I'm sorry, dear. But if I'm to make tonight's rehearsal, I do have work to finish up."

"Of course. I understand." She felt a burning at the back of her throat and needed to leave quickly, lest she make an even bigger fool of herself than she already had.

"Rod," he said behind her, "I'm going to escort Miss Allenhouse downstairs. I'll be right back."

"Duly noted, sir."

"No," Vada protested without turning around. "I'm fine."

"I insist," Garrison said, and she felt his hand on the small of her back, guiding her out the door and across the hall. The staircase was too narrow to allow them to walk side by side so Vada took the lead, never once separating herself from his touch. Only a dim gaslight kept the stairwell from utter darkness, though its light barely touched the landing between the two flights.

Here there was room for two, and as the faint touch encircling her waist expanded, she was brought against his body. When she closed her eyes, the blackness increased only a little, and she felt Garrison's mouth on hers, kissing her as he had on the rarest occasions, with an urgency against her lips that she was more than ready to answer.

She brought her hands up around his neck, feeling the strap of her pocketbook slide to her elbow, and tried to bring him closer. Not just to deepen the kiss, but to take him in—to fill her up and banish the images that swirled in her darkness.

No matter how ardent the embrace of this man, her mind wrapped around another. One with broader shoulders and coarse, curling hair. It was his hands she imagined roaming the breadth of her back, underneath the plum-colored shawl, which now seemed unbearably cumbersome. His voice, filled with his tainted French, lurked beneath the small contented sounds she made. She wanted to kiss Garrison forever, if it meant a chance to meld the two.

But too soon he released her from their kiss, though he drew her close enough that she could smell the efficiency of the office on his shirt.

"I'm sorry," he said, his hands still trailing along her back, "that I didn't have time for coffee."

She craned her head back to look at him and smiled, hoping to banish her thoughts. "That's quite all right. But you must hurry back now. It has to be nearly ten-twenty."

"Until tomorrow night?"

"Until tomorrow night."

And please, God, keep me true until tomorrow night.

She reached up and straightened his glasses. "We don't want Rod to get the wrong idea."

Minutes later, when she stepped out into the sunlit street, she brought her hand to her lips, returning to the moment. Now the tears that had threatened to spill upstairs in his office appeared unbidden, and she stumbled, head sagging, down the sidewalk. Vague mutters of concern echoed from the strangers who passed her, but she ignored them and eventually was able to walk upright, her shoulders back, the last tear whisked away with the corner of her shawl.

She had a list of errands the length of her arm, but right now she couldn't keep them straight. All the tiny slips written in Herr Johann's precise hand were jumbled in her pocketbook, but she couldn't face opening the little snap and seeing Katrina's accusatory note. There was very little to do at the office until the afternoon, and she couldn't go home. The kitchen would be full of Molly and Vada's bedroom full of Eli. How was it she'd come to this age without a single place to call her own?

She found herself back at Moravek's bakery—welcomed by the tinkling bell, enveloped by the warm, yeasty aroma.

"Well, now," Mrs. Moravek said, already taking a small plate from the stack on the shelf behind her. "I know you would come back. What can I get you?"

"Coffee, please." Vada dropped her pocketbook on a table by the window.

"Sit, sit. I bring it out to you. How about a nice piece of lemon cake?"

"That sounds good." And it was, perfectly tart with a thin layer of sweet vanilla icing. She doled it out in tiny bits, alternating with sips of hot coffee, letting all of it—the bitter, the sour, the sweet—melt together and dissipate before the next bite.

Oh, Lord, I need— But the prayer went no further. Eyes open, her serene face guarding the chaos within, she eased a corner off the cake. *I don't know what I need. But forgive me, Lord. For my thoughts*—LaFortune and his charming crooked smile looked back from her coffee—*like that one, Lord. I told him to stay away. Keep him away, and I can overcome this temptation. But if You don't*—

The knock on Moravek's window startled her, sending the empty fork clattering to the plate. She looked up to see Hazel, stiffly corseted in a severe brown suit, waving. For a few seconds, both sisters beckoned the other to the other side of the glass, and in the end Hazel settled in across from Vada on the other side of the table.

"What happened to you?" Hazel asked, breathless from the act of sitting. "I didn't know you'd be gone all morning. Have you been here the whole time?"

"Yes." Vada didn't miss a beat. "I needed a little quiet to plan out my day. Who's sitting with Eli?"

"Cupid himself. It was that or Molly was going to make him paint the shutters."

Mrs. Moravek came over with a slice of cake and coffee for Hazel. "Be sweet to your sister. She seem sad today. And who wouldn't, with such tragic story?" She walked away, tsking and shaking her head.

Hazel's round, soft face burned with curiosity, and Vada reported the contents of Eli's note.

"You know what that means?" Hazel spooned sugar into her coffee. "He's dying from a broken heart."

"He's not dying. And if he were, it would be of a broken head."

The sisters shared a guilty giggle, and Vada felt the cloud of the morning lifting. Thoughts of Garrison and LaFortune and even Alex Triplehorn drifted away with it, and Hazel and Vada settled into speculation about the story behind the note.

"To think," Vada said, "he came all the way to this country to find her in love with another man."

"Unless she found another man in the old country, and that's why he came here."

"He wouldn't carry that note across an ocean."

Hazel held up three envelopes. "I don't know...a single letter can carry a lot of weight in a romance. At least I hope it will."

"Really, Hazel. It's rather cruel of you to lead these men on. You can't marry all of them, you know."

"That's why all of these letters send my regrets. I'm returning their pictures too."

"To all of them?"

"Not all." She sifted through the envelopes and held one up. Her face flushed crimson above the ruffles of her shirt.

"Barth the mountain man turned sheep farmer?"

"I'm still holding out some hope."

"That's good," Vada said. "Hope is good."

"So," Hazel leaned in with a conspiratorial air, "should we tell Althea about the letter? Perhaps she's the woman worthy of Eli's love?"

Vada thought for a moment, then shook her head. "No. Not yet."

"So, it's another secret to keep?"

"For now, yes. Hope is good, but let's give her just one thing to hope for at a time. Now, tell me, why are you dressed like a suffragette on parade?"

"No parade. Just a meeting. At the Junior League Hall up the street. Want to come?"

"Thanks," Vada said, "but I think I'll leave the world changing up to you."

"Oh, it's not so much about changing the world as it is Mrs. Noratelli's peach sorbet. Come on, Vada. A cup of tea, a few speeches. What else have you got to fill your morning?"

"I have responsibilities." She pressed the back of her fork to the plate, picking up crumbs. "Things to do."

"None of it can wait until the afternoon? The meeting's only an hour. You might learn a little about being a woman in the next century."

Vada offered a weak smile. "I'm having a hard enough time being a woman in *this* century."

"Please?" Hazel had a wheedling tone Vada could rarely refuse for long, and she finally agreed.

"But no picket signs."

"That's a promise."

They finished their cake and coffee while Vada recounted the wedding party outside of the church, giving an especially amusing account of the reluctant little boy.

"I'm afraid the experience will turn him into a bachelor for life," Vada said as they stood to leave.

"I figure every man's a bachelor for life," Hazel said. "Until he meets the right woman."

They left Moravek's with their arms linked and chatted all the way to the post office, where Hazel gave one envelope a kiss before handing the stack of letters over to Mr. Witherspoon.

The Junior League Hall was just two doors down, a pretty white-brick building with a rosebush-lined walkway out front. Hazel led Vada up the front steps and through the ornately carved front door, where an older woman in a pale lavender suit sat at a small table, her pale hand resting atop a wooden box.

"Oh, right." Hazel fumbled through her pocketbook. "I forgot to tell you. There's a nickel donation to the cause."

"Well, then, find a dime," Vada said, keeping her smile sweet. "It's your cause, not mine."

If the lavender lady heard them, she gave no indication. She simply took Hazel's dime in her hand and raised it, a shaking fist, above her head. "Votes for women!" she cried in a thin, creaking voice.

"Votes for women!" Hazel raised her own fist. Over her shoulder she whispered, "Now for sorbet and a seat in the back."

Vada followed her sister's lead, nodding greetings to several women she recognized from the neighborhood. Soon she was being handed a delicate glass dish with one rounded scoop of peach sorbet and a small spoon with which to eat it.

"Thank you," she said, accepting the treat.

"Votes for women!" the table hostess replied, holding the next glass high above her head.

The sentiment was echoed on banners and ribbons strewn across the walls of the grand room, and a statuesque woman stood at the front of it, pounding a wooden gavel on a podium, encouraging the others to finish their refreshment and take their seats.

Hazel and Vada chose to take their sorbet with them, holding the dishes close, shielding them from the prying eyes of the hostess.

There was a brief surge in conversation as the women complied, and Vada noticed every one there seemed dressed in the best her wardrobe allowed. Certainly Hazel did, and Vada, wearing a simple shirtwaist and skirt, felt positively dowdy beside her.

"Don't worry," Hazel whispered, reading her mind. "Nobody cares what you look like."

But the sidelong glances said differently, and Vada stuck even closer to her sister.

They found their seats in the back row —as promised, and by the

time they settled in, the gavel and podium had worked its magic, bringing silence to the room.

"Good morning, women."

Vada craned her neck to get a better look but could not come up
with the name of the gavel wielder.

"Welcome to the Wednesday morning meeting of the Terrington
Heights Women's Suffrage Association. If you will join me, please?"

The room was full of rustling as fifty or more women took to their
feet, Vada and Hazel among them. From somewhere at the front of the
room, a piano pounded the familiar opening chords of "Onward, Christian Soldiers," and soon the hall exploded in soprano passion:

> *Like a mighty army moves the church of God;*
> *[Sisters,] we are treading where the saints have trod.*
> *We are not divided, all one body we,*
> *One in hope and doctrine, one in charity.*

Vada, unfamiliar with the lyrics, barely moved her lips, but Hazel
joined in with lusty enthusiasm, offering a sorbet toast when she sang
"Sisters," forgetting for the moment that she was not supposed to have her
refreshment at her seat.

When they were once again seated and attentive, the minutes from
the previous meeting were read, and Vada spooned the icy peach treat
into her mouth, grateful she hadn't been hogtied and dragged here last
week. The woman's voice became a droning nuisance, incapable of diverting Vada's attention the way she'd hoped.

She sloped further down in her seat, seeing nothing but the bunch
of silk azaleas on the hat of the woman in front of her until the smattering of polite applause called her attention, and she sat up to see Mrs.

Cordelia Thomas—the *widow* Cordelia Thomas—making her way to the front of the room.

Vada leaned over and whispered, "What's she doing?"

"Every week different women speak or give some little presentation."

"What could she possibly have to say?"

Hazel shrugged and then twisted herself, seeking a comfortable position.

The last time Vada had seen Mrs. Thomas, the older lady had been chastising her unruly behavior, and now a whole room of women were going to be subjected to her insufferable arrogance.

"Well, I'm not listening to her."

At this point, the bundle of azaleas disappeared from view as the woman in front of Vada turned around and scowled.

"Pardon me." Vada smiled sweetly until the flowers reappeared.

"My fellow women of Terrington Heights," Mrs. Thomas prattled in her overly cultured voice, "I am both pleased and honored that you would select me to be the bearer of feminine truth this lovely morning."

"'Bearer of feminine truth,'" Vada said, mocking. "And just what exactly is that supposed to be?"

The azaleas twitched again.

"I find it intolerable," Mrs. Thomas continued, "as should you all, that this day and age, when women are on the cusp of being seen as the political, social, and economic equal of men, so many of our young sisters see no greater fulfillment in their life other than marriage."

Vada nearly choked on a delicious chunk of fruit-flavored ice, even as the azaleas in front of her bobbed in approval.

"Did you hear that?" she hissed once her throat was cleared.

"Every now and then we get one of these," Hazel replied. "Last week it was all about equal wages for equal work. You just never know—"

"Shhh!"

It was impossible to tell just where the hushing originated, and Vada responded by staring straight ahead.

"They seek nothing more," Mrs. Thomas intoned, "than to hitch their lives to one of the very same sex who would seek to keep us mired in subservient silence."

"Hear, hear," the ladies chirped from their chairs.

"Oh, for the love of—" Vada twisted in her chair, turning to face Hazel head on. "We cannot possibly sit and listen to this. Of all the hypocritical—"

"Will you please be quiet?" The azaleas now hovered above, and half a dozen from the row in front of them were also turned around. Reactions rippled through the room, punctuated by the pounding of the gavel.

"You! Back there!" Mrs. Thomas called from the podium. "What is this disturbance all about?"

Suddenly Vada felt a hundred eyes turned on her and heard her sister groaning.

"See here, I demand to know the nature of this disruption."

The audience concurred with Mrs. Thomas, and Vada dug her elbow into Hazel's side. "Say something!"

"Me?" Hazel was incredulous. "You're the one making all the comments."

"I just think, given how she's always snooping around our father…"

"Don't tell me." Hazel spoke from behind her hand. "Tell them."

By now the crowd was on the verge of eruption, and poor Hazel looked like she was trying desperately to disappear, bending her head so low the rim of her hat almost graced the ruffles of her blouse.

"I'm sorry." Vada reached out a comforting hand. "You brought me here to support you and I've—"

Hazel recoiled at her touch, and now every woman knew the precise source of the commotion, including Mrs. Thomas herself, who called out from the podium.

"Vada Allenhouse! I should have known. You and that sister of yours."

The woman's insulting words from Saturday afternoon rankled inside Vada's head. The woman could say whatever she wanted about her, but Hazel had done absolutely nothing to deserve such derision. Slowly, Vada stood; the crowd grew quieter and the sorbet warmer with each passing second.

"I'm...I'm sorry," she said to the sea of turned faces. "I simply cannot see how the desire to be married has anything to do with the suffrage movement. Would married women be any more or less likely to vote?"

To her satisfaction, there were scattered mutterings of agreement.

"My dear Miss Allenhouse, had you been able to restrain yourself for the entirety of my thesis, you would know that I make no such assertion. I simply believe that a woman should have higher ambitions."

"But weren't you married once, Mrs. Thomas?"

At once the faces—even the azaleas—turned to hear the response.

"I was," Mrs. Thomas said, without the slightest hesitation. "But that was a different time. I had nothing better to aspire to."

"So, shall I tell our father that he is safe from your pursuit?"

"Oh, no..."

Vada looked over to see Hazel bent fully forward in her chair—perhaps to shield herself from the onslaught of laughter that burst forth from the women in the audience.

"Come on, sis." Vada reached for and found Hazel's hand and pulled her from the chair. They stopped briefly at the hostess table, depositing their empty sorbet dishes before dashing out the door, the laughter behind them nowhere near dying. They themselves didn't laugh, not until the lady in lavender, still holding her station at the registration table, lifted her hand in salute, proclaiming, "Votes for women!"

At that, as they spilled onto the front steps, the sisters dissolved, barely able to stand straight enough to walk down the perfectly paved pathway out to the sidewalk, taking a block to fully recover.

But once she recovered a sobering breath, Hazel asked, "Do you think she has a point?"

"Who?" Vada said with one final splutter. "That sack of hot air? Of course not."

"You don't think maybe we should want something more?"

"Than what? Love? Security?"

"Marriage?"

"You, of all people, Hazel, should realize what a buffoon that woman is. Look at the lengths you're going just to get one up on the vote."

"Maybe." Hazel's steps began to slow. "But I have to admit, it's just as much for love as for—"

"*The Cause?*"

"You make it sound silly."

Vada instantly regretted her sarcastic tone. "It's not silly, Hazel. Not at all. It's important. And I think you believe in it more purely than anyone else in that room. Certainly more than Mrs. Thomas."

She seemed satisfied, and for a while neither said anything.

"Do you hope to marry Garrison?" Hazel asked after a time.

"Yes. I mean, I hope to marry. And I love Garrison. So…"

"Does it hurt you that he's never proposed?"

"Sometimes," she said, and all of the morning threatened to wash over her again. "But if he did, he might just try to mire me in subservient silence."

These final words she delivered with a near perfect impersonation of Mrs. Thomas, and the two were still chuckling when they staggered through the kitchen door for lunch.

"Well, I must say it's good to hear some laughter comin' out o' the two of you," Molly said upon their arrival. "It's been too long."

Indeed, laughter reigned in the kitchen throughout the meal as Vada and Hazel stumbled over each other's words, trying to relate the story. Even Althea, risen from her late-morning sleep, participated in wide-mouthed glee, scribbling short jabs on the pages of her little notebook and passing them to her older sisters who shared them and howled until tears came to their eyes.

Never, in recent memory, had there been such a meal at the table, though the food was nothing extraordinary. It was a simple repast— chopped egg and ham salad with a dozen rolls baked that very morning in the Allenhouse oven. Perhaps the informality of the food added to the levity of the conversation. But when Doc arrived midway through, his very presence made for the final outburst, causing Molly to wipe away tears from her reddening cheeks.

"Girls! Molly! Just what is all this noise?"

"Oh, nothin' you'd be likely to see the humor in, Doctor. Now," she continued, her breath even, "will one of you take this up to that poor boy sittin' with our patient?"

But right at that moment the poor boy himself walked into the kitchen, his face glowing. "He–he opened his eyes."

Vada's heart recovered from its tumbling mirth and soared. The most welcoming silence fell all around the table.

"He looked right at me, and I told him I was sorry. That I…" Kenny broke down sobbing.

While Molly grasped him to her ample bosom, the rest of the

Allenhouse family clattered up from the table and ran right past him, following Doc in a mad rush to Vada's room, only to be stopped abruptly at the threshold.

"All of you," Doc held up his hands, "stay here. The young man won't be able to take so much stimulation."

He went in and shut the door, leaving the three sisters in the hall. Althea's face was one of rapturous joy, and she immediately clasped her hands and bowed her head. Vada went to her, as did Hazel, and all three sisters' hands intertwined, their heads bowed to a common center.

This, surely, was a moment that called for corporate prayer.

"Thank You, Father!" Vada spoke aloud, but words seemed inadequate for the gratitude she felt for this healing. Still, she repeated her thanks over and over as the sisters drew closer. In her heart, she saw it as more than just the waking moment of this young man but an awakening for herself.

This is Your power, Lord, she prayed behind her vocal repetitions of thankfulness. *This is Your promise, Your faithfulness, Your answer to Althea's prayer. Hear mine too. Deliver me from my temptations. Keep me…*

She paused, hearing the sweet strains of "Amazing Grace," made all the sweeter because it was Althea making the music. Here, in their presence, she hummed a sound sweeter than any prayer that could ever be uttered. More articulate than any spoken word.

For the moment, Vada abandoned her prayer, adding her own voice—the tune, not wanting to mar the moment with some other poet's lyrics. Soon Hazel joined them, bringing a sweet, low harmony. With their eyes squeezed shut, all their senses imbibed this sound, verse after verse, until Vada felt a hand on her shoulder and turned to see her father's face.

He gave only a terse shake of his head and peeled her away from her sisters, bringing her into the room and closing the door.

"I don't doubt that young Kenny saw what he says he did," Doc said, looking drawn. "It happens sometimes; they go in and out of these states."

Vada stepped over to the sleeping figure, noticing a renewed air of peace ruled his countenance. In a gesture she hadn't attempted before, she stroked his cheek with the backs of her fingers, taking comfort in the growth of new, soft whiskers.

"Does that mean he'll wake up again?"

"Not necessarily. But it doesn't mean he won't. The fact that he regressed shows that he needs to fight. I just hope he has something to fight for."

Outside the door the music continued.

"I think he does, Doc. We should tell the others."

"Not yet. Might be good for them to have this time."

Vada agreed. "In the meantime"—she drew her father into the farthest corner of the room and dropped her voice to a whisper—"I know the story of the letter."

For the next several minutes, the door to Vada's room divided worship from whispers.

Although Vada would have liked nothing more than to sit at home waiting for Eli to come to light again, neither the revelations of the morning nor the lunchtime miracle impacted the responsibilities she had for the afternoon. Today's box-office receipts could be recorded tomorrow, but Herr Johann still needed his tuxedo picked up from the laundry, and the reserved seating still needed its embellished velvet coverings. All of this needed to be accomplished by four o'clock, the time Lissy would be home from school to sit with Eli when Althea left for her job at the telegraph office.

The fact that there'd been a glimmer of consciousness made Vada all the more anxious about leaving him in her youngest sister's care; she was apt to say something so snide, he might slip back into his coma as a means of escape. Goodness knows Vada had often wished to do so.

Armed with a list and an envelope filled from a quick stop at the office to raid the petty cash box, Vada set out to fulfill her obligations. She journeyed to the store farthest away from the theater, planning to work her way back, starting at the laundry up on the corner of Cash and Cleric, where Mr. Ping presented her with a long, flat box. He opened the top, revealing a pristine black wool suit folded within layers of tissue paper.

"Look good?"

"It's lovely, Mr. Ping. Thank you."

He wrapped the box in brown twine, and Vada tucked it under her arm before setting off for Madame Grenier's shop on the next block.

"Bonjour mademoiselle!" The tiny French woman bustled all about her the minute Vada walked through the door. Madame Grenier's Stitcherie felt like an ornate front parlor—plush chairs and windows dressed in velvet and lace. Madame Grenier herself sat at a white and gold-leaf desk, while three assistants wearing stiff pink aprons sat in the chairs, hunched over their needlework.

"I have everything ready for you." She clapped her soft hands and a startled assistant jumped from her place and ran to the back room accompanied by the sound of Madame Grenier's, *"Rapidement! Pour l'orchestre!"*

Minutes later Vada's arms were draped with beautifully quilted velvet pieces, each large enough to drape over the back of a theater seat. The corners were embellished with gold tassels, and the word *Reserved* was stitched in gold thread. And of course, Mme Grenier was quick to point out, "Réservé" on the opposite side.

"Because sometimes only *le français* will do."

The more Mme Grenier spoke, the more Vada heard LaFortune's voice. For that reason alone, she felt a mounting desperation to escape. Bad enough the man had taken up permanent residence in her mind; she should not have to endure his presence in her ears. Still, she endured the fountain of conversation politely, silently urging the jumpy assistant to quickly wrap and tie the beautiful pink and white striped paper around the rolled bundle of velvet. .

Finally released, Vada once again tucked the long box under one arm and looped three fingers through the string tying the package from Madame Grenier's.

The walk back to the theater took her right past the printer in charge of the programs, and her mind flashed to Dave Voyant's flirtatious promise to have them finished by today. Tempted as she was to pop in and see if he could live up to his word, she had no way to carry them back.

Tomorrow. Something more to occupy her time.

It was well after three o'clock when Vada staggered up the stairs and back to her little office where she dumped the packages unceremoniously on her desk. The afternoon had turned warm, and a thin trickle of sweat made its way down her back, settling at the waistband of her skirt.

There wasn't another soul in the building, save Mrs. Greenville down in the box office who hadn't even offered to step out and help when it was obvious Vada was struggling to open the door. How was it that just hours ago she'd been searching for a place of solace, and now she couldn't bask in the silence?

She took Herr Johann's freshly laundered tuxedo to his office. Praying he wasn't in, she knocked softly on the door. When, thankfully, there was no answer, she walked in, deposited the box on his otherwise empty desk, and scribbled a message on one of his telltale blue notes.

Suit inside.

Will see you Friday, barring any emergency.

V. Allenhouse

Then to home, sneaking out the back entrance and through the alley. Strange how sunlight and solitude made the walk home so much longer. By the time she arrived at her front door, she wanted nothing more than to fall through it, to be carried up to Hazel's room later in the day.

Unless, of course, Eli had treated them to another moment of wakefulness. Then maybe he could be moved to Doc's patient bed downstairs, leaving her own free for a long night's slumber. Just the possibility of such a thing sent a final burst of energy that propelled her through the front door, and she was rewarded with a delightful sound from the top of the stairs.

Laughter. Sweet, giggling laughter—obviously Lisette's. And in between the bouts of mirth, a man's voice. Not her father's, and as bold as the girl might be, she'd never bring one of her many suitors up to her room. It was either Kenny, choosing somehow not to play in that afternoon's game, or…

She bounded up the stairs, ready to welcome Eli back to the land of the living, but every step she took made the man's voice more familiar. Before her foot reached the top, she knew exactly who the voice belonged to, and the recognition spurred a different energy altogether.

"Mr. Voyant," she said from her bedroom doorway. "What an— unexpected surprise."

"Well, Miss Allenhouse." He'd been sitting on the chair next to the headboard and stood the moment she walked in. "Or should I clarify— the *eldest* Miss Allenhouse?"

This evoked both a whoop and a giggle from Lisette, who was sitting on the foot of the bed, possibly *on* Eli's feet, with her own tucked up beneath her skirt.

"Isn't he just hilarious, Vada? He's had me in stitches all afternoon."

"Really?" She looked back and forth, matching him smile for smile. "All afternoon."

"Well, since I got home."

"Ah, since you got home," her eyes settled on Mr. Voyant, "from *school.*" Back to Lisette. "You did mention that you were still in school, didn't you?"

"I figured he knew since he met me on the corner and carried my books."

Vada swallowed hard, hiding her frustration, and suggested that Lisette go downstairs and begin her studies. "Mr. Voyant and I have some business to discuss."

Lisette unfolded her legs, exposing more than a little of her ankle as she did so, evoking a brief appreciative grin from Voyant, who had the good sense to look away almost immediately.

"Have a lovely chat, you two." Lisette gave Vada a broad wink on her way out the door.

Once she was gone, Vada smoothed the bedding around Eli's feet and tugged the blanket up further on his chest. He was once again lying flat, his breath slow and steady, but present.

"He's got to be the easiest houseguest I've ever seen." His voice was deeper, more resonant in this little room.

"What are you doing here?"

He gestured with his thumb toward a box sitting on her bureau, his cap squarely on top of it. "I told you I'd have them by Wednesday. Guess I failed to mention my delivery services."

"You could have brought them to my office."

"Tried that. You weren't there."

"So you snuck into my house?"

"I was invited."

"You should be ashamed."

"I'm not the one hiding a corpse."

"Shh!" She held a finger to her lips and checked to see that Eli hadn't woken. "He's sleeping."

"According to your sister the princess, he's been *sleeping* for a while now."

Vada gave up, releasing the breath it seemed she'd been holding since she walked into the room. "What does it matter to you? Why do you care?"

"I need one good story, Miss Allenhouse. Just one, and I can stop covering local ballet recitals and amateur musicians. No offense intended, of course."

"None taken. But there's no story here, Mr. Voyant."

"Not now, maybe. But if he"—his voice dropped to a whisper—"doesn't make it, well, then, that's something. All I know so far is he was conked in the head during Monday's game, and one Kenny Cupid is"—he took his small notepad out of his shirt pocket and flipped to a page—"'stupid with guilt' about not catching the ball that hit him. And might I say, your youngest sister is a lovely little source."

"Not to mention unreliable."

"And," he flipped back a few pages, "it was Brooklyn Bridegroom Louis LaFortune who hit the ball. Got that from listening to some of the regulars down at the park. The only thing I don't know is why nobody on the team's ready to talk about it."

"It's a private matter—a simple, unfortunate accident."

"So, why hide it?"

"Perhaps to keep men like you from printing a story that would make everybody in the city look at those two men like they're some kind of criminals. They feel awful enough as it is."

"Is that right?" He rubbed his chin, intrigued. "I know Cupid's been hanging around here, but you've been talking to LaFortune?"

"Don't be ridiculous." She flushed, answering too quickly.

"So, he wasn't the"—he consulted his notes again—"the 'delicious French redhead' on your front porch this morning?"

Oh, she could kill that girl.

"You know," he put the notepad away and sounded quite serious, "I understand your need to protect your father."

"He hasn't done anything wrong."

"Really? Are you positive this guy can get the same treatment here as he would at a hospital?"

"Just what are you insinuating?"

He put his hands on her shoulders, and the gesture was oddly comforting. "Listen, if he doesn't wake up—ever—this could look bad for your father. And it won't be because of what I write; it'll be because of the circumstances. Don't you think it might be better to get it out in the open now, when he can still be seen as a good Samaritan, rather than later and have him risk looking like some sort of quack?"

"You wouldn't do that."

"I wouldn't, no." He dropped his hands. "But I can't guarantee that for every journalist out there."

"I see." She cocked her head and gave him the look that Garrison always likened to a cat about to delve into a saucer of milk. "But you're not every journalist, are you? So tell me, Mr. Voyant, what exactly do you want?"

He bent at the waist, lower and lower, until his nose was not quite an inch from her own. "I thought you'd never ask."

She didn't flinch.

"What I want, my dear Miss Allenhouse, is a story. Any story. Miracle recovery. Tragic death."

Lost love? New romance?

"And I'd like you to give that story to me."

"But you understand that today, right now, there is no story?"

He nodded, slowly, and soon she joined him, their heads moving in unison. "But you'll let me know," he glanced down at the sleeping form, "when there is?"

"You have my word. Now, thank you for delivering the programs, and I'd like you to leave."

He picked up his cap and stooped to look in the mirror hanging above it, taking a luxurious time settling the cap at a perfect angle. "I suppose," he said, not turning around, "that I would not be welcome to call on your sister at some later date."

"If by 'later' you mean when she is eighteen, maybe."

Satisfied with his reflection, he turned and leaned against the bureau, his elbows resting on its surface.

"By then it'll be too late. Cupid will have caught her."

Vada snorted. "If that's the best your investigative powers can do, Mr. Voyant, I'm afraid you have a long future of writing about the latest happenings at the Junior League." Although, she hoped he never heard about *her* latest happening there. "I'll have you know Lissy can hardly abide Kenny's company."

"Really?" He dragged the word out like an invitation. "Have you not read your Shakespeare, Miss Allenhouse? Something about protesting too much? It's a well-proven fact that the more the sparks fly, the greater the flame."

Vada's face flamed then, and she hazarded a glance over her shoulder to the sleeping Eli to be certain he hadn't been exposed to such a flirtatious jab.

"I'm afraid my sister doesn't have the emotional capacity to be ironic. If she is cruel to Kenny Cupid, it's because she doesn't care for him. Pure and simple. She has some of the most eligible men in Terrington Heights squiring her around. Why would she waste her time on a ballplayer?"

Something flinched in Dave's face, and he slowly brought himself to stand upright, pushing his cap further back on his head. "Tell me, Miss Allenhouse, do you see all ballplayers as a waste of time? Or just Cupid?"

"Well—I don't mean—it wasn't my intent to disparage an entire group. I simply think Lisette has her sights set a little higher than what a ballplayer can give her."

"Always about the money with you women, isn't it?"

If the first flush was receding, it was back again as she fought to protest. "No! Not at all. I can't speak for Lissy, but we don't all—I mean, I don't—"

He reached out and gripped her arm, a gesture both comforting and playful.

"Relax. I wasn't trying to get you riled. Just talking."

"I'm sorry," she said, calmer. "Now I've just played into that hysterical woman stereotype. But, honestly, very few of us care about such things."

"What do you care about?"

She shrugged, never leaving his grip. "Love, really."

"That simple? Nothing exciting? No element of surprise?"

She struggled to find an answer. Not for him, of course, but for herself.

The seconds ticked away measured by Eli's steady breath. Dave's steady gaze held her, amusement lurking behind his eyes. And something else too. A challenge—one to be met with her response. Somehow, through the whirling of her emotions, enlightenment came.

"I believe all of that falls to passion. The love, the excitement. It's the passion that surprises us sometimes."

"Pops up when you least expect it, eh?"

"Yes." She thought about Garrison in the stairwwell and Mr. LaFortune on the field. It was as good an answer as any.

13

Given the chaos of the day, Vada was more than ready to welcome a calm, quiet evening at home.

Althea returned from the telegraph office full of hope that Eli had yet another moment of wakefulness, but she held in her disappointment with a thin, stoic smile. She immediately went to his bedside with a cup of broth, specially prepared by Molly as she stewed tonight's chicken, to begin the arduous process of maintaining the sleeping man's strength.

"Remember," Doc told her, "just a tiny drizzle. Drops at a time."

She nodded, but Doc's reminder was unnecessary. Althea had proven to be the only one of them able to perform this task. Vada tried one turn earlier that day, simply giving the man a drink, and after five minutes she'd been ready to throw the glass across the room. Lisette probably would have done so, and Hazel claimed to spend quite enough time at sickbeds during her work with Doc.

So Vada found herself curled up on the parlor sofa, no sound but the clock ticking somewhere in the shadows. With each passing moment— each stitch made to darn a pair of stockings, each page of *Ladies' Home Journal* read—Vada thanked God for the foresight to spend this evening at home.

Her mind played through the events taking place at the Dresden Street Theater. This is when Herr Johann would assemble the musicians.

This is when he would lift his baton to drop them into the first number. This is when he would stamp away from the podium in his first fit of rage. Any other evening she'd be there in the midst of it, and until this evening, she'd be happy to be there. But right now it was pure joy to have her body as still as Eli's, her mouth as silent as Althea's, and to know that she was welcome to remain so until she went to bed.

Earlier, before supper, they'd received word—from a frantic telephone call from Patsy Tebeau—that the Cleveland Spiders had been hopelessly trounced by the Brooklyn Bridegrooms. Almost as if a different team had turned up to play, he'd said, and it was largely due to the performance of Lucky Louis LaFortune.

Doc shared the information at the table, prompting Vada to complain that they'd never had to suffer sports talk at supper before, and she saw no reason to begin now.

To everyone's surprise, Lisette had the strongest reaction, pouting all through the meal and leaving a honey-covered biscuit untouched on her plate.

Now Vada sat in the dimming front parlor. If she was to continue reading her magazine, she'd have to light the lamp. But seeing as the table was much more than an arm's reach away, she contented herself to remain in the gathering darkness. She leaned her head against the back of the sofa and closed her eyes, ready, even this late, to take the little nap she'd been longing for all day.

No sooner had her eyes closed than she felt another presence in the room. She opened one eye to see her father's rotund, whiskered silhouette in the doorway.

"I thought you were down in your office," Vada said through a yawn.

"I can't look at another book. Not another page. It's all so frustrating."

"Here, sit with me." She patted the cushion next to her on the sofa and sat upright to better accommodate him.

"There's simply no reason. No explanation for his condition. There's no way of knowing what damage has been done to his brain, if any. No telling when or if he'll wake up."

"So, today, that wasn't a good sign?"

Doc made a dismissive gesture. "No way of knowing, given that his condition is completely unchanged. No way of knowing if…"

"If?" she prodded.

"Lord forgive me for such suspicions, but I can't help but think that our young Mr. Cupid may have imagined…"

"Why would he do such a thing?"

"Guilt. Wanting so badly for Eli to wake up. Breaking under the pressure from his teammates. With today's loss, I'm sure he feels even worse. But perhaps a walk with Lissy will do him some good."

"What?"

"He called for her. At the back door, which is unusual for courting. But we are living in unusual times."

"And she went? Voluntarily?"

"Oh, if you could have seen the boy. Head hanging so low he'd get mud in his hair. I guess she felt sorry for him."

"I suppose so," she muttered. Eli could fall through the ceiling dancing a jig, and she wouldn't be more surprised. Perhaps Mr. Voyant was right after all. The mere thought of that made her shudder.

"Shall we light the lamp, then? In the window? Surely Lissy won't let the boy leave her at the kitchen door."

Vada made her way cautiously across the room. When she got to the table in front of the window, she felt for the box of long matches, but before striking it, she pulled the curtain aside, risking one peek.

There they were. Any hint of past acrimony undetectable. They strolled, not arm in arm, but hand in hand, with Lissy looking sweeter than Vada ever remembered. In fact, the girl seemed almost timid, her eyes downcast, their hands swinging in half the time to their steps. Right at that moment, Kenny must have said something witty, because Lisette's mouth burst in laughter.

"For goodness' sake, Lissy, cover your mouth," Vada said from her side of the window.

Almost as if she heard, Lisette brought her free hand up to her face. Kenny captured it in his own and brought it to his lips.

Vada looked over her shoulder. "You'd better get out there to chaperone, Doc. I'm afraid our Mr. Cupid is taking liberties."

"He's a good boy. Better than those rapscallions who usually hang around here."

"Whatever could have changed her mind?" Vada said more to herself than to her father. Still, he answered.

"There's no telling the mind of a woman, I guess."

"She's not a woman, Doc. She's a girl. And you're her father. You might not be able to wake Eli, but you can certainly stick your head out the front door and tell Lissy to come inside before the neighbors have a field day."

"Maybe you should do that. You're better with her than I've ever been."

Vada chose not to reply. She'd been Lisette's mother since the girl was born and obviously, given the girl's behavior, she'd done an abysmal job.

She struck the match and touched it to the wick, then replaced the globe, bathing the room in soft light. When she peeked out the window a second time, Lisette scowled and made a shooing gesture, but Vada simply leaned on her elbow on the windowsill, as if settling in for the evening.

Lisette responded by stamping her foot; Vada rested her hand on her chin. Pouting, Lisette gave Kenny a quick kiss on his cheek—an amusing sight, given that the boy was a good two inches shorter than she. Perhaps this would be the end of her spool-heeled shoes. For tonight, though, there was no mistaking the frustration in the clatter of those spool heels immediately after the front door slammed.

"Vada Allenhouse!" *Stamp, stamp, stamp, stamp, stamp.* And Lisette was in the parlor. "You embarrassed me to death, spying out the window like that."

"You certainly should have been embarrassed. But it has nothing to do with me."

Lisette turned to a more sympathetic ear. "Papa, did you see her spying on me?"

"Now, darling, she didn't mean any harm."

"Doc!"

"Well, maybe she didn't, but honestly, what's a man like Kenneth supposed to think when he can't even take me out for a walk without having the whole family staring out the window?"

"Kenneth, is it?" Vada smiled. "It seems earlier this morning you had far choicer names for the boy—er, excuse me. *Man.*"

"Don't be bitter, Vada. It ages you."

"Just tell me," Vada said, controlling her voice, "when did you start roaming around, hand in hand, unchaperoned with boys you presumably hate?"

"People change, Vada. You might not realize that since you've been such an old fussbudget since you were—"

"Girls!" Doc instantly brought them back to childhood, usually a comforting place to be, though tonight his intrusion felt condescending. "Why don't we go into the kitchen and see what Miss Molly has for us in terms of pie?"

"None for me," Vada said, her eyes boring into Lisette's.

But to no surprise, her sister was more than willing; she and Doc left the parlor, whispering together. After they left, Vada studied the picture on the mantel, the one that once held a photograph of her mother and now kept the image of little Lisette. Not for the first time, Vada felt a pang of jealousy over the closeness between the two of them.

She hadn't been much older than Lisette was in this photograph when their mother left. Vada had to take on the role of motherhood right at the moment, whereas Lisette was allowed to be a little girl to this very day. She, Hazel, Althea—all of them held jobs when they were Lisette's age—at dressmaker's, sweeping up shops, setting type. But heaven forbid the baby sister use even one moment of her time usefully.

Suddenly she was exhausted. Maybe she was the old fussbudget Lisette accused her of being. She certainly felt bent and old, like her very bones were dissolving within her. She'd lay money down that Lisette had never been this tired. Not a day in her spoiled little life. This wasn't a fatigue that came from dancing and ice cream socials. This came from a day of having a head battered with one decision after another and a heart pulled back from certitude.

She left the light burning in the parlor, in case Doc decided to come back in, and fairly staggered out, grasping the banister preparing to climb the stairs when she heard a soft knock at the front door.

"What's the matter, *Kenneth*?" She spoke to herself in low, breathless tones. "Not enough spooning for one night?"

Fully intending to send Cupid out into the night, she grasped the front door handle and yanked, immediately wishing she'd thought to check through the window first.

"*Bon soir*, mademoiselle." LaFortune leaned against the door frame. "I didn't think that little Spider-boy ever gonna leave."

"I believe I asked you not to speak to me again." Vada tried to close the door, but he blocked her effort, filling the gap with a soft wool sweater—green, from what she could tell in the darkness.

"I aim to come give you a *bon merci.* Now, I could charge in there or—"

"You're not coming in here."

"*Alors,* no choice." He bent low, assuming the form of a bull ready to charge his way through—including having fingers posing as horns—and made a menacing snorting noise.

"Mr. LaFortune, please!"

"*Cinq minutes.*" He held up an open hand. "Five minutes, or prepare to suffer the consequences."

Now it was she who pushed her way through the door, squeezing out the narrow opening, as if that would keep the others in the house from hearing the skirmish. Once Vada was on the other side, she found her hand clasped in his, and she was being pulled down the steps and around into the dark alcove beneath them.

Soon after, her face was pressed against soft wool covering hard muscles; her feet were clear off the ground and she was twirling—whispered laughter floating through the top of her hair.

She wanted to yell, "Put me down!" Knew she should yell it, in fact. But it happened so fast, by the time her feet were firmly on the ground again, she could only wish for one more twirling moment.

"I was amazing today," he said, holding her steady. "First at-bat, home run! Second time, triple! Third time, triple again. It was magic. *I* was magic! And all because of *ma belle ici*!"

Again her feet were suspended. Again the world spun beneath her. And this time, when he set her down, she clung to him, forgetting for a moment why she ever tried to send him away.

"Don't be silly. I didn't do anything."

"Beg *contraire.* Have you forgotten *les boutons?*"

"I refuse to buy into your superstitions."

He took her face in his hands, her chin resting against the heels of his palms, his thumbs grazing the apples of her cheeks. "Is that all you do, *cher,* refuse?"

She thought—well, as close as she could come to thinking with his face, his body so close to hers. There wasn't room for logic; she had to choose between thinking and breathing. Instead, like a pellet wedged at the base of her neck was this pinpoint of resentment. A life full of people-giving and asking for less than she wanted. Never had there been a wanton moment—not even when she wanted one. And maybe there never would be again.

The distance between them was so small, and it was getting smaller all the time, until he was nothing more than a blur. Nothing more than sweet clove-scented warmth coming toward her. She realized the clove scent was his breath, and then, it was her breath too.

Once more, the ground gave away. But she wasn't swirling. In fact, she was stock still, the brick wall of her home at her back, the brick wall of his body pinning her there. The hands that cradled her face now roamed at will, as did hers, delighting at the ripple of muscles, the softness of his sweater. Garrison's body felt nothing like this. Garrison would never wear a sweater. Garrison wouldn't even walk her home, not all the way, lest he—

Oh, Lord! Vada pulled herself as far away as she could get, given the intimate quarters. "Garrison!"

LaFortune laughed, a dangerous sound that seemed to originate in his nose. "It is impolite to say the name of one man when you are kissing another. But I choose to forgive you."

He swooped in again, but she dove under his arm, ending up behind him.

"I can't believe I let you—what was I thinking?"

"You weren't." He put his hands on either side of her waist and pulled her close again. "Which is what makes it so enjoyable. Now, turn off that little brain of yours—"

And he was kissing her again, one hand holding her close at the small of her back, the other tracing fire along the side of her neck. His lips trailed behind, nuzzling her jaw. Garrison never nuzzled—

"Stop it!"

And to his credit, he did, dropping his hands into his pockets and leaning back against the wall, leaving her free to leave. But she remained, still trapped by whatever force compelled her to follow him outside in the first place.

"No need to *fait fâcher* with me." His voice was low and drawling, just short of teasing, obviously trying to soothe her anger.

"I'm not angry with you. It's me. I should know better. I never do anything like this."

"But you such a beautiful young woman. You should be doing things like this every day."

He looked about ready to come for her again, and she held up a warning finger. Instead of backing away, though, he took that one finger and crooked it through his own, creating an open link between them.

"I'm watching you earlier," he said. "Through the window, looking quite the little mother spying on her chick. And I think what a shame for her to be the little flower behind the glass."

"I may as well be her mother. I've practically raised her since I was eight years old."

"Your *maman*, then? She dead?"

Vada nodded. "But she left before she died."

"Comment?"

She owed him no explanation as to how these events unfolded, but soon she found herself speaking into that great cavernous shadow under the stairs, telling him everything. About being a little girl waking up to a motherless home. About her father's unrelenting pain. About she and her sisters growing up—each alone beside the other. Althea's silence. Hazel's discontentment. Lisette's dangerous, wild nature.

"And you, *cher.* What are you in all of this?"

"I'm…" She looked for the word. "I'm lost. Everything I ever wanted—" She let out a soft, rueful laugh. "I can't even remember what I ever wanted."

"You and *les belles soeurs.* Just four little duckies on a pond, eh?"

"Duckies?"

"It's something we say. *En baseball.* When you have men on base, waiting to run home, and the last guy gets up to bat, and *whiff, whiff, whiff.* He strike out or hit a pop fly, easy out. And those three men, they just standin' out in the field. Can't do nothin' but walk on in. And all them runs they were gonna score, just—*pfft!* Gone."

"Yes. I guess that's us."

"Your *maman,* you never hear nothin' from her again?"

"No, not from her."

"And this man who took her?"

She didn't know why she told him, but soon every detail she knew about Mr. Triplehorn, every moment of that disastrous luncheon and yesterday's confrontation, spilled out unchecked. Maybe because LaFortune seemed worldly enough, impetuous enough to help her understand. Maybe because he was recessed so far in the shadows, with only the tiny link of his finger connecting them, she felt she was speaking into a void, saying out loud everything she'd been forced to repress. All of her questions. All of her fears. And, finally, her resolve.

"I'm going to see him again."

"Pourquoi ça?"

"To tell him to go away."

"Which you did already, non? Twice?"

"Things have changed."

"How, that?"

She stepped back into the shadows with him and brought her hand up to touch his face. "It would be so easy…" To give in to this temptation, claim this moment for herself. But the denial of it made her stronger. Stronger than she'd been at the hotel that Monday afternoon. Stronger than she'd been on her steps last night. Stronger than she'd been just moments ago.

He captured her touch, turned, and kissed her palm. Lingered at her wrist, her pulse pounding against his lips.

"I am here just two more days." His words felt delightful. "Will you spend them with me?"

"No."

"It is far less dangerous than to run away, non?"

She extracted herself, slowly, lingering, until she knew the darkness held nothing for her.

"Good-bye, Mr. LaFortune. *Et bonne chance.*"

THURSDAY

A SECOND ENCOUNTER

"Memories of My Mother"
By Althea K. Allenhouse, Age 12

In summer, she smelled of wildflowers,
In winter, of evergreen
In fall, of late, cool showers
And of lilacs in the spring.

Late at night when I called her name,
She'd be quickly at my door.
A participant in my childish game,
To see her just once more.

Now, as memories start to fade,
I can scarce recall her features.
I, silent, silent as the grave,
And she, giv'n back to nature.

14

Vada hadn't slept. Not a bit. And it wasn't because Hazel snored, and it wasn't because she knew Althea was across the hall sitting straight up in the chair at Eli's bedside. Vada didn't spend time worrying about the Lisette and Kenny affair, except for a few minutes feeling a bit sorry for the young man, because he did seem sweet. Unlike her body, which remained comfortably settled and still next to her sister, her mind tossed and turned, reliving every moment of the day, all of it cowering in the encompassing shadow of Louis LaFortune.

How many nights had her mother done this same thing, lying in bed next to Doc, filled with longing for Alex Triplehorn? Because certainly she longed for him. A woman doesn't leave the life she created unless she longs for something else. And why would she invest the time in growing this family—marrying Doc, raising three daughters, conceiving a fourth—if she was going to be so easily uprooted?

And yet, this was the stock Vada came from. The fruit of that kind of woman. And here she was in bed, longing…

She would go to Alex Triplehorn today and tell him he must not attempt to make amends. Indeed, there were no amends to make. He hadn't dragged Mother hogtied and kicking away from this family. She simply left. He hadn't held her prisoner during the time they roamed and lived together, she simply stayed. He certainly didn't ban her from stationery and pen, hadn't withheld postcard privileges, barred her from telegraph offices. If Mother's desertion proved anything, it proved that she was a woman who knew—and got—exactly what she wanted in life.

Seventeen years ago, Mother decided she wanted Alex Triplehorn. Last night, in the alcove beneath the front steps, Vada understood why. Because there in the dark, when she wasn't dwelling on her mother's choices, she was facing her own.

Long after the time she'd spent on her knees, her face now buried in the mattress beside her sleeping sister, she confessed, *Lord, holy Father in heaven, forgive me. For my dishonesty with Garrison, for my behavior with him. And tonight...* She couldn't bear to form words around her shame. But God had been watching. He knew. *Take away this taint of lust that has settled on my spirit. And have mercy on me, Father. And keep Mr. LaFortune away...*

But hadn't she prayed that very thing over tea and lemon cake in Moravek's? And hadn't God allowed LaFortune to wander, unfettered, right up to her front door? She lifted her head from the mattress, looking up and out into the moonlight through the window.

"Then be my strength."

As much as she knew that her Savior granted grace, that her sins were forgiven, she felt no comfort. Confession to Jesus wasn't enough to grant her peace. That would only come with confession to the man she betrayed. The man who, if the embrace in his office stairwell was any indication, was just as capable of passion as was this passing stranger. How could she tell him, after all these years of faithfulness, that she'd chucked it all away for one moment of reckless abandon?

Well, more than one moment, if she were to be truly honest. Her willful surrender to LaFortune seemed, in light of the circumstances, an inevitable misstep. She would need to acknowledge the enticement at the time she gave him the buttons. No, to the conversation at the ball field. In truth, at the moment she first laid eyes, then a comforting hand, on him.

For three days he'd been a plague on her thoughts, slowly casting a pall on the heart that once was so full of love for Garrison. The love was still there, to be sure, but in light of these past days, it was a shadow of what it once had been. How would she tell him?

Or should she?

Two more days, LaFortune had said. Two days and he'd be on the train to Brooklyn or Chicago or Philadelphia—anywhere but here. Gone, and no doubt forgotten all about her. For three days she'd protected Garrison from this pain, surely she could shield him for two more. It would be easier once LaFortune was out of town, when she knew he wouldn't show up unbidden on her doorstep. And then she and Garrison could continue on as they were before. The same slow, steady path of understanding. In time, this monstrous mass of self-loathing would diminish, become a pebble of memory she'd carry forever, like the shiny, smooth stone in Eli's pocket.

She might even come to forget about it for days on end. After all, that's what happened with the pain she felt when Mother left. Althea allowed it to steal her voice, and Hazel wrapped herself up in it. But Vada had stamped it down, down, down, becoming stronger—the strongest person in her family by any measure. If she could walk away from that pain, she could walk away from this. Her life, as far as anybody knew, unscathed.

What would her life have been if her mother had made the same choice all those years ago?

Which started the cycle of thoughts all over again.

The moment she heard Molly's heavy step through the back door, Vada gave up any pretense of trying to sleep. She took her pink floral wrapper from its hook and tied the belt as she walked across the hall to observe the scene in her own bedroom. It was as familiar now as any other—Eli, still as a corpse, his hands heavy against his sides, and Althea, slumped in the chair, her head resting against the wall.

Moving in, Vada noticed a new addition to the tableau as Althea's thin, small hand rested on Eli's bare shoulder. She thought immediately of LaFortune, how his body felt beneath the thin layer of wool. Here was a touch far more intimate, yet without a hint of salaciousness. What she wouldn't trade for such innocence.

Her first instinct was to pad across the room, take Althea in her arms, and lead her, sleepwalking, to bed. Either her own or in with Hazel. But as Vada approached and Althea's face became more distinct in the pale predawn light, she was struck by the peace she saw there. This was a choice Althea had made—to stay by this man's side no matter the cost. Who was Vada to judge what constituted comfort?

So, as silently as she entered, she backed away, padding barefoot downstairs to the kitchen.

"Well, don't you look like somethin' the faeries rummaged out of the slop house last night?"

"Good morning to you too, Molly."

"I'll be gettin' the coffee on as quick as I can, but it looks to me like what you're needin' is to march yourself back up those stairs and finish sleepin'."

"I tried." Vada made her way to the table. "But I woke up a while ago, and it's useless."

"Was it a bad dream?"

"No. No dream."

Molly opened one of the drawers underneath the narrow table to the right of the sink where she stored her apron. "Sometimes there are things in this world that strike such fear in us; the only way to face them is in our dreams. Not sleepin' is how we run away."

"I'm not afraid of anything."

"Oh, of course not." The effort of wrapping the apron strings and tying them behind her left Molly a little breathless, and she sat in the chair opposite Vada to continue. "Known ya goin' on fifteen years now, isn't it? Even when you were just a little bit of a girl, you was always fearless. Protectin' everyone. And ya know what?"

"What?"

Molly leaned close and rapped her knuckles on the table. "You didn't fool me then either."

If only she were ten years old. She'd crawl into Molly's ample lap, nestle down in her soft bosom, and talk and weep and sleep. Not that Molly would ever allow such piffery.

"I guess I am worried about Eli."

"Him? Now how is he goin' to add a single day to your life?"

"Althea loves him."

"And that's naught to do with you."

"Were you there to witness Lissy's change of heart in regards to our young Mr. Cupid?"

"I think 'tis a matter of your own heart you're wrestlin' with. Like Jacob with the angel. 'Bout to break your own leg too, from what I can tell."

"I'm fine. At least I will be once I have some coffee."

"Well, then," Molly braced herself against the table to rise to her feet, "let me put the pot on."

Vada buried her head in her arms and let her loose hair form a dark cave around her. Outside of it, a match was struck, a stove lit, a kettle filled.

"What d'ya say I make us a special breakfast this mornin'? Maybe those French puffs you like so much."

"I'm not hungry."

"I'll let you dip them in the sugar."

Molly's tone was wheedling, almost playful, making Vada wonder if the woman used up all her softness in the first hours of the day, before anyone was awake.

Vada lifted her head high enough to peer through the strands of hair that had fallen in front of her eyes. "Can I lick the bowl?"

"If you help me get them stirred up before your sisters come down. I don't want any fussin' over it."

It was the same bargain they'd struck since Vada could remember, and she hauled herself up from the table, though she wouldn't be much help. The measurements proved too complicated for her sleep-deprived brain, and in the end she did little more than shuffle from the pantry to the counter where Molly whisked the ingredients together with a swift, strong arm.

"Now," Molly waved that same arm inside the oven to test its readiness, "while these are bakin' up, why don't you go upstairs, wash your face, and comb your hair."

"What about the bowl?"

"You'll enjoy it more if you're cleaned up a bit. Coffee'll be done then too."

"All right," Vada said, "but do you mind if I just wash up down here?" Being in this kitchen was the safest, the warmest she'd felt in days, and she was reluctant to leave.

"'Course not, dearie."

Molly stepped away from the sink, leaving Vada to turn on the tap and cup her hands beneath it to capture the cool water. At first she simply stood, staring at the tile on the wall, as if she'd never seen the delicate blue designs scrolled around the border of each square.

Eventually she splashed her face, feeling immediately less fuzzy, and even took in two or three great gulps to soothe her throat. Refreshed, she ran her wet hands through her hair, smoothing it away from her face. She gathered it in one hand and fastened it with a bit of ribbon she'd found stashed in her wrapper's pocket.

"Better, then?"

Vada nodded, truly feeling a bit brighter than she had when she first stumbled into this room.

"Then come on, coffee's ready."

Vada made her way back to the table where the large mixing bowl sat with Molly's favorite tall wooden spoon. A generous amount of the muffin batter had been left along the sides, and Vada dragged the spoon around the rim until it was covered. The taste of the sweet batter flavored with nutmeg instantly made her feel like that little girl again. She washed it down with a sip of Molly's good, hot coffee and wished for just a minute that she could spend the rest of her life—or at least the rest of this day— right here, eating nothing but what she scraped from this giant bowl.

Apparently she made some sound of contentment, prompting Molly to say, "Good, is it?"

"Wonderful," Vada said, her mouth full of batter.

Then, to her surprise, Molly came around behind and embraced her, planting a firm, dry kiss on her cheek.

"You're a good girl, Miss Vada. Always have been."

While the muffins baked, their sweet, spicy aroma gave way as Molly fried slices of bacon on the back burner and on the front, scrambled a pan full of eggs to a golden fluffy mass. She left the bacon draining on sheets of newspaper and covered the eggs with a dishtowel to keep warm until the rest of the family came down for breakfast. Once she determined the muffins were done, she took the pan out of the oven and, with a deft flip, dropped them onto a large oblong platter.

"An' you're sure I can trust you to finish them up?" Molly untied her apron.

"Of course. I do have some culinary skill, you know."

"All the same, I've measured out the cinnamon and sugar, and the melted butter's on the stove. Now I'm off to the market before the best o' the fish are gone."

Once Molly was out the door, Vada set to work, dipping the top of each muffin in the melted butter, then rolling it in the mixture of cinnamon and sugar. It was hard to resist eating one right there and then, but the lingering sweetness of the batter still satisfied her tongue.

Just as she placed the last muffin on the plate, Lisette came traipsing into the kitchen, perfectly coiffed and ruffled for the day.

"Mmm! What smells so yummy?"

"French puffs." Vada carried the platter to the table. "Baked fresh this morning."

"How astonishingly appropriate." Lisette picked up a muffin and licked the top before taking a big bite of the steaming muffin. "Ooooh! S'ot!" She formed her pretty mouth into a perfect oval and waved her hand in front of it, making no attempt to either chew or spit out the bit of pastry inside.

Normally, Vada would have found this sight endlessly amusing, but she couldn't forget what Lissy had said just before the bite.

"What do you mean by *appropriate*?"

Once fully recovered, Lisette planted her coyest smile, now rimmed with sugar. "Seems like there was a lot of French *puffing* going on last night."

Vada may just as well have stumbled from her sleepless bed into this very moment. Every bit of warmth gathered during this cozy morning dropped far and away. Molly's comforting food and healing words vaporized like steam.

"Oh, look at you," Lisette said, teasing. "Your face! If you could see it…but better you can't, because you look kind of a mess. I could pack groceries in the bags under your eyes." Then, as if seized with genius, she clapped her hand over her mouth to contain a squeal and spoke through her fingers. "Don't tell me you snuck out again last night!" She leaned in close. "Did you sleep at all?"

There didn't seem to be a point in arguing. Indeed, the strength to do so had long since fled. Vada attempted a casual pose, leaning against the table, and would have picked up her coffee for a nonchalant sip if she'd trusted her hands not to shake.

"How do you know about—What did you see?"

Lisette pouted. "Not much. I heard the knock at the door and thought it might be Kenneth. By the time I got into the hall, I saw that guy practically haul you outside. And oh, Vada, he's such a—"

"He came to check on Eli. He's concerned, just like Kenny."

"Of course he is." She made no attempt to soften the sarcasm. "But then when I went to the window to spy on you the way you did on me, the two of you were nowhere to be seen. Not on the steps, not on the sidewalk. Which leaves only one place." She pinched off another bite of muffin and said, "In-the-alcove," before popping it triumphantly in her mouth.

"What do you know of the alcove?" Vada hoped to redirect the conversation.

"I know it's dark. And small."

"We were talking."

"And I know you have to stand really, really close to talk in there."

"Well, it seems you're quite the expert, then. Doesn't it?" Desperate to escape, Vada turned away, walking briskly to the cupboard to take down plates and cups to bring to the table. Hopefully, Lisette's short attention span would kick in the minute she saw the bacon.

"Now don't worry, sis." Lisette met her at the cupboard and took the plates from her hands. "I'm not judging you. In fact, I think it's marvelous that you're giving yourself a break from stuffy old Garrison."

"I'm not—oh, Lord." She tried to gather her thoughts. "Lissy, shut up."

"Relax, I'm not going to tell anyone. Ooh, is there bacon?" She lifted the top plate from the stack and dropped her half-eaten muffin on it before moving to the stove, where she picked up one, then two slices of bacon and scooped a heap of eggs from the bowl. "Secrets are fun, aren't they? Kenneth and I were going to keep our—shall we say, *truce*—a secret, but I guess you found us out, didn't you?"

"He seems like a nice boy."

"He's hardly a boy. He'll be twenty in June. And, no offense, Vada, but he's nowhere near the rogue that your man is. What's his name? LaChance?"

"LaFortune. And he's not my—"

"That's right. LaFortune. Kind of rolls off the tongue, doesn't it? Well, I guess you would know…" She collapsed into a fit of giggles, not at all fazed by the double entendre of her joke.

But Vada had to turn away, suddenly wishing she were having this conversation fully dressed with her hair properly combed and pinned— anything not to appear as slatternly as she felt.

"What's so funny this morning?" Hazel's breezy entrance into the kitchen testified a long night of sound sleep.

Vada meant to say *Nothing;* in fact, she did say it, but the denial came a bit slow, catching in her throat, and got lost behind Lisette's exuberant reply.

"Vada had quite the fling in the alcove last night."

"Lissy!"

"In the alcove, eh? I thought old Garrison always stopped at the corner."

"*Old* Garrison does," Lisette said. "*New* LaFortune apparently doesn't stop at anything. Looks like our big sister might find herself juggling two bridegrooms."

"Lisette Allenhouse!" Vada rarely raised her voice, but she did now, and the effect was immediate as Lisette paused, a forkful of fluffy eggs poised in midair. "I've always known you to be a mean, small-minded, heartless snipe, but I never thought I'd see you so stupid and, and—cruel!"

She pushed past Hazel and marched upstairs where Althea came out of the bathroom, looking confused and pointedly asking what the disruption was all about.

Vada mocked her sister's silence giving only a shrug as she stormed into the bathroom, closing and locking the door behind her. The repeated knocks were answered with the turning on of water—first hot, then tempered with cold—intending to let it run until it was within an inch of the top.

She took the wrapper off and hung it on the hook on the back of the door, then pulled her nightgown over her head, dropping it to the ground. When she stepped out of it, she looked up and faced her reflection in the mirror above the sink. Her hair, still bound loosely by the ribbon, spilled over one creamy white bare shoulder.

She touched her cheek, where LaFortune had touched her last night. Closing her eyes, she tried to remember every moment spent with him and tried to trace her fingers across every place he'd ever touched. Her face, her neck. She crossed her arms and caressed her shoulders, reaching to her back, her waist.

Here, without the barrier of blouse and corset, her flesh burned with the shame she should have felt last night, and her reflection now revealed a bright red flush reaching to her collarbone.

Hazel pounded on the door and with an impatient voice said, "Vada! What is wrong? Talk to me!"

Did that mean Lisette hadn't told her? Or that she didn't elaborate? Whatever, it meant no peace until she spoke to Hazel. She went to the door and pressed her face against the wood.

"I'm going to take a bath, Hazel. Then I'm going out. I promise, I'll explain everything later."

"Open the door."

She did, just a couple of inches, enough to see Hazel's wide, concerned face.

"Are you—"

"Yes, I'm naked. I'm about to take a bath."

"No, I just wanted to see if you were all right."

"I will be."

Without another word, she shut the door and stepped high into the claw-footed tub. Before sitting down, she reached up and took hold of the rose-patterned curtain and drew it around, encircling her in a floral cocoon. Finally, she sank into the water after lifting her hair up and over the edge. The tub's rim felt cool on the back of her neck, and she focused on that coolness as the hot water enveloped more and more of her.

When it was in danger of sloshing over the edge, she lifted one leg out of the water and reached for the faucet, turning it off. The act ushered a new silence into the room, save for a few echoing drips, so Vada took the washcloth draped over the tub's edge and pressed it close to her face before she opened her mouth for the first of many long, shuddering wails.

15

Each step made her feel a little stronger, maybe because each one took her farther away from the house, the stairs, the alcove, the corner. Vada kept her eyes down for the most part, especially in familiar neighborhoods where somebody might make the mistake of reaching out and asking such an innocent question as to how she was feeling that day.

She headed north on Huntington Street and felt absolutely absorbed by the city by the time she hit Euclid Avenue. Absorbed, that is, and exhausted, as everything within her began to protest her sleepless night. There were seedier parts of town where people slept flat out on the street, and she didn't doubt that she herself, given the opportunity to rest her head on a coffee-shop table or even to recline on a park bench, would be snuffed out like a gaslight at dawn.

A large clock outside of the Cleveland Bank and Trust building showed the time to be ten thirty. It seemed like a perfect time to call on a gentleman staying at a fine hotel, although she had no experience from which to gauge this conclusion. It was still a formidable walk—probably more than a mile—and she could only hope to look somewhat present-able when she arrived.

For now, the back of her hair was still damp from her bath, and her crying jag in the bathtub did nothing to lessen the puffiness of her eyes. She'd left the house purposefully hatless, hoping the sunlight and breeze would work a little color into her face, although today's choice of a somber, fawn gray dress begged to be set off by her black ostrich-wrapped hat. Last she knew, though, Lisette had borrowed that very one to add an air of respectability to an outing for ice cream with Reverend Dickerson's visiting nephew. After managing to maneuver through the rest of the morning without seeing any of her sisters again, Vada wasn't about to reignite their questions for want of a silly hat.

After looking at the clock, however, she hazarded a glance at her reflection in the bank's window and was appalled at what she saw. If anything, she looked worse than when she left the house. She hadn't noticed, for example, that her hair had been swept up and pinned askew—the carefully coiled knot sitting low behind her left ear.

A glance in the small mirror from her handbag confirmed her suspicion that the brisk morning walk hadn't infused her face with a healthy dose of color; instead, she had amorphous red blotches standing harsh against the pale. If anything, her eyes had swollen smaller, and the bags beneath them had taken on an almost purple hue. Her actual violet eyes—long considered her most attractive feature—were washed away in the red rimming of her lids.

She'd had an idea of exactly the person she wanted to present to Alex Triplehorn. Not the panic-stricken, hysterical female who had to be ushered out of the Hollenden Hotel dining room. And not the pathetic, needy woman whose life had been devastated by his action. No, above all, she wanted him to see somebody strong, confident. A representative of a family of survivors that managed to weather the wake he left behind. No need for his apology. No need for his intrusion. No need for him to think she was protecting their father or her sister. She wasn't protecting anybody. She wanted to appear to have the upper hand. To be the one assuring *him*.

For that, she needed a hat.

A quick check into her pocketbook showed her to be carrying nearly six dollars within the lining. She'd had plans for that money—a boutonniere for Garrison to wear at the concert tomorrow night, and maybe, if he didn't think it too bold, a quick late supper at a restaurant after. But she had more stashed away in a single rolled black stocking in the top drawer of her bureau.

When she came to the street where she should have headed north to the Hollenden Hotel, she continued moving forward. A few blocks more, and she was at The Arcade.

She was infused with energy the minute she walked between the entrance towers. The long, narrow building, four stories of balconies looking down on the open floor—all of it illuminated by a full-length vaulted glass ceiling—hummed with life. Men and women bustled within its wood-and-steel frame like so many bees in a hive, popping in and out of the little shops that lined the walls.

Along with the jolt of energy came a pang of guilt, for this was truly one of Lisette's favorite places to be, and right now Vada heard the last of her angry words echoing in her head, piercing through the hundreds of partial conversations around her. The sisters had spent countless hours here, sometimes zipping from store to store looking for the perfect birthday gift for Doc, sometimes simply strolling, barely acknowledging the offered wares.

This morning she was on a mission. She bounded up the first flight of stairs at the far end, then took the second set to the left. Four shops down was a small, familiar hat shop, cleverly named *Deux Mesdames Chapeaux,* though there was only one owner, and she was far from French. The proprietress was actually a middle-aged woman from Kentucky named Elmira Capstone who would suffer each customer exactly ten minutes before sending her away either completely satisfied or empty headed.

There was one woman in the shop ahead of Vada, so she strolled about, looking at the various styles perched on the smooth wooden forms, trying to decide what she wanted before falling into Mrs. Capstone's capable hands.

"I simply cannot decide between the green and the blue." The customer was a young woman, probably Althea's age, holding out two nearly identical boater-style hats, one of dark green straw, the other navy blue. The crown of each was festooned with silk flowers, the green sporting the addition of a tiny, bright-eyed red bird.

Mrs. Capstone took a step back and surveyed first the green hat, then the woman, then the blue, then the woman, and said, "Take the blue, or buy nothing at all."

Minutes later it was Vada's turn. She offered her hand to Mrs. Capstone and wished her a good morning.

"Good morning. Aren't you one of the Allenhouse girls?"

"Yes, ma'am." Vada felt like she'd somehow stumbled back into school.

"And are you looking for anything special today?"

"Just something…" She had no idea how to ask for a hat that would erase the ravages of a sleepless night, so she simply stared straight into Mrs. Capstone's eyes and said, "…something that will go with this dress."

"And will you be wearing the hat out today?"

"Yes, ma'am."

Mrs. Capstone pointed to an upholstered bench along the window that looked out into The Arcade. "Then sit. I'll be right with you."

She obeyed, leaning against the cushioned back and allowing herself to close her eyes for just a moment…

"Miss Allenhouse!"

Vada scrambled to her feet, a bit disoriented, and blinked several times before the woman in front of her had any meaning.

"Are you all right, Miss Allenhouse?"

"Yes, I —" She interrupted herself with an enormous yawn. "I didn't sleep well last night."

"So I gathered. Here." Mrs. Capstone thrust forward a beautiful piece — midnight blue felt, the brim, with an alluring iridescent quality, lifted up along one side creating a flattering angle. Shooting up from the crown was an array of peacock feathers. The feathers gave a much-needed shot of bold color to counteract the rather dull color of the fabric of her dress, while the hat itself perfectly matched the piping.

Vada followed Mrs. Capstone's pointing finger to the straight-backed chair in front of an oval free-standing mirror and sat down. Her reflection in the artificial light of the store was even more depressing than what she'd seen outside, and somehow plopping a shock of peacock feathers did nothing to brighten it.

"I'm not sure this is exactly —"

"Just wait."

Then Mrs. Capstone did the most amazing thing. Working her fingers along the brim of the hat, she showed the iridescent quality of the brim to be the result of a layer of fine, gray silk netting that, when not wrapped around the brim, created a lovely, encompassing veil that could be cinched and tied just below her left ear.

"What do you think now?"

"Oh, it's perfect." And it was. Her face was now a beautiful, mysterious blur. "I, um, didn't see a price."

Of course, that's because Mrs. Capstone never advertised her prices on any of her merchandise. She crouched down behind Vada and connected their gazes in the mirror. Then, as if some kind of sideshow medium, she squinted her eyes, thought for a minute, and said, "Four dollars and twenty-five cents."

Thrilled but suspicious, Vada turned in her seat. "You can't be serious."

"You will buy this hat for four-twenty-five, or you will buy nothing from me today."

Minutes later, another woman was in the chair, and Vada, renewed, walked out of the shop. The stunning headpiece garnered more than one admiring glance from the women she passed, though to be true, some of their whispered comments might be due to the eccentricity of wearing such a veil in this setting.

Despite the generous light allowed in through The Arcade's glass ceiling, the sheer gray fabric proved to be cumbersome—as did a few low-level plants—so she decided to brave baring her face a little while longer and folded the veil back up over the hat's brim.

Any time she and her sisters came shopping here, the tradition was that whatever shop was officially declared the "last" of that outing, they would walk the entire circumference of that level before taking the stairs to the bottom level.

Perhaps it was a matter of stalling before heading out on such an unpleasant errand, or perhaps it was a feeling of guilt for her outburst this morning. Or for her behavior the night before. Whatever the motivation, she'd paid such a surprisingly reasonable price for her hat she felt she could splurge on a little something for each of her sisters.

So, as she made her way along the second-floor balcony, Vada stopped at her favorite stationers and bought a box of pretty letter paper for Hazel and a box of pretty painted pencils for Lisette. For Althea she found a beautiful tiny notebook with gold-winged cherubs painted on the cover. Nothing seemed appropriate for Doc, but she reasoned she'd done him no wrong, and an unexpected gift would bring more questions than anything.

Satisfied, she took her paper-wrapped bundle and listlessly strolled the rest of the second story before heading out to the street. Once there, she paused long enough to bring down the veil before fixing her steps toward the Hollenden Hotel.

Although she had no way of knowing precisely, it must have been after noon when she walked into the lobby. The lunch hour. The sheer gray netting made it more difficult for her eyes to adjust to the dark, rich interior of the lobby; still, she made her way to the restaurant without mishap.

Bad enough that she hadn't planned exactly what she was going to say when she came face-to-veil with Mr. Triplehorn; there was one other con-frontation she hadn't planned on. The minute she saw the large podium outside the double doors leading into the dining room, she remembered the stubby maître d' who seemed so smugly satisfied to escort her and her little party out of here three days ago. And there he was.

All the weight of anxiety she'd carried all day settled in her shoes, and by the time she arrived at the podium, her feet were too heavy to pick her up and run her away. But it was too late to turn back as his face had already folded into a broad smile.

"Are you meeting somebody for lunch, mademoiselle?" The cordial reception indicated a total lack of recognition on his part, as he stretched *mademoiselle* into five syllables, much different from LaFortune's com-pact *mam'zelle*.

"Do you know if Mr. Triplehorn is luncheoning in the dining room today?"

Either her voice or the mention of Triplehorn's name brought a spark of recognition, but still, he consulted the enormous book on the podium before responding, "I'm so sorry, mademoiselle. *Monsieur* Triplehorn has not made an appearance since breakfast. Perhaps," he laid one finger to the side of his nose and raised an eyebrow, "mademoiselle will be visiting him in his room?"

Ordinarily, Vada would have delivered a gasp along with an injurious retort, but the hat and the veil elevated her above the moment, and she simply inclined her head. "I don't believe so, thank you."

She turned slowly and glided back to the lobby, counting on her pace and posture to blend her in with the other hotel guests milling about on the marble floor.

At the far end of the room was a long counter made of highly polished maple, armed with a regiment of uniformed bellboys in perfect formation along its front. Now it was just a matter of handing one of them a note to be delivered to Mr. Triplehorn's room and keeping the courage needed to wait at the bottom of the wide, carpeted staircase for his arrival.

Taking a deep breath, she approached the first boy on the line, a lad of no more than fourteen with a smattering of blemishes underscored by the chinstrap of his bell cap. She cleared her throat, getting no response. "Excuse me, boy?"

He said nothing. She maneuvered her body directly in front of his, bending down to meet his eyes, craning her neck with each attempt at his avoidance.

Finally, she opened the clasp of her handbag, and before she could reach in for a dime, he clicked his heels together and delivered a crisp, "Help you with something, ma'am?"

"Yes." Her fingers pinched the coin within her purse. "I need you to deliver a message to Mr. Triplehorn."

"You mean a note?" His voice cracked with the question.

"No, just a… If you'll please tell him Miss Allenhouse, Miss Vada Allenhouse is downstairs to speak with him."

He fished a square of paper and a pencil out of his pocket and wrote a reasonable spelling of both names. "And what room is Mr."—he consulted his note—"Triplehorn in?"

"I don't know. He's not quite expecting me."

"Are you a guest in this hotel?"

She was more appreciative than ever of the veil to hide her blush. "No."

He clicked his heels again and returned the paper to his pocket. "Then you'll have to request your message be sent from the front desk." Still standing ramrod straight, he jerked his head back, as if she could possibly miss the massive redwood counter behind him.

"Thank you," she said, backing away. At least he had the decency not to extend his hand for a tip, but she held out the dime anyway, which he took, looking her in the eyes for the first time and giving a curt nod.

Vada took just two steps toward the desk before turning back. Asking help from a bellboy was one thing, but approaching the stuffy, stiff-buttoned clerk behind the counter was quite another.

The lobby was full of lush green plants of varying shades and sizes, many of which grew tall in stone planters surrounded by round, plush sofas. The nearest one called to her, and the moment the back of her knees touched it, she collapsed in the velvet cushions.

She should leave now. No one would be the wiser. She could explain her day's absence with her new purchases. Just a few more minutes here to collect her strength and gather her resolve.

Safe behind her veil, she allowed her gaze to roam openly, observing the hotel's patrons, wondering about the wealth and power behind each. Which unassuming man was actually a state senator? Which woman was the wife of a financier? Whenever she allowed herself to plan a future with Garrison, she envisioned the life of a successful attorney, possibly a future politician, and they would stay in places like this—or better, maybe in New York or Washington. But now, even as she sat within the possibility, that life never seemed so far away. She was no more deserving of being his wife than he was eager to make her so.

She was just about to get up and leave when she saw him. Along with her breath, that tight feeling in her skull went away, filling her with an unsettling relief. Not to mention curiosity.

What was Louis LaFortune doing here?

Dressed as she'd never seen him before, he wore a rich brown suit with just a hint of green thread running through it. His starched white collar stood out against his tanned face and neck; the tie twisted into a perfect bow. Most men would wear a bowler hat with such a suit, but his head was bare, the reddish curls disciplined with a part above his left temple and shining with tonic. All of these details became clear as LaFortune settled within two feet of her before he sat not two cushions away.

He didn't speak, and neither did she. Though he hadn't made a move toward her, she felt inexplicably trapped. Slowly, she scooted to the edge of the cushion, stood, and attempted a nonchalant stroll toward the front entrance.

"I thought that was you, *mam'zelle*."

She could have kept walking, just left him to sit and wonder about this mistaken identity, but the thought of him following her, creating some sort of scene, seemed infinitely worse. So she stopped.

"How did you know it was me?"

She hadn't turned around, but the next thing she knew, LaFortune was right behind her, one hand on her shoulder, speaking down the back of her neck.

"I wasn't sure until you started to walk away. That walk, *cher*, I would know it anywhere."

"What are you doing here?"

"You told me last night of your intentions. I didn't think a woman such as you should be in such a situation alone."

"I'm fine." She took one step, but his grip on her shoulder held her back. "Let me go."

"You have talked to this man?"

"Let me go."

The hand was lifted; still she went nowhere. Then he was in front of her, his finger beneath her chin, tugging her face upward. She could feel the warmth of his skin through the netting. "*Allons, ma chère.* I'll go right on up with you."

Vada moved away from his touch. "I don't know what room he's in. And I—"

"Too much a flower to ask? Settle up here, I be right back." He moved with a confidence just short of a swagger, and two seconds and a handshake later, he was back at her side.

"Room 714. Look like we're takin' us an elevator."

He reached for her, but she wasn't about to walk across a hotel lobby arm in arm with this man. She shouldn't walk with him, period. In fact, he shouldn't even be here.

Lord, why couldn't You keep him away? Yet she couldn't deny the bit of comfort LaFortune brought.

Around the corner from the front desk, they found the tall mahogany-rimmed glass doors of the hotel elevator attended by a young man who was taller, though not much older, than the bellboy she'd spoken with earlier.

"Going up?" he asked in a clipped, crisp tone.

"Floor seven," LaFortune replied, and without any ceremony whatsoever, he gripped Vada's free hand.

The operator slid the tall doors open, revealing an accordion-folded iron gate within. He grabbed the handle at one end, folding it completely before stepping back and ushering them in with a wide, gesturing arm.

"Après-toi." LaFortune nudged her ahead without letting go of his grip. He followed her across the threshold, and when she turned to face the front of the elevator, there he was, his breath heavy and close enough to ruffle her netting. They stood for a few seconds until a tiny little sound prodded them to action, and she backed in farther to allow him to stand next to her.

The sound repeated itself, and for the first time she noticed the ghost-like man in the corner of the elevator. He was tall and thin and pale, like a wisp wearing a little round hat. His age was well beyond being merely "old," and his voice so slight, it seemed that very word was destined to be his last.

Vada leaned closer. "I beg your pardon?"

"Floor?"

"Seven," LaFortune said.

With arms no wider than the gearshift he commanded, the operator lurched the car into motion. The opaque darkness of the shaft slid by the iron filigree of the inner doors, bringing the little party up and up. With each passing floor, LaFortune's grip grew tighter and, surprisingly, wetter.

"Oooh, I feel me the *mal pris* in here," he said, bending low. "These things make me cat-scared."

"Elevators?"

"We don't have nothin' the like of them back home. Don't seem natural."

"Seventh floor," the operator said with all the remaining strength of a man who had actually climbed all seven flights. Once again the accordion doors were opened, and the outer doors as well.

"Merci, papère," LaFortune said to the old man as they exited.

Room 714 was to the left, and the minute they stepped into the hall, Vada extracted her hand and openly wiped it dry on her skirt. "I don't want you to follow me. There's no reason for you to be a part of this. How would I ever explain exactly who you are?"

"How you explain that other fellow?"

"You are not *that other fellow.* Now you can take the stairs down, or get back in the elevator, or jump out a window, I don't care. But this is where we part ways."

"First floor, sir?"

Both Vada and LaFortune jumped, neither having seen the young man standing ready at the door.

"*Yi, non.* I take my chances with her."

So it was that he followed her down the hall anyway, though she never looked back to give him the least encouragement. Her thoughts were too full of exactly what she was going to say once Mr. Alex Triplehorn opened the door to room 714.

Right now, all she envisioned was herself, standing strong and a little mysterious, insisting that he leave their family alone. That he had no claim on her sister and no score to settle with her father. They were healed and whole, and even if they weren't, which she would never reveal, there was nothing he could possibly do to help, no matter how well-intentioned his offering of apology. Yes, that sounded good, *No matter how well-intentioned your offer of apology.*

She worked her lips around that phrase, mouthing it silently over and over until she was facing a door with the numbers 714 embossed on a gilded plate.

Time to knock.

"I be just right here," LaFortune said over her shoulder. "Right outside the door."

"Thank you," she whispered, not sure if she was more grateful that he was staying outside or that he was staying, period. After taking a deep breath, she delivered three quick raps. Three long breaths. Then three more. She ventured a sidelong look at LaFortune, who gently pushed her to the side and delivered a series of knocks no one could ignore.

Nothing.

"He must be gone." And she felt the first twinge of relief.

"Clerk say he is still a guest here."

"Well, we can't simply stand here in the hallway. Perhaps I'll leave a note with the porter." If she started running right now, she could be out of this hallway before Mr. Triplehorn made an appearance. "Let's go."

This time it was *she* who grabbed *his* hand. In her haste, though, she soon realized they were heading in the wrong direction, and after a few twists and turns, they were lost.

"This way?" she said, breathless.

"Par-ici." He tugged her in the opposite direction. He led them to an open door. Not wide open, but enough to give a good glimpse into the room, and to show that it was unoccupied. "Let's go."

"Are you insane?" She dug in her heels. "We can't go in there."

He held a finger up to his lips, bringing her hand along with it. "Shhh. We say we made mistake. Got lost, which is true *alors.*"

"You are insane." But, for reasons she would never understand, she followed. One step over the threshold, then another. And soon the door was behind them. Soon after that, the door was closed. Then all she could say was, "Oh, my."

They were standing inside the most exquisite little parlor she could ever have imagined. One wall hosted a fireplace with a mantel of carved pink marble and an ornate brass grate. Beautiful works of art adorned the other walls, soothing pastoral scenes and lovers strolling along French river banks. The furniture struck the perfect balance between comfort and taste, the fabric an understated pattern of creamy stripes on even creamier silk.

Almost every surface held a vase of flowers. Some crystal, some brass, others a delicate, detailed porcelain—all filled with roses and lilies and carnations in every shade imaginable. They lent a fragrance to the room like she'd never experienced, and she took it in. Was this the early stages of pure intoxication?

"What you think of all this?" LaFortune moved around the room at a pace akin to prowling. "What a man's got to do in his life to stay in a room like this one here?"

"You mean you don't?" she said, grinning. "Not even in the exotic, exciting life of a professional baseball player?"

"*Shoo-non!*" He traced one finger along the length of the mantel. "Most times we're stayin' in somethin' more like a hole."

"Well, we've seen the room. Let's go." She had her hand on the doorknob, ready to turn it, when she noticed he'd slipped into the little hallway.

"*Cher,* come see this!"

"No, thank you." What was she thinking even walking through this door?

"Oh, but you must." Suddenly he was back, grabbing her and taking her by such surprise that her package flew from her hand, and she was standing in what she imagined bathrooms looked like in heaven. All white, from the pristine tiles to the fluffy towels hanging from racks that appeared to be made of solid gold. *Everything* looked gold, even the commode pull chain. And the tub, if she wasn't mistaken, seemed large enough for two—

"Yes," she said. "Extraordinary. Now, let's go." But she was already alone, and when she walked out of the bathroom, his hand snaked out into the little hall and pulled her into the only room left.

It was dominated by the largest bed she'd ever seen. Easily four times the size of her own. The four bedposts—all clean, varnished wood, no fussy, old-fashioned carvings—stretched nearly to the ceiling. The mattress itself was at least waist high, covered with a thick cream-colored quilt scattered with stitched pink rosebuds. One large dresser ran the length of the wall, and an imposing armoire dominated the other. Cornered between them was a free-standing mirror, and Vada happened to get a glimpse of herself reflected in it, wearing what now looked like a completely ridiculous hat, her face blurred beneath it like a ghost. Just as well she couldn't make out her features, she didn't know who this woman was, sneaking into expensive hotel rooms with a Cajun madman.

And then, there he was behind her, and she heard the sound of the ribbon just below her ear, amplified, as he pulled it, untying the bow. The veil was lifted, the hat removed, tossed onto the bed, and there she was. There they were. Then they disappeared as she turned, and there was nothing—no brass, no gold, no flowers—only him.

Oh, and she should run. Or even walk. Or even move. But the air around her seemed thick and heavy as a dream. A faint hope flickered within her, that maybe she was still sitting on the little sofa in Mrs. Capstone's shop, and none of this was real. Perhaps if she opened her eyes…

But her eyes *were* open. So she closed them. And that's when everything broke loose.

She felt her little pocketbook drop to the floor. She would have dropped right along with it if not for one strong arm wrapped around her waist. And then the other. She would have cried for help if not for the warm mouth covering hers. She reached for the door but found her hands full of brown wool interspersed with green thread. She would run, but her steps brought her right up to him. Her heart pounded against his. Blood pounded in her ears.

"*Si belle. Si, si belle…*"

But deep inside, deep within the core of her that coiled upon itself, she knew she wasn't beautiful. Not here, not now, and while her mouth was free, she told him, "No."

"Oh, but see. When again do we ever have this chance? A room like this? A woman as beautiful…"

The tight, twisted feeling she held puddled into something else, and the lingering taste of his kiss turned bitter.

"Did you plan this?"

"*Comment?*"

"All of this. Meeting me at the hotel. This room. Is it yours?"

He threw back his head and laughed, seeming to pull the mirth from his toes. As embarrassing as it was, at least it caused him to loosen his grip, though she didn't move away.

"Ah, *cher.*" He reached deep inside his pants pocket and pulled out several bills. "This all I have in the world. Nine dollars. All I'm gonna have until the first of July. I'm just lucky Barnie buy me supper."

"I'm—I'm sorry, Mr. LaFortune."

"'Bout time you called me Louis, *non?*"

"Louis. Like the king?"

"*Non.* Like the wolf. My name given is Petit Loup LaFortune."

She thought a moment. *Petit loup.* "Little wolf?"

"For the howlin' I did when *ma mère* bore me."

She couldn't help it. She laughed, and before she knew it, she was back in his arms. Loosely this time, feeling no need to run.

"*Voyons,* don't you see? Moments like these ain't nothin' but a gift from *le bon Dieu*. And you, *ma petite,* have been some little bit of heaven each a-one of these days."

"No, Mr. LaFor— Louis. This is not from God." She didn't have the heart, somehow, to tell him that she'd actually prayed *against* these moments. In fact, if she was truly honest with her Lord, she would confess being a little angry with Him for allowing the *very* thing she'd begged Him to protect her from. "What this is, is a diversion."

"But fun, eh?"

"Maybe a little," she confessed.

"And why would the good Lord not want you to have a *bon amusant*?"

"He doesn't want me to have this desire. For you. It's just—not right."

"It feel right a few minutes ago." He drew her closer.

"How can it be when you're leaving? We'll never see each other again."

"I'm here tonight, after the game. Don't leave 'til sleepin' train tomorrow. And then," he brought his nose to hers, "you sure you don' want to slip off with me? Stay in lots of little holes until it's time to head back down to *le bayou* for the winter?"

"I'm sure," she said. To her surprise—and relief—she was.

"Well, a shame, that. Because I could look into those eyes for—" He stopped, turned his ear toward the door.

She heard it too. A woman's voice: throaty, cultured, giving orders to somebody to take something back to lay out on the bed.

"What do we do?" She was surprised she could speak at all, given her throat seemed to have shriveled to the width of straw.

He reached around her and snatched the hat off the bed. She picked up her pocketbook from the floor.

"Run!"

And just like that, he grabbed her hand, yanking her out of the bedroom as abruptly as he'd yanked her in. Acting on instinct, Vada held the hat over her face. Looking straight down to the floor, allowing herself to be led blindly into the parlor, trusting him completely to guide her steps.

"What on earth!"

That same cultured voice now took on a screeching quality, and Louis said, *"Pardonnez, madame!"*

Vada watched the paisley-patterned carpet roll by beneath her skirt but was momentarily distracted by the glimpse of the plain little package on the floor. Determined to protect her identity, she screamed, *"Attendez!"* bringing Louis to a halt long enough for her to reach down and grab it.

Then they were out in the hall.

"Elevator?" she asked, panting.

"No to that." He pulled her down the hall, turning right and, to the stairs. They clambered down two flights before daring to slow down for the next two, where they came to a complete stop on the landing. It was dark, lit only by a small window near the top of the wall, and their laughter echoed from floor to floor.

"You see what I tell you? Is fun, *non*?"

It was then that she felt every moment of the day, every hour of the sleepless night before, and she was ready to curl up and sleep like Eli on the third-floor stairwell of the Hollenden Hotel.

"Cherie?" The playfulness was gone from his voice. "You feel well?"

"I need to go home."

"Come. I have to be at the field by three. We get a cab and take you home."

"I hate to cost you any of your nine dollars," she said, knowing there wasn't nearly enough left in her pocketbook to cover the fare.

He patted the breast pocket of his jacket. "I have tickets to the game. I pay with those."

She fully relied on his strength to get her down the final flights and didn't dare sit in the lobby waiting for him to hail a cab. Instead, she stood next to him on the street and, for the second time that week, found herself being driven home from this place. This time, though, she rode with a different man. And while she could recall every moment of the ride home with Garrison and Hazel, this one would be lost to her forever. She barely remembered climbing in.

16

Strange how the cab seemed to still be jostling along, though she couldn't hear the hooves of the horses or the jangle of chains. In fact, it was quiet, absolutely quiet, save for a warm, teasing voice telling her to wake up.

She was home.

Little by little she clawed her way out of the fog and opened her eyes to see nothing but a field of brown wool infused with green thread. His suit, his shoulder. At some point during her sleep, her mouth had gone slack, and she attempted her best ladylike swipe of her chin as she pulled away. Doing so, she felt the imprint of his jacket on her cheek and could only imagine what a mess she was.

"Look like someone need to *fais do-do*."

His face was so close; she closed one eye trying to bring him into focus. His chuckle rippled through her. "Meanin' I need to get you up to bed. To sleep," he added quickly. "You was out before the first wheel turnin'."

"I didn't sleep last night."

"Because of me?"

Much as she hated him knowing his effect, she nodded.

"Do you know what I think?" He tugged at her chin. "I think you far too beautiful to lose sleep on me. So with me leavin' tomorrow, best we part ways right here."

It seemed kinder, somehow, not to remind him that she'd tried to tell him that very thing three times already. She took his hand and planted a soft kiss on the back of his knuckles. "For luck at the game."

"And I will long treasure *les boutons* and carry them always, thinkin' of you."

"Speaking of the buttons, would you like to come inside, just to check on Eli one last time?"

"*Non, cher,* I wan' remember you just like this."

"I'm a mess!"

"Ask me, you should spend more time messin'." He opened the cab door, then stepped out and handed her down. With almost fatherly attentiveness, he straightened her hat and held out her pocketbook so she could loop its handle over her wrist before handing her the package from the stationer's.

Her mind drew a blank. "What is this?"

He shrugged. "*N'sais-pas.* But you been clutchin' at it all this time."

Then she remembered the gifts for her sisters and clutched it again. "*Au revoir,* Mr. LaFortune."

"*Au revoir, ma belle.*" He took her in his arms one more time, crushing the package between them, and gave her the sweetest kiss he ever had, just at the corner of her mouth.

Suddenly she didn't want to leave his embrace, knowing just beyond it was nothing but explanation and confession. At this point she was just as far away from the cab as she was her house, and perhaps she would have given herself over to reckless abandon if the front door hadn't opened, and if she hadn't turned around to see Hazel standing on the top step.

Shock registered on Hazel's face, and then something else. Despair? She spun around and ran inside, leaving the door wide open behind.

Louis LaFortune dissolved around her, and Vada ran from him, not knowing if he said another word. She bounded up the front steps and looked around the front hall before hearing Hazel's footfall on the second floor.

Grabbing the banister, she took the stairs two at a time, heading straight into Hazel's room to find her sister standing, fists clenched at her sides.

"Get out."

"Hazel, let me explain."

"Everything Lissy said was true. I thought for sure the girl was exaggerating. I even told her she had imagined it all. But then, here, with my own eyes—"

"It wasn't— He was just saying good-bye."

"Oh, well, then! By all means a kiss is completely appropriate."

"Of course it isn't—"

"All your talk about love. What have you told Garrison?"

It was the first time his name had been said aloud in the context of this madness, and it stopped Vada cold. "Why, nothing, of course. There's nothing to tell."

"What I just saw," Hazel pointed to her window that looked out onto the street, "was not *nothing*. He deserves better."

"You're right," Vada said, shaken by the depth of that truth. "He does. But you have to believe me, Hazel. This is all meaningless."

"It's not fair!" With that, Hazel burst into tears and moved to her bed where she sat on the edge and sobbed.

"Oh, sister…" Vada sat beside her and draped a comforting arm over her shoulder, despite Hazel's attempt to pull away. "That's so sweet of you to be concerned about Garrison, but I think it would only hurt him to—"

"I mean, it's not fair to me!"

"To you?"

"Here I peddle myself to some stranger in the godforsaken wilderness—"

"That's your decision, Hazel."

"Well, I'm never going to find anyone here, am I? Not with you around anyway. Who's going to look past you and see me?"

"Don't be—"

"So it's not enough you have a sweet, wonderful man who adores you. You have to go running around with that, that— I don't even know what to call him."

"Don't call him anything. He doesn't even deserve your attention."

"Then Lissy tells me about that reporter who was sniffing around here—sniffing around *you* more like it. I thought she was exaggerating that too. But now I'm not so sure. How you'll ever have time to fit in a third is beyond me."

"Now hold on just a minute!"

"And you know what?" Her voice was elevated now, screaming straight into Vada's face. "You are just like her!"

"I am nothing like her!" Vada matched her sister's volume. "Lissy is a mindless twit of a flirt who doesn't care about—"

"I don't mean Lissy! I mean Mother! You are just like her. You're doing to Garrison exactly what she did to Doc."

"That is ridiculous." She'd taken her arm away shortly before Hazel started screaming, and now Vada stood up, pacing the room, collecting her thoughts. "Garrison and I are not married. He won't even propose. I haven't left him, and I have absolutely no intentions of doing so."

"Not now." Hazel's voice was eerily void of emotion. "But you will. You've proven yourself capable."

The shock of what Hazel said stole Vada's breath and turned her blood to a cold, slow slush. The humiliation of it compounded by Althea's silent presence in the doorway, her face retelling the entire sordid conversation.

"You can't mean that," Vada said when she could speak again.

"Don't tell me what I mean," Hazel said. "You're always complaining about being everybody's mother. Well, congratulations. You are now our mother in every single way."

Maybe it was the fatigue or the fact that her brain no longer seemed capable of forming words, but the next thing Vada knew, there was a sharp stinging sensation on her palm and an angry red mark on Hazel's cheek.

Hazel lifted her hand to respond in kind, but Althea leaped between them.

"Get out of here, Althea!" Hazel screamed.

"Don't talk to her like that!" Vada yelled in kind.

Then came an eerie quaking to the floor, the trinkets scattered across Hazel's bureau began to shake, and Molly Keegan burst through the door.

"What in the name of Saint George and his dragon is goin' on up here? Not since I heard my own brothers findin' themselves with nary a pint and only a nickel have I heard such clamorin'! Keep it up and I'll do just what I did with them—give each of you a pipe and send you to the alley to settle it out 'til the last one's standin'!"

By the time she finished her diatribe, all three sisters were huddled together—Althea behind Hazel—and it was quite a while before Molly's coloring lost its lobster hue and her nostrils returned to their nonraging width.

"Now then," she said, after several even breaths, "I've come up to say you might want to step away from the tavern brawl because the doctor has a distinguished visitor downstairs."

"What visitor?" Vada asked. Doc never received company in the parlor.

"Good glory, the man's been here once already this week, but with all the comin's and goin's, there hasn't been a chance to—"

"Who is it, Molly?" Vada insisted, though the sinking feeling in her gut already provided a name.

"Oh, somethin' exotic. Trippenshire? Trip—"

"Triplehorn?" Vada and Hazel spoke in perfect unison.

Molly snapped her fingers. "The very one! And with your father out again—back to that ballpark, Lord bless him. Stayin' for the game today he is. I told him he should do that very thing. Poor man needs to enjoy himself a little more."

"Mr. Triplehorn's downstairs now?" Hazel asked, her voice shaking.

"He is, indeed. And I told him I'd fetch one of the young ladies to speak with him, and then I come up the stairs to find the souls of my sweet girls taken over by a pair of brawlin'—"

Vada pushed past Molly and turned to see that Hazel followed her into the hall.

"Stay here," Vada said. "Talk to Althea. And Molly."

"What should I tell them?"

"Everything. Some secrets are easier to share."

Vada had long ago perfected the art of descending the stairs quietly, knowing exactly which ones were likely to elicit a protesting squeak. She moved slowly, stealthily. *Lord, give me the words to say.* She paused at the hallway mirror long enough to smooth her hair and give a quick pinch to her cheeks.

As impressive as Alex Triplehorn's size was when she met him in the Hollenden Hotel restaurant, and as menacing as he'd appeared in the streetlamp shadows, nothing compared to the mass he claimed standing in the Allenhouse parlor. His eyes were level with the uppermost book-shelves, and he ran a thick finger along the titles.

"Mr. Triplehorn?"

He turned around, clasping his hands behind his back. "Miss Allen-house. We meet again, under less confusing and startling circumstances, I hope."

Vada replayed the escapades of just hours ago and smiled.

If he only knew.

"What is the reason for your visit, Mr. Triplehorn?"

"I would prefer to speak to your father."

"He isn't here, and quite frankly, I think it would be best for all of us if you were to leave right now before he comes home."

The pounding in her head had narrowed to a sharp, precise pain, and it served to truncate her conversation, making her sound more powerful than she felt.

He moved to the mantel, strolling the length of it, looking at each picture in turn. "No picture of your mother."

"No. There hasn't been for some time." Still, even then, she could see her mother's image—so much like her own—buried in the top drawer of her bureau, now nestled next to Eli's letter.

"Too bad. Marguerite was a beautiful woman."

"We really must insist that you leave. Again."

He raised an eyebrow. "You speak for your father?"

"I'm speaking for our family."

"A family I have wronged. And I feel I must make amends."

Whatever threat he'd represented, whether his size, his stature, or his-tory, diminished with the ticking of the clock. He seemed to shrink to the room, or maybe the room grew to encompass him. Either way, before her very eyes, he became nothing more than a man, a tormented one at that, and her own tormented soul reached out to him.

"Why?" She approached him. "Why now?"

"My business kept me traveling much of the time. And I guess"—he looked up to the ceiling—"I didn't want to face what I did. But when I happened across your sister's advertisement in the Cheyenne paper, and I knew I was coming to Cleveland…it seemed like a sign."

"From whom?" she asked, remembering LaFortune's powers of spiritual interpretation.

"I'm not a man to believe in God."

Until that moment, it was a question she'd never allowed herself to ponder, but now, facing the man who might have the answer, she asked, "Did she?"

A bittersweet smile curved his full lips. "After she got sick— Do you want to hear this?"

She clenched her jaw and nodded.

"After she got sick, she used to say she felt like God was punishing her. For"—his voice caught in his throat—"for leaving you. All of you." He looked closely at the picture of Lisette. "Is this the baby?"

"That's her. She is twelve years old in that picture."

He lifted the frame and brought it closer to his face. "What color is her hair?"

"It's like caramel."

"Then I saw her. One afternoon when I was waiting for your father. She's a lovely girl."

"Yes."

"And she looks nothing like me."

"No. So it would appear that your business here is concluded."

He replaced the frame but made no attempt to leave. "I still would like to make some restitution to your father."

"And what restitution could you make, Mr. Triplehorn? Can you bring his wife back?"

"Of course not. But, having been alone for so many years now, I think I better understand what I did to him."

"Is that what you think? That our lives just stopped the moment you—the moment she left? Because it didn't. Yes, we were all very sad for a while." She thought about Althea's lingering silence. "But we're stronger than that. We're fine. And for the pain that lingers, well, there's nothing you can do about that. Only God can touch our hearts that deeply."

"And has He?"

"Perhaps, because of your visit, we're in a place to ask Him to. But I know this for sure. Your presence here, unannounced, can only cause our father pain. And I think we both agree that he's been hurt quite enough."

"Still I—"

"Take heart in this. Whatever happened all those years ago, it was my mother who hurt him. He didn't love you, Mr. Triplehorn. Your actions alone could never have left so deep a wound. You did not betray him. You did not leave him. If she had the sense to seek God's forgiveness for her actions, then she must have been content to meet Him without asking the same of my father. You owe us nothing. We wish you no ill will."

"But will you tell him I stopped by?"

She thought about that evening, all those years ago, when she and her sisters learned of their mother's death. All those questions. How? And when? Could Doc have somehow saved her? The man who held the answers stood before her, but she no longer desired to know. There was quite enough pain to erase already. No need to add another circumstance.

"Someday. When we are happier than we are now and sitting and talking of inconsequential things. When he is stronger."

"He has a right—"

"To peace. Which he has worked very hard to find. I think it best neither of us take that away."

He twirled his hat for a moment, before reaching his hand out to Vada. "Then I wish you good afternoon, Miss Allenhouse."

She offered hers in return, feeling it swallowed up in his massive palm.

"And give my best to your sister."

"I will."

"And to that young man of yours. He seems quite attentive."

"He is," she said, unwavering. "Let me show you to the door."

They said nothing else as she walked with him to the front door, which he opened, hesitating on the threshold. "Do you think I might write your father a letter?"

"Address it to me," she said before closing the door behind him.

Once he was on the other side, she rested her face against the cool smooth wood, gathering strength before climbing back up to Hazel's room. There she could see that, even if they hadn't strained themselves listening at the stairs, Hazel had informed them of who Alex Triplehorn was and why he was here.

"Oh, ya brave soul." Molly lifted her apron to wipe an errant tear.

"What did you tell him?" Hazel asked.

"I told him to leave us alone." And that would have to do for an answer. The three women parted for her like she had just freed a nation. She collapsed on Hazel's bed, flinging her arm over her eyes to block out the light.

"Everybody out," Molly said. "Poor thing's not slept a bit, I'd wager. Althea, it's time for your young man to start on his supper. I strained a little bit o' prunes into the broth, just to keep things movin' along if ya know what I mean."

"Vada?" Hazel sat on the edge of the bed. "I'm so, so sorry for those horrible things I said."

Vada dropped her arm but was unable to open her eyes. "It's all right. And I'm sorry I slapped you. It's been a really terrible day."

"Do you want to tell me about it?"

She lolled her head from side to side.

"Would you like to hear something nice?"

"Very much."

"Okay." The weight lifted, there was a rustling of paper, and the weight returned. "I got a new letter from Barth today."

"Another one?"

"Which is why I had no right to be so cross with you this afternoon. Listen?"

"Please."

Hazel gave something between a squeal and a clearing of her throat before beginning. "'My darling Miss Allenhouse. Although I have not yet received a reply from my previous letter—in truth I put it to post just two days ago—I've taken barely a breath since then that was not taken in your presence, for indeed you are with me always. I drink the words off your page, carry them in my heart. Speak your name. Hazel. Hazel. Hazel. You surround me here—your name the color of the sage when it sparkles wet with rain. And I imagine your scent to be as sweet. I hear your voice as on the breeze, and with it I hear the voice of God compelling me to declare my love…'"

That was the last word Vada heard. *Love.* And she carried it with her into the black.

17

Vada's first thought was that she'd slept through both the day and night, waking to the predawn darkness. But the unmistakable odor of Molly's Irish cod cobbler hardly heralded breakfast fare. It must be evening, and suppertime at that.

An entire day without food following an entire night without sleep raised a debate within her about which of the two needs she should meet. If her body would cooperate and get her downstairs, there was little doubt which would win.

Now, to move.

The right arm that had been flopped above her head was still there—or so she assumed, given no trauma had occurred to sever it. She could feel nothing beyond her shoulder, and even that was a knot of numbness. It simply would not move on its own, so she was left with no recourse but to bring her left arm over her head to scoop the right one off the pillow and drop it down by her side.

Sitting up was an arduous task, given only one functioning elbow, and she struggled until her legs dangled over the edge. Somebody had seen fit to remove her shoes. She wriggled her toes, thinking that, until her arm recovered, she'd remain shoeless.

A chorus of popping sounds sang out as she rolled her head from side to side. Not even the slightest tingle invaded her right arm, so she braced herself with her left hand and rose to her feet. The sticky-sour taste of hunger filled her mouth, and she worked her tongue along the inside of her lips, first opening them, then smacking them once, twice, before erupting into an enormous yawn.

A thin ribbon of light outlined the door just before it opened, revealing Hazel's distinctive silhouette. "You're awake?"

"Just barely."

"Garrison is downstairs."

"What?"

"Thursday night. Supper."

"Oh, of course."

She began a stumbling walk toward the door, only to be corralled back by Hazel's guiding arm.

"Let's clean you up a bit first, sis." Hazel guided Vada to her desk and sat her down in the chair. Then, one by one, she took the remaining pins out of Vada's hair until it tumbled loose around her shoulders. The only sound in the room was that of the brush working first through the knots, then making long, smooth strokes from the top of her crown down to the ends splayed out against Hazel's palm.

"Do you want me to put it up?"

"No," Vada said. "Just plait it."

She felt Hazel gather her hair and separate it into three sections, creating a long, loose braid hanging straight down her back.

"You want me to wrap it around? Or leave it so it's all ready for when you go back to bed?"

"Leave it." Her arm was just beginning to tingle.

"And why don't you just put on your housedress for supper?"

"My housedress? With Garrison downstairs?"

Hazel giggled. "It can't be any worse than what you're wearing now. And I think he'll understand. He knows you've been sleeping."

"Oh, what he must think of me."

"He thinks nothing, Vada. Just that the stress of the past few days caught up with you. And by the way," Hazel said as she helped Vada undress, "I talked with Lissy and told her I personally would shave her head at midnight if she even hints to Garrison that something might be wrong between the two of you."

Vada braced herself against her sister's shoulder, wincing at the pain in her wakening arm, and walked out of her skirt. "Thank you for that. Do you think there's something wrong between us?"

"I know Garrison loves you."

"Really? How do you know that?"

"Because he looks for you. Every time he walks into a room, it's like his eyes can't rest until he sees you."

"Then I'd better get downstairs." She stepped into the soft cotton dress and allowed Hazel to fasten the plain wooden buttons that crept up one side of the bodice. A contrasting ruffle hid the row of buttons, forming a three-sided square under her bust and up to both shoulders. Nowhere near as fashionable as what she'd worn all around town today, the dress was nonetheless infinitely more comfortable, and the thought of putting shoes on underneath it seemed completely superfluous.

"How do I look?" She assumed the fashion pose of a *Harper's Bazaar* model.

"Like you and Garrison ought to follow me to the frontier. You'd be high fashion out there."

Every Thursday, the Allenhouse family ate in their formal dining room. And if ever there was a night to invite a guest, Thursday was it, as this was the final meal of the week to be prepared by Molly. Often she cooked two entrées, several side dishes, and even more than one dessert—all intended to see the family through the weekend.

When Vada and Hazel came down, everybody was seated at the table—Doc at the head, with Lisette and Althea to his right. The chair to his immediate left was empty, waiting for Hazel; Garrison sat in the chair next to her. Vada's place was at the foot of the table and had been since Garrison first came to dinner. Before that, there had always been an empty space at family dinners.

They walked in with Lisette in midcomplaint about her Kenneth not being invited to supper. "It was the most awkward thing telling him I couldn't go walk with him because we have this family dinner. And then not to invite him. What must he think of me?"

"I courted your sister for three months before I was invited in to dinner," Garrison said. "It was mid-December and Molly made corned beef and cabbage. I ate so much, children thought I was old Saint Nick and followed me all the way home."

Only Doc granted a polite chuckle.

"And what a fine pleasure it was to see me boy-o with such an appetite after feedin' all these girls." Hazel's voice was a perfect match for Molly's, and the two sisters came to the table in the midst of laughter.

"Well, look at you, Vada," Lisette said, absently tapping her spoon. "Planning to do a little dusting after dinner?"

Oh, how she wasn't in the proper humor to suffer Lisette's jabs, but before she could open her mouth for a retort, Garrison was on his feet, taking her hands and leading her to her place. Good thing he did too, as she couldn't bear to look up to find it for herself.

"I think you look perfectly lovely, darling," he said. "I'll never understand why you women don't dress more comfortably all the time."

"Because you *men* wouldn't look at us if we did," Lisette said, prompting Doc to deliver the first admonishment of the evening.

Soon after, Molly came in with a soup tureen clutched in the crook of her arm and asked if anyone had thought to say the blessing.

"Not yet," Doc said. "We were waiting for Vada."

"An' bless your souls you did," Molly said. "Looks like the rest did you a bit o' good."

Doc asked Garrison to say the blessing, as he often did, and Garrison stood at his place, reaching down to join hands with Vada and Hazel. Molly plopped the tureen down on the table, bringing forth a blurp of bright orange soup, and quickly made the sign of the cross before stepping between Althea and Doc.

"Kenneth is Catholic too, you know," Lisette whispered broadly over her sister.

"Saints be praised for that," Molly replied before dutifully bowing her head.

"Our Father in heaven," Garrison began. Vada felt the first tear squeeze through her closed eyes at the sound of his voice. "We thank You for this bountiful meal, and we ask a blessing upon the hands that prepared it. We thank You for bringing us safely to gather here, and we pray for those who have no one with whom to share their food, and for those who have no food to share. Gather us close unto Your bosom, Lord, and may we be ever mindful of Your presence. Grant us wisdom, and bind us together in Your love. Amen."

A chorus of *Amens* followed, and Vada quickly swiped away the tear before Garrison was back in his seat.

Molly moved along behind them, ladling bright orange soup into the shallow bowls at each place.

"Carrot?" Doc asked after taking the first sip.

"Creamed with some of that sweet canned milk," Molly said, bursting with pride.

"Well, it's delicious." Just as the table was quick to chime in their agreement with Garrison's prayer, so did they show their appreciation for the soup with short, mumbled sounds of satisfaction interspersed with clinking spoons.

"I hear you made it out to the ballpark today, Marcus," Garrison said. "Beautiful day for it."

"Indeed it was."

"And I begged him to let me go too," Lisette said, "but he *refused*."

"Now, my darling daughter, you already missed one afternoon this week to attend a game, and with rather disastrous results, I might add."

Althea looked up from her soup, stricken, but Lisette was nonplussed.

"I wouldn't say disastrous. After all, I did meet Kenneth. I think I might be his good luck charm."

"Really?" Hazel chimed in. "At the first game you attended, he missed a catch and a man was seriously injured. Tuesday he was benched. Yesterday they lost. And today— how did our Spiders do today, Doc?"

"Abysmal. Nine to three, but if it's any consolation, Lissy darling, your young man did absolutely nothing to contribute to it."

"Kenneth says that miserable manager of theirs is keeping him out until…" She rolled her eyes up to the ceiling.

"Well, well," Doc jumped in, "if it's any comfort, I don't know that there's anything he could have done. It's that Cajun Bridegroom who seemed to be on fire."

"Why are we talking about this?" Hazel said, much to Vada's relief. "We've never talked about baseball at supper."

"We'd better get used to it." Lisette licked the back of her spoon. "I have a feeling we'll be having a player at the table a lot more often. When he's not on the road, of course. And on Sundays, which means somebody will have to learn how to cook."

"I've never known any of your beaus to stick around long enough to earn a place at the table." The warmth in Garrison's voice carried a big brother quality taking the sting off the jab. Lisette's retort, however, had no such cushion.

"And I've never known any of Vada's beaus to aspire to anything greater."

Normally Vada would jump to Garrison's defense at such an attack, but right now it was all she could do to swallow spoonful after spoonful of Molly's orange soup. Luckily, Molly herself arrived at that moment, distracting everybody with her announcement of the main course. Althea was dispatched to carry the stacked soup bowls to the kitchen, while Hazel and Lisette were ordered to help bring in the rest of the meal, leaving a quiet interlude for the remaining three at the table.

"Are you all right this evening, darling?" Garrison made to touch her arm, but she snatched it away, reaching for her water glass.

"Just very tired. I didn't sleep well last night, and then I napped too long this afternoon." She took a sip before turning to him and offering a weak smile. "I'm a bit off, I guess."

Molly and her sisters returned, each carrying a steaming dish of some sort: a bowl of broccoli, another heaped with fluffy white potatoes, a basket with a mountain of brown crispy rolls—all designed to surround Molly's delicious Irish cod cobbler.

"And where were you off to so early?" Doc brought the napkin to his whiskers. "Already gone before I came downstairs."

"Shopping." She forced herself to look at him. "A new hat and some things at the stationer's." She looked around at her sisters. "If you all can behave at supper, you'll each get a prize."

"You didn't make it to the theater at all?" Garrison asked.

"There's nothing I can't take care of tomorrow."

"Might be good for you to have something to keep you busy."

Her hand shook as she set down her glass. "Why would you say that?"

"If you're anything like me, you'll be a nervous wreck all day. You know, half of me can't wait until the concert starts, and the other half can't wait until it's over."

Plates were filled within an inch of their edges, but when Vada's once again sat in front of her, she could do little more than pick her fork through the creamy fish and sauce spilling out from under the flaky scone topping. Still, lack of eating would only lead to more questions, as this was one of her favorite dishes. After a few valiant bites, her appetite awakened, and for a time superseded her conscience.

She sent several grateful glimpses to Hazel, who worked doggedly to keep the conversation away from troublesome topics. Unfortunately, given the circumstances, that left very little safe territory. And when, for the third time, Lisette batted her eyes and asked Vada exactly what *did* she do all day, Hazel slammed her fork down on the table.

"Okay, family. I didn't want to break it to you this way, but there's something I must share."

Vada's potatoes stuck in her throat, and everybody else at the table looked equally surprised.

"Yes, Hazel?" Doc set down his own fork, giving over his full attention.

"I have been, well, corresponding with a young man for quite some time now. It seems we may have developed feelings for one another. He has asked me to marry him, and I intend to accept."

Vada managed to smile before her jaw dropped. "You didn't tell me this."

"You fell asleep before I got to the end."

"What makes you think I will stand by and allow my daughter to marry a complete stranger?"

"He's not a stranger to me. And I know you trust me not to do anything foolish. Tomorrow I'll post him a letter suggesting I go out to meet him face to face. I thought, Doc, that you might want to come along with me. You could use a change of scenery."

"Exactly what scenery are we talking about?"

Hazel hesitated and brightened her smile. "Wyoming."

Lisette choked on something, drawing Doc's temporary attention. "That is the craziest thing I've ever heard!"

Only Althea seemed genuinely pleased, leading Vada to wonder if Hazel had been confiding in her too.

"I know it might seem insane," Hazel said, "but it's been on my mind for months. Do you realize if I move out there this summer, I'll be able to cast a vote for our next president?"

"As long as it's for McKinley," Doc said. "I wouldn't want any daughter of mine voting with the Democratic party."

"Hazel," Garrison wisely interceded, "I had no idea you were so involved in the suffrage movement. Seems to me there's a much less radical step you could take to show your support for women's voting."

"It's not about that. It was just a lark at first, and then…"

Lisette twirled a long strand of hair. "So, he doesn't know what you look like?"

"No." Hazel caught Vada's eye, and Vada knew she was reliving the humiliating moments with Alex Triplehorn.

"Do you know what he looks like?"

"No," Hazel lied. Vada could only imagine what Lisette would make of the mountain man in the picture.

"Well," Doc said, as if winding up for a proclamation, "it seems premature for a strong reaction. But it is a diverting topic, I'll grant you that."

Just like that, the case was closed; in fact, all conversation came to a halt, so that nearly everyone startled when Molly strode in with pie.

"None for me." Garrison brought his napkin up to wipe his lips. "I have an early day tomorrow—need to wrap things up before the concert, you know."

"Then let me send a piece home with you on a plate. Not a word! 'Tis not a problem. I'll be back in a jiff!"

"Thank you as always, Molly." Garrison stood. "You're a saint among women."

Doc stood too and shook Garrison's hand.

Vada touched Garrison's sleeve. "I'll walk you to the door." It was the first she'd spoken since the soup, and Vada walked away from a plate half full of food. She'd hear about that later.

Once they were in the front hall, he reached for her. "Are you quite sure you're all right?"

"Yes, I—" She cast a furtive glance into the dining room, satisfied at the level of conversation. "I finally had a chance to talk with Alex Triplehorn this afternoon."

"You went to the hotel?"

The question came out of concern, not suspicion, and the truth clogged like wool in the back of her throat. "He came here."

"Oh, darling. How terrible for you. And your father?"

She shook her head and lowered her voice. "He doesn't know. And I don't think he will. I—well, I put the matter behind us."

He took her chin in his hand and studied her, close, the way she imagined he pored over the massive law books he sometimes carried around, looking for the elusive detail. "There's nothing you want to tell me?"

Nothing I could bear.

His very eyes touched her, and it was unfathomable to think he could not see through this thin veneer of control straight to the burning bedlam within. Unable to endure his scrutiny, she threw her arms around his waist and buried her cheek in his lapel. "Just that I love you, Garrison." She would have said it again if doing so would make it truer.

"Oh, darling." He kissed the top of her head. "You know that I love you too."

"And don't I just love the both of ya." There stood Molly, wielding a small plate covered with a bright blue napkin. "Now leave the boy to get his sleep. You could use a bit more yerself."

"Let me walk you outside." Vada stood back so he could take the plate.

He looked down at her feet. "You're wearing house shoes."

"I won't cross the street. Just to the porch."

"Just behave yerselves." Molly winked, reassuring Vada that she knew nothing of her indiscretion.

Once they were on the other side of the door, the memory of the previous night washed over her, and she wished she'd stayed to clear the dishes. Side by side they walked down the concrete steps—he to the sidewalk below, she to the bottom step. Her braided hair fell over one shoulder, and he reached for it, prompting her to come down and close the gap between them.

"I've never seen you looking like this, Vada."

"You mean, like an utter mess?"

"So natural. You're lovely, you know."

"I look like a common housewife."

"Housewife, maybe. Common? Never."

She tucked a few stray hairs behind her ears, before remembering how much she hated the way they stuck out. He'd never seen those either.

"Do you think she'll really do it?" he asked.

"Hazel? I don't know. I suppose she's like Lisette that way, impetuous. But to *marry* someone she barely knows? You and I have known each other for years and…" *And I behaved as if you didn't exist.*

"I'm sorry if I've hurt you."

"You don't know what it is to hurt me, Garrison."

"I'm well aware people expect—that you probably expect—we'd be married by now."

"Don't be silly." She attempted a dismissive laugh. "I've never given it a thought."

"You're a horrible liar." He balanced the plate on the concrete banister and took her in his arms. "You deserve so much more than I can give you."

"No," she whispered. "I don't—"

"But it's all about to change. I should be partner by the fall. And then—"

"And then?"

"And then I'll speak with your father. If Hazel follows through, he might not like the idea of losing another daughter so soon."

"And then?"

He kissed her forehead. "And then, my silly violet-eyed goose, we'll become engaged. And when I've saved enough money to buy you a proper home…"

He couldn't even say it. He looked at her and cocked his head, inviting her to complete the story, but tonight, she couldn't either. Guilt weighed down her tongue, making it impossible to speak even the emptiest of promises.

"Well," he said finally, uncomfortable with the silence, "I guess after all that, it's just a matter of God's timing."

"Oh?" The bitterness in her voice surprised her. "*After all that* you'll put it in God's hands?"

"You know what I mean. My life—our lives—are in His hands. When the time is right, He'll make it clear."

"To you?"

"Of course."

"And what about to me? What if it's clear to me now? What if He tells you to marry me tonight? And you don't? And tomorrow, you just don't—don't want me?" Her pitch rose with every question, thick with tears, and she folded her arms tight around her in an attempt to keep herself intact.

"Darling, that could never happen." He attempted an embrace, but his cajoling tone burned as much as his touch. She backed up three steps, until she was safely out of his reach.

"You don't know that. You can't predict how your heart will change. Look at Kenny and Lisette. One day they hate each other, and now—"

"They're different. They're young."

"So am I!" She stopped herself just short of screaming. "So are *we*. But I've been your girl for so long, and everybody's mother for so much longer—it's no wonder nobody thinks I'm worth marrying. You just don't realize how much I want—"

By then he was next to her, and she fell into him, her mouth pressed against his shoulder to stop the words that would speak her desires. Oh, if he would drag her into the alcove for an ardent embrace. Entice her to the corner for a kiss under the streetlight. Leave Molly's pie on the banister and carry her into his life. She wouldn't stop him until they reached his bed. If then. But she needed something to protest. Something to fight against. And he offered her nothing.

"I believe," he said, his hand caught up under her hair, "you are overly tired."

No!

"What with the day you've had."

"No…"

"I know Mr. Triplehorn's appearance has been upsetting all around—"

Lord! Please let him hear what I cannot say.

"—and we've all been a bit on edge with so many rehearsals. So what do you say we table this until tomorrow night?"

She knew his touch was meant to bring comfort, his voice to soothe, but now she recoiled against both and slowly stepped away.

"You're probably right." She stared at the tips of her well-worn house shoes.

He stooped to look up at her. "Until tomorrow?"

She nodded. "I'm all yours."

Until tomorrow.

FRIDAY

FIRST CHAIR

"Your Name"

I'll write your name upon this page,
Its letters singing of my love.
I'd sing your name if——

Althea K. Allenhouse, Unfinished

18

Vada awoke and counted three chimes. It was dead of night outside, and the three chimes could mean three o'clock, or three-quarters of any hour. She would know in fifteen minutes when the clock chimed again, so she propped herself on one elbow and prepared to wait.

"You're awake?" Hazel's voice came out of the darkness.

"I could probably go sleep in Althea's bed. She just sits at Eli's side all night."

"But she has that tiny room with the sloping wall. Makes me feel like I'm in a coffin."

"Yes. Much better to be in here like a couple of sardines."

"Or one sardine and one whale."

The last word was lost in a sob, and Vada reached over to touch her sister's face, only to find it wet with tears.

"Hazel? Honey, what are you…" But she knew, of course, and she doubted talking would do much to ease the pain, so she took her sister in her arms and rocked her until the crying slowed.

"Lissy's right, you know," Hazel said, her voice wet.

"Lissy's never right about anything."

"No, no. She is about this. It's crazy, Vada. Crazy. And I'm crazy to think that any man would w-w-want me. It was bad enough when I thought Mr. Triplehorn didn't want me. How am I going to live if I travel all the way out to some sheep ranch, and Barth does the same thing? What if I get off the train, stand there waiting for him, he sees me, and he just leaves?"

"I think you're getting a little ahead of yourself."

"I'm going to tell him. When I write to answer his proposal, I'm going to tell him that I'm—I'm fat. That I'm big as a house with a pretty face and give him the opportunity to rescind his offer."

"Hazel, you're not—"

"Don't say I'm not, Vada. Because you know I am. Nobody ever says it out loud, but they cannot possibly look at the four of us and not see that I'm the fattest of us all."

Vada considered the weight of the sister in her arms, the rounded shoulders and the soft flesh wrapped around her body. "But you get a much more ample bosom in the bargain." She sensed her sister's smile.

"No more so than Lissy. That girl has my bust and your waist."

"Too bad she doesn't have Althea's mouth."

The sisters dissolved into laughter, and Vada was so glad she hadn't chosen to sleep in the tiny coffin room.

It was quiet again. "Hazel?"

"Yes?"

"I'm starving."

"Me too."

"I didn't get any pie."

"I did."

They laughed again, rolling into each other, then simultaneously trying to hush themselves.

"I'm going downstairs to have a piece right now," Vada said. "Do you want to come with me?"

"May as well."

They climbed out of bed and tiptoed into the hall, wearing only their nightgowns. A low light flickered in Vada's room, and she poked her head inside. Althea sat in her customary chair, writing in her journal.

"*Psst!*"

Althea looked up and closed her book, marking the page.

"We're going downstairs for pie," Vada said. "Want to join us?"

Althea looked over at the sleeping Eli. Satisfied, she looked to Vada and nodded.

Hazel took a taper from a wall sconce by the door and lowered it down the lamp's globe to light. Then, like a scene from a suffragist's version of "Wee Willie Winkie," the sisters passed silently through the hall and down the stairs. Once in the kitchen, Althea set about getting plates and forks while Hazel looked for a holder for the candle. Vada found the pie in the safe, its apple filling puddled into the middle of the dish. There was plenty left for the three of them, even given generous slices, and she looked in the icebox, happily finding milk.

The cozy light from the single candle warmed the room. The pie was flaky and delicious, with the tartness of the apples buried deep within each baked slice. They made no conversation other than satisfied "mmms" until Hazel pointed her fork at Vada and said, "When are you going to tell us about your day?"

Vada looked first to one sister, then the other. "Did you already tell Althea everything about Mr. Triplehorn? About that afternoon at the restaurant?"

Hazel nodded. "Her and Molly—no, it's all right. Molly won't say anything. She loves Doc too."

"But did you mention that he thought he might be Lissy's…?"

This time, Althea indicated that, yes, she'd heard that. But she didn't believe it.

"He doesn't believe it anymore either." Then, between bites of pie and sips of milk, she relayed the entire parlor conversation—from the moment she walked in until the closing of the door behind him.

"Do you think we should tell Doc?"

Vada looked to Althea for confirmation before saying, "No."

"So, we just keep it a secret?"

"Not all secrets are bad, Hazel. Besides, who are you going to tell? The sheep and buffalo?"

"And moose. Don't forget moose."

Althea splayed her fingers out from the side of her head and stuck out her lips in a very impressive impersonation of a moose. She was giving a kind of wild-eyed expression when her face stretched into a mask of terror while her mouth formed a silent scream.

Hazel followed the direction of Althea's gaze and she, too, let out a yelp.

"What on—" But when Vada looked, her throat was too clutched with fear to scream. There it was, a face on the other side of the darkened window. No, two faces. The pie was threatening to come up, bringing her heart along with it, and she clutched at the table to keep upright.

Then Hazel was out of her chair, storming across the kitchen toward the door. Vada wanted to cry out for her to stop, but she couldn't make a sound. She could only watch in horror as Hazel yanked open the door, ushering in the intruders.

"Lisette Marie Allenhouse!" Hazel grabbed the girl's arm and pulled her through the door, to be followed by one Kenny Cupid who looked twice as terrified as Vada felt just seconds ago. "Just what were you doing out there?"

The boy crushed his cap in his hands. "We were just out for a walk, ma'am."

"Do you have any idea what time it is?"

"I know it's past midnight."

"We don't have to answer to her, Kenneth," Lisette said. Then to Hazel, "We don't have to answer to you."

By this time, Vada had sufficiently recovered her breath and joined the little gathering at the door. "Yes, it's well past midnight. And no, you don't have to answer to us, but you do have to answer to our father. Both of you."

Kenny's eyes grew wide, and now he looked about ready to eat his hat.

"Now, I have no doubt that this late-night stroll was entirely Lissy's idea, but you have to remember that she is just a girl. A young girl. Seventeen. And it's very important—"

Vada's thought was interrupted by a sound from upstairs. A footstep? Surely Hazel's scream hadn't been loud enough to waken their father. To be certain, though, Vada lowered her voice, feeling much more threatening in doing so. "I don't know what kind of girl she herself has led you to believe she is, but she simply isn't—"

There it was again, more distinct this time. A voice, unfamiliar in this house, and then a long, clattering thump.

The feeling of the recent fright coursed through her, but then it was clear just where the sound was coming from. Her room. The man in her room. She turned to Althea. "I think your man's awake."

That ended the last relatively peaceful moment in the kitchen. Hazel snatched the candle and led the way, her soft bulbous body undulating beneath her gown. Althea followed on her heels, and even Lisette looked mildly interested. Vada grabbed her hand, telling Kenny, "Wait down here," and dragged her through the darkened house.

"Slow down!" Lisette protested. "I don't even care about this guy."

Vada kept up her pace. "I know. I'm taking you to your room. And I want you to stay in it until morning." She gave Lisette a little push in that direction and waited, hands on her hips, until the door was closed. Then she turned to her own room, where Hazel waited just outside the door.

"Is he?" Vada said, approaching.

"Yes. Doc's in there with Althea. Here, hold this." Hazel thrust the candle into Vada's hand.

Nervous, Vada surveyed the scene that had become so familiar, but it was gone; her bed, empty. It seemed he'd fallen to the floor, and there he still was, pale and thin, but undeniably awake. Doc was crouched down, his arms hooked under Eli's. Althea stood to the side, her hands clasped to her heart, her eyes filled with tears.

"Hazel, help me get him back into bed."

"No, no! Please!" His voice was weak, but he seemed strong enough as he clutched at the blanket and pulled it down in an effort to cover himself. In doing so, a dozen or so small papers fluttered up and down to the floor, sending Althea to her knees in a frantic effort to collect them.

"On second thought, girls, why don't you all wait outside?"

Vada set the candle down on the bureau before joining her sisters out in the hall. They gathered together just as they had a few days ago, right outside this door, waiting to hear news from Doc. But this time, instead of hopeful anticipation, they embraced each other in joyful relief.

"Thank You, God, for the healing You have brought to our home." Vada knew her prayer spoke for everyone, and Hazel echoed, "Thank You, Jesus."

Vada took Althea into a special embrace. "Sweetie? Isn't this wonderful? What we've all been praying for?"

Althea pulled away, nodding, and Vada could tell she was a different girl. In the harsh gaslight of the hallway, it was plain to see that the undercurrent of fear ran deeper and more powerful than it had that day. Althea clutched the papers she'd gathered to her breast, and with her hair loose about her shoulders, she looked almost mad.

"What have you got there?" Vada reached for a paper, causing Althea to clutch it tighter. "Show me, darling. Why are you so upset?"

With an insistent tug, Vada managed to loosen a sheet and opened it from its careless folding. The edges along one side were rough; it had obviously been torn from her journal.

> *Lord, I pray that it might be*
> *His soul remaining here with me.*
> *And the moment he once again sees light,*
> *'Tis I he'll seek with this new sight.*
> *For in Your hands—*

"This is your poetry?"

Althea nodded.

"Everything that you wrote for him? To him? Have you been *reading* these?"

Althea acknowledged each question to that point.

"Not reading, exactly, but...*giving* them to him?" She could picture it, all those still, quiet hours. No sound but her pen scratching on the page. The verses, once perfected, torn from their seclusion and slid under his hand. Next to his heart.

"You've never shared your poetry with any of us. You really do love him, don't you?"

As an answer, Althea threw herself in Vada's embrace, and the reason for her fear became clear. If Eli could walk, he could leave.

The door opened and Doc walked out. Even in his nightshirt, he managed to look the part of the authoritative sage as he wiped his glasses on his sleeve.

"So, he's awake?" Hazel asked. "For good, you think?"

"I'd say so, yes," Doc said. "At least until it's time to sleep again. But it's impossible to know for sure."

"And he's…" Vada searched for the correct word, "…functioning? Mentally, I mean?"

"Oh yes. Sharp as a tack, as far as I can tell. He was able to let me know his name, where he came from, where he lives—"

"So, who is he?" It seemed a safer question than whether or not he still pined for Katrina.

"A better question is, *what* is he? And what he is, is easily tired and extremely hungry. So if one of you ladies would please, go downstairs and make him something to eat. Nothing heavy. A scrambled egg, maybe. Or oatmeal and a cup of weak tea."

"I'll take care of it, Doc." Vada quietly handed the journal page back to Althea, who was sorting and straightening the little bundle.

"And he shouldn't be alone for long; I'll need one of you to go in and sit with him while I get dressed. He needs a more thorough examination, which I'd rather conduct with pants on."

Althea moved behind Hazel, nudging her toward the door.

"Now, I'm not sure exactly what this means," Doc said, "but he asked me about the girl who wrote poetry. Was that from a dream, I wonder? Or could that possibly be one of you?"

Hazel stepped aside. "Well, what do you know?" Grinning broadly, she nudged Althea. "He was paying attention all along."

In her excitement, Vada had forgotten all about Kenny until she walked into the kitchen to see him dutifully waiting at the table, finishing off the last of the pie in the dish.

"I'm sorry, Miss Vada," he said, his mouth full. "I eat when I get nervous."

"And just what do you have to be nervous about, Mr. Cupid?" She filled the kettle and lit the stove before moving to the icebox for eggs. "Should I be in fear for my sister's reputation?"

"Oh, no ma'am. It's nothing about that. I was just worried about him upstairs."

"Well, you and your team will be relieved to know that he's fine. He's up, and awake, and hungry."

"Oh!" He quickly crossed himself and, hands folded, said, "Thank You, Lord!" before crossing himself again.

"You really are a nice boy, aren't you, Kenny?" She cracked two eggs in a bowl and began whisking them with a fork.

"I try to be, ma'am."

"Then stop calling me 'ma'am.' I'm not quite six years older than you."

"I'm sorry, ma' —, sorry."

"So with that settled, tell me why I don't need to worry about my sister. My *baby* sister, just seventeen years old."

"I can hardly explain it." He had one of those smiles rarely seen on men, full lipped and wide, with corners that actually turned up. His dark hair curled around his head, and his eyebrows danced with expression. "The first time I saw her, it's like the rest of the world just disappeared for a second. I mean, I've devoted my whole life to playing baseball, even though my parents hate that I do it, but the moment I saw her face, I didn't even remember being on a field. I feel bad for the consequences, but my mother always said the good Lord works all to the good."

Vada listened, adding a splash of milk to the eggs and melting butter in the pan before pouring the scrambled mass in, creating a satisfying sizzle.

"This might seem unusual, but Lisette's really not the one I'm worried about."

"How's that?"

"I'm not sure quite how to put this, but you should know that Lissy has had—shall we say—several suitors. I'm afraid you might be one of her more passing fancies. And on the other side of it, well, she's not always, er…kind."

"I know. The first real conversation we had, all she did was tell me about all those other guys who took her dancing and bought her stuff."

"That doesn't bother you?"

"No, not really. I'm confident I can give her more than they ever could."

Vada turned away from the stove and gave him a leveling glare. "As a baseball player? No offense, Kenny, but I have some insight into the salary you fellows make."

"I don't exactly mean that. I mean love. I love your sister, Miss Allenhouse."

She turned back, scraping the wooden spatula along the edges of the pan. "Isn't it a bit soon to be talking of love?"

"It's never too soon for love. It comes across you in a moment. Hits you right between the eyes." At that, he smacked his forehead with the heel of his palm, then cringed. "Oh, sorry. Horrible analogy."

She couldn't help it; she laughed, and he did too.

The kettle started to make the sounds of boiling, just as the eggs made their final fluffy transformation. She filled the pot and dropped in a packed tea ball before scooping the eggs on a plate. She put the plate, the pot, and a sturdy cup onto a tray and Kenny, ever the gentleman, offered to carry it upstairs.

"No, I have another errand for you." She set the tray down on the table and ran upstairs, returning with her pocketbook. It took a little digging, but she finally found the small business card with Dave's address carefully printed on the back.

"Go to this address, and knock on the door until somebody answers. Ask to speak to Mr. Dave Voyant, and when you see him, tell him that his story just woke up and seems ready to talk."

Kenny looked confused. "It's one o'clock in the morning."

"Tell him I'm a woman who keeps her promises."

When she got back upstairs, Vada found her door closed but not latched, so she combined a knock and a nudge before walking in with the tray.

He was wearing pajamas—her father's, she believed, the very pair she'd given him for Christmas two years ago. They billowed about his spare frame, but the pale blue stripes seemed to bring a little life to his face. Althea sat in her customary chair, though it was now turned to fully face the bed. Their hands were clasped, causing Vada's heart to leap to her throat when she noticed that his fingers were intertwined with Althea's, rather than lying limp and heavy at his side.

She hesitated, not sure exactly what to say to a man brought back from the brink of death, finally settling on, "Hello."

"Hello."

"I'm Vada. I've brought you something to eat."

"I am Eli. Eli Prochazka, and I am very grateful because I am very hungry."

His voice was pleasant, perhaps softer than usual because of his weakness, with the faintest Czech accent hugging the corners of his words. He seemed instantly friendly, as if the days spent sleeping under their roof allowed him to bypass the formalities of introduction. Eli was already a fixture; now he was simply one who spoke.

"Well then, I hope you enjoy this."

He was already sitting straight up in the bed, well-propped with pillows. By the time Vada made it to the side of the bed, he had dropped Althea's hand in preparation for the tray soon to be set on his lap.

"It looks delicious."

"Just scrambled eggs. And tea." She turned to Althea. "And be careful. The tea is hot."

He picked up the fork, but it became immediately evident that he lacked the strength, or perhaps just the powers of concentration, to manage feeding himself. Althea took the fork from him, separated a bite of egg, and speared it onto the fork's tines. After a sheepish grin, Eli opened his mouth, allowing Althea to feed him like a child.

But there was nothing childlike about the atmosphere in the room. Vada felt every bit the voyeur, and she backed out, determined to stay away until she was invited back.

It seemed impossible to imagine that half the night remained for sleeping, yet Hazel was already well on her way there when Vada came back to their shared bed.

"Aren't they adorable?" Hazel whispered.

"Who? Althea and Eli?"

"They already look like an old married couple. Oh, what I wouldn't give to have a man look at me that way."

"Scoot over." Vada crawled in. "Did you learn any more about him?"

"I helped Doc a little bit, not really cleaning him up, but just helping, you know…and Doc told him what happened at the ballpark and that he's been here unconscious for four days—"

"But did you learn anything about him?"

"He's lived here since he was fifteen. Then he went back to his home country for a while and just came back."

"Did he mention Katrina? Anything that might explain the letter?"

"No, but Althea was in the room part of the time, and he kept looking over at her. Like he didn't want to talk in front of her. Anyway, he says he rents a room down on Harper Street and that he's trying to save money to finish his last years of school. Engineering."

"My goodness! You managed to find out quite a bit."

"Doc kept asking him questions, I think to keep him alert and to check his memory."

"Did Doc ask how he knew about the poetry?"

"No. But he didn't have to. It was in his eyes."

"What do you mean?"

"It was like he read those poems before he ever opened them."

Vada lay there, awake, desperate to sleep. The clock downstairs chimed three o'clock. Her body didn't know what to do, though her eyes burned and her mind begged for respite. Every time she felt the first faint tugs of sleep, she'd hear Eli's voice, sweet and low, coming from across the hall.

Sleep. Sleep. Sleep.

Maybe, if she could shut everything out, sleep now, and stay there through dawn, through breakfast, *she* might wake up in love.

Or, at least, in love enough.

Suddenly, she had to know what it felt like to be in the path of that much passion. Not the lust she'd felt in the throes of LaFortune's embrace, but true, pure desire. She slid out of bed and crept over to Hazel's desk. After a modicum of searching, Vada found the letter Hazel had been reading the last time Vada had fallen into any true, restful slumber. And, certainly, Hazel wouldn't mind. She'd read most of the letter to Vada herself.

Positioning her body so the page could be illuminated by the street-light, Vada allowed the words written in the precise, strong hand to tell their story—of Barth's longing, his love, and finally his urgent promise. By the time she came to the signature—*With all the love I dare send right now*—her own heart was racing by proxy.

Maybe she and Garrison had it all wrong. Too much talking, too much familiarity. Maybe if they spent hours in silence, or sent letters, or threw caution to the wind to be together—no matter what the hour. Maybe…

She wished she had moonlight—pure, natural, God-given moon-light—rather than the eerie saffron glow of the streetlight. Somehow, that might lend the touch of romance this moment needed. Might make her feel like more of a tragic heroine rather than the woman who simply couldn't sleep. Not with this matter so unsettled.

The top drawer of Hazel's desk protested as she pulled it, but she didn't have to open it far to find what she wanted. One sheet of thick, good paper. One envelope and a pen—one of those new-fashioned ones with the ink stored in the barrel. She drew her hand through three empty circles before touching its nub to the paper and writing, *Dearest Garrison…*

Pausing, she thought of those words written to Eli. The acknowl-edgment of childish promises, the sincere desire for his happiness. If only she spoke the language, she could copy it verbatim. As it was, she imag-ined she was Katrina, wishing that sweet, loving boy to find a woman worthy of him.

Mere moments and a few lines later, she signed her name to that same sentiment and was practically asleep before the ink dried.

19

"And the music stands have all arrived?"

"Yes, Herr Johann."

"And they are assembled on the stage?"

"Not yet, but they will be in time for the final rehearsal."

"And you have warned the ushers not to seat late arrivers?"

"They know not to open a door until they hear applause."

"And the——"

Thankfully the bell at the delivery door rang, giving Vada a chance to squirm away from Herr Johann's barrage of questions. She'd been in her office since eight o'clock that morning, keeping herself busy by bundling programs to distribute at the ushers' stations and running the Bissel over the lobby carpet. That's where she'd been when the conductor caught her, and she'd been running around behind him ever since.

But it was better than being at home. With Lisette and Kenny mooning over each other at breakfast and Eli making his way downstairs supported by Althea's birdlike shoulder, the atmosphere had just been stifling. Not to mention Molly's drilling Eli about his religious convictions. It was good of her to come on a Friday—her usual day off—to help tend to the young man, but once the excitement of the early morning summons had worn off, she'd become insufferable. At one point she'd even pulled Vada aside, claiming they might be lookin' at a double weddin' in the summer.

"O'course not you and your young man," she'd said. "But that'll come in its time." She then took Vada in her arms, in what could only be a gesture of sympathy, before going back to her hash.

Yes, mindless chores at the theater were just the thing for rescue.

Now the ringing at the delivery door provided rescue yet again, and she excused herself from Herr Johann and ran downstairs to answer it.

The dark, stocky man on the other side wore a starched white shirt and a bright green apron. Behind him, parked in the alley, stood a patient mule with petunias laced through his bridle. He was hitched to a small, white cart with the name *Flore di Dante* painted in elegant script.

"Flowers." He held out a small ledger book for Vada to sign.

"How lovely!" Once she'd signed for the delivery, Vada propped the door open, and he walked in with two enormous sprays of carnations. She instructed the delivery man to follow her to the main lobby and set the flowers on the long, narrow refreshment bar. "Is there a card?"

"Look for yourself. I got more."

She followed him back to the door, and he came from the cart carrying four long boxes tied with peach ribbon.

"Sign."

"Who are these for?"

"Lady, I just bring 'em. The cards? They's up to you."

Such unpleasantness hardly warranted a dime tip, but she fished one out of the coin bag in her skirt pocket anyway before taking the boxes out of his arms.

"*Buon giorno.*" He touched the dime to his head in salute.

"Good day to you too," she replied, struggling to unprop the door with her hip.

She managed to carry the boxes over to the counter and untied the ribbon on the first. Inside, nestled among the white tissue paper, were a dozen long-stemmed red roses. The fragrance brought her back to the intoxicating room at the Hollenden Hotel, and for the briefest flutter of her heart, she wondered if these had been sent by Louis LaFortune.

"Stop it, Vada. Lord, forgive my weakness."

Lifting the top layer of tissue, she found the tiny pink envelope addressed to *My Darling Vada from…G. W.*

Garrison Walker. She thought of her own envelope, now sitting in the darkness of her pocketbook, with its passionless, dismissive letter within. Her hands trembled as she picked up this tiny one, opened the unsealed flap, and pulled out the miniscule card.

May this night be the night of our dreams. — G.

Certainly, as he pondered for hours and hours trying to decide just what sweet, loving phrase to write on the card, he envisioned her clutching it to her breast only to read it again and again through rapturous eyes of love. Instead, the words sat flat on the page, hardly earning a second glance. The roses, however, were beautiful, and she would ask Althea to fashion them into a corsage to wear that evening.

The other three boxes were flatter and narrower than this first one, and before she took the first tug on the string to open the next, Vada had a vague idea what they might hold. Sure enough, the next box contained three yellow roses for Hazel, the next three peach-colored for Althea, and the last three white roses for Lisette.

She stopped herself from reading the individual card written to each—the girls were entitled to some privacy, after all—and felt the first splash of guilt as she picked up one rose. He was such a kind and thoughtful man. Perhaps last night's resolution had been little more than a product of sleeplessness. An emotional overreaction. She looked at the card again while stroking her cheek with the silky red petals. She spoke his name aloud, "Garrison," and inhaled the rose's scent, engaging all of her senses in this man, waiting to feel something akin to what she'd felt in the arms of Louis LaFortune.

"I'm afraid you win."

Startled, she gave a little jump before hastily returning the rose to its box.

"Hello, Mr. Voyant. And just what did I win exactly?"

"The beauty contest between you and that rose. Poor little flower didn't stand a chance."

"Well, I'm sure she must be devastated. What does one send a flower by way of a condolence?"

He thought for a moment. "A weed?"

She snapped her finger. "The very thing. I shall arrange a bouquet of dandelions to be delivered tomorrow."

"Those from Walker?"

"They are, indeed."

"Must have cost him a pretty penny."

"Apparently, only the prettiest will do." She folded the tissue back over the flowers, replaced the lid, and retied the ribbon to a facsimile of its initial pretty bow. "Did you have a chance to talk with Mr. Prochazka?"

He broke into a huge smile of mock gratitude. "I did. And I really must thank you for sending your messenger boy to wake me from a most magnificent dream."

"Half-dressed dancing roses?"

"Something like that. Anyway, I've just come from your house after a long, fascinating interview with the immigrant Lazarus."

"Don't call him that. Lazarus was dead."

"Yeah? And so is this story." He affected a huge yawn, which prompted Vada to produce a real one. She covered her mouth and giggled, excusing herself.

"I tried to tell you there was no story."

"No, three days ago there *was* a story. This is only human interest if the humans are interested. They don't care about a guy who just woke up. But they would have cared about a guy who might not."

"And then we'd have them camped around our house morning, noon, and night. Bad enough to have the few that we did hovering around our door. But, you have to admit, the love story is pretty compelling." .

"Love story?"

"He woke up in love with Althea. She sat with him more than any of us did, and he was apparently aware"—she broke off, not wanting to reveal the role her sister's poetry played—"aware of her presence."

"Bah! Love stories. I'll never be considered a serious journalist writing that kind of drivel."

"No, but perhaps I can convince Herr Johann to write an opera around it, and you can cover that."

"Ha, ha." He was devoid of mirth. "But I did, however, manage to get a dream of a story—a bit of a love story, I guess—that I'll be able to sell and possibly get me out of the newspaper business for good. And for that, I thank you."

"Thank me?"

"I don't know what prompted you to send K. C. Cupid to my house in the middle of the night, but I will be forever grateful. In fact, I'll dedicate my first byline in *Baseball Express* to you."

Vada furrowed her brow, trying to follow his logic. "I had no idea Kenny was that valuable a player."

"Let's just say his value is not in his playing, and he's never talked to anyone about that until last night. I'm glad I didn't take his head off when he was pounding on my door. That's one family I wouldn't— Wait a minute, you don't know about any of this, do you?"

"Not a clue."

"Does she?"

"She who?"

"That Gibson girl baby sister of yours." He clapped his hand over his mouth and dragged it down over his chin. "I'll bet she doesn't. Of course she doesn't. I spent five minutes with the girl and had your entire family history. That girl couldn't keep a secret if she was shackled to it."

"What secret?"

"Do you know who K. C. Cupid is?"

"Apparently not."

"First of all, it's a reversal. Cupid's his middle name. Mother's maiden name, I believe. He's really Kenneth Cupid Chentworth."

She waited a moment, letting the name sink in and take hold. When it did, her head began to spin. "As in *the* Chentworths? They're as rich as the Rockefellers."

"At least," he said. "You know all that property the Rockefellers bought on Euclid Avenue? Guess who they bought it from?"

"And he told you this last night?"

"I always knew the basics of it, but last night—well, this morning, I guess—he filled me in on some of the details. All off the record, of course, for now. But he guaranteed me a story in time, and I figure now I have an 'in' with the family."

"An *in*?"

He gently touched a knuckle to her chin. "Come on, doll. Isn't it about time you walked away from that lawyer of yours and ran away with me?"

Oh, how tempting, if she thought there was anything serious behind his invitation. In fact, it might be fun to accept, just to see how quickly he back-pedaled out of the proposal. But she already had one cruel act to perform, so she simply invited him to carry the flower boxes home with her and join the family for lunch.

"You sure?" he said. "I don't want to impose."

"There's no such thing, and I don't believe you anyway. Molly always has plenty."

Quickly, though, first she ran upstairs to tell Herr Johann she was leaving and, caught up in a current of goodwill, asked if he would like to join her family.

"You think I could eat on this day?"

"Shall I bring you back a plate? I think we're having ham."

"It wouldn't be a problem?"

"None at all," she said before following through on an impulse and giving the stiff little man a kiss on his warm, dry cheek. "Everything's going to be marvelous tonight, Herr Johann. Simply perfect."

"You really think so?"

She pulled back to look into his iron blue eyes and saw fear there she'd never imagined existed during all the weeks of ruthless rehearsal. Perhaps Garrison mixed up the cards and sent the conductor a tiny missive of unending love.

"I know so."

She grabbed her pocketbook and ran back downstairs where Dave Voyant had already restacked the boxes and tied them all together with the long red ribbon.

"After you?" He gestured to the front entrance. "Because you have the key."

He filled her in on the walk home—off the record, of course, with her binding verbal agreement not to approach any other reporter with the story as a third-party informant. The story began with a young Kenneth living in an exclusive boarding school in New Haven, Connecticut, playing shortstop on the campus team. On a lark, he tried out for the Cincinnati Reds and earned a spot—to the outrage of his father.

"So they struck a deal. Chentworth senior lets the kid play until he turns twenty-five, or as long as the league'll keep him, and Kenny promises not to shame the family name by telling anyone who he is."

"Playing baseball is shameful?"

"To a Chentworth it is."

"But if he made it on the Cincinnati team, how did he end up here in Cleveland?"

"That's baseball. Always trading."

He swore her once again to secrecy at the foot of the concrete stairs, then up they went to be greeted like heroes at the door.

"Flowers? For us?" Hazel ripped the ribbon and the lid off her box and held up one of the long-stemmed beauties. "And we'll put Lissy's in water until she gets home."

"I'll take care of them for you ladies," Molly said. "I'm just about to put luncheon on, and I'll get to it while you're eatin'."

Eli and Althea were in the parlor, sitting side by side on the sofa looking through Althea's favorite book of birds. When Vada walked in, Althea rushed across the room to wrap her thin arms around her.

"Well, hello to you too," Vada said. "Go into the kitchen. I've brought a surprise for you from Garrison."

Althea pointed to herself and gave a quizzical look before giving Eli a short wave and flying out.

Dave crossed the room to shake Eli's hand. "How are you feeling, Prochazka?"

"Good. But please, for a while, no more questions. My head still hurts."

"That's all right. I have more than I need. Which reminds me." Dave turned to Vada. "Do you have a telephone I could use? I need to clear some space for this story."

"Right at the foot of the stairs," Vada said. "It's local, right?"

"Just downtown."

Once he left, Vada had an opportunity to focus her attention on Eli, who had politely stood the moment she walked into the room. He looked none the worse for wear in a pair of well-tailored slacks and a clean shirt. True, both garments fit him a little loosely, as his pants seemed to be literally held up by the suspenders, but certainly a few days of Molly's cooking would cure that. Or at least it would starting Monday.

"You seem to have a little more color in your cheeks today, Eli." She sat in one of the chairs opposite the sofa, inviting him to sit too.

"Althea and I went walking. Just to the corner and back."

Did he kiss her at that corner? "You know, my sister is a very sweet, very special girl."

"I know. And very quiet too."

"She doesn't speak. She can—or she could. But she was badly hurt a long time ago—"

"When your mother left."

"She told you?" Vada couldn't imagine how much Althea would have to write to explain this.

"In a way. We were in here looking at the photographs, and I asked if there were any of her mother."

"That's when she stopped speaking. And I can't imagine what she would do to herself if she were ever to get hurt again. Do you understand me?"

"I'm not sure…"

"She's very innocent. Never had any kind of beau or suitor. Never been courted, never asked to be. Nothing. And I'm afraid—"

"I understand, miss. It is hard to explain, but all that time when I was…asleep…there would be moments—almost like coming to the surface when you are swimming. And I would hear the sound of that pen scratching on paper. And I would hear the writing. Not the words, but the…oh, I cannot think of English word…but the *sense* of them. The emotion of them."

"The essence?"

"Yes. Exactly. The whole time too, I hear God's voice talking to me, telling me to sleep a little longer and heal, and He would have a great gift waiting for me. Then you can imagine when I open my eyes and see nobody there, when my heart was waiting to meet this beautiful woman with the beautiful words."

"What about Katrina?"

He frowned. "What do you know of Katrina?"

Vada told him how she'd found the note and taken it to Moravek's to have it translated in an effort to find out more about him.

He brightened. "Moravek's bakery?"

"You know it?"

"When I lived here before, I used to eat there all the time."

"And what about Katrina? Why were you still carrying around that note?"

"True, she was a girl I loved in the old country. And when I went back, I hoped to return here with her. But she was very young, and how can any love survive that distance? And in truth? When I see her again, I noticed her voice was so high and shrill. I almost pity the poor man who has to listen to it for the rest of his life."

"So, why were you still carrying the note?"

"I didn't know I was. Perhaps it had fallen into the lining?"

Vada took this in, allowing her protective instinct time to accept this explanation. When Molly's booming voice summoned them into lunch, they stood, smiling a truce. Once at the parlor door, he gestured for her to precede him, which she did, until one last thought entered her mind and she turned back.

"By the way, I'm afraid I took your buttons."

"My what?"

"The buttons that were in your pocket. It seems silly, but I had a…friend—one of the players, the one who actually hit the ball that…well, he wanted something of yours for a kind of good-luck charm. So I gave him your buttons. I'll gladly replace them."

He threw his head back and laughed, a pleasant sound that she hoped to be hearing for years to come. "I bought those pants secondhand just…well, the day before the game. I didn't even know I had buttons in the pocket."

Then she laughed too, all the way into the kitchen, but when Hazel asked her to share the joke, she couldn't. Not without telling the whole story, and she couldn't do that yet. Luckily, Eli seemed content to go along with her explanation of, "Nothing, just some silly thing not worth telling."

Molly had indeed outdone herself on a Friday lunch, serving three kinds of salad along with slices of cold ham and enormous soft rolls.

"These are from Moravek's," Vada told Eli, who was soon ready to eat his second.

Dave Voyant seemed equally comfortable for his first meal in the Allenhouse kitchen. He joked with Hazel and teased Molly, asking why a good Catholic girl like her could bring herself to serve meat on Friday.

"No scandal in servin' it, sir," she said good-naturedly. "Just a sin in the eatin' of it."

"Nothing sinful here." Eli speared his third slice.

Vada looked at Hazel. "Is Doc out visiting patients?"

"I don't think so. At least none were on his schedule."

Just then, as if hearing his name called, Doc walked into the kitchen, causing all of them at once to stop their conversation.

"Doc!" Vada jumped up from the table and ran to her father, barely recognizing the man with the newly clean-shaven face. The whiskers that had sprouted from his cheeks and chin for as long as she could remember were gone, leaving only a tidy, fashionable mustache. "What prompted this?"

"Well," Doc said, giving the ends of the mustache a twirl. "I figured we are on the brink of a new century, and I should be ready to meet it."

"Or," Molly said from her place by the sink, "our writer friend wanted a picture for his story and you didn't want to come off lookin' like some sort o' mountain man."

"That too," Doc said before taking his place at the table.

After lunch, Dave excused himself, saying he had to drop by the newspaper office before cleaning up for the concert.

"It is formal dress, I presume?" he asked as Vada walked him to the door.

"For the audience, yes, preferred. But since you're the press…"

"I'll see if I can't dig up a suit."

20

Vada had reserved five seats for the concert: one for her, one for her father, and one for each of her three sisters. It had been quite the fight to get Althea to agree to take the night off of her telegraph office job, and even a bigger one to convince Lisette to spend a Friday evening listening to an amateur orchestra of mostly middle-aged men. Now, of course, circumstances had dramatically changed. Doc insisted on staying home to monitor Eli, and Althea seemed wounded at the thought of being away from him.

"You should go," Eli insisted when the subject came up after lunch. "I believe you have already spent too many nights sitting and watching me."

Just like that, he established himself as Althea's newest authority, and she silently agreed.

Lisette, however, walked through the door after school complaining. "Do I still have to go to this thing?"

Vada assured her that yes, indeed, she did have to go to *this thing*, and that furthermore, Garrison had been kind enough to send her flowers to commemorate the occasion.

"You can wear one in your hair, that would look lovely with your spring gown," Vada told her, hoping to sound more enthusiastic herself.

"Oh, all right. Kenneth was going to meet me there anyway, just in case I couldn't get out of it."

"That's lovely," Vada said. "He can have Doc's seat with us."

Promptly at two o'clock, under Molly's firm insistence, the four girls took to their beds for an afternoon nap before the night out. Eli, exhausted after so full a day, also agreed to take a rest, after a good-humored promise to wake up by next Tuesday at the latest. In the meantime, Molly would pop down to the laundry where their gowns had been sent to be cleaned.

Up in her room, Hazel stripped out of her corset and down to her chemise and pantalets, but not Vada. She was too weighted with worry to sleep. She took her letter to Garrison out of her pocketbook and read it for the first time that day. Clear, succinct, but no admission of her straying into another man's arms. She could spare him that, at least.

Oh, Lord, there's still time for You to change his heart. If I thought he really loved me. Loved me like…like he couldn't bear to live another day without me. And that's it—I hurt. Lord, let him see how he's hurting me. Show him, Father, today. Because my heart is set. I cannot wait for three years to finally be worthy. I deserve better than that.

A nagging voice behind her heart dared to ask *Why?* But she ignored it. That meant revisiting those moments with Louis, and she couldn't do that. After all, didn't Garrison betray her a little every day that passed without a proposal? He may as well have pushed her into LaFortune's arms.

She read the letter one more time before sliding it back into the envelope. On it she wrote, *Garrison—to be read after the concert.* She owed him that much. Before she could change her mind, she opened her violin case and placed the note within. She would take both tonight.

That evening's concert was the first spring social outing for the Allenhouse sisters, and whatever hesitation any of them may have had about attending disappeared within the excitement of preparing for it.

Hazel spent the day with her hair in rag curls. Even Vada put on a brave enough face to keep any misgivings at bay, and Molly hardly grumbled about spendin' an extra evenin' with her girls with nary an extra dime of pay.

Each bedroom door—save Vada's, of course—had a newly pressed and steamed spring gown hanging from it. Molly kept vigilant command of the curling tongs heated on the kitchen stove, and each sister took a turn in her chair, nibbling on cheese sandwiches intended to tide them over until the late postconcert supper.

Lisette was the first to get her hair done, as she had decided to wear it up this evening. Vada, Hazel, and Althea sat at the kitchen table and watched Molly's masterful handling of their baby sister's long, luxurious tresses. She divided the hair into three thick strands that she intertwined into a knot right at the crown of Lisette's head. The ends of those strands were left loose and were curled into ringlets that seemed to spill from within the bun. As a final touch, she took one of the white roses Garrison sent and set it at the top of the cascading ringlets, securing it there with the oyster comb Lisette received for her sixteenth birthday.

The end result was breathtaking, even with the girl wearing her pink cotton wrapper. Moments later, she walked into the kitchen wearing a gown of white satin with a sage green lace overlay. The neckline extended from one creamy white shoulder to the next, with the lace flounce at the bust creating a more modest silhouette for her generous figure. Capped sleeves fluttered at the top of her bare arms, and the skirt swirled perfectly around her feet.

"Saints preserve us." Molly held a handful of Althea's hair. "You look like you just walked off a fashion plate."

"Do you think Kenneth will like it?" For the first time ever, Lisette carried an air of insecurity.

"He's going to love you," Vada said, thinking how beautifully she would fit into the Chentworth world. "More than he already does."

"What do you think, Papa?" She did a twirl for Doc, who had just walked into the kitchen.

Doc was speechless for a second; Vada could see the valiant fight against tears being waged in his eyes and his throat. Finally, he said, "This cannot be my little baby girl."

"Oh, Papa!" Lisette wrapped her arms around him, careful not to mess her hair. And when she looked up, Vada had a perfect view of the two of them, just as if she were looking at a new set of pictures in a double frame. With Doc's whiskers gone, the soft planes of his face were exposed, including the tiny bump of a chin. An identical profile between father and daughter. In fact, in forty years' time, she would look just like him—minus the mustache if she was lucky. The thought of that would probably make Lisette furious, but it brought a certain peace to Vada's heart.

When the tender moment was interrupted by an insistent knock on the front door, Lisette leaped out of Doc's arms. "I told Kenny to meet me at the theater, but I suppose he couldn't wait."

She skipped out of the kitchen, until Vada called after her to remember she was a lady.

Molly returned to her task at hand, fixing Althea's hair in a much more subdued, conservative style, creating a pretty twist that ran from her crown to the nape of her neck and pinning individual curls at her temples.

"Now you know I'm not a one for meddlin', Dr. Allenhouse, but it seems to me you'd better get that one married off soon as you can. For the sanity of all of us."

Doc took a cheese sandwich from the platter and munched it thoughtfully. "I'll certainly take that into consideration, Molly."

Lisette was back at the kitchen door, an odd look on her face.

"Why don't you ask the young man to come back here?" Molly said. "Let him get a snack."

"It's not Kenneth. I don't know who it is. Some man, tall, dark hair, very sophisticated and handsome. Said he needed to talk to Miss Allenhouse? But not me."

Vada and Hazel locked eyes across the table. Molly held the curling tong in midair, and Althea twisted in her chair. They all knew who it was, and the thought of the man here to ruin this evening burned the wick of Vada's anger to the explosive end.

"Do you want me to go talk to him, Vada?" Hazel asked.

"No, I'm sure he means me," she said, rising to her feet.

"Girls? Is there something I should know about?"

"No, Doc," Vada said. "Just some last-minute concert business, I'm sure. Sit down and finish your sandwich."

Her stomach roiled with every step, intensifying at the sight of the familiar silhouette on the other side of the front door glass. What would she say? How could she keep him away from Doc? What if he overpowered her, knocking her down and barging right in? That was the trick. Don't let him in. Open the door just a crack and slip out onto the front porch. So what if she was wearing her robe? It certainly wouldn't be the first time.

Pressing her face close to the jamb, she twisted the knob and opened the door, planning to ease it open no more than it took to scrape through. But the wider she opened the door, the better the look she got of the man on the other side, and the clearer it became that this wasn't Alex Triplehorn on the front porch.

This man was as tall as Triplehorn—perhaps taller—and probably broader across the shoulders. His hair was black as raven's wings and his hands, clasped loosely in front of him, looked like they could strangle a lion if given the chance. His face, though, was somewhat familiar. No, not his face, his eyes. She'd seen those eyes before. Tonight, standing this close, she could see that they were an icy blue, but it wasn't the color that was familiar; it was the shade. She'd never seen them in color before, only staring at her from a photograph. And, like her father, this man had taken advantage of a barber's trade, sporting a perfectly clean-shaven face with just the hint of shadow that must have grown during the train ride from Wyoming.

"Are…are you…?" She swallowed. "Barth?"

"At last!" His voice rumbled up from deep inside that massive chest, and all of Vada's plans to disallow his entrance vanished as he strode across the threshold and grabbed her, both of his hands easily encircling her waist. Before she knew it, she was being held high above his head, looking down into an extremely handsome, smiling face.

"Mr.—" Not only did she not know his last name, the grip and the angle in which he held her made speaking nearly impossible.

"Shoulda sent a telegram, but the wires was down, and then—"

"Put me down!"

"Beg pardon?"

"Put me down. Now, please."

Barth did as he was told, holding her steady until he was sure she'd found her footing.

"Sorry." He stepped back out onto the porch. "Been picturin' this moment in my mind for so long now, and that's how I always imagined it. Bet your family thinks I'm crazy."

"My…" She turned around, and there they all were, packed at the end of the entrance hall, Doc in the very front. "Oh, my family." Vada could barely see Hazel's stricken eyes behind Molly's shoulder.

"Maybe I oughta leave now and try again in the mornin'?"

"No," Vada said. "Come in, and let me introduce you to the woman you've been corresponding with all these months."

Realization registered on his face, and to her delight, a bright red flush spread from his cheeks to his ears. "You mean, you aren't Miss Allenhouse?"

"There are four of us, actually. So, yes, I am Miss Allenhouse, but I am not *your* Miss Allenhouse. Let me introduce you to Hazel."

Behind Molly's shoulder, a little mass of rag curls bounced.

"Come, Hazel. There's somebody here to meet you."

Doc, in a fiery moment of authority, reached behind him and grasped Hazel's arm, pulling her to the front, then giving her a little push ahead.

Step after step she took, until she was even with Vada, and Vada handed her over. "Hazel Allenhouse, I'd like to formally introduce you to Barth…"

"LaRoche," Hazel filled in. "So nice to meet you." She spoke with the quality of having some other entity forming her words within her, and it wasn't until Vada prompted that she held out her hand, which he immediately took and kissed, looking straight into her eyes even as he held her hand to his lips.

"You," he said, "are the beauty behind all those letters?"

The rag curls were shaking again, nodding.

Without another word, he dropped her hand and walked out the open door, closing it behind him.

Never, not even as Vada imagined those long comatose nights shared by Eli and Althea, had there ever been such a mass of pure silence in their home as at that moment. Then, a tiny sound broke through—the same tiny sound Vada heard all those days ago at the hotel when Hazel felt the pang of rejection. Her sister's lip quivered, her whole body shaking, in fact.

Housecoat or no, Vada was ready to storm onto that front porch and break him in half. That is, if she could beat Molly to it. The Irish woman's arms were exposed now as she rolled up her sleeves, and only Doc's restraining hand kept her in her place when once again a knock sounded at the front door.

"I'll take care of this," Vada said. This time, she threw open the door, exposing Mr. Barth LaRoche to the wrath of the Allenhouse clan, but he seemed nonplussed by their presence.

He breezed right past her, walked straight to Hazel, and said, "At last!" before picking her up in his arms, lifting her high over his head, and spinning in one slow complete circle. Once he set her down and had assured himself she could stand steady, he dropped to one knee and took her hand in his.

"My darlin'. I could not wait another day to know your answer. I must know now, will you consent to be my wife?"

Vada looked past them to the family still assembled in the hall, where everybody stood with looks of shock and amazement on their faces. Again, the thick silence until Hazel made that tiny sound once more, only this time it carried with it joy, and later it transformed into, "Yes."

He rose to his feet and kissed her gently first on one cheek, then the other. "Now then, my heart, perhaps I should meet your father."

"Come, girls," Molly gathered them like so many chicks, "come to the kitchen and I'll finish your hair while they talk."

The atmosphere in the kitchen was vastly different than it had been before the knock at the door. Althea had gone upstairs to dress, but Lisette asked question after question, chastising Hazel for keeping such a secret for so long.

"Here I was feeling sorry for you, old maid, and you were sending love letters across the country for months."

"They weren't all love letters," Hazel said, wincing as Molly pulled out the bits of rag from her hair. "We wrote about all kinds of things."

"But mostly love?"

Hazel smiled at her youngest sister. "Yes, Lissy, I guess mostly love."

"Oh, and he's a handsome thing, isn't he girls?" Molly said. "Looks just like a paintin' come to life."

"Or like a statue," Lisette added. "He's so tall! And strong. Goodness, he picked you up like you were—"

"Careful," Hazel warned.

"Like you were a feather," Vada said. "You should feel very happy."

"Oh, I do. I do." Hazel cocked her head sideways, easing Molly's task. "Are you sure I should even go to the concert? It just seems like, since he's here…"

Vada thought about Hazel's dress hanging on the back of the door, a sage-colored silk gown appliquéd with thin black velvet ribbon sewn into a swirling design across the bodice, narrowing at the waist, and cascading down the front of the skirt. Already her jet-bead earrings flickered through the curls Molly arranged around her face. "Of course you should go. If only so Barth has a chance to see you in that dress."

"Do you think…is there any chance he could come with us? I've never had an escort to anything before. Are there tickets available?"

"Oh yes," Vada said, picturing the ledger. "Plenty available. But I don't know that you'll be able to sit with us."

"Well, that's good," Lisette said, "since nobody would be able to see over his head. But do you think he has anything to wear?"

"Go fetch the iron, Lissy, and put it on the stove. When I'm done with you girls, I'll have your father send him in and I'll give that suit a pressin'."

Althea made a subdued entrance into the room, wearing a pale blue gown trimmed with a white satin ruffle that crossed her bust at an angle, giving the appearance that the gown was wrapped about her. A length of the same material wrapped around her waist and fell down the top of her skirt. She'd fashioned a corsage from the roses Garrison sent and had it fastened at her waist, weaving the stems through the knot.

"Oh, and doesn't my quiet one look lovely? And cheer up, girl. Your young man needs his rest."

Unconvinced, Althea held out the corsage she'd created from Vada's roses. Four of them were arranged on a bed of pink satin and lace threaded with a thin, wine-colored velvet ribbon. She held up her hand and indicated that it was intended to be worn on the wrist, which best suited Vada's gown.

"Thank you," Vada said, wondering how she'd ever bear the weight of it. "If you like, why don't you sit upstairs with Eli until it's time for us to leave? We still have an hour, at least."

With a grateful expression, Althea stood, took a sandwich, then another, and bounced out of the kitchen.

"Oooh," Lisette said, admiring Vada's corsage. "That gives me an idea. Are you finished with Hazel?"

Molly stepped around to observe her handiwork and declared that yes, she was.

"Then come on!" She grabbed Hazel's hand and dragged her away.

"That's how it's to be then." Molly returned the curling iron to the stove. "One after the other just flyin' out."

"We should take a photograph."

Molly snapped her fingers. "The very thing! They say that's the time to sit for a photograph, when you're sittin' on the brink of life changin'. I'll make an appointment tomorrow."

"Sounds marvelous," Vada said, trying to sound brave.

She took her place in Molly's chair, imagining an evening one year hence with just the three of them—the spinster, the Irish maid, and

Doc—sitting around the table, perhaps playing cards. The infuriating aspect of that picture was its inevitability. No matter if she ended her relationship with Garrison or not, she was guaranteed to be a free woman long after her sisters settled down with the men of their dreams.

May this night be the night of our dreams...

"What are you scowlin' about? You're goin' to ruin your face etchin' in all those lines."

"Nothing." She grabbed a sandwich and sunk her teeth into the soft bread and cheese.

"Feelin' sorry for yourself, are you, that you don't have some dashin' young man in here sweepin' you off your feet?"

"Don't be silly."

"I ain't bein' silly, and don't think I don't know about the sweepin' that's been happenin' with you of late. That Lissy'd tell a secret to a stone just for the joy of speakin' it."

"Oh, Molly. I've ruined everything."

"I doubt it's as bad as all that." She pulled the brush through Vada's hair, the feeling oddly familiar and comforting. "You're a good girl, after all. I'm sure nothin's been...undone."

The weight of Molly's statement hit home. "Of course not! I just feel like my affection has been... It's just not the same. Just not as strong."

"Nonsense." She gave Vada's hair a painful tug, eliciting a yelp. "Sorry, had a bit of a knot. It's just as much as it's ever been. What you're feelin' is sorry for yourself after you had a little taste of somethin' new."

"It's not that...well, not *only* that. I just worry that Garrison doesn't love me. Not really. Because if he does, why won't he marry me?"

"He will, lass. In his time. And o'course he loves you, much as any man ever loved any woman. Some fires burn slower, is all. Doesn't mean they don't burn as hot."

Thirty minutes later, at precisely quarter past six, Vada was the last Allen-house sister to descend the staircase fully dressed for the evening. Her gown was a pale pink chiffon, falling in four tiers, with a bodice trimmed in burgundy velvet. The neckline wrapped around the tops of her arms, with narrow jeweled straps over her shoulders.

Where most young women would carry an elegant silk clutch, she clutched the handle of her violin case. She wished she had the spirit to carry the regal nature of the gown, but not even the admiring gazes of her family puddled at the foot of the stairs could lift them. Not even Doc, who took her hand as she descended the final steps and gave it the most gallant kiss.

"Planning on joining them onstage?" he asked.

"Hardly. Just makes me feel better."

"Then it's the music world's loss."

She ran the backs of her fingers over the new smoothness of his face, still not accustomed to this visage. In many ways it seemed the past few days had brought a new man into this role, and part of her longed to forget about the evening that lay ahead and fulfill her destiny of long, cozy nights at home.

"Thanks, Doc."

"I've ordered the carriage for you." He led her to the door. "Pete's waiting outside, already paid and tipped, so you all just enjoy your evening."

Sure enough, parked in front, the Allenhouse carriage waited, with young Pete Darvin himself gussied up for the evening with a black jacket and top hat.

"Good evening ladies," he said from his perch. "Gentlemen."

He made no move to come down from his seat, so one by one, Barth and Doc handed the girls up, before Barth settled into the place beside Pete. The springs groaned under his weight, and for a moment Vada worried Pete might be sent catapulting over the roof of the house. From the look on his face, Pete seemed to have the same concern.

"And no worry thinkin' you need to be home by midnight!" Molly waved vigorously from the porch. "I believe our Pete would do just fine drivin' a pumpkin!"

The sisters laughed, remembering their favorite fairy tale. It was the one Molly used to tell them, leaving off with the moral: 'tis better not to have a stepmother at all than one who treats you wicked. As little girls, it was an odd comfort to be found at the end of a long, sad day.

With the first few turns of the wheels, a voice cried, "Althea!" and Vada looked up to see Eli leaning through the second-story window. "You'll tell me all about it when you get home?"

Althea blew him a kiss, which he feigned to catch in his outstretched hand.

21

The lobby was a teeming mass of beautiful people. Or at least, people beautiful for that evening.

The hems and trains of pastel gowns graced the carpet, making Vada glad she'd taken the time to give it an extra sweeping. The cloakroom did some bustling business, though many of the women chose to keep their wraps—colorfully embossed velvet shawls and light wool capes.

Interspersed within the colorful sea, men in black evening suits and tuxedos dotted the crowd, filling the air with the smoke from thin cigars and lending a low, steady rumble to the sound of countless conversations.

Vada made her way through, smiling and greeting all those she knew, and even a few she didn't. Hazel and Barth peeled away the moment they entered the lobby, as Barth claimed he'd never seen so many people gathered in one place. Sheep, maybe, but sheep knew enough to walk in one direction. All this milling made him nervous. Because of this, Vada recommended the two of them take a seat toward the back—last row, if possible—so they could be the first ones out when the concert was over.

Althea, too, expressed discomfort at being a part of the multitude, and Vada offered to escort her to her seat—fifth row, marked with one of the pretty "reserved" flags—but Althea mentioned that she could find it on her own and disappeared through the middle set of doors.

Lisette leaned close to Vada's ear. "Where's Garrison?"

"Backstage, I imagine."

"Shouldn't you go find him? Wish him good luck, or break a finger, or whatever?"

"I'll stay with you until your escort arrives. As pretty as you look, you need a chaperone."

It was true. Lisette had drawn more than one interested eye. Only Vada's protective glare served to keep them at bay.

"I'm afraid I'll miss him." Lisette craned her neck and looked around. "He's so short."

But then Vada spotted him, making his way purposefully through the crowd. What a difference a jar of pomade and a three-hundred dollar tuxedo made on a man.

She caught his eye and sent him a wide, approving smile; he held a finger to his lips and continued walking, right up behind Lisette. He stood to her left and tapped her right shoulder, drawing her to look over it, only to see no one.

Meanwhile, he moved in front of her, so when she turned around, Vada had a full view of her delight. Although she looked quite the woman with her piled hair and sophisticated gown, Lisette's face took on the expression of an enchanted child.

"You look beautiful, Lisette," he said before kissing her offered cheek.

"So do you, Kenneth. You're sure your manager doesn't mind that you aren't taking the train tonight?"

He took her hand and tucked it up into his arm. "It doesn't leave until nine, but I told him I'd take the next available tomorrow. They'll get along fine without me for one more game."

The two stood, drinking each other in, until Lisette, in a surprising display of etiquette, cleared her pretty throat and said, "Kenneth? My sister?"

"Of course." He looked truly embarrassed. "I'm so sorry. Good evening, Miss Allenhouse."

"Please, it's time you called me Vada. And good evening to you."

"And our victim? Mr. Eli? He is still doing well?" Already, with the change of clothes and a beautiful girl at his side, Kenny Cupid transformed into Kenneth Chentworth, speaking in mature, clipped tones. There was a certain swagger about him, not at all unpleasant, that endowed both the height and the years he lacked.

"He is well, indeed. Just at our home resting."

"And is Dr. Allenhouse here?"

"I'm sorry, no. He's home with our patient, keeping a careful watch."

A shadow of disappointment crossed Kenny's face. "I had hoped to see him here. My parents were unable to attend this evening—"

"Oh, I didn't realize your parents lived here in town," Vada said, proud of her ruse.

"Neither did I," Lisette added with pure wide-eyed innocence.

"They do, but they had a previous engagement this evening—a little gathering in our home. I was hoping to ask your father's permission to take Lisette by after the concert to meet them."

Vada fought to keep her face straight. If everything Dave Voyant said was true, Lisette would cap off her evening in a most unexpected way. To her credit, she had a look of mild terror on her face.

"Don't you think it's a little too soon for me to meet your parents, Kenneth?"

"No, my darling." He kissed her hand. "No I don't."

"I don't know," Vada said, enjoying this bit of power, "that'll have her out awfully late."

"I'll have her in by midnight. You have my word as a Spider."

"Very well. How could I doubt something as auspicious as that?"

The couple looked at each other in pure glee, then to Vada in gratitude. "Now, Althea's in our seats sitting alone. It would be nice if you two would go join her. I'll be there directly."

If Lisette had captured people's attention alone, her coupling with Kenneth proved even more enticing, and more than one head—men and women—turned to follow their progress.

One man in particular took note—Dave Voyant. But when he looked up and saw Vada, his eyes seemed full of appreciation for her alone.

"My, my, my Miss Allenhouse. And how I do wish you were *my my my* Miss Allenhouse."

"You need to be careful, Mr. Voyant, or one of these days I'm going to take you up on your offer and make an honest man out of you."

"Sweetheart, I don't think there's enough good in you to do that."

"And I don't think there's nearly as much bad in you as you want people to think."

"Yeah," he said, leaning close and putting his hand right on her bare shoulder, "but wouldn't it be fun to find out for sure?"

The shiver that ran through her for a moment made her think that, yes, it would, but when she held up her hand to push him playfully away, she caught the scent of roses from her corsage, taking her back to the last time she fell for such temptation.

"More fun for you, I think, Mr. Voyant, than for me."

He pulled away, thrusting the stub of his pencil into his lapel like an arrow. "Ouch! You wound me, Miss Allenhouse."

"Good thing my father's a doctor then, isn't it?" She started to walk away but turned around and said, "Stick around after the concert and I'll see if I can't get you an interview with Herr Johann."

"Please tell me he's an international jewel thief living as a conductor to escape Scotland Yard."

"Sorry. I'm afraid he's a washed-up Austrian musician trying desperately to keep his delusions of grandeur alive."

"Ouch!" The pencil was back. "This time it's mortal!"

Vada laughed, as she always seemed to do whenever she talked to him, and she wished they *could* love each other.

Her ears quickened to the sound of the tuning orchestra and her heart too. Her feet followed suit as she zipped through the side doors leading backstage. Though the sound coming from the stage was full, a few musicians still milled about like so many wasps in cheap black suits. Some matronly wives were here too, licking their fingers to slick back thin, wayward hair and holding more than one irritated child at bay.

"Ten minutes!" barked Mr. Messini, the head usher also engaged in the task of managing the backstage. It was the only warning the orchestra would get; from here he would go from one octogenarian to the next, yelling, "Ten minutes!" in their ears too.

Vada peeked through the back curtain, delighting at the cacophony within. Oboes chased flutes, scales skipped from violin to cello and back. Bows rose and fell with no discernable pattern. Garrison sat among them, erect and proper in his third chair, staring straight ahead.

Not caring what Herr Johann's reaction would be, Vada walked onto the stage, crossed behind the seats, and came right up to Garrison's row, the *tap-tapping* of her silk evening boots lost in the wayward noise. She ignored the disapproving glances, sat right down in the vacant first chair, and—much to his surprise—leaned across the jowly Mr. Pennington to whisper in Garrison's ear.

"Are you nervous?"

He didn't startle at the sound of her voice, merely turned his head slowly, his eyebrows rising above the rims of his spectacles as he took in the vision next to him.

"Darling!" He scrambled across Mr. Pennington, temporarily trading seats, and placed both of his hands on her bare shoulders, his thumbs gracing the straps of her dress. "You're a vision."

"Well, thank you." She tugged at his white bow tie. "You look quite handsome yourself."

His hands shook as he fussed with his jacket buttons. "Look at that. I may need you to take my place."

"Sorry, darling. I left my violin in the carriage, just so I wouldn't be tempted. Don't tell me you're nervous?"

"Not nervous really. I just—" He leaned closer, taking her in confidence. "I just want to do well."

"That's you." She was surprised at the hint of tears she felt. "Always wanting to do the right thing."

"Is that bad?"

"No." And she meant it. "It's quite admirable, actually. But remember, I've been listening to you for weeks now. You'll do fine." She leaned over to Mr. Pennington. "You all will."

Garrison took her hand and noticed the corsage. "You got my flowers."

"Oh yes! Forgive me for not thanking you yet. Thank you, from all of us. They're quite lovely. Lisette is wearing hers in her hair, Althea has hers pinned to her dress, and Hazel…"

"Yes?"

"It's a long story, there. Suffice it to say that Hazel's escort is wearing hers as a boutonniere."

His gaze intensified, seeking more information, but it was clear none was forthcoming. "You'll have to tell me that story after the concert then."

"I hope I will."

She could see Erik Vlasek, first chair, glowering from the wings. He tapped his bow against his leg with a simmering impatience, and she knew Herr Johann could not be far off.

"I'd better be going."

"Wait. Where are you sitting?"

"Fifth row. Seat three. Like always."

"Because I look for you, you know. If I get lost, or if I'm not sure—"

"You need to look to Johann."

"I love you more than I love Johann."

Vlasek's expression now could only be defined as furious, and Herr Johann came up behind him, looking Vada straight in the eye as he raked his baton across his throat in a threatening gesture.

She gave Garrison a quick kiss on his cheek before running offstage in a most unladylike manner. When she reached the wing, she ran right past Vlasek and paused just long enough to give Herr Johann a kiss in kind, then continued running before he could either protest or return the gesture.

She went through the door that opened out to the back hallway, then out through the lobby, pleased to see the crowd greatly dispersed, and when she walked through the door into the theater, equally pleased to see the house nearly full.

"Vada!" Her name carried on a guileless whisper, and she turned to give an encouraging wave to Hazel and Barth, who seemed quite cozy in the back row.

Vada made her way down the aisle, spotting their seats not only by the decorative flags, but also the distinct style of Lisette's hair set off by the beautiful white roses. Kenny sat on the aisle, and like a gentleman, he vacated his seat allowing easy passage for Vada to take the third seat, in between Lisette and Althea.

Soon, the curtain opened and the discordant sounds of the orchestra's tuning continued. She loved that sound. It seemed to herald such an impossibility. How could all those instruments, all those sounds ever come together in anything close to cohesion, let alone harmony? But they always did. Every night, even though from time to time there might be a slight problem. One musician playing too fast, another too slow, another with an instrument out of tune. But those moments were fleeting, and by the next measure, the problem was solved. The difference undetectable. Chaos given over to harmony once more.

Was that what just happened onstage? As she listened, she couldn't help but think of the chaos of the past few days. Eli gone from the world. Althea in isolation. Barth clear across the country; Hazel in despair. Alex Triplehorn looming. Lisette submerged in a sea of flirtation while Kenny waited for her on shore. And she? Floundering through her own music. Out of tune, missing the constant steady beat that was Garrison. He alone remained constant.

Then silence, until the auditorium echoed with the footsteps of Erik Vlasek. By day he taught music at Cleveland High School, and here he was, violin and bow tucked under his right arm, holding the second most powerful position in the orchestra. Oh, how Garrison hated him.

Still, she clapped along with the audience as he gave a twirling flourish of his left hand as he bowed. He signaled the oboe player to play an A. The woodwinds echoed the note, followed by the brass, and finally the strings. It was Garrison's first official note in front of an audience, and she clutched her sisters' hands, beaming.

Vlasek, satisfied, took his seat, and Herr Johann came onstage, getting taller and taller with each step, as if elevated by applause. It died down as he turned his back and took his place. All around her, programs fluttered as the audience lifted them to read the title of the first piece. But not Vada. She knew this one by heart. She knew it so well, she could be on that stage in minutes with her violin and play it along with the men. Bach's *Brandenburg Concerto no. 5.*

Three taps on the music stand. Baton poised. Such an eternal, excruciating moment, as everyone—audience and musician alike—held a single breath. All bows primed, lips graced precious silver and brass, mallets held inches above taut, stretched skin—all ready to touch down at one command and make music.

Then…

Oh, it was lovely, and perfect. The sound of a beautiful creation. More beautiful now that it was received by the people who loved such a thing. She scanned the musicians, her heart full of love for each of them—accountants and clerks, dock workers and tailors. And lawyers. Well, one in particular.

His pale brows knit together in concentration, his thin frown, his long fingers holding the bow with that soft grip. A few tendrils of his thin hair floated straight up from his head, and she wished she'd been one of those women with the right to paste it down.

Because she loved him.

Oh, Lord, she offered up from her seat, *I love him.*

And when she brought up her hands to wipe away her tears, the scent of the roses brought only one memory—that of a handful of new spring lilacs pilfered from a neighbor's yard.

She moved to the edge of her seat. All those moments of the past few days when he'd been excluded from her thoughts came in a flood as she could see, hear, think of nothing but him. His nubile fingers dancing up and down the violin's neck, his elbow at that peculiar akimbo angle he favored, maneuvering the bow across the strings.

She longed for the touch of those hands, to walk with her hand in the crook of that elbow. More than that, she wanted a life in harmony with him, his steadfast nature to counter her impetuous one. His love so firmly rooted in his faith in the future God planned for them.

Slowly—as if she were coming out of a five days' sleep—the image of such a future took hold. She didn't see a partnership. She didn't see a house. For the life of her, she didn't even see her veiled self walking down an aisle. Every person on the stage and around her disappeared. For her, the entire concert—the whole world—receded behind the third chair violin.

And then, with all the abruptness of that first glorious note, the music stopped. Not all of it, just him. Somehow, something had gone wrong, and there he sat, a world away, his bow suspended over the strings, useless.

He was lost.

If it were rehearsal, Herr Johann would be pounding his fist on the podium, screaming, "Does the third chair need an invitation to continue? Shall I punch your ticket?" But no such outburst would do now. Only Vada knew the meaning behind the new sharpness in the conductor's gestures, the *jab, jab, jab* as if spearing the notes with his baton. At the end of this piece, Herr Johann would probably make Garrison leave unless something happened.

Look at me.

Onstage, his eyes were glued to the floor, and her fellow patrons, who just moments ago were lost to her, began shifting in their seats.

Garrison! Look at me!

His fellow musicians labored valiantly on, the music swelling all around him. He lifted his eyes, and Vada leaned forward. But he didn't look to the house. Instead, he focused his gaze on the music, but by now he was hopelessly behind.

To her left, Lisette snickered into her hand; to her right, Althea slouched down into her seat. Behind her, people wondered what was wrong with that man. In front of her, they shifted from left to right.

On the conductor's box, a murder was being plotted.

Please! Look at me! Lord, let him look at me!

Forgetting all protocol, she braced her hands on the seat in front of her and stood. Now, there was commotion all around her—most of it quite unkind. Lisette covered her face with her hands, and Althea slunk even lower. Certainly, if he didn't look to *her,* he'd look to *this.*

Soon, maybe four or five measures away, would come the point in the performance when all violins would cease, save for Vlasek, who would carry on the part alone, and that's when he would—

Everything in her stopped as Mr. Pennington, jowls quivering, took that brief respite to poke first Garrison, then Garrison's music with his fleshy finger. That was all it took. Seconds later, right on cue, his bow touched strings, and all was as it should be.

Onstage, at least. The fifth, sixth, and probably seventh rows were all in a lather. She should sit down, join Garrison in feeling sweet relief, but she couldn't. He hadn't looked to her. Hadn't even tried. This one thing they shared. The one part of his life he let her fill, and she'd been given over for Mr. Pennington's fat finger.

She felt a tugging on the back of her skirt and turned around, ready to scold the offender only to look down into the tiny, angry face of Mrs. Babbeth, grandmother of Reverend Dickerson who sat beside her. Looking up, she saw Mr. Messini striding down the aisle, his small feet comically in time with the orchestra.

Turning back and sitting down no longer seemed an option, so Vada began the task of climbing over Lisette and thanking Kenny for vacating his seat. Head down, she followed the elderly usher up the aisle and out the door, a sea of faces turned to watch her shameful exit. Once in the lobby, she ignored the old man's query as to what, exactly, had gotten into her. If she told him, he'd be dead before intermission.

No, she continued on, straight outside where a row of carriages awaited, horses hanging their patient heads. The various drivers leaned against them, smoking cigarettes. A few let loose a low, approving howl at her appearance. Any other time, she would have taken them to task, but now she marched right up to a group crouching around a pair of dice and asked where she could find Pete Darvin.

"Come on, lady." One rose to a full height that barely cleared her shoulder. "I can drive you home quick as he can."

"Don't pay him no mind. He couldn't drive you to the corner," said another, not bothering to stand. He jerked his thumb behind him. "Pete's about five rigs down."

Vada thanked them and strode down the sidewalk to where Pete sat, straight up in his driver's seat, head thrown back and dozing.

"Pete!"

He responded with a snore and a shake of his head before scrambling down. "G-Good evening, Miss Allenhouse. Is the concert over already?"

"Not quite. I need you to take me—" Where? Home? "I'm not quite sure yet."

By the time Pete made the first move to come down and help her, Vada had already gathered a handful of pink chiffon and was climbing up. She wished she'd thought to bring the wrap that now sat in the theater coat-check room, but for now the blue plaid driving blanket would do. She turned and dug around behind the seat until she found it, and when she did, she folded herself in its woolen warmth.

"Where to, Miss Allenhouse?"

"Just drive."

And with a lurch, he obeyed.

May this night be the night of our dreams…

This night? Our dreams? Strange, selfish words coming from the man who would be on the stage making music to write to the woman reduced to cleaning the floors for the audience. What dream did he think she was harboring? The dream to watch him? Applaud for him? To walk home on the arm of a third-chair violinist? What dream did they possibly share together? Not music. And apparently not marriage—at least not any-time soon. Not until *he* was ready. Until *his* dreams were fulfilled. It prob-ably never occurred to him that she had dreams of her own.

"Pete? Take me to the train station."

22

Vada leaned back, her feet propped up on the opposite seat, her head resting on the back of the seat. Stars rolled above her, their light competing with the saffron tint of the streetlights.

"Hey, Pete. You have any idea what time it is?"

The boy touched his finger to his cap. "I'd say eight fifteen."

Not that it mattered. She had no idea what she would find at the train station. Possibly an empty platform. Or a new life. One thing for sure, there was no three-year plan. No circus act of balancing on a promise. This was barely even a hunch. Not quite a whim. This was foolishness at its best. Or worst. This was putting out a fire, or starting one, or simply knowing if one burned at all.

"Eastbound or westbound station, Miss Allenhouse?"

Brooklyn. "East."

Pete brought the carriage around to the area just outside the platform. She could hear the great billowing sound of a train sitting on the tracks, the steam from its engine floating up through the night sky.

"Need help with your bags, Miss Allenhouse?"

"I don't have any bags, Pete. Remember, you picked me up at the house?"

"Oh, right. So, are you meeting someone?"

"I'm not sure."

"If you do, will she need help with her bags?"

She sighed. "No, Pete. You won't be carrying anybody's luggage tonight. But I would appreciate your giving me a hand down."

Pete heaved a sigh of his own and, with sluggardly slowness, slid down and met her at the carriage opening, holding up his hang-nailed hand. Although the night was now quite chilly, she chose to leave the riding blanket wadded up in the seat. There were few people around this late at night, but those who would see her deserved to see her in this dress. She did, however, reach back to grab her violin case.

"So, you want me to wait for you here?" The boy seemed genuinely, pathetically confused.

"Yes, Pete."

"How long?"

"Until I give you word to do otherwise."

She walked into the station, right up to the ticket window, and inquired as to where the sitting train was bound.

"East," came the reply of the lethargic man behind the glass.

"New York?"

"Among others. Look, lady, you buying a ticket? Because this window closes in ten minutes."

She had nothing with her but a violin and a letter, but he didn't care about that. Ten minutes would have to be enough.

Opposite the door she'd come through was one leading to the tracks. Squaring her shoulders, feeling the weight of the embellished straps of her gown, she grasped her case and walked out onto the platform.

A conductor stood next to the folding steps and barked, "Train leaves in ten minutes!"

As she approached, he graciously moved aside, offering her a hand up the steps. "I hope you have a wrap on board, miss."

She inclined her head, saying, "Thank you," and stepped onto the train.

Judging by the men and women aboard, this car must be for first-class passengers. The seats were wide and tall, upholstered in red leather; the windows adorned with Roman shades. Stewards in white jackets were pouring cups of tea or walking down the aisle with glasses of wine held high on a tray. She smoothed a hand down the front of her dress. No wonder he'd let her walk right in.

But the team wouldn't be here. No troublesome troupe of baseball ruffians would be allowed passage in this car. Turning slightly to avoid causing a collision, she strode down the aisle, out and over the coupling, onto the next car.

In here, she could barely see through the smoky cloud brought on by cigars and cigarettes, floating as freely as the laughter. She bent her ear, listening for one voice in particular. She'd know it anywhere—she'd hear it in her dreams if God ever allowed her to sleep so deeply again.

At first, finding it seemed as impossible as finding a—well, who was she to say? Hadn't Althea and Eli found each other? Hazel and Barth? Lisette and the life of her dreams? So she closed her eyes against the stinging smoke and walked down the aisle, listening...

"So if you choke up on it more, you'll get a faster swing..."

"...little linseed oil on the leather, then stick it in the oven. Honest to Moses, right in the oven..."

"...anyway, we start dancin' and the next thing I know..."

"...then I say *gar ici, mon frère,* I'm doin' no harm—"

"Mr. LaFortune?"

The man jumped in his seat, like he'd seen a ghost rising from the mist. It took only one long glance, from the top of her head, past her bare shoulders, to her pink silk toes, and back again for his face to move from fright to fancy.

"*Fais-toi?*" He stood from his seat, surrounded by the appreciative sounds of his fellow passengers, and enfolded her in a protective embrace. "What are you doin' here, *belle*?"

"I-I had to talk to you."

"I hear already about the young man. This, Eli? He wake up, *merci á bon Dieu.*"

"It's not about him. It's about...us."

"*Allons.*" He steered her down the aisle, growling at the hoots that followed, and soon they were right back out on the platform.

"Train leaves in five minutes, folks." It was the same conductor, this time looking a little more suspicious.

"*Cherie*, you should not be here." But he touched her as if she should, his hand cradling the back of her neck. She felt it there, a warm spot on her otherwise cold body, but it did nothing to penetrate the numbness.

"Just one question."

He glanced over at the train, at the line of men plastered at the windows looking like they'd just paid a hurly-gurly nickel. "I hope you do not want *les boutons* back. I leave them in the dugout when I hear the good news. To leave the curse behind."

His tone was light, cajoling, but she only had four minutes, and that left little time for banter.

"I need to know if you ever, at any time—did you love me?"

It was amazing—maybe admirable—how his expression didn't change. The shallow half-smile brought forth for the voodoo buttons didn't flinch a bit in this turn of conversation. He simply said, "Ah, *cher*," and began to press her toward him.

"No!" She pushed him away. The action was cheered on by the men at the windows. "What if I said I wanted to go with you, tonight? That I have a ticket in this bag"—she held up her violin case—"and I intend to go back with you to New York. And we can spend every night together there. And I'll be there when you get back from the road. And I'll spend the winters with you in the bayou."

There, a bit of a waver in the grin.

"Because no man could hold me the way you did. Kiss me the way you kissed me. Look at me the way you looked—the way you're looking at me *now*." She stepped closer, brought her hand up to touch his face. "Because no man could ever, ever make me feel the way I felt when you touched me unless he loved me. Am I right?"

She steeled herself for his answer, promising not to be hurt, no matter what he said. She was prepared for humor, for flirtation, for flippant denial, but not pity. *Oh, please, dear God, don't let him pity me.*

By the time she got to the end of her speech, the crescent smile was gone, and he simply looked sad. He caught the hand that touched his face and brought it to his lips—the last time he would ever touch her.

"Ah, *ma belle mam'zelle*." His lips moved against her fingers. "A man should be so lucky to love you. I, for you, am not that lucky."

It was enough. Not love, but worth, and she'd treasure the revelation.

"All aboooooard!" The conductor made a point of shouting the command so the words seemed to cut right between them.

"This ticket? You have it?"

"I doesn't matter, does it?" She curled her fingers within his grip, and just like that, they were no longer touching. The train's whistle blew, and three bounding steps later, LaFortune was just a fuzzy image behind a smoky window, moving along until he dropped out of sight.

"Ma'am? You must board now."

She looked into the conductor's wide, brown, kind eyes. "I've changed my mind, again."

Pete was curled up like a baby in the driver's seat when Vada returned. The jostling of the carriage as she climbed in did little to disturb his slumber, and it wasn't until a violin case hit him on the side of his head that he shot straight up and asked where to next.

She, unfortunately, didn't have an answer.

"Back to Dresden Theater, then?"

"No, not there. Just…home, I guess."

He seemed relieved at the answer and clicked to the horses to start them on the journey. But they hadn't gone more than two blocks when she knew she couldn't go home, not yet. So she hollered up at Pete, giving him a new address.

"What are we gonna do when we get there?" he asked.

"We're going to wait."

"How long?"

"Until I tell you otherwise."

She found the ratty carriage blanket and wrapped herself up in it once more. The ride was slow and smooth—not many drivers out on the street, and no hurry to arrive at the destination. Taking advantage of the luxury of having such an enormous vehicle to herself, she leaned up against the far side and stretched her legs the length of the seat. Having one ear pressed up against the upholstery further muffled whatever noise drifted in.

She gave herself one more long look at the stars before the enormous weight of her eyelids prevented her from seeing them more. The *clomp* of the horses' hooves was every bit as regular and soothing as the sound of the distant parlor clock, and the tattered wool blanket sealed in a warmth that dissipated at the slightest movement on her part. So, she didn't move. She sank, a little. Curled a bit. But didn't move. No movement until…

"Vada? Darling?"

Coarse wool tickled her nose and scratched her shoulders; a block of pain wedged itself in the small of her back.

"Vada?"

A coolness came to her cheek, long graceful fingers whose touch she'd know anywhere. They moved the blanket, letting her be awakened by the chilly evening breeze.

"Wake up, darling. It's me."

Garrison.

She opened her eyes to see only his face, pale against a backdrop of stars. In those first seconds, his expression melted from concern into mild amusement. The stiffness in her back stilted her movement. She grasped the back of the seat and maneuvered her body—crackling and all—to sit up. The blanket fell away, as did one of the straps on her dress, leaving her shoulder bare.

His eyes flickered away from hers, distracted by the fully exposed moonlit skin. Slowly, he reached out, found the strap, and settled it back in place.

"Where's Pete?" she asked, still trying to make sense of the setting.

"Who?"

"Pete, my driver. Where is he?"

"I'm right here, Miss Allenhouse." She leaned to the right and saw the boy sitting straight up in his driver's seat. "You said to wait, so we've been waiting."

"What time is it?"

"Ten thirty." Pete and Garrison answered in unison, though Garrison had to check his watch beforehand.

"I must have fallen asleep."

"It would appear so."

"I should get home."

"But I haven't seen you all evening. Where did you go?"

It all flooded back then, the last time she'd seen him, and the frustration she'd felt in her concert seat bristled alongside the pain in her back.

"You didn't look for me."

He settled back in the opposite seat. "Oh, but I did. After the concert, I went straight out to where you were sitting, but your sisters said you'd left during the first piece. And the carriage was gone, so we walked to your house, but you weren't there. Everybody's half-crazed with worry."

"I meant onstage."

"What?"

"Onstage. When you were playing. You got lost, and you said you'd look to me, but you didn't."

"Vada—"

"You looked at the music and you looked at the floor and you even looked at fat old Pennington."

"Darling, you'll wake—"

"I was begging you to look at *me*! Just once. I stood up! I would have called your name if—" A shifting in the driver's seat caught her attention. She looked up at Pete who was staring at the stars, but the stars alone would never completely entertain him. Lowering her voice she asked, "Can we go inside?"

Garrison glanced over at the fussy, garreted Victorian house. Every window was dark, save for a faint light coming through the front door window. "I don't think so."

She leaned across and whispered, "I have to talk to you."

"Mrs. Paulie is quite clear on how she feels about female guests. She doesn't approve—"

"You are a grown man, Garrison Walker. That room in there is your home. If you want to have a female guest in your home, you may do so!"

She threw off the blanket, grabbed her violin case, and tumbled out of the carriage. By now so many unaided entrances and exits had frayed the hem of her dress, and the contortion of her body as she slept left the entire gown rumpled and askew, as was her hair. The roses of her corsage were now limp and crushed—though no less fragrant. Still, she yanked the ribbon loose and took it off, throwing the whole lot into the street.

"Now, I'm going through that front door and into your room. You may follow me, or wait here, but I'm not leaving until I talk to you."

"Do you know which room is mine?"

"No, but I'll knock on every door until I find it. Are you coming with me? Or shall I wake the whole house?"

"I'm coming." He swung his long frame down to the ground and plunged a hand into his pocket. "It works best if you have a key." He turned, speaking up and over his shoulder to Pete. "And you, driver. Just wait here."

"Oh no, sir." Pete pulled his cap low. "Pa'd kill me for bein' a part of anything like this." He slapped the reins and the horses took off at a brisk clip.

"Well, now," Garrison watched the rig disappear, "it seems we are alone at last."

"Take me to your room."

"It wouldn't be—"

"Rumors will be what they will, Garrison. But you know me. Do you honestly think I'm the type of girl who—" She broke down then, sobbing, her shoulders shaking, because she didn't know herself what type of girl she was.

"There, now...there..." He tucked her head into his shoulder, and she sobbed, her mind ready to split with confession and pleading.

"Please," she said, her words wet against his lapel, "take me inside."

Without a word he'd taken off his jacket and wrapped it around her, folding her into an embrace beside him. The front door, unlocked, opened into a warm hall with a cozy, fussy sitting room just to the left. The only sound was the click of the door behind them.

"Mrs. Paulie goes to bed promptly at nine thirty." He whispered directly into her ear, tickling. He took her hand and led her up a wide set of carpeted stairs to the second floor and the first door across on the left. His body shifted against her as he fumbled for the key, which he silently inserted.

Neither spoke. In fact, it seemed neither was breathing as they crossed the threshold. She waited for the sound of the closing door; instead, she heard the strike of a match as Garrison touched the flame to the wick of a brass-based lamp with a plain glass dome. She moved to close the door, but he stilled her hand. "Better we keep it open."

The room filled with light from corner to corner.

"I've never been in here before." An unnecessary thing to say.

"Nobody has." Equally unnecessary.

She turned slowly, taking it all in. A small, cold stove stood in the corner; above it were three narrow shelves, two of them empty, one with a neat little row of glass bottles, a shaving mug, and a stack of shoe polish tins. The lamp itself sat on a round table with two straight-backed chairs tucked beneath it and covered with a dark-checked cloth. Probably blue, but in the lamplight it was hard to tell.

Across the room, underneath the single square window, sat a comfortable-looking stuffed leather chair, draped with a crocheted Afghan. Beside it, another small table with a neat stack of books, a black Bible on top. And finally, against the wall to her left, his bed. Black iron headboard, cheerful quilt. Not a big bed by any description, but easily as large as the one she'd been sharing with Hazel these past few nights.

One step after another, she moved around the room, touching the base of the brass lamp, running a finger along the unused shelves. No dust. Touched the cold stove, studied the pattern of the Afghan, laid a palm against the cool leather of the chair. She picked up the Bible in order to see the book beneath it. *"The Time Machine?"*

He cleared his throat. "I—um…I enjoy the fantasy."

Imagine, after all this time, a surprise. A covert passion. Vada balanced the Bible on her forearm and thumbed through the pages of the novella, skimming a few lines, imagining Garrison doing the same. She'd never sought her fantasies in pages; they'd never left her own head. If he harbored this secret delight, what others might await?

"Tell me," she said, "would you rather take a time machine to the past or to the future?"

"That depends." He took the books from her hands. "Wherever you are."

She waited for him to return the question, but of course he didn't. He didn't have past mistakes to erase, and he didn't have a future in question. She longed for the feel of the book in her hand, something to relieve her of this undeserved, burdensome trust. But he'd put them back, neatly, with finality, so she moved around him and studied the quilt.

"This is a log cabin pattern."

"Is it?"

"Did Mrs. Paulie do the quilting?"

"I don't believe so. She did, however, make the Afghan. On the chair. Why don't—I mean, would you like to sit down?"

"No." She set her case on the bed, filling the room with the sound of its clasps as she opened it. There, on top of the violin, was the envelope. She held it out to him, her hand absolutely steady.

"What's this?"

"Read it."

His eyes first scanned the words on the envelope, the instructions to read it after the concert. A slight tremor came to his hands as he slid out the note, becoming eerily steady as he read.

She stared at the log cabin quilt, replaying the words in her mind. He must have finished it by now. And again.

"Vada?"

"I was going to give that to you. Leave it in your case. But then, right before the concert—I just couldn't. Because I remembered how much I loved you. And how much I thought you loved me."

"I do love you. I don't understand—"

"And then you wouldn't look at me—"

"I couldn't see past the lights, Vada. They've never been that bright before. But I didn't need to see you, because I knew you were there."

"I know…I mean, I must have known that. Should have known that. Oh, Lord forgive me." Her knees buckled and the tears came again. She fell to the bed, burying her face in a sea of log cabin stitches. "I have been such, such a fool. You can't possibly know—"

He was at her side, kneeling beside the bed, moving the damp wet hair off her face. "Vada, where did you go when you left the concert?"

She lifted up on one elbow, focusing on a single orange square.

"There was a man…" And she told the whole story. Her voice, a listless monotone, narrating the events of the week—every moment since they took a cab ride from the Hollenden Hotel. Even the ones they shared, because she wanted him to see, wanted him to know how important he was to her life.

Louis LaFortune was reduced to *this man. This man* touched her knee at a ballpark. *This man* kissed her in the alcove. *This man* brought her within inches of a bed. *This man* never loved her. And she never loved him.

By the time she finished, Garrison was no longer beside her. She sat up, turned around, and found him sitting on his stuffed leather chair, elbows resting on his knees, holding the envelope loosely in one hand, the note in the other.

"I knew there was something," he said.

"You must hate me."

"No. I couldn't. I just don't understand why."

"I guess I thought you didn't love me."

"Darling, how could you think such thing?"

"Look around you." She stood, his jacket falling from her shoulders, and made a tour of the room. "Two chairs here at the table. One for me. Empty shelves, room for me." She came to the bureau behind the chair, and he craned his neck to follow. "Yes, we'd need to get another dresser. A small one. And," she swallowed, "your bed…"

She held no fear of being taken for a seductress. Oh, her head pounded, her eyes burned. Her mouth filled with the salty, gummy taste of tears. No mirror anywhere in the room, but she knew she looked a blotchy, swollen, puffy, disheveled mess. The strap on her dress would not stay up, and she felt the stray hair on the back of her neck and stringing past her eyes. Still, the air was thick with certain promise.

"Of course," she said, in an effort to break the tension, "there's only one really comfortable chair."

"Well then, we'll just have to share it."

The next thing she knew she was snatched at the waist and pulled right into his lap. Her outcry stifled by his kiss, and his long arms holding her together.

"Don't you see?" She snuggled into his collar. "There's room for me in your life now, Garrison. This is enough for me."

"But I want to give you so much more."

"Do you love me, Garrison?"

"You know I do."

"And can you—will you ever be able to forgive me?"

He lifted her chin and answered with a kiss, deeper than the first, and with it he claimed her, leaving no room to question if any other man would ever have such privilege.

"Oh, Vada." His finger traced along her jaw, down her neck, dabbling in the well of her collarbone. "My darling, I need to take you home."

"Before Mrs. Paulie finds us out?"

"Before I break my promise."

"What promise?"

"Every time I see you, I promise God to honor you. And I've promised to keep my thoughts pure—as pure as I can, given the circumstances. So, now, I need to get you home."

"I felt like I was home the minute I walked in here."

"But you aren't. Not yet." He began to stand, and she stood with him. They faced each other, hands clasped loosely. The lenses of his glasses were smudged, obscuring his eyes, so she reached up and took them off. The gaze behind them affected her every bit as strongly as his kiss, and it seemed the final barrier had been removed.

"Vada Allenhouse," he said, his voice choked. "I loved you the moment I saw you in Moravek's. And every day since. And never for one minute more than I do right now."

"That's enough for me, Garrison. All I ask for is enough."

"Then you shall have it." He gestured grandly around him. "All of this, my darling, I'll share with you."

"Even the chair."

"Especially the chair."

"Oh, darling!" She moved to her toes, eager to throw her arms around him, but her grand romantic gesture faltered when her foot slipped and she fell into his arms. There was a brief moment of laughter, until the two glanced down to see what had caused her to falter.

It was the letter, dropped when he'd pulled her to him. It spoke to them from the floor, filling the space between them with questions and doubt.

"There is," he said, "this one other matter." He knelt and picked up the note, folded it, slid it back into its envelope, and rolled it into a tube. With two short strides, he crossed the room to the table and lowered the rolled envelope through the glass globe, igniting the words within. He lifted it out, flaming, and, with no more urgency to his stride, dropped it inside the cold stove. Back at the lamp, he leaned over the globe and, with one quick breath, extinguished it.

The room was dark, darker it seemed than it had been when they walked in. Soon she felt a jacket being draped over her shoulders, long fingers entwined in her own, and his voice reaching to her through the night.

"Shall we?"

Back out on the street, she was surprised to see the carriage once again parked in front of Mrs. Paulie's house and Pete, looking sleepier than ever, at the reins.

"Mr. Allenhouse says I was to come back to fetch you. Says I was to wait here until midnight if I had to."

The relief of his presence sapped the last of her strength, and it felt like Garrison was pushing her up into her seat. He settled in beside her, draping his arm across her shoulders, and arranged the wool blanket across their laps before giving Pete the word to start.

"But take it slow, Pete," he said, drawing her close. "Midnight's a while off."

READERS GUIDE

1. Vada has grown up in the shadow of the loss of her mother. How do you see that affecting her relationship with her father? With her sisters? Ultimately, with Garrison?

2. Why does it seem sometimes that those people who are absent from our lives can have just as big of an impact as those who are present? Can they have more?

3. *The Bridegrooms* is full of several illustrations of grace. Which one did you find most touching?

4. What do you think of Garrison's reluctance to make his relationship with Vada "official"?

5. As if the advances of Louis LaFortune weren't enough, Vada also has to contend with the flirtatious Dave Voyant. Do you think he was ever a serious contender for her affections? Why or why not?

6. Althea has been living as an elective mute for most of her life. Do you see this as an exercise in discipline or as a means of escape?

7. Vada, Hazel, and Althea seem to have been raised to be up-standing young women. To what do you account Lisette's wild streak?

8. Hazel claims to be following the trail of women's rights in her quest to find a Wyoming groom. What else do you think is fueling her decision?

9. More than once, Vada prays and asks the Lord to simply keep Louis LaFortune away from her. Yet, he continues to pop up. Why do you think God chose to answer her prayer in this way?

10. Besides housekeeper and cook, what role does Molly Keegan play in the Allenhouse home?

11. Throughout the story, we see Vada unraveling. In what areas of your life do you have a hard time "letting go"?

12. Why do you think Dr. Allenhouse has never remarried?

AUTHOR'S NOTE

My stories always start with something small. This one began with one word. *Bridegrooms.* While I was in the midst of researching for *Stealing Home,* mixed in with all the teams and stats and players and scores, I saw them. The Bridegrooms. I was hit with the humor of the team name and caught up in the romance of the early days of professional baseball. More than that, the word—that plural, *bridegrooms*—really brought to mind the idea of chaos. Of choices. Ultimately, the chaos of choices, especially when we fail to factor the Lord's wisdom and guidance into those choices.

Of all the characters I've created, it's safe to say that Vada Allenhouse is the most like me. We're both wound a little too tight, both prone to think we have more control over situations than we actually do, both prone to call on God after we've made a mess out of things. I loved taking this journey with her, and I loved stocking a story with such a cast of strong, vibrant women. And, I must say, I was so excited to bring each girl to her own "happily ever after."

For the past year, whenever anybody asked me about my next book, I'd say, "It's a story of four sisters. And it's so much fun!" I hope you had fun with it too. In fact, I hope you'll continue on the journey with me. Please visit my Web site, www.allisonpittman.com. Drop me an e-mail, leave a comment on my journal, or sign up for my newsletter. The Allenhouse girls have come to the end of their tale, but I'm far from finished with mine!

ACKNOWLEDGMENTS

Many, many thanks to you, my readers, who bless me beyond my own imagination.

Thank you to all the great people at Multnomah—especially Alice Crider, who heard this story over breakfast and believed in it before it was fully formed.

Thank you, Bill, agent extraordinaire, who "gets" me, even though I'll never, ever bait a hook.

Thank you, Julee Schwarzburg, for seeing everything I can't and showing me everything I should. So cool to work with you!

Thank you, my Monday Night Group—especially my fellow fiction-ators. Twelve pages, twelve pages, twelve pages…

And, of course, my bridegroom, Mike! Thank you for twenty amazing years.

Finally, my Bridegroom, Jesus Christ. Author of my life, lover of my soul. Thank You, Lord, for giving me the words, the people, the stories—and covering it all with Your grace and Your power.

A LARGER-THAN-LIFE HERO
and the
Small Town That Awakens His Soul

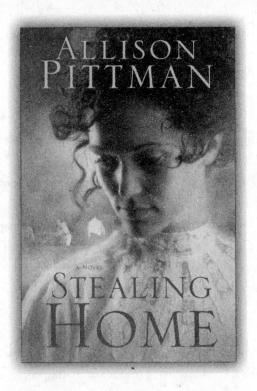

The 1905 Cubs need Duke Dennison to win the pennant.
Only one thing stands in his way: alcohol. To get sober,
Duke is whisked to a small town. There, four unique lives
intersect and something devastating happens that will
change each of them—forever.

www.waterbrookmultnomah.com

Sometimes man's best friend is also
the best teacher.

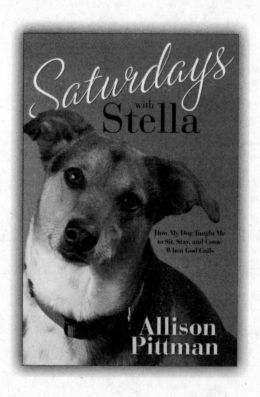

In this heart-warming, thoughtful, and often hilarious tribute to her beloved canine, Allison Pittman introduces readers to Stella—a slightly neurotic yet curiously adorable mutt who bears a striking spiritual resemblance to many Christians who want to please their Master but often miss the mark.

www.waterbrookmultnomah.com